# Curio's Summer

(The Curio Chronicles)

Robin John Morgan

First published (Paperback) in the UK in 2022 by Violet Circle Publishing.

Manchester, England, UK.

Print ISBN: 978-1-910299-34-0
Digital ISBN: 978-1-910299-35-7



British Library Cataloguing in Publication Data.
A catalogue record for this book is available from the British Library.

All paper used in the production of this book are sourced only from wood grown in sustainable forests.

www.violetcirclepublishing.co.uk

# Also by Robin John Morgan.

## Heirs to the Kingdom.

Book One, The Bowman of Loxley.
Book Two, The Lost Sword of Carnac.
Book Three, The Darkness of Dunnottar.
Book Four, Queen of the Violet Isle.
Book Five, Crystals of the Mirrored Waters.
Book Six, Last Arrow of the Woodland Realm.
Book Seven, Bridge Of Sequana.
Book Eight, The Circle of Darkness.

## The Curio Chronicles.

Part One, Abigail's Summer.
Part Two, Curio's Summer.

## Other works.

Rise of the Raven.

*Few see the darkness and hidden anguish, of spoken words.*

*For all those who endured them, and the pain they suffered.*

*You are not alone.*

Had we made a change? I really was not sure, maybe we had just played our part in starting the process, like Birch has always said, there are times when you need to plant a seed, and watch out for what grows in your sunlight, and I think one or two seeds had been planted this summer.

(Abigail Jennifer Watson)

Chapter 1

# Return to Summer.

I sat on my bed, feeling completely alone, looking at my black tear streaked mascara, that had run from my eyes. I held up my phone, 'CLICK!' and took the selfie, as I gave a huge sob.

"I miss you so much, and I am so lonely, I am so sorry Birch, I failed you."

My head was spinning, and the tequila bottle slipped off the bed, and hit the floor with a thump. I fell back on the bed, and the pill bottle slipped from my other hand, as I stared at the ceiling. The whole room of the guest house was spinning, I felt drowsy, and then suddenly, everything went black.

The phone fell to the floor, it landed screen up, showing the picture of my rats' nest hair, and the black tracks my tears had traced down my face, from my blood shot, unfocused, dead eyes. This picture, was the proof, that she was not coming back, and I had lost her forever. Why had I lied to myself, after all we had been through, why could I not just admit the truth of who I was, why could I not tell her how deeply in love with her I was?

Nothing changes in the way you expect it, when you see an acorn on a tree, it is fresh wholesome and green, but as the year moves on, the colour fades, as it falls to the floor, and gets lost in the pile, and it ends up brown, and rotting in the grass. It was sort of how I had been feeling, lost in the pile and left to rot.

That was last night, and having awoken this morning, and feeling afraid of being by myself, and afraid of being alone in the house, I wandered out, and into the village, feeling lost, lonely, utterly broken, and a complete failure. Coming home that summer with Birch, was hard, but I was so happy surrounded by her care and the love of my new friends, my Curio's. Before that, everyone who had ever hurt me, had met me with a smile, and called themselves friend, and Birch had changed all that for me, but now she was gone, and I was utterly alone, living in hell.

I guess it is the saddest part of life, the hardest part of life, people grow apart. No matter how much you want someone, the truth is, a great beginning can only lead to a sad ending, it is inevitable, things eventually always go round in a full circle, nothing remains open ended, the circle must always close and in a way, today I was feeling like my circle had closed, that part of my life was over, and this was a new start, but to what, I had nothing left inside me?

I stood outside the salon, having been lectured again for letting myself go, by Anthony, as he slipped out his scissors, and again, I refused for the one hundredth time to let him do my hair. He had given me that look, the one he only had because of Birch and me, and tutted.

"Abby darling, I never thought I would see the day when someone in this village, would have hair like a rat's nest, even to rival Ronald." He heaved an exasperated sigh, and reached a hand towards me.

"Darling, you simply must pull yourself together, for the sake of every Curio that has ever been, you have to dig deep girl, and find the sparkle that lit the way for all of us."

I get it, I do, and yes that summer was the happiest time in my life, which in itself is bizarre, considering I came back as a transient, hated by the village, and filled with the ideals of changing the world, and being true to myself. Like all bright flowers, they wither and die, and as I look round the village today, it still looks exactly the same. Wotton Dursley survived the onslaught of the Curio's, and like all seed, we were scattered in the wind to flourish elsewhere.

We all came together that following November, to help mum campaign, and she won the election. She is now chair of the Parish Council, and she has made sweeping changes.

The following February Martin Hinkley appeared in court. Birch and her mum came down, as Birch and myself had to give testimony in court. It was an horrendous time for me, as I cried several times on the stand, as Martin's solicitor said some vile and horrible things about me, as I relived my moments alone in that room with him. Mum cried all the way through it which made it even worse.

Martin was found guilty, after a private video link testimony was given by Julia, he had raped her just the same way he had tried with Chloe and me. The jury was unanimous in their verdict, although I did not see it, I felt sickened by it all and sat outside with Chloe who felt the same. I had really bad nightmares alone for some time, although I do feel guilty, as I never told Birch about them.


The village under mum on the council, is better maintained than it has ever been, people are a lot more liberated, Peter and Mary are now a little more open about their naturist's lifestyle, they even have a flyer in the Post Office, for the local Naturist Retreat, outside of Oxendale.

Modern life has moved onward, and although there is little sign of it, as I stand here, having stopped outside the dress shop, there are small signs that times have changed.

The Fish Monger is closing after forty years, and even the Charity Shop is moving. The news agent, run by the post office, has less paper boys, and where the village had one taxi in my youth, it now has four, that run out of an office above the Deli. Lillian and Celia have two young girls helping in the Tea Rooms waiting on the tables, and the hardware shop, has an online catalogue for those bigger items, and screws and nails come in bags, where they had once been sold loose.

Jessops craft shop has been taken over by Anabel, because her dad Tom, was arrested for running a cannabis farm in the back. Some say it was an anonymous tip to the police that got him busted. I did not think it took much effort to know who, and yes as always, she is still here, frowning and intimidating the villagers, even though she has been demoted to Vice Chair on the council.

Tom's wife Fiona, stays pretty much out of the public eye, avoiding Marjorie, although she does run a lovely little plant area at the back of Jessops, in what had been the Cannabis farm, selling flowering plants for Norman and Daisy, out of their nursery.

Norman never changes, his business is as booming as are his loins, he has two children now, Tulip, his daughter, and Denzel his son, who is three. Tulip is almost two. Daisy is pregnant again, although no one here knows that yet, it is information held by just a few, God knows what Marjorie will say when she finds out?

Apart from that, little has changed, except Hatty... I am delighted to see she is finally happy; she met a sculptor by the name of Harrow Temple, actually that is his artistic name, his real name is Clive Stourton.

He came into Oxendale High to give a presentation to the students on sculpting, and in true Hatty style, she got him drunk, took him home, and screwed his brains out. He surpassed my Uncle Jeremy in his ability to sate the beast that was Hatty's libido. She told me it was a love at first fuck, which made me really laugh.

They are very similar, he lives alone with a studio, like she does, and both are opposed to marriage. They now spend their time commuting to shag each other, between here and Tethering Dibley, twenty eight miles away. Personally, it looks like a match made in artisan heaven, and I am happy for her.

With Hatty gone most of the time, and a vacancy for Village Harlot, I was the obvious choice, the scruffy female writer, who drinks, and as it appears these days, gets laid occasionally, and I really do mean occasionally. It's been months since I last had the attention of a decent male, and I dumped his ass, because I turned up to his flat, let myself in, to find him snorting coke off another girls' tits.... God life is depressing, I miss Birch.

Birch has done really well; she got her doctorate, sadly I was not there to see it, as I had a booking on the same day. I left Uni and came home to write, Katie became my agent, whereas, today nothing I have published has had any sort of interest. Birch has in true Birch style, gone on to bigger things. She has been working for three years part time with her mum, and has really excelled as a therapist, although she now has long white hair, and no black patches, which is so disappointing.

I see her on our video calls, and I find it unsettling, I have no idea why, because I am not much better. The black and red grew out, and I had it cut off. The fringe has also gone, and I am back to a blonde ponytail. I wear ordinary jeans, and baggy jumpers and tops, I think the only thing left from that summer now is, I still refuse to wear a bra, and I always swim and sunbathe naked.

I suppose we all grew up; it was bound to happen? I often think, is this what it was like for my mum, when I came home that day. Had she drifted into the dullness, and lost her yen for life, and just become ordinary? Maybe that was life, and the bumps in the road she told me about, but it just feels recently like my bumps are mountains.

My saving grace is that I am twenty four, and my trust fund has kicked in, I will give my dad his due, he is as dull as grey paint, but he certainly knows how to invest. My income from the fund is massively larger than I will ever need to live. I thank him for that, at least I won't starve. God what has happened to me?

I left Uni with such honour, I aced everything and got distinctions all the way. Birch stayed on to pursue her doctorate. I missed her so much that when I came home, I moved permanently into the guest house, and converted it into a writer's retreat. Sadly, gothic fantasy is no longer in vogue, and even though the two books I have put out have done okay, I am not sure I will ever make the best sellers list. I feel bad about that, Katie put in so much effort, I feel like I let her down, when the sales did not even cover the promotional packages.

I miss Birch, it has been almost a year since I saw her, I miss the Curio's, we have not really been together since that November campaigning for mum, we have all expanded our horizons and moved on.

After Veronica recommended Anthony on stage five years ago, the salon has expanded, and he now has two new hairdressers working for him. I do see him, but only in the salon, he is so busy these days he never has much time, and what little he does, he spends with Brent.

Edwina runs her own business freelancing graphic design, and internet services, she is as always living up to her reputation bedding everything male or female she comes across, although she now runs a site for Unicorns. I am not too sure what that is, I just know it has nothing to do with rainbow coloured horses with a horn on their head. I really should look it up.

Chloe is still single and lives and works in Oxendale in an art shop. She has sold a few paintings, and as far as I can tell, is in hot pursuit of Hatty's reputation. I have often wondered, if the Hinkley incident became too much for us all, and not being together is easier, as for some of us, it is still traumatic to remember?

Deb's never changes, she aced everything as expected, and now works for the large pharmaceutical company in Cambridge. I see her on some of the weekends she comes home, and she has crashed occasionally with me, we email a lot. We went to Glastonbury last year with Birch, it was a pretty wild weekend, and hey you will never guess, she ended up in the caravan of Jimmy.

Battered Taco are a massive hit in the east, especially Japan, they have also just about broken through in America, not so much over here yet, they did have one hit with 'I want the girl in my hat back.'

It was a pretty big hit for them, and was written by Jimmy, and dedicated to Deb's. He saw her in the crowd at Glastonbury, and he jumped off stage, fought his way into the crowd, kissed her, and then dragged her wearing his hat, on stage with him. It was pretty cool to see the look on her face, as he told the crowd, how he had lost her contact details, and thought he had lost her forever. He then sat her on a stool at the front of the stage, and sung the song to her.

The poor girl, she was beetroot, and hated by every single woman in the arena. Birch said it was the most romantic thing she had ever seen, and cried buckets, I could not help but laugh, although it was pretty cool.

It is another reason why I am feeling down; Deb's is getting married at the village church in August. The village is preparing for the wedding of the year. Isn't it strange, the village has accepted the wedding because firstly Mr Wheeler is loaded, and Jimmy is an internationally well known musician? No one appears to mind the fact he is obsessed with steam punk, and wears all the clothes and styles, including his top hat and goggles, and is a poor boy done good. The hypocrisy never ends here in Wotton.

I miss Birch, but she has a busy life, her text messages are
further and further apart, it has been well over a week since
her last text, and last night she did not come online and talk to
me on video call. It felt like the end of the world, on the never
ending slide downwards in the abyss of darkness that is my life
of utter loneliness. God, I miss her so much, it is hurting deep
inside, and I am not coping at all well, as I cannot stop thinking
of her and feel this huge ball of pain inside me. I know she is so
disappointed in me, I should have achieved more, but I think I
have really let her down and dashed her high hopes for me, hell, I
have let myself down, I miss her so much.

"Are you going to stand there looking like a sight all day, or will
you be moving, you are making the place look untidy?"

"Huh! What?" I came out of my thoughts to Marjorie staring at
me in her usual disapproving way, she gave a frustrated sigh, as
she scowled disapprovingly at me.

"I asked, if you would be moving any time soon Abigail Watson?
Good grief, just look at you. I understand your absolute lack of
care for anything, especially yourself, but in fifteen minutes,
we do have a funeral arriving. Around here, it is considered
respectful to at least make an effort, for the final passing of the
deceased."

I had forgotten, today is the funeral of Mrs Perkins. As you
will remember, Mrs Perkins lived at number three Waterside
Lane, almost right across the road from us. She would watch the
coming and goings of the lane through her binoculars, and report
her findings directly to Marjorie.

She died a couple of months back, but due to the nature of her
death, she has been disposed of in a special way. Her son had
been working in Africa, and on his return, she had contracted a
rare tropical unidentified disease, and suffered in hospital for a
while.

Eight times her son had been told she would not last the week,
and yet the old bat came through. My dad told me she was just
'too dammed nosey to die,' which I cannot deny, made me laugh,
and was possibly true. However, she was assigned a room at the
care home, and her property was placed up for sale.

Then on the day she was supposed to be discharged from

hospital, and taken to the care home, she woke up in her hospital bed, allegedly healed, and ate a full breakfast, only to projectile vomit it back up, in a scene reminiscent to the Exorcist, and then dropped dead in her bed.

Her body has been in a lab for a while, and then cremated for reasons of safety, and then her ashes were placed in a sealed container. Today her sealed remains were to be placed in a coffin, and brought to church for her burial shortly, and apparently, I was too unsightly to view this.

Some things just do not change, no matter how hard you wish for them to. You would have thought after that summer, and the revelations that followed, about changed votes, Marjorie would have stepped down from public life, but no, the woman has no understanding of honour.

Losing to mum was a blow, but like a flat tyre, once she got her wind back, she simply reinflated her ego, played the victim card, and bounced right back up. For the last couple of years, I have been her favourite target, and verbal punch bag. Normally I would fight back, but to be honest, today, I just do not have the spirit or will power to bother.

"Well?" I gave a sigh, and looked at Marjorie.

"Okay... I am going."

"Good... Get a move on."

I turned to say something, but something at high speed and lilac, caught my eye, and held it as it hurtled past the Post Office, was that what I thought it was? I narrowed my eyes and focused on it.

"No frigging way!" Marjorie gasped.

"OH MY GOD, SHE... SHE.... SHE IS BACK!"

BEEP.... BEEP.... BEEP.... BEEP...................... "SWEETIE!"

I could not believe my eyes, as a lilac Land Rover covered in daisies and rainbows, came tearing and screeching, round the bottom of the road by the Hunters Arms, with the wild green eyed, and long flowing blonde haired, figure of Birch hanging out of the window, waving like a lunatic.

She came hurtling up towards me, as Marjorie staggered back on the path, and Petal, came to a screeching halt, skidding sideways on the road. Her door exploded open, and suddenly, I was wrapped in her, laughing and cackling like an escaped mental patient, and I burst into tears. I felt her, and wrapped my arms around her.

"Sweetie I am back and I missed you, did you miss me?"

I could not talk, I just held her tightly, feeling her warmth and smelling her scent, as a tsunami of emotion ripped through me. She pulled me back, and lifted her arms in the air, and her eyes burned with fun and frolics, and her smile was huge.

"SURPRISE!" I wiped my eyes, stunned, and yet happy.

"Birch what are you doing here, I thought you were in London?" She smiled.

"I was, mum is taking a few days sightseeing, so I thought I would come and see all my favourite people." She looked at Marjorie, who was staring at her, with horror in her eyes and smiled, and looked back at me, and lowered her voice.

"Well obviously, not the Bell Twats. I missed you Deads, and it has made me unhappy, I need us to talk, so I drove here, so I could see you and hug you." She smiled a soft smile, and tilted her head to one side as she looked at me.

"Look at you... Oh Deads what has happened, have you missed me that much?" I nodded, and burst into tears again.

"Yes.... Oh Birch, you have no idea."

I did not want to cry, but seeing her brought it all back, and those deep feelings inside me, everything came rushing up. She pulled me back into hug.

"Oh, Sweetie so little has changed... Come here you silly."

Beep...Beep! Birch sighed, and turned, and looked back at the road.

"Seriously, can you not see we are having a moment here......? Oops, my bad."


The long black hurst, with a coffin, decorated with pink and yellow flowers, was stopped on the road in front of Petal, who had skidded right across, and was blocking the road. The door was open and the engine was still running. Behind the hurst a long line of black cars waited, with frustrated scowling people inside. Birch let go of me.

"Give me a moment Sweetie." She walked onto the road, and

sighed at the driver of the hurst.

"Seriously… She is dead you know; she is not exactly looking at her watch now, is she?"

Birch climbed in, and reversed back, then spun the wheel, and pulled Petal to the side of the road, and smiled as she got out, and waved the funeral procession through. Marjorie turned and skuttled off up the street cursing under her breath.

"She is back less than a minute, and already there is chaos in the village."

I just smiled as she walked back towards me, she gave me that big beautiful smile of love and fun.

"I have vodka, and I am here until tomorrow, but then I have to go home, so how about we head back to your place, get naked, drunk, and talk, you can tell me all about it?" I nodded as I smiled, and gave a long breath out.

"Yeah…. I would love that."

God, she looked so good, she had hardly changed, although I missed the patches in her hair, but I could live with that, just hearing her voice, and being able to hug her and smell her, it was like a tonic. She winked.

"Come on Sweetie, jump in, I want to terrify your dad, when he gets home, and sees Petal across the gates."

I pulled her back into a hug, and just squeezed the life out of her, I guess I was making sure this was real, and she was actually here. I mean, I have fantasied about it so many times, I had wondered if I had slipped out of reality for a moment.

I opened the door, wow, Petal had been completely transformed, she looked like a brand new car. I could not believe it, the seats were rainbow striped, thick, and fluffy. As I slid in, the dash was completely new and covered in a bright flowery vinyl, and from the mirror hung a small blue rosette. I still say curd is not jam. Just getting in felt like home. Birch gave a giggle, and suddenly I was pinned to my seat, and tearing at high speed towards Manor Road, and home with my eyes closed.

Chapter 2

# Birch Returns.

Do you ever have that feeling like everything is not real, and you have to pinch yourself? Well, that is my life at the moment sat looking at Birch, as she drives at high speed towards my house. To be honest, there is a little bit of good sense looking at Birch, as it avoids me seeing out of the windscreen. I learnt five years ago that it is easier to not see all the hazards she misses by inches; it makes for a calmer, and more relaxed journey.

We moved on to Waterside Lane, and slowed down, for the last month there had been a constant line of trucks parked outside number three. The house had been sold, and whoever had bought it, had obviously decided to remodel the house. They had become my equivalent of the Bell Twat, as they hammered and drilled all day, which when you are a writer, and you are trying to focus, is just dammed right annoying.

Birch slowed down, yet again the residents had to wait, as another delivery was parked in the road, and a man handling a large pallet on a trolley, was guiding it through the gates. Finally, we had a clear run past, and Birch drove up to our gates, I got out and looked back across the road.

"Frigging hammer twats, I cannot wait until the new owner moves in, I am going to smack them in the mouth, for the month of endless noise." Birch gave a chuckle.

"Really Deads, what if they are nice and sweet, for all you know the new owner might be lovely and bangable?" I watched the delivery man pull his pallet down the drive.

"I doubt it, if they can afford to buy that house, and then knock the shit out of it, like they have been doing, you can bet it is some rich coke snorting twat from London. No other type can afford to live on this drive."

The gates opened, and Birch drove in, and parked Petal in front of the side gates. Birch leaned over and grabbed her bags, and we jumped out, and I opened the front door into the hall.

"Mum are you home?" Her voice sounded back from the kitchen.

"In here Abby."

We walked up the hall towards the door. Once we arrived, I stepped back, and pushed Birch through with a smile, she stepped into the kitchen. Birch gave a giggle, and spoke quietly.

"Hi mum, I am home."

There was a loud squeal, and as I walked in, mum rushed across the kitchen, and swept Birch into her arms.

"Oh Birch darling, why didn't you tell me you were coming? Oh it is so lovely to see you, it is far too long young lady, oh it is so nice having you home again."

I smiled, mum had missed her as much as I had, life had never felt the same since she went back home to Manchester. It is funny really, five years ago we had stood here, whilst my mother had a minor breakdown, accusing me of tattooing my eyeballs and taking heroin. Had things really changed so much? It felt strange, the times had moved on, and yet inside I still felt the same, except, there was a tiny part of me that was different.

I was happy she was back, I had missed her so much, and seeing her in the street had blown my mind, and stirred up all of my emotions. Maybe it was just that, but I somehow felt there was something missing, a closeness if you like? Yes, I think that was it, there was a strangeness to both of us. It was nothing you would notice, the bond was still there, I had felt it in the car, but it was like a small part had been chipped off, and I felt it, and missed it.

We sat inside for ages, talking at the counter with coffee's, mum and me asked a million questions, and poor Birch must have felt like she was being interrogated, but she loved it.

I sat watching her as she spoke, the way her hair, which was much longer now and touched her waist, fell across her shoulders, her long eyelashes, her green eyes, that just glided across her face as she noticed everything, she was different, and yet the same. I felt she was a little more mature, a little more like her mum, and yet in an odd way, more Birch than Birch had ever been, or at least more than I remembered her.

Her skin was as white as alabaster as always, her boobs looked a little bigger, and she had gained a little weight, or maybe it was she was just more toned. I was fascinated and yet perplexed, she was the same, and yet very different, and I just could not put my finger on it. She saw me looking, and turned to me and smiled, lifted her hand, and swept my hair back from my face.

"You okay Sweetie?" I smiled.

"Now you are here, I am fine." Her eyes just for a second clouded, I think it hurt her to know that, but she smiled at me.

"You should put the fringe back, it suited you." My mum agreed.

"Oh Birch, you have no idea how many times I have told her, although I have to say, it feels odd that you do not have Birch hair." I agreed and looked at my mum.

"Yeah, it does not feel the same now does it?" She gave a chuckle and looked at me, there was a little sadness in her eyes.

"No one calls me Birch anymore; I am Jemi to everyone."

That just did not feel right at all, only Birch had called me Deads, so in a way I had not missed it, although in those first few minutes during our meeting, I had been relieved to hear her say it. I think if she had called me Abby, I would have felt hurt, no scratch that, it would have been devastating. I looked at her, with her beautiful green eyes.

"You will always be Birch to me." She gave a soft smile, my mum agreed.

"I am not sure I could call you anything else, I mean Birch suits you, it is something natural, something wild and free, a part of this world that will always create beauty wherever it grows. I am sorry, but I absolutely refuse to call a daughter of mine Jemi." I saw the tears fill her eyes, they just welled up as she smiled.

"I have missed you both so much…. I love the name, I do Flick, but since Uni, and working in the office, it has kind of disappeared, it is so nice to hear it again, thank you." Mum smiled, as I leaned in and hugged her, she dried her eyes.

"I am so happy to be here, I needed this." It felt like an odd remark, but she stood up, and I slipped back from her.

"Can I see the house; I really want to see what you have done with it?"

It was raining, somewhere between us arriving it has started, I looked for an umbrella, Birch walked to the doors and looked out.

"You have no idea how much I have wanted to be here, there

have been so many times I dreamed of being out there by the pool." I looked out through the window, and saw it streaking down the glass.

"Well not today, it is probably not the best day."

She turned to me and smiled, and there was that grin of mischief. She grabbed her blouse and started to open the buttons, I looked at her like she was mad.

"Birch... What the hell?"

Her blouse came off, and she undid the buttons on her slacks, she winked at my mum and me.

"Water is just water, it's either up there or down here, and I have waited too long for this, what say you my dark little beastie, are you in?" My mum gave a laugh and looked at me.

"Go on, what are you waiting for?"

I grabbed my jumper, and pulled it up, and Birch started to laugh, a few minutes later we ran screaming through the rain, across the patio, stark naked, over the grass and dived into the pool. My mum stood at the door laughing, as we both surfaced and screamed out with delight, but hell it was cold. She swam over to me, with wild excited eyes and hugged me in the water.

"You have no idea how much I have missed you." She pressed herself into me, and hugged me until I could not breathe.

Felicity sat at the desk in the study, holding the phone to her ear.

"Hi Roni, just wanted you to know she arrived here safely. I know it is probably none of my business, but as you know, she is like a daughter to me, especially after that long summer. She made such an impact, she really made Edwin and myself look at ourselves, and try to work things out. Roni she is hurting, I see it and I feel it, can you tell me what has happened, or should I leave it alone?"

Roni was quiet on the other end of the phone for a few seconds.

"Flick... You cannot mention anything to Jemi, she needs some time, and has taken a leave of absence whilst she adjusts. Look Flick, the thing is, Jemi has lost a client, not just any client, it was her first one, and it has hit her really hard. She has been working with a young woman for two years, if I am honest this girl was very like Abigail, and had suffered a similar experience. Honestly

Jemi was brilliant with her, and she was flawless in her work, but last week out of nowhere, the girl took her own life. I have not had all the medical reports, so I do not know the specifics, but it has hit her really hard, and she is hurting badly." Flick sat back in her seat, and closed her eyes.

"Poor girl, I sensed it the moment I saw her, alright, what does she need to help her?" Roni gave a sigh.

"If I am honest, she needs Abby, I suggested she go visit Abby whilst we were in London. I brought her down here because I needed some time alone with her to help her, and I have done all I can. I knew getting her closer to where Abby was, would be a massive help. I have told her to take a break until September, I think being around Abby will help her work things out on her own. It is impossible to get her to confide how she is really feeling to anyone up here. Flick, Abby understands this better than any of us, it happened to her, and so at the moment being with her is the best thing for her. If Abby struggles, tell her to talk to me. I know it sounds crazy, but she needs to leave Jemi behind for a while, this is something only Birch, Deadly and Goggles can fix, or at least I am really hoping so." Felicity understood.

"Alright Roni, I understand, and I will keep you posted on how she is doing." Roni sounded a little relieved.

"Flick.... Thank you.... Thank you for noticing so quickly, it makes me a little more relaxed knowing you love her so much. You are like another mum to her, because that is something only a mum would spot, I am so grateful." Felicity smiled.

"She is a wonderful girl Roni; you can relax knowing I will be watching to make sure she is fine. They are in the pool, and laughing at the moment, even though it is raining, no doubt they will head into the guest house shortly, and then they will be alone to talk. We will talk again soon, so do not worry, she is in safe hands." Roni chuckled.

"This is Jemi we are talking about; she may get a little wilder than normal, but thanks, William and I will sleep better knowing where she is."

"Yes, relax, I am sure we can handle whatever crazy she brings."

Not long after, Felicity gathered up their clothing with a smile, as she heard the screams and laughter from the pool. She folded them neatly, and then picked up Birch's bags, and with an umbrella, she walked to the guest house, and placed the clothes on the bed, and the bags at its base. Above the bed was the painting Hatty had done for Abby, and next to it the rosette Abby had won at that year's fete, she smiled

"Birch, Deadly and Goggles... Why does that feel like it fits?"

She walked out of the small house, lifted her umbrella, and then walked to the side of the pool, whilst we splashed and frolicked around.

"Girls... I have put your clothing, and Birch's bags in your room. I will make some dinner soon, and bring it down when it is done. Don't catch cold, Abby, I turned the heating up in the house a little, it felt chilly in there." I gave mum a nod.

"Thanks mum."

Birch dived under the water, and grabbed my legs, and pulled, and I went gasping under the water, this was so much fun, even if I did panic for a moment. I came up gasping but still smiling, God it felt so good just having her back with me, no one will ever know or understand how much I have missed her.

I have learned that you really do not fully appreciate something, until you have lost it. I spent two years at Uni, and every day she was there. When we returned for a second year, we pushed the beds together and created a double bed, and moved the desks so that we had a smaller version of the guest house, albeit with more shelves, we did have a lot of books at the dorm.

When I left, Birch moved into a single room dorm, and shared with no one, and I came home. I spent my first night home in my own room, and hated it, and so in the middle of the night, I grabbed my duvet and walked down to the guest house, and curled up alone on the large king sized bed, and hugged the pillow Birch had slept on. It still smelt faintly of her perfume, and I missed her so badly, just that was enough to make me feel at ease. That Summer dad took us away to Greece for a month, and it was beautiful, it even had nudist beaches, but it was not the same without Birch.

The guest house was all I had left of her, so when I returned, I told my parents I wanted to convert it into a writer's retreat, a place I could be solitary, and have the space to think. It took a while, but eventually with all my things moved in, and some new furniture, and a new desk, it once again felt like home.

The thing is, that because this had been the centre of what I now refer to as the Curio's, it helped me to feel safe.

I have spent so many nights alone, sat at my desk, or sat on the floor with a pillow behind me, leaning against the wall between the kitchen and the bedroom doors, that if I closed my eyes and concentrated, when I opened them, I could see them all again.

Anthony on the old comfy chair, Deb's leaning against the bathroom wall, Birch sat in the wooden chair next to the small table, and Chloe and Edwina lay on the floor with pillows or cushions, as I relived those happy times. It was all I had to keep me going, in what felt like endless loneliness, and it did ease the pain I felt in my chest.

I began writing my stories, but I also wrote a diary of sorts, it was the story of us all, and how we survived that summer when everything felt against us. Reliving it helped ease the pain of isolation, because with low book sales, and everyone so far spread apart, I was falling apart inside, being attacked even more in the village, and so lonely it was unbelievable. My life became a living hell, and my biggest demon was Marjorie.

It got so bad I started to take sleeping pills, to help me close my mind and feelings off at night. My mum did her best, so did Hatty when she was around, and on those weekends when Deb's crashed here, it was nice, but the truth of it all was, none of them were Birch.

Every Thursday without fail, we would video call each other, and for the rest of the week she would text, and every time became a spike of joy for me. Recently she had texted less, and then last night she was not able to video call, because she was in London, and it felt like the longest night of the last four years. I sat on my bed, slightly drunk and in tears.

My day had been the worst, as Madge's comments in the village had been more hurtful, and I had been so looking forward to seeing her, and she was not there. I had started to think she was so disappointed; she couldn't handle seeing me anymore, and I fell apart. It had felt like the worst week, I had tried to write, but I was losing my confidence, and I really needed to see her face, and could not.

It is not that easy to explain, it makes no real sense even to me, except it was two am, I was sat in my panties on the bed, hugging a pillow which was pretty much devoid of most of her scent now, drunk, and crying my eyes out, and holding a bottle of sleeping pills.

I had been here only once before, it was when I first told my mum I wanted to go to Uni in Manchester, and she had thrown the fit of a lifetime. I thought about it then, but swore I never would again, and yet here I was back to square one, a failed writer, in love with a person I could never hold, and at the loneliest I had ever been. Thank God for tequila, because I passed out, before I could do anything stupid.

That was last night, and today is today. It is crazy, Birch once told me, that the one good thing about hitting rock bottom, was after that moment of realisation, you can only go in one direction, and that was back up, and she was so right, because look at me now. It is raining like crazy, I am freezing my tits off in a pool, in my own garden, and laughing like a crazy person, looking at her beautiful green eyes, as she smiled at me. I had no idea she was coming, I walked into the village just to be out of the house and get some air, and suddenly there she was, it was almost as if she had known.

"GIRLS.... GIRLS! YOUR DINNER WILL BE READY IN TWO MINUTES, COME ON YOU NEED TO GET OUT." I waved from the pool.

"WE HEAR YOU!"

She shook her head, and smiled, she must have thought we were as mad as hatters. I swam to the side and pulled myself up, Birch grabbed my hips and yanked, and I went flying back into the pool, as she giggled and climbed out. I came back up to the surface, and saw her running for the house, I climbed out behind her, and ran dripping across the lawn.

I came panting into the bedroom, to find Birch wrapped in a towel, holding up the small metal frame, which I kept on the side of my dresser, the picture was of all of us the day we left, stood next to Petal outside the salon, she smiled as I walked in.

"This was such a bitter sweet moment for all of us, I miss them, oh god I have really missed everyone, you have no idea how hard it can be without them."

She put the picture down, and lifted up the bottle of sleeping pills, and turned to me, her bright eyes stared at me, and I felt exposed.

"Maybe I should rephrase that, you know too... Seriously Deads, why didn't you say something?"

I had forgotten, I know how she feels about medication, especially addictive ones. I had been so happy to see her, I had not thought. She had caught me out, I was busted, her bright green eyes shone with life, and she wanted an answer, and I did not really know what to say. I didn't want to spoil the moment, I just stood there with my head down, shivering like crazy, and dripping on the carpet, completely naked, showing my unshaved vagina, which had grown into a small shrubbery to rival even Deb's, and feeling more exposed in her gaze, than I would if I walked naked through the village fete. My eyes filled with tears.

"I thought we were over, and I missed you.... I was so incredibly lonely.... So frigging heart broken. This village hates me, and has made my life a nightmare, it got to me... I needed you, you have no idea how much I really needed you, and it hurt so badly, because you were not here with me. What the fuck do you want me to say Birch.... I fell in love with the one person I can never truly be with, and I lost her, and it hurt so badly, I could not deal with the pain of it all, is that what you want to hear?"

Two tears ran from her eyes, and rolled down her cheeks, and she just exploded, and screamed at me.

"YOU CAN NEVER.... NEVER.... NEVER EVER DO THAT TO ME DEADS!"

She shook her head, as more tears rolled down her face, and her voice dropped to an almost inaudible squeak.

"Not ever."

She came round the bed, reached out, and snatched me into her arms, and almost crushed me, she held me so tight. Her face buried into my shoulder and she started to sob.

"No matter what happens, you must never leave me, promise me Deads.... Promise me you will never leave me alone in this world, because I would not survive if you left me alone?"

Her sobs became bitter and painful, and I was wrong footed now. I stood there with my arms around her, as she cried like I never thought was possible, and all I could do was hold her.

I noticed movement, I saw my mum through the doorway stood in the living room, behind her, two hot steaming plates were on the table. Her eyes were fixed on us, and she smiled, and gave a gentle nod, and then backed away. It was almost as if she knew something I didn't. Mum turned, and quietly left, as Birch sniffled into my shoulder.

"How did our world get so fucked up Deads?" I had no idea; I gave her a squeeze.

"You tell me… You're supposed to be the bloody expert." She gave a gasp of a chuckle and then sniffled.

"Yeah… But I still have a lot to learn, trust me your mum was right, life has bumps in it, I just never realised they would be this sodding big." She slipped back and wiped her nose on her hand.

"I screwed up Deads… I really screwed up big time, and all I could think of was I need my dark little beastie, if I am with her, the answers will come." I looked at her and sighed.

"While you're at it, find a few for me too… Dinner… Manchester tea, is here, let's eat whilst it's hot." I pointed behind her. "Tissues are there." She started to giggle.

"God, I have missed this Deads."

I got it, she had no idea of how much I missed this, I looked at her as she turned to grab a tissue, and felt the surge of my truth explode inside me. I looked at her as she wiped her nose, and it just slipped out.

"Then stay with me Birch, and don't ever leave me again."

Chapter 3

# Surprising Revelations.

The house was different and the same, the comfy chair and
wall unit were gone, and I now had a new desk with my desk top
computer, with a small side table, on which was my laptop. Above
the desk, my dad had a carpenter come in and build a large book
case, to surround above, and down both the sides of the desk,
which was now home to my books and DVD collection. I kept
the table and two wooden chairs, mainly because some of my
happiest memories, had been sat at it, or watching it with Birch
sat there framed by the window.

The wall that ran along the bathroom to the door, now had a
big soft comfy sofa, which also pulled out into a double bed, I had
offered it Deb's when she stayed, but she had blushed, and asked
if it was okay to sleep in my bed. She too missed us all jumping
in at night together. The underfloor heating was upgraded, in the
sense that a quieter and more economical heater was added, but
apart from that, little has changed.

I left the bedroom pretty much as it was, it is silly, but for me it
was a sacred place. I hung my large painting of us by Hatty over
the bed, and I swapped the wardrobe with the one from my room
as it was bigger, and had a section with draws in for panties and
socks etc. My bedside table has booze on one side of the bed, and
on the other side, sanitary towels, baby wipes, and tissues, as well
as thousands of condoms, left by Birch.

We sat at the table eating, and watching the rain outside, as
Birch told me the story of Melody Pritchard, a bright, very clever
university student, who had come up from Bristol to study at
Manchester. I cannot deny I got a few shivers, as Birch filled me
in on what she was like.

She had arrived at the practice, after being referred there by
Birch's dad, she was lonely, afraid, very geeky, and insecure,

naive way more than Deb's, and from a sheltered background. She was struggling with anxiety and panic attacks, because two years before Uni, she had gone to a party and passed out, and three boys had for want of a better word, screwed her.

She had told no one, she had been a virgin before that night, and only really understood what had happened when she woke up to find semen leaking out of her. Birch told me how hard it had been to get her to talk, she pointed out that Melody had not been unsimilar to me. I got cold shivers just hearing that.

Birch had worked with her for two years, and she really thought she was making progress, Melody had finally admitted that she had a boyfriend at home. He had been the one that had found her weeping at the party, and walked her home, and been kind to her, and each day, he had checked on her, and so over time they began to date.

Even though she was miles away, they talked every day, and on her term trips home they spent a lot of time together, there was obviously more, but Birch could only tell me so much, after all, she was a client, and even though she had died, Birch still kept her deepest confidences secret. Birch sat back and lifted her glass of gin, and gave a long sigh.

"At our last meeting, she was quieter than normal, but final exams were on the horizon, and she was anxious. I missed something Deads, I must have, we talked about how much she had changed. Her anxiety was a hundred times less than it had been, and she had not suffered a panic attack in four months, and yet two days after our last session, they found her dead from an overdose in her dorm, and a note that said life this way is less painful, sorry."

She breathed in a deep breath and swallowed hard, I had seen the emotion that had surged up in her, I knew that feeling all too well, I reached across the table and grabbed her hand.

"Birch how could you know, how many times have you said to me, it is those who never mention it that do it, and the ones who threaten, who never will? She said nothing Birch, you could not have seen it, I am sorry but you are brilliant and so great at spotting things, but you had no hope of ever seeing that." She looked up at me as I leaned across the table.

"You and her are so alike, and you were going to leave me too."

Tears rolled down her cheeks, and it tore me apart, nothing is worse than seeing Birch with tears in her eyes, she gave a sob.

"You did not tell me either, you would have left me without saying goodbye Deads."

Her shoulders shook, and she gave out a huge sob, and looked down at the table, where her tears dripped onto her empty plate. I felt wretched inside, it was heart breaking to watch, I squeezed her hand.

"Birch I am still here; I am not going anywhere… See, your dark little beastie is sat right in front of you."

She gave a huge gasp, and just wailed, as more tears flooded into her eyes.

"You are blonde with no fringe, and I frigging hate it… My dark little beastie has gone to the light, and I want her back."

Actually, that was a low blow, and if I am honest a tad pathetic. Melody I get, but wailing the house down because my hair grew out, and I was blonde again, why the hell was that a crime, or reason to break down?

Her shoulders shook as her sobs got faster, I could see her lip trembling, it was ridiculous, a quick trip to the chemist, and it was fixed. I watched the tears drip onto her empty plate, who the hell was she crying for, Melody or my fringe? I just sensed this was actually doing her good, it felt like this had been bottled up for a while, and so I just left her to cry a little longer, and refilled our glasses, from the bottles on the table, and got the tissue box ready.

She grabbed a tissue without even looking, and pulled it under her long hair, and blew her nose. If memory served me right, it was as loud as her morning farts. It appeared to me, all air expelling from Birch was indeed very noisy. She dried her eyes and looked at me, she tried to smile but failed miserably.

"I am sorry, Deads." I nodded.

"What for crying and shaking the house, or trashing my hair?" She snorted her nose.

"Crying… I do frigging hate your hair; you look like Axel Rose's lesbian cousin." She giggled, and found her smile.

"Well, if we are being honest Birch, I got to tell you, I frigging hate your blouse, you look like a receptionist for a dominatrix."

She gave a gasp of a giggle, and looked at me.

"It's designer, I wear it for work." It was a low blow, but I risked it.

"Christ Birch, if I sat in a room with you wearing those clothes, week in and week out, I would frigging want to kill myself too." She gasped, and looked shocked, and then burst out laughing.

"That is so cruel Deads."

"Feel better now?" She nodded.

"Yeah tons…. Thanks, Deads."


Weird as it sounds, I got a text from dad, he had seen the 'jeep' I have no idea why he cannot understand it is not a jeep? Anyway, he asked if we would like to come up to the house, as he would love to see Birch, so whilst Birch cleared the table, I got dressed, and went for a pee.

I was relieved to see when Birch came out of the bedroom, she was more Birch like, in a long flowing top and skirt, I cannot deny, the blouse and slacks was creepy. I mean she looked really professional, but it was too Roni like, and as much as I love her mum to bits, it suits her, but not Birch.

We made our way to the house, and the living room, where my dad gave her a huge hug, he was smiling and jolly, and not at all like the dull boring walking greyness he had been for the last few months. He sat back looking at us, and actually appeared to approve of the jeep.

"I must say Birch, it is a remarkable transformation, I mean it looks like new."

She appreciated such high praise, considering how much he had hated it before.

"I have some really talented friends, they specialise in Land Rovers, especially the Defender. My first year back at Uni I was too busy, and after that, I had so much on my plate I got very little done and she just sat in the garage. So, they had her for almost a year, and stripped her down to the basics, and then literally rebuilt her, and restored her, from the frame up. I chose the colour, and they sprayed her, and even the roof, which I love, I was never happy with it white." He gave an agreeable nod.

"I see you left the artwork on the back door; I was glad to see that." Birch gave a slight chuckle.

"Actually, that is a decal, the door was leaking and damaged, so they replaced it. I got them to cut out the metal sheet off the back, and it was in fact Edwina who helped me. She was up with Katie and saw it in my room. Edwina took it to a friend of hers, and they scanned it, cleaned up the edges to sharpen it, and turned it into three special decals, one of which is on the back door. Flick's original art is back in my room at home." My mum was amazed.

"I could not tell, I went out to look at it, I just thought you had varnished over it, the detail and depth of the paint are still clearly visible." Birch smiled.

"I am thrilled with how it turned out, Edwina is pretty well connected now, she has really done some amazing work for Katie. After the respray, I got all the bumpers and accessories chromed, added the flowers, rainbow decals, the Petal scrolled name on the bonnet front, and then mum and dad helped completely redo the interior, and as you can see, she is as glorious as I said she would be." My dad chuckled.

"I cannot deny, I had my doubts it could be done, but your vision of what could be done is inspiring." He lifted his glass. "Here is to the Jeep." I had to giggle.

"She is called Petal." My phone buzzed, it was a text, and I had wondered when the news would travel. I looked at Birch.

"Guess who?" She gave a huge smile.

"Where is she, home, the front gate, or already in the guest house?" Mum laughed. I looked at my phone.

"She saw Petal, as she drove past, and she got home to find out you were back here, so I think looking at the message time, she is probably somewhere between her house and ours." Mum stood up.

"You two head back, and I will buzz her in, go on, you three need a reunion, in your club house." Mum understood us so well, we said good night to dad, and we both hugged him, and then excitedly hurried back to our house, and waited for her.

It did not take long, she came charging down the garden, I opened the door, she sped straight through, and launched herself into Birch, with a happy squeal.

"I MISSED YOU BIRCH!"

It was nice to see them, as they both hugged with happy smiling faces, as I closed the door. I think it was important to Birch, she appeared happier and less worn if that makes sense? Birch released her with a huge smile.

"God, I missed those hugs Goggles."

I reached for the gin, and she stepped back looking at us both side by side, and gave a long contented happy sigh.

"I have really missed you guys, life without you is really dull and boring, which is why I quit today." I stumbled, and almost dropped her drink.

"What... I mean.... What?" I could not find the right words; Birch found the right words.

"What the hell Goggles?" She gave a huge smile, and sat on the sofa. I was still trying to find words that would join in a sentence that made sense.

"I have been talking with dad for ages now, I mean, I enjoyed the work at the lab, but if I am honest, it just is not as exciting as I thought it was going to be, and some of the other lab techs are so dull, it's just life draining. Agatha Willington is retiring, and so she has put her bookshop up for sale, and I have bought it. I mean, to be honest the steam punk section is really lacking, the whole place needs dragging out of the dark ages, and into more modern times." I sat on my desk chair.

"That is a big step Deb's." She shook her head.

"Not really, if you look at it from my point of view. I hate Cambridge, I hate living there, I miss everyone at home, I really have missed you guys, and I am getting married to a rock star." She looked at me with a pleading expression.

"Abby, I hardly see you, think about it, I have done three years on a 70K a year wage, and not had a life to spend it on. Your dad handled the trust fund dad set up for me, and I have shit loads of cash in the bank. I really do not even need to work, but I want to. I thought if I am going to work, I want to be close to you, and do something I love, and let's be honest, all three of us love books, it's like the coolest place on earth to hang out." Birch sat on the wooden chair by the window.

"I must admit, I love therapy, but if I had to do something else, a bookshop would be ideal." Deb's agreed and took a swig of her drink.

"It will be cool after the refit, and it will have a section for your mums' books, and a good self help section. I would like more fantasy and sci fi, and it defo needs some good books on herb lore and witchcraft." She giggled. "I probably won't sell any, but when Madge finds out I have books on witchcraft, she will never enter the place."

And so it began, the three of us settled down, just like old times, and talked as we drank. Debs pointed out all the benefits of owning a bookshop, and the plans she had. Apparently, Bradly Wheeler had got my dad to do a full appraisal of the business and property, and under dads' instruction he bought the building and everything outright. The bookshop would officially change hands on the first week of July, and would close for two weeks, to be refitted. Deb's just bubbled with enthusiasm.

"Well, you know, this could be a shrewd move, because with the fish monger closing, I mean let's be honest here, no young guy is going to take on that, I mean, old Higgins always smelt funky, even after he had showered. Well, it looks like the charity shop is going to relocate there, they say they need a cheaper premises. I mean, they get high class stuff from round here, but I never really understood why we needed one, everyone round here is loaded. Anyway, it looks like there is a buyer for the shop when they move in August, although dad has tried, and cannot find out who has bought it. If it is a decent business with loads of trade, they will be going right next door, and I bet I can grab a lot of extra passing trade, especially during the fete."

It made sense, she had said nothing I could argue with, and I was actually impressed at how much behind the scenes work she had put in. Like all things Deb's, she was smarter than she looked, and I could not deny, having her closer would be so nice, especially because Birch would only be here for a day, although I really did not want her to leave.

The clocked ticked and Deb's passed out, and so we carried her to the bedroom, and stripped her and put her in bed. It was funny how quick things could get back to normal, I went for a pee and Birch already had the middle. She sat back with a beaming smile. I pulled my top off, and then slid off my jeans.

"Holy shit Deads, you wear a G string with that, it looks like a kite that came down in a dead bramble bush."

I looked down at it and smiled, she was not far wrong, I slipped off the string and climbed into bed.

"I will do it tomorrow." She sniggered.

"Are you going to use your dad's lawn mower?"

I could not help but giggle, as I slid down in the bed, and she snuggled down and pulled me close, and I felt her hand slowly move round and grab my boob. I relaxed into the pillow.

"I have missed this so much." She wriggled around to get comfy and slipped her leg over mine.

"Me too, I have not had a decent night's sleep in three years." I looked back.

"What about Kev, you two are still seeing each other aren't you?" She opened her eyes.

"Yeah, we still have the open relationship thing going, well you see, he is skinny, his boob is not as nice as yours, and I have missed it."

It was not long before I drifted off to sleep, and for the first time in a long time, I knew I would sleep deep and happy. It was so deep it was gone twelve when I woke up, Deb's was awake and nursing a headache as she came in naked with a coffee. How quickly things get back to normal, Birch was still flat out, I looked at her, with her hair everywhere. Deb's stood at the end of the bed and whispered.

"Hey Abby, I have a really cool idea, don't laugh, just watch." I blinked, I had a headache, she put down her coffee, and stood by the bedroom door, she winked.

"OH MY GOD, BEV IS HERE!" Birch shot up in the bed, with her eyes still closed.

"Guard your vagina's."

Deb's exploded into laughter, and collapsed on the floor, in hysterics, I cannot deny, I was laughing too, even though my head had almost exploded, as Birch turned slowly round, opened her eyes and smiled.

"Hi Sweetie."


It took a lot of coffee and paracetamol before I felt anything like alive, but it was a fun morning. It felt just like old times, there was all the usual banter and shenanigans, I walked into the bedroom where Birch was hanging some of her clothes from her bag in my wardrobe.

"Won't you need those back at home?"

"I told you, I will not be long, I just have a few things to sort, and then I will be back, it is pointless taking them home just to bring them back." I shrugged.

"I still wish you didn't have to go; it has been so long and I loved last night, it was such fun, and I slept better than I have in years." She gave a sigh and turned, and pulled me into a hug.

"Oh, Deads, little has changed in five years. Look Sweetie, I promise, I will be there and back before you know it, but I have to go home, honestly this time it's not forever." I gave a long sigh.

"I know, I am being selfish."

She pulled back and looked at me, her eyes were so close they looked huge.

"It is not selfish, I want it too, this is as important to me as it is you, and I will be back in a flash, please Deads work with me on this." I smiled.

"The last time I asked you that, you dressed up like a satanic garden gnome for the vicar." She giggled.

"It was fun that day, that's when people could actually see your vagina, although the vicar did almost get an eye full." Deb's leaned round the doorframe.

"Never mention that man and his weird perversions again, you promised Birch, I still get wobbly legs when I think about it." I looked at Birch and lowered my voice.

"She does know it will be him who marries' her doesn't she?" Birch sniggered.

"I am not sure she has realised yet... Shush.... Let's wait until the penny drops, it will be fun."


Saying goodbye is never fun. Deb's drove Petal onto the road, and then got out, and walked round admiring the fully restored work she had done. I walked through the back gate with Birch holding her hand.

"You will be fine Deads, Deb's will be around more, so at least you will have each other, I will be as fast as I can be." We got to the open front gates, and dad and mum came out to say goodbye.

As always it was a big round of hugs as we stood next to Petal. Mum kissed her cheek.

"Hurry back, I want you around for more than a day." Birch gave me a huge hug.

"I love you my dark little beastie, I won't be long."

She finally climbed inside Petal, and waved as she pulled off. Birch drove five yards down the road and turned left, the gates of number three opened, and she drove in. I frowned, my dad looked confused, Deb's turned to me.

"Is she lost; I am not sure she is allowed in there?"

I shrugged; it made no sense to me either. Bradley Wheeler appeared at the gates, and I looked again, Petal drove back out and stopped on the pathway. Birch got out and walked round Petal to Bradley, he handed her some papers, and she placed them on the window, and wrote on them. My dad looked even more confused, my mum was all smiles, I looked back at my dad, he shrugged.

"What the blazers is going on?"

I turned back to number three, where Birch had got back in Petal, and drove onto the road, indicated right and came back down the road, and pulled in outside the house, she got out with a beaming smile.

"I am back.... SURPRISE!" I had no idea what to say, Deb's pointed at number three.

"That was my dad, you said you were going home?" Birch looked back at the house where Bradley stood smiling.

"I did Sweetie... I bought it.... That is home.... Or at least it will be when your dad has finished working on it, as I said, I had to go home to sort a few things out, well I just did."

My brain crashed. Birch walked to the back of Petal, opened the door, leaned in and took out her case. She snapped the handle so it came up, and walked round to me with a huge smile on her face.

"Hi Sweetie, see, I told you I would be back in a flash." In my mind, it was still mashed, I lifted my hand and pointed at number three.

"You are the hammer twat?" She walked up close so her eyes looked huge.

"Hmm... About that... So, tell me, what is it going to be, hit me or screw me?" My dad snapped his head round.

"I beg your pardon?" I just started laughing, so did my mum, she looked at my dad and rolled her eyes.

"Edwin, I have told you a thousand times, it's a Birch thing, you will get used to it." Birch slipped her arm in mine, and winked.

"Take me to your place and sleep with me."

She gave a cackle of a laugh, and we walked back through the gates, as she dragged her case behind her.

"Sorry Flick, I don't have any pegs or fortunes on me today, although I did find a great pair of binoculars yesterday." Mum smiled.

"You know I did see a purple coloured car drive out of there yesterday, when I was cleaning the bedroom. I should have known it was you, I just did not recognise it was Petal." Birch snuggled into my arm.

"I am on leave for the summer, and I am feeling very curious, how about we call for an early reunion?"

Chapter 4

# Sweetie's Retreat.

My head was spinning, as we walked into the kitchen, my dad firing question after question, poor Birch was swamped, and mum came to the rescue.

"Edwin, give the poor girl a second to think, I say let's all just sit down, relax, have a coffee, and let Birch tell us just exactly what has been happening."

She was watching me all the time, her eyes filled with happiness, and I may add some devilish delight. Finally, Mum, and Deb's, joined me at the counter with Birch, and dad got a chair from the dining table, and sat at the end of the counter. Mum and Deb's made coffees, and we all calmed down a little, exactly as she had told us. Once we were seated with drinks, Birch looked at me.

"Are you alright with this, you know me owning a house here?" It felt like an odd question, she took my hand in hers.

"You are quieter than I thought you would be."

The truth was I was simply blown away, I mean, I knew she had cash, I just never realised it was enough to buy a house here. I shook my head and smiled.

"Birch I am blown away; it was a hell of a surprise. I am actually delighted about it; I suppose I am lost for words." She gave a huge smile, and her excitement bubbled over.

"You will live with me won't you, I mean if I am going to live here, you have to move in with me Deads?" Again, my words caught in my mouth.

"Wow, Birch... I do not know what to say... I mean, I don't exactly have a lot coming in at the moment, and these places have a lot of costs, but yeah, if I can afford it, I would love to." She gave a huge giggle and dragged me into a hug.

"Deads don't worry about money, I have shit loads, it will be like Uni all over again but bigger." She slipped back on her seat, and looked at Deb's.

"You can stay too when Jimmy is on tour, it will be so much fun, it will be like a sorority house, all girls together." Deb's looked like her eyes would pop out, and her smile was so wide I thought her head was going to split.

"REALLY? Oh guys, I would love that so much, you have no idea how cool that would be." Dad gave a slight cough.

"Pardon me if I interrupt, but how exactly did you acquire this house without anyone knowing, I would imagine there will be a few raised eyebrows in the village?" Birch smiled, she understood how things worked with dad, he smelt money, and was on the trail of it.

"Bradley handled everything for me. I contacted him a few years back at work, and met him in London. I have been looking for something since I was here that summer, because that was when I talked to mum about setting up a second office here. I knew I had to serve my training time, and finish my doctorate, so I contacted quite a lot of people around this area. To be honest Ed, when they found out I was in Manchester, and only twenty two, they did not take me seriously, and gave me the run around. I knew Deb's dad was in property, so I rang him, and we met and talked, and he has pretty much handled me as a client since. I set up a holding company, transferred the funds to it, and he has taken care of everything." Edwin suddenly understood.

"You are aware I am his accountant?" Birch smiled.

"Yes I am... We knew it would be a risk, and I was afraid you would work it out, but I have to say Ed, I still got ya." He nodded and started to chuckle.

We all looked at the both of them, what was this inside joke Birch had with my dad? He noticed all of our attention was on him. He gave another chuckle.

"I challenged Bradly about a company I checked out in his accounts. I didn't like the sound of it. It looked a little too good to be true, I was concerned it was a front for illegal activity. He assured me it was solid and told me not to worry, so I watched it carefully, but my initial concern was I could not find out who the owner was, I was convinced it was something illegal. I have to admit, I hounded him a lot about it, then I saw the funds appearing in the company, I honestly thought it was a front, so I dug deeper and found out...." He looked at Birch. "Is it alright to tell them, I am assuming you have not?" She gave a happy giggle.

"The cat is out of the bag, you might as well." He shook his head.

"I cannot believe I did not see it; I mean it had you stamped all over it."

"Edwin for god's sake stop blabbering and tell us." I looked at mum and giggled, she was as excited as we were. He smiled.

"The bloody company was called 'Sweetie's Retreat' They purchased the charity shop property in outright cash, and as it now appears, number three."

Birch giggled, as I let out a long gasp, and looked at her, Deb's was even more blown away, her eyes were expanding in her face, and I was convinced if they did not stop, they would explode.

"You are going to be my neighbour?" Birch gave a happy chuckle and put out her hand.

"Hi, I am Dr Jemima Dixon, I do hope you have a good self help section, and I would hope a very well stocked erotic section, because I aim to fill your shop with every kinky pervert from a radius of fifty miles." It suddenly hit me as Deb's shook her hand with a beaming smile and replied.

"I am going to have the filthiest books ever written, you can bank on it." Birch turned with a smile, and I was staring at her.

"You okay Sweetie?" I nodded.

"Birch I am so sorry I completely forgot.... You are a doctor now." She winked.

"Yes dear, now lie back on the bed, and drop your pants."

We all burst out laughing, and it took us a long while to settle down. She looked so happy, and more of the Birch I knew, she looked at all of us.

"I have really missed you all, I wanted the practice open sooner, but it takes time. Anyhow, Bradley found out that the shop was becoming empty, and we snapped it up, I held interviews in London at his offices in March, and I have three great therapists joining me at Sweetie's Retreat. This is my own business, but it is connected to mums' company, which is sort of the umbrella organisation, but it is all my investment, as I decided I wanted to be more independent. After that, I got the house, Bradley negotiated the price down as the guy wanted it gone fast, and I have been video calling him on site as he walked me round it, and telling him what I want doing to it, that is why I had to go over and sign the papers, it was in his care until I signed for it, so it is now officially mine." Deb's sipped her coffee.

"Wow you are pretty shrewd, and rich, so where has all the cash come from, I mean, we did once think you were a secret bank robber?" My mum frowned.

"I am not sure you should ask such a question Debbie; I mean a person's money is private."

I looked at Deb's, she was interested, I knew dad was, and to be honest I didn't care if it was rude, I was pretty interested. Birch chuckled.

"My grandad used to buy shares in all sorts of new start ups, because he thought he was helping young people. He would always buy them in my name, he never really paid a great deal of interest in them. Anyway, when I was twenty one, my dad told me about the portfolio in my name, that he had left me in his will. We did not think it would amount to much, because he only bought a handful of shares of each company, his broker managed it all for him, and kept reinvesting the profits into more of the shares. It turns out he bought shares early on in companies connected with online payments, book retailers, social media pages, search engines, and electronics. Then they all hit big, so there I was at just twenty one, with shares valued in the millions, and eighteen million in the bank."

I almost fell off my seat, mum gasped, Deb's almost fainted, and my dad gave out a mighty roar of a laugh, although that did not surprise me, he could see the motherlode was sat in his kitchen. I was impressed, she was so calm about it all, it was almost like it did not even matter to her at all. She turned to me and gave a really beautiful smile.

"Deads, do you want to come and see our new house, it is still a bit dirty, they are finishing it off before decorating, but I can show you round the place if you want?" I nodded, and felt the excitement building inside me.

"Yeah... I want to go explore." I looked at Deb's who looked ready to explode.

"Come on then." Birch jumped up with a squeal, and grabbed both our hands, and we ran down the hall laughing, and out the door. Edwin smiled and looked at Felicity.

"It is nice to hear that again." She smiled.

"I think this will be good for both of them, although I am not so sure the neighbours will be happy about it, they can get a little wild Edwin." He took a sip of his drink.

"Stuff them, this is the first time I have seen Abigail smile since last year, if a little trouble with the neighbours is the price of her smile, then I for one will gladly pay it."

Number three Waterside Lane was big, it was one of the biggest plots in the area. It was set in a huge piece of land that backed onto the manor, with high stone walls, all the way round it. It was about twice the size of my house, with four huge bedroom windows, and a very large windows above the door. The roof was high in large pointed peaks, above each window, and it was rendered in a pale grey. The garage alone could house three cars, and there was a huge workshop with big windows attached, apparently it had once been a stable, but Birch had converted it, into what she called a studio. Above the front door, was a slated porch way, with small glass windows, that kept the rain off the entrance, with an umbrella stand, and a shelf, with a dead plant on it.

The front door was enormous, and inside was a massive entrance hall, with a central staircase that went up, and then split, and had stairs going left and right, it had eight very large bedrooms, all ensuite, a separate guest toilet, and linen cupboards. Downstairs either side of the main hall, were two huge front rooms, both with double doors. One had been converted into a library, and Birch had arranged carpenters to come in and fit the whole room out with bookcases. Birch and myself had a serious book addiction, and this meant only one thing, book buying binge.

There were dust cloths everywhere, as an army of men worked on about a million things around the whole house, and it smelt of plaster and fresh timber. Wires stuck out of walls waiting for light covers, and there was sawdust and plaster dust everywhere.

I found it all a little overwhelming, it was so big, and for just the two of us, it felt a little too much, I was used to compact and close quarters.

The kitchen and dining room, were huge, you could cook for a hundred, and seat thirty, but it was so beautiful, fitted out in dark wooden doors, and marble surfaces, I had no problems imagining myself sitting here drinking coffee. Along the far wall was a bank of patio doors, set either side of a long wall, onto which the kitchen units, cooker and sink was fitted, with a huge window looking out across the garden.  We crossed the kitchen, and walked out onto a wide stone patio, with a newly built outdoor kitchen, a full size swimming pool, that had a long pool house along one side, with changing rooms, and vast gardens that stretched all the way back to the manor property boundary. Deb's and me were just lost for words, Birch bit her lip, and looked nervously at me.

"Did I get carried away again?" Deb's looked round.

"Just a tad Birch, but sod it, if you have the cash, splash the ash." I frowned and looked at her.

"What the hell does that mean?" She shrugged.

"No idea, my dad says it all the time."

It was at that moment I realised; Deb's was in fact used to a bigger house. Mr Wheeler owned the largest property in the area. I looked round at the vastness of what would become my new home.

"I am not sure you will feel that comfy here Deb's, I mean compared to your house, won't you be slumming it moving in here?" Birch started to laugh; Deb's gave a titter.

"Oh... The sacrifices I have to make for my friends, I am sure, I can just about squeeze my shit in to this kennel."

It broke the tension as we all started to laugh. We walked round the house giggling, there was still a lot to be done, Birch as always had endless enthusiasm.

"I know it looks huge, but once it is all decorated and we have furniture in, it will feel more lived in and homely." We walked up the stairs, and stood on the top landing.

"Obviously guys it is eight rooms, so I figured we could let some others come to live here with us, I mean I know Chloe hates her flat, and I did sort of build the studio for her if she wants one, well actually, I know she does. It would be nice if Edwina had a permanent base, she could have loads of room for her computers, and do a lot of her work from here, although keep quiet for now,

I want it to be a surprise for them. Izzy is coming down from Manchester, she will be helping me run the practice, so she will be here too, I mean what do you guys think, I would love to have us all girls together again?"

It made sense, it definitely needed more people in it, Deb's looked down the long hall.

"So, which will be my room?" I laughed.

"She probably has her dad already packing her shit up at home." Birch smiled, and pointed in front.

"I thought this would be my room, and that one to the right would be Deads," She linked my arm.

"It has adjoining doors to a shared bathroom, which we can leave open, and there is loads of room, so you can have a desk in there to work privately, and in peace. Debs I thought you might like that one next to mine, it looks out on the gardens, and it gets loads of sun on it, the whole place is private, so we can be naked as much as we like." Deb's was in, and she bolted off to look at her room. Birch walked me to the door and opened it.

"This will be your room, see how much space you have, it is about the same size as the guest house, but has no kitchen, but I thought we could arrange all your furniture, so it looked similar, to make it more homely for you." She suddenly looked really nervous.

"Deads Sweetie, please tell me I have not gone too far, and you like it, please tell me this is not too much and you can live here, I really want us to live together again?"

I cannot deny it was a lot to take in, I always knew I was pretty privileged, I mean hell I live right across the lane, but since living alone in the guest house, I have become very simplistic, and needed little to live, this place was massive, and it felt intimidating. I could feel the tension in her, she turned and pointed to two large double glass doors, and hurried towards them, as I stood and watched her. She looked back at me, and I could see the panic in her eyes.

"There is a balcony, and we can put a table on it, I thought the house would be like a dorm, you know lots of people living together, going about their lives, and up here you can sit out in private, you could even write out here. Deads most of us will be at work, so you will have lots of quiet time, like when we went to class. Please tell me it is alright?"

She was making more sense, and I could see how much she had thought about it, it was clear this was not a hair brained scheme, and she really had given everything a lot of thought. She turned back into the room, and pointed.

"Look that is my room, we can come and go, and we will have two beds, so we can take it in turn sharing."

Birch had put a huge amount of thought into it, I turned and looked at her, and suddenly there was that frightened little child side to her, those bright green innocent eyes, her biting her lip, looking worried. Hell, she was now a doctor, and yet here she was, shy and vulnerable, I gave a sigh.

"You are impossible to say no to, you know that right?" She burst into tears, and threw her arms round me.

"Oh, Deads, you have no idea what that means to me, I was so afraid you would hate it. I missed you so much, I miss living with you, I miss sleeping with you, my life has been horrible. All the time I was doing this, I was thinking of you, it will be such fun, I promise. You will never need to look over that abyss again, I promise, I could not live if anything happened to you."

I held her tight, this was just not like her at all, I had never known her be so unstable, actually scratch that, she has always been a little unstable, but this, this vulnerability, this was not a Birch thing. I cannot deny it bothered me more than I was willing to admit.

"You are aware I am a writer, and I love peace, and you are going to invite Chloe to live here, and we already have a Deb's?" She gave a snort and giggled.

"It won't be boring, will it now?"

That is what worried me, I was already envisioning Chloe and her sexually deviant friends, just about shagging in every corner of the house. Either that or she would be skate boarding up the hallway, actually, I fancied that myself, I made a mental note to buy a new skate board, it had been a few years, but it's just like riding a bike I have heard.

"Alright I have seen as much as I can for one day, let's go home and get you unpacked, I am assuming it will be a while before it is ready?" She gave another snort and wiped her eyes.

"Yeah, mid to late July they say…. Look Deads, I am serious you know, this is not a game for me, I really mean what I say? I want us together every day, things have got strained a little between us, and I do not want that, I want us back together, but this time for good, me and you, and the girls." I understood as she stood there looking at me, she smiled.

"I love you Sweetie."

She lifted her hands and then held my face, moved in and kissed me. It was warm and soft and loving, and I felt a huge wave crash over me, and instinctively lifted my arms and kissed her back, and it was long and delightful. Oh god I was getting way too turned on, I could feel myself getting wet. She pulled back and smiled.

"Us… Together, forever, that is the deal sealed." She smiled. Deb's was stood at the door smiling.

"Bout time… Jesus you two really are slow, it only took you five years." I felt my cheeks heat up, Birch winked, and I smiled.

"Us… A deal is a deal." She slipped her hand round my waist and leaned into me, and whispered.

"You are wet, aren't you?" I felt suddenly really shy and embarrassed.

"Fuck you Birch." Her hand slipped onto my bum and gave it a squeeze, I jumped and Deb's giggled as she smiled.

"I really love you guys; I am so happy at the moment I could burst." I shuddered, as pictures of Rosie came back to mind.

"The toilet is that way, and no walking out till you are done." Birch started to snigger.

We came out of the house, and crossed the road towards my house. Birch was happy, and I realised that she was worried, but having secured my agreement, she relaxed. We reached the gates to my house, and she fumbled in her bag.

"Deads Sweetie, I have to just run an errand, you and Gogs go and head in, and I will be back in ten minutes. Okay Sweetie, make mine a strong gin?" I looked at her with that what are you up to look, she smiled.

"I will literally be ten minutes." She pulled out her keys and jumped in Petal, and before I could even reply, she spun Petal round, and was driving at high speed away from us.

Antonio was chattering away, as he played with the girl's hair, he lifted his wrist and examined the look.

"Oh yes, I mean, it looks like perfection darling, those eyes and those waves, no red blooded man alive could resist you, am I not right Cynthia?" She glanced across from the chair at his side.

"Oh yes... Yes.... Yes, Antonio I don't know how you do it, it's perfect."

Outside there was screeching, as the lilac form of Petal ground to a very swift halt. The door to the salon burst open, and in marched Birch, Anthony's face lit up with happiness.

"BIRCH... DARLING YOU ARE BACK... Ooh what the hell have you been doing with your hair, oh dear." He spun his wrist in the air. "That cannot be left unattended, it simply will not do." She smiled.

"Anthony, I have a deadly emergency, you have to come now, you need red, and you need black.... Lots of black, and possibly shampoo and anything that gives life to the dead, because her thatch is dried to tinder." She turned to Delphine and hugged her.

"Delphine Sweetie, lovely to see you, how are you?" She turned back to Anthony.

"Well come on... Toot sweet... I do not have all day." He froze and gasped.

"Birch darling, I am creating.... You would not interrupt Harriet whilst she was painting, well darling, this is my art." Birch turned to Delphine.

"Who is better, you or the new girl?" Delphine smirked.

"Well I am obviously; it is why I am a partner." Birch gave a nod.

"Brilliant, his canvass is not that good, you finish it, I am stealing him, it is a matter of life and death for a scalp." Birch walked up to him and grabbed his arm.

"Remember I have a knife... You need dye, red and black, and shampoo and conditioner, come on man, I don't have all day, this is a real life emergency, lives depend on it, so hop to it." He jerked on the spot.

"I am not sure I like this bossy type, Birch; you are kind of scary at the moment darling." She smiled.

"Nowhere near as scary as I will be if I am not at Deads house in four minutes with you." He recoiled.

"Oh dear I am being kidnapped… Oh… Oh Delphine, she is stealing me, but what can I say, I love dominant women." She dragged him roughly, off into the back room, and he squealed.

"Red and black, lots of black, now grab your shit, we are on a tight schedule here."

Birch tapped her foot, and he grabbed what he needed, and packed them quickly into his bag, she crossed to the door pulling him roughly along, and smiled.

"Thanks Delphine Sweetie, you are an angel."

She opened the door and dragged him out to Petal, she swung the door open, and pushed him in, he sat there jumping and twitching in his seat.

"Oh I say darling, I love what you have done with her, she looks positively lively." Birch hit the pedals, and Petal sped off, and then skidded round.

"ARRRRRRGH!!!!"

She rocketed down Church Rise, past the Hunter's Arms, as Anthony who had been in Petal several times, but never with Birch at the wheel, screamed out with fear, he stuck his head out of the window and looked back.

"OH MY GOD, YOU JUST MISSED THAT CYCLIST BY INCHES, you are mad… I tell you mad…. Why are you not banned?" Birch giggled evilly.

"How do you know I am not?" Petal swerved violently to the right, into Manor Road.

"ARRRRRRGHH!!!!!" Then left into Waterside Lane. "ARRRRRRRGHH!"

She came screeching to a halt outside number six, and Anthony was thrust forward towards the dashboard, then his seat belt yanked him back into his seat, where he sat shaking with utter terror, and whispering prayers to his lord. Birch jumped out, and walked round with a smile, she opened the door.

"Hi Sweetie, we are home." He stared at her with suspicion.

"Are you on the run, is that what it is… Your mother had you committed didn't she, and you have escaped?" He put his hand on his chest and took a deep breath.

"Birch darling, I love you, I do, but I am too pretty to go to prison, I can change your looks, but please, I beg you, tell no one it was me." Birch gave a chuckle.

"Anthony this is not for me, it is for Deads." His hands flew to his face, and he looked horrified.

"OH MY GOD WHAT DID SHE DO!?"

I sat cross legged on the floor talking to Deb's as she curled on the sofa with her drink, Deb's smiled.

"I thought it was lovely, you two have always had something so special, and I saw her take you so gently and kiss you. Honestly Abby, there was so much love in that kiss, oh god, I am telling you, it took my breath away, it was a beautiful moment." It was, my whole insides were reeling.

"Deb's I was so in love with her, and all through that second year at Uni, I wanted something to happen, but it didn't. I came home, and had to leave her, and it was terrible. You will never know how much I missed her, I cried every night, it broke me Deb's, it was the hardest thing I have ever done." She gave a nod of understanding.

"And you thought you were over her, and now she is back, and she kissed you, and I may add, now you are questioning what if I lose her again, am I right?"

Sometimes I hate smart people, I looked down at the floor, my stomach lurched just thinking about it.

"I have lost her before, what if I screw up again?" Deb's emptied her glass and sat forward.

"Abby, she has spent millions to be here, she has bought a house, and business not ten minutes' walk from here. God, I thought you were smart.... Abby for Christ's sake wake up? Do not sit there and tell me you are over her, look at you, you have shitty hair, crappy clothes, you have been miserable, locking yourself away, that's the bloody point, you never got over her. You never will, you two belong side by side, and everyone knows it and accepts it. What do you think Chloe, Edwina, and me have not talked about it? We have hundreds of times, none of us understood why both of you were so God dammed stubborn, when it is as clear as day to all of us? Abby, I saw the way you kissed her back, I saw the look on your face, why can you just not say the frigging words, and admit it. Abby you are, and have always been in love with her, you will never get over her, do you think she is any different, why the hell is she here?"

I looked into her eyes, and could see the belief behind them, I took a deep breath and tried to relax.

"Deb's, I have never had sex with a woman, if I am honest, I have no idea what to do." She gave a snort and sat back.

"Trust me it just flows, when the time is right you two will know it, and it will happen, and your head will explode, or at least mine did when I slept with Edwina."

I had to titter, suddenly she was the master and I was the student, although I had to ask.

"So how are things between you two, I mean has it not got in the way?" She shrugged.

"Why would it, we are great friends who really care about each other, the last time we hooked up was in Cambridge, she spent a weekend with me. I love sleeping with her if I am honest, she is really gentle and tender with me, I like how that makes me feel, if anything it is the only thing that worries me about Jimmy. I really do love him, and the sex is mind blowing, but when we get married, I will have to give her up, and I will miss it. I am not bothered about any others, but giving Edwina up will really be hard for me." I was pretty shocked.

"Does Jimmy know?" She nodded.

"Yeah, we had a threesome together." I gasped with surprise.

"Holy shit Deb's.... Well, if he knows why don't you talk to him about it, and tell him how you feel, I suppose it is worth a try, if he says it's not cool, you will know won't you?" She gave a sigh.

"Life can be really tough don't you think?" I hear that, I have spent the last four years alone with that conundrum and I still had no idea about any of it.

"Yeah, there are too many bumps, and not enough smooth rides." She smiled, and her voice softened.

"Abby, Birch is back, talk to her, be honest with her, and with yourself, she is going nowhere, and you will be living with her. This is real, it is happening, it is not a gothic fantasy, the way I see it, you can be as you always have been, with or without sex, or you can have the same as she has with that Kev guy, but closer, it really is up to you."

Chapter 5

# Back to us.

I was refilling Deb's glass when Birch reappeared, she was holding Anthony by the arm, and he appeared to be objecting.

"Birch I am here, I am not going to run away, I said I would do it; I do not need to be man handled, well not by a woman."

The door opened, and in staggered Anthony twitching, then in stepped Birch behind him. He looked back at her with glaring eyes, and then turned to me.

"She is insane, whatever it is Abby, whatever trouble you are in, I have promised to help you. For you I will do anything, but I am not going to prison for her, she is completely bonkers."

"Huh!" I was pleased to see Deb's looked equally as confused.

"Why are we going to prison?" I looked at Birch.

"What have you done now?" Anthony looked stunned.

"Kidnap, for starters, and road rage and driving without a licence to boot."

"Huh!" Birch gave a sigh, and her green eyes twinkled.

"I did not kidnap him; I used my feminine charm to convince him.... I made it quite clear, his services were required. Well, yeah, so okay, there may have been talk of a knife, and I do have a driving licence, and it has no points on it. Honestly Anthony, you were the one screaming out of the window, I was simply driving." Anthony looked stunned, as he looked at me and pointed at Birch.

"She is insane, she drives like a maniac, we almost maimed a cyclist, the woman has no understanding of speed, or safe driving distance." He looked at Birch and then looked back at me, sharply in a double take, it was almost as if he suddenly understood.

"Eh... What... You want me to do Abby's hair.... Why didn't you say so, I was almost done with that client, she was the last of the day?" He twitched, and I shook my head.

"I am sorry Anthony; she has been a little excitable all day."

Birch walked over to me and lifted some of my lank hair.

"I am sorry Sweetie, but I cannot stand this another second, it is not you, not at all who you are, and it has to go." Anthony joined her, and grabbed the other side.

"She is right Abby darling, I have told you a thousand times, these rats' tails are just damaging to your persona, as much as I hate agreeing with this lunatic, she is right, it is simply a major disaster."

I stood there in the middle of the room, and as far as I am concerned, I was having my hair fondled by two lunatics. I gave in, I know Birch, and she was not going to stop until I did something.

"Okay so what do I have to do?" Birch smiled.

"Well my Dar... Bland little beastie, I think a shower, a shave, and washed hair. I will help with the shave and washing, and Anthony can get ready and organise." I gave a frustrated sigh, and turned for the bedroom, I knew when I was beat.


Ten minutes later I was stood in the shower.

"Ow, for God's sake Birch!" I looked down to see her pulling at my blonde pubic hair, she looked up at me.

"It is definitely longer than Deb's was." She held up a pair of scissors. "You want me to do the honours?" I stepped back.

"I have seen you with a knife, it's fine, I will do it myself."

I stood in the shower and snipped, and handed it to Birch, who was sat on the floor, holding a large paper towel. When I had finally removed enough to see a clear outline, of my twenty four year old womanhood, Birch handed me a razor, and then sat back on the floor and watched as I shaved. She kept tilting her head from side to side.

"You know watching me do this is seriously messed up right?" She smiled.

"I think it is fascinating, you see I do it in a completely different way, but I can see why you do it that way, it makes sense." Anthony was right, she is really strange.

Finally, I got it as clean as I could, and Birch reached in to stroke it for smoothness, my whole body tingled, and I slapped her hand.

"Pack it in pervert."

I ended up sat in the shower with my back facing out, and she sat crossed legged on the floor, and applied the shampoo. The feel of her fingers on my scalp felt familiar, like some memory from the past, and I relaxed, albeit in a cramped up fashion, as the water ran over me and her hands caressed me.

"I have missed this Birch."

"Yeah, me too, we have waited four years Deads, you know you should have come to live in Manchester with me, I would have handled things better if you were there." I closed my eyes and leaned back as she washed out the soap.

"Are you going to be alright Birch, you know considering events?" I had my back to her, but somehow, I felt she was softly smiling.

"I have taken a leave of absence to sort the house out, and organise the shop, Izzy will be coming down when the shop opens to help, but yes, I will be fine, how could I not be, I am back with you, which is where I belong?"

I sat there as she rinsed off my hair, the water pounding down on me, and thinking of what Deb's had said, she was right, I was so busy and hung up looking for negatives. Had I not spent four years aching and lonely, because she was not there?

Maybe it was the feel of her fingers, mixed with the water pounding down on me, I don't know, but in a really weird way, I felt everything was going to be fine now, she was back, and this time it was for good, and that was the best thing to happen in four years.


My hair was clean, in all honesty it had been ages since I washed it, and just looking at the pale colour in the mirror proved it, it looked five shades lighter and a million miles off Birch's colour. I wrapped in a towel, whilst Birch stripped and got in to wash hers, and when I was ready, I walked into the living room. Anthony had a chair on the floor, stood on a large sheet, he had taken his jacket off, and he smiled as I sat down.

"Right Abby darling, we will put that last hack to shame, get yourself mentally prepared, because my favourite person in the whole world, is about to get the best of my talents."

Deb's sat cross legged on the sofa, in front of me and smiled, and Anthony pulled out his comb, and went to work, it was time for a certain dark little beastie to return.

It felt like it took forever to get my hair done, but finally wrapped in a towel, I stood in the bathroom and looked in the mirror, and Deadly was there to be seen again, and Anthony was right, it looked a thousand times better than it had done before. The dark hair, the fringe, and the really brightly red tipped hair, it looked natural and right, and I cannot deny, I felt a little of the old me, the me I had forgotten, had found its way back.

In the living room, on my desk top, Birch had pictures of birch bark on display, and Anthony had scrutinised every one of them. This for him was a first, and Birch had no memory of how it had been done in the past, as she explained, she had been really pissed when she had first had it done.

It took him quite some time, less dye was involved but it was very tricky. When she walked out of bathroom with him, and he dried her hair, I was blown away. This time it looked almost three dimensional, and it was so close to the images he had looked at, it was surreal, but it looked incredible.

She finally stood up and flicked her long hair, and I felt tears in my eyes. I had not realised how much I had missed her; it had felt like something was missing, and that was it, the dark patches had seemed to steal a part of her. She stood in front of me with that patched hair, and her bright green happy eyes, and smiled, and that was Birch, the real Birch.

"What do you think Sweetie?" I filled up, and oddly enough so did Deb's, it was like both of us had felt the same.

"I think you are beautiful, that is what I think Birch." She gave a shy smile, Debs bounced up with her phone.

"I want a picture."

Both of us leaned together and smiled, and she took the picture, it was uploaded to Insta immediately, with the hash tag '#look who is back together' and she showed us with a beaming smile.

"That is how things should be." Anthony stood grinning, as we all posed for yet another picture with him, #this guy is the best stylist ever.

For the next ten minutes her phone went mad, as like after like, and endless comments hit her Insta account, it appeared we were a hit, especially with Chloe and Edwina, and also my mum. I didn't even know she had an Insta account? Her comment simply read, 'about bloody time' I smiled, my mum was cooler than she looked.

As with all things us, we cleaned up, and then sat around having drinks, talking. We had not been together anywhere near as much as we had in the past, and so there was a lot of catching up to do. I was thrilled to find out that secretly Anthony had moved in with Brent. He had kept it very quiet, they were still going strong after all this time, and as the night slipped through the evening, with take away delivered, we ended up on the subject of festivals. Deb's was leaning over the arm of the sofa.

"It was great fun, we did Oxendale and Glastonbury, all crammed in our tent, screwing and drinking, it is a shame there is not another festival. We could all get together again, and put the tent up, and watch great bands."

I was sat on the floor, Anthony at the table, and Birch was on my desk swivel chair, she spun round with excited eyes.

"Guys... We can take our own music, so why don't we all just camp? It will be crazy, we can go somewhere filled with cool people, set up the tent, get pissed and shag, just like the old days, it will be like a reunion camping trip. I mean come on guys, with the bookshop and the practice, and the house to organise, not to mention the wedding, it will give us all a break to chill and reconnect and just have fun."

I looked at the other two, it sounded like fun, and it had been years since I had been camping, Anthony looked a little hesitant, but Deb's was suddenly alive.

"Yeah, what a great idea." Anthony looked a little awkward.

"To be honest, it would feel mean to Brent, I would hate to leave him alone." I shrugged.

"So, talk to him and bring him along, if there are men there, we will feel safer, and he is a big guy, and let's be honest, if we are getting laid, it is only right you do too." His whole attitude changed.

"He is a little bit of an outdoors type, so I know he will love it." Birch smiled.

"Okay, I will get right on it, camping it is, we will need at least three tent pitches, let's have a look at what is available, and then

Deads, you find out when everyone is free."

By eleven o'clock we were pretty drunk, and sadly Deb's had to go.

"I really want to stay, but I have to be in church tomorrow, they will be reading out the bands, and I promised mum I would be there while Jimmy is away in Singapore."

We understood, and hugged her goodbye. I thanked Anthony yet again, I was really happy to see Birch back to normal, and I was also my darker self, and I had actually missed it.

He was as always lovely, but he also wanted to get back to Brent. Deb's walked up the road, and Anthony jumped in a taxi, and together Birch and myself made our way back to my tiny home. She flicked out the living room light, and we moved into the bedroom, it was the first time we had been alone together since her return, and it was nice. She slipped into bed and lay back and watched me undress.

"You are not mad at me then for the hair?" How could I be, I had felt normal again for the first time in ages.

"No, I am not mad, he did a fantastic job, and actually I am glad I finally redid it, I don't like bland little beastie." She giggled, as I slipped in beside her, God this felt so normal, she had no idea how much I had missed it.

"You were never bland Deads, you have always been my sunlight." I lay on my side looking at her.

"That has been the problem, when you left, I felt like I was living in the shade. I have regretted so much Deads, I sat alone for days at home riddled with them."

It felt strange to hear, Birch had always been honest and never apologised for anything, how could she have regrets? She turned on her side to look at me, her bright green eyes shone from her birch bark surrounded face.

"I knew you would have to come home, and I would continue. I did not want to hurt you before leaving you alone, and I thought it would be easier. I mean, I had another four years to go before I could come back here. I hated you leaving Deads, it tore me apart, my mum thought I was mad, she actually told me to come down here alone, and do online counselling. I hope you understand that I have wanted this for my whole life, and I have had to make sacrifices to get here, and for a while as painful as that was, you were part of that?"

"Birch, you do not have to explain, I understood all that."

"Did you, I mean honestly? Deads you thought of killing yourself, you were in so much pain, and that is my fault." I lifted my hand to her face and cupped her cheek.

"Birch that is done with, look where we are, and what we have planned." She smiled.

"You need to know this Deads, you need to hear it from me.... Deads I really do love you; I have hated being apart, and I cannot deny, I was a coward back then, I was afraid to be straight with you. I never lied. I wanted you, I don't want any other female, but I do want you, and it is as new to me as it is you, but I am here now, and I have done what was needed."

I did understand her, I always had, I know I was selfish, I was just so lonely stuck here on my own. She smiled and then reached out, and gently pushed me back into the pillow. At first, I did not understand, she slid over me and sat up on my waist.

She was above me in the lamp light, her pale white skin gleaming, and her hair filled with lines and patches hanging down in front of her, this was the girl I loved so much, she smiled, and tilted her head to one side.

"You are so beautiful my dark little beastie." I smiled as I looked up at her.

"So are you." It felt precious and special, she leaned forward and came closer, her eyes danced just inches from me.

"I love you Sweetie."

Her lips locked onto mine, and my whole body exploded. Oh god kissing her was so wonderful, I had spent most of the day thinking about her last one, but this one just blew me away. I was so turned on it was unbelievable, and my heart started to race, I was loving it, going with the motion and feeling hotter and hotter, and then she slid onto my neck, and kissed softly below my ear, my toes curled, and I felt breathless.

"Oh Birch!" I gasped for air. "Please don't let this be another prank."

She slid down on to my left nipple, and gave it a gentle suck, my whole body felt the twinge of electric that ran through me, and I sucked in air and arched slightly.

"Oh Jesus... Oh god!"

I felt her slide down me a little, and her knee moved between my legs, and then spread, pushing my legs apart, and she slid into the gap, as she continued to swirl her tongue around my nipple, her hand slid over to my other boob, and stroked the nipple. My body was burning as the heat intensified, I was slipping out of control, I was breathing faster, and trembling, my back arched a little more, it was like I was on auto pilot, and a million senses ignited inside me. My vagina gave off a deep throb. I felt her hand glide across my stomach, and slide slowly down.

"Oh my god Birch, I am going insane, I am not sure I can handle this kind of pleasure."

Her chuckle vibrated through my chest, as her hand slipped over the top of my pelvic bone, and her palm slid over my vagina. She looked me right in the eyes, and smiled, as her hand slid over it.

"Oh Deads, it is so smooth."

My heart was already bouncing out of my chest, but those eyes, those sexy sultry eyes of hers, drove me rapidly towards insanity. She moved her middle finger, and my lips parted, and then a bolt of lightning exploded in my head, and electric shocked every nerve I had, and my hips bucked forward.

"Aar... Oh God, OH GOD BIRCH!"

I was breathing so fast, I felt like I was drowning, as her finger began to slowly gyrate around my button, and it sent fizzing pulsating spasms into my thighs and hips. I gasped in more air, as she continued to move her hand, as I felt that need grow inside me. The beast that needed to be sated, it was like Eric, but way stronger, and my legs shook, as it built and built, and it was becoming so intense, I thought I would die.

"Oh god.... Oh god... OH GODDDDD!"

I was losing control as my body took over, it was so amazingly wonderful, and at the same time driving me insane. I looked down at her watching my reaction, I could see her arm moving, our eyes were connected, as she smiled, and then her head went slowly down.

"Oh Christ... Oh Jesus... OH GOD BIRCH I AM GOING TO CUM!"

Her hot breath, wafted between my legs, and then suddenly I

lurched up, as her tongue entered me.

"OOOOOOHHHHHH SHIIIIIIIIIIIIIIIIT!" And boom, I lost all control. My body jerked and jumped, my mind went blank, and my legs twitched wildly.

All I could do as the huge wave crashed over me, was gasp, and feel the massive burst of electricity surge through every limb, and render me powerless. Time stopped as she continued, and I just lay back in the pillow, unable to move as the wildness of the moment, flooded me with euphoria, and I lay there shaking, pulling at the headboard, unaware of what was happening, I was cumming like crazy.

I was gone, spaced out, lost to anything, staring at the ceiling, drifting through space, I was not aware of the sweat on my brow, or the speed at which I was breathing, as I gasped in more air, or the vibrations, that shook my whole body. I vaguely became aware of Birch, as she kissed between my boobs, and then her smiling face appeared over mine, and she smiled. I locked eyes with her as I panted. She was remarkable, I lifted my limp arm to her face, and smiled. She looked so happy.

"That was my first time, I was a bit nervous Deads, did I do Okay?"

I swallowed trying to breathe, I was exhausted, and could hardly speak, my mouth was so dry, I licked my lips as my whole body quivered, and I pulled her face down and kissed her. My words were breathless and faint as I broke apart.

"That was mind blowing... I love you." She smiled.

"I think you pissed the bed." I gasped a giggle.

"I cum a lot." She sniggered.

"Well, you frigging drenched everything in cum Sweetie."

I really didn't care, I was knackered and happy, oh god I felt so happy. My body was still twitching, little bolts kept shooting up through my stomach, and it felt glorious. Birch slid over to Deb's side of the bed, and I shuffled back towards her. I flopped on the pillow, and she snuggled into me, I was only just starting to breathe properly. Her hand came round me and cupped my boob, and I relaxed into her. The truth was, I really wanted to return the favour, but I was just so dammed exhausted. She gave me a squeeze.

"Are you okay with this Sweetie?" I lifted a limp arm and

pattered her leg.

"Birch, it is the best thing that ever happened to me, honestly, I have dreamed of this, I am just frigging exhausted." She squeezed me tight.

"Good, I am happy... You know Deads... If you cum like that every time we do it, then it is probably better we have two beds in the new house." I smiled.

"Or we buy rubber sheets." She giggled.

"And a life raft, you nearly bloody drowned me." I had to laugh; I felt her tummy wobble behind me.

I closed my eyes feeling the best I had in a long time, and I was gone, I think she did say something else, but it was too late to hear it.


I woke feeling alive and full of energy, and I had no hang over which was weird, Birch was flat out at the side of me, her soft breathing gently blowing on the back of my shoulder. I took a few moments for everything to return from last night, as my head cleared, my mouth still felt really dry, and the clock said 11:22. That was odd, church had started and the bells had not woken me, although I was pretty exhausted.

I wriggled free of Birch's vice like grip, I really needed to pee, although when I pulled back the duvet, I wondered why, it looked like most of my bodily fluids had decorated the sheets. I staggered into the toilet, even now my legs still felt weak. I sat there expelling yet more liquid, and simply enjoying the pleasure of the fast flow, licking my lips in need of more liquid. I wiped, flushed, and washed my hands, I smelt of sex.

I wandered into the kitchen, and clicked the kettle, and got out two cups and proceeded with coffee. Moments later I lifted the cups and walked to the bedroom, I kicked the door closed, I knew what was coming.

I put a cup down for Birch, and sipped mine, licking my lips to bring them back to life, and then took a really good swig, it was hot, but my throat, which was so dry felt the joy of new liquid, the clocked ticked, it was 11:39, and I smiled. I put my cup down, and waited. The bells began, and the closed door made no difference, Birch twitched, and then sat bolt upright in bed with her eyes closed.

"Oh Crap, I have got this every Sunday for the rest of my frigging life."

I crawled onto the bed, and took her hands, and lifted them to her ears, she blinked, opened her eyes, and I smiled, she smiled back, her hands pressed tightly against her ears, muffling the sound. I pulled back the duvet and pushed her back onto the pillows, and she frowned.

I slid across her and opened her legs, spreading them apart, her eyes opened wider, as she suddenly realised what I had in mind. I smiled and lifted both legs slightly, and then dropped into place.

I have to say at this point, I really was not sure I could do this, but she had done it to me, and I was going to try. I lowered my face and kissed her tummy, she wriggled, her eyes still wide open, and then I pushed out my tongue and ran it across her tummy. Her tummy bounced up and down and she closed her eyes. I found her belly button and ran it around it, and she gave a squeal.

"Oh, Sweetie it tickles." Her belly bounced up and down, and I slid my tongue right inside and wiggled it, she lurched and screamed and let go of her ears, and grabbed my head.

"No, no, it tickles…" Her hips wriggled like crazy, and she lay back and squealed. "No Sweetie stop, ha-ha-ha-ha-ha-ha!"

I lifted my head, and she looked at me giggling wildly, and gasping for air.

"Deads that's not fair, it tickles like crazy, and I cannot stand it."

I slid back lower down the bed, as I watched her, she swallowed hard, and breathed in.

"Oh god…. Sweetie you know yo…"

I dropped down, in between her legs and took a deep breath, and then kissed her outer labia softly, she flopped back and gave a slight moan.

"Oh Sweetie…… Oh god."

And I moved slowly up and down, I really wanted to do this, I had no idea what to expect, my heart was thumping inside my chest, and I swallowed hard, and then slipped out my tongue, she gripped the sheets tight.

"Oh Deads…. Oh my god!" Her hips lifted.

The bells rang out to mark the end of the service, and Edwina,

Chloe and Deb's, jumped into Deb's car, and drove towards number six, Waterside Lane. They fell out of the car laughing and giggling, and Deb's key padded them in, they moved quickly through the side gate, and came down the garden towards the guest house, and as Deb's reached for the door, all of them heard it.

"Oh.... Oh.... Oh.... OH GOD!" Deb's looked back at the other two in shock, Edwina smiled.

"OH GOD...... OH MY GOD SWEETIE!" Chloe sniggered, and covered her mouth. Deb's swallowed hard, and lowered her voice.

"What should we do?"

Chloe grabbed the door and opened it; Deb's panicked trying to whisper.

"Jesus Chloe no!" It was too late; she was inside grinning from ear to ear. Edwina pushed past, and Deb's dithered at the door.

"Oh shit!" She followed the other two in. The bedroom door was closed which was rare, Birch was squealing at the top of her voice.

"OH.... OH.... OH... OH!" Chloe looked uncomfortable.

"Oh god, I really wanna screw something, this is really getting me going." Edwina sniggered, and slipped into the toilet, Deb's looked at Chloe nervously, and took two steps away from her.

"OH GOD DEADS, OH SWEETIE!" Deb's swallowed hard.

"I think we should leave, but weirdly enough, this is turning me on, and I am wet as hell." She turned to Chloe. "Is that weird of me, I mean are you getting wet too?" Chloe shrugged.

"Fucking everything turns me on, I got banned from that large Mesco supermarket in Millington for stroking a marrow." The toilet door opened and Edwina appeared.

"Psst!" She held out a huge black dildo. Chloe smiled and grabbed it.

"Fuck yeah!" She walked into the kitchen and closed the door, Deb's gasped in shock, and turned to the toilet.

"Why the hell would you give her that?" She gasped trying to keep her voice down, and pointed. "And why the hell are you naked?"

"Oh GOD...............SWEEEEEEEEETIE!.....Oh.... Oh.... OH FUCK!" Edwina looked at the bedroom door.

"Oh god this is too much." She leaned out grabbed Deb's by the collar, and dragged her into the toilet, Deb's gave a muffled squeal and disappeared

Birch was tearing at the sheets, her face and chest red, and sweat pouring down her face, as her head turned, and she bit into the pillow, she thrust up her hips.

"Deads baby I am cumin. O... o.... o...OOOOO DEADS!"

I cannot deny seeing Birch cum from that angle, was a real eye opener, from nowhere liquid flooded out, it filled my mouth, washed my face, and it really turned me on, how messed up is that? My brain just kept on ticking over and over saying 'you did it, you did it, you did it, you made her cum'.

She collapsed back, and quivered on the bed, and I lifted my head and looked at her breasts, which were heaving up and down, her nipples pointing up to the ceiling, and I could just see her chin. I slowly slid up her, as she panted, her head back in the pillow, she was smiling, she was happy, although she was panting like a steam engine. I looked down at her, her eyes were sparkling like I had never seen them. I smiled.

"Was that okay?" She nodded.

I flopped on top of her, my jaw ached, and I just lay sprawled across her, with my head on the pillow at the side of her. Her arms came round me, she turned, and gasping for air, kissed my cheek, her rapid breathing filled my ears. She was happy, I was happy, we were happy. Birch patted my back and I rolled off her, she sat up and grabbed the lukewarm coffee and downed it in one.

I grabbed the cup and slipped off the bed, I walked through to the living room, and pushed open the kitchen door. At this point I have to say, I did blink, actually several times. I was so not mentally prepared for what I saw, I froze for a second, unable to fully comprehend what I was looking at.

Chloe was stood frozen on the spot, her skirt hiked up, and her knickers round her ankles, looking sheepish, whilst holding a frigging huge dildo, which was half inserted inside herself, she smiled, and looked sheepish.

"Hi Abby."

I stepped back, I had so many feelings surging up in me, shock, horror, confusion! She looked a little guilty, and so slipped it further up inside. I stepped back further into the living room, feeling horrified.

"DON'T TRY FRIGGING HIDING IT…. JESUS CHLOE, I HAVE SEEN WHAT YOU HAVE!" She looked down.

"Yeah, I see what you mean!" She went to pull it out, and I panicked, and shook my hands, one with cups and one without.

"FOR CHRIST'S SAKE, DON'T PULL IT OUT… NO ONE WANTS TO SEE THAT!"

My head was reeling as I tried to grab the reality of my situation, why was she in our kitchen doing herself with a bloody huge dildo? I mean, it was the frigging kitchen for god's sake. I screwed up my eyes, as she looked at me semi crouched, holding the end of the dildo.

"Chloe, why… Why would you do that…. I mean it's our frigging kitchen, we cook food in there, Jesus Chloe, the last thing I need is your fanny batter spraying all over the bloody place?" She looked a little guilty, and looked round the room.

"Sorry, I will clean up when I am done."

"THAT'S NOT THE FRIGGING POINT CHLOE, IT'S THE FRIGGING KITCHEN FOR GOD'S SAKE!"

Birch appeared at the bedroom door looking puzzled, she saw where I was looking, and leaned round the corner.

"Hi Sweetie…. Holy shit…. Jesus Chloe, if you shove it in any further, you will damage your tonsils."

I heard a rustling near the toilet door, and rapid panicked whispering, I walked over and pushed it open, I could not believe what I was seeing.

"For God's sake, you two as well, what is this, a secret banging session, can frigging no one round here control their carnal activities?" Birch looked back as a very bright red Deb's walked out, with her panties still round her knees. Edwina was still naked, she shrugged.

"Hi Birch… Sorry we got here, and just listening to you guys, well it sort of turned us all on a bit." My jaw dropped.

"A bit… Chloe is trying to reshape her uterus, and you two, well looking at Chloe, God knows what weird screwed up shit you two were at in there?"

I was lost in all of this; I was surrounded by perverts; I was lost for words. Birch smiled.

"Oh Sweeties, were we that good?" I shook my head in complete disbelief and looked at Birch.

"That is what you frigging took from that?" Deb's blushed even more.

"You guys were really hot, I mean wow Abby, you were really giving it to her good."

Birch smiled and winked at me. I turned to the kitchen where Chloe kind of penguin walked out, Deb's gave a gasp and stepped back, and screwed her face up.

"Holy shit Chloe, does that not hurt?" She looked down and went to grab it, and three of us all screamed.

"NOOOOOO!" She looked up looking frustrated, clenched her fists, and shook them hard.

"WILL YOU PLEASE MAKE UP YOUR FUCKING MIND, IS IT FUCKING IN, OR IS IT FUCKING OUT?"

She stamped, and there was a 'clunk' on the floor, everyone squealed, and recoiled away from her in horror.

"EEEWWWWWWWW!" She looked down, and gave a sigh of relief, Birch turned to the bedroom doorway.

"You can have that Chloe; I no longer want it." Deb's smiled, suddenly understanding something.

"Oh my God... I get it now... So that's why they banned you from the Mesco supermarket!?"

Chapter 6

# Honest Conversation.

Having overcome, the sudden rise in hormonal activity, brought on by my apparently 'giving it to Birch good' behaviour, we all settled down, and Deb's and Birch filled the two sisters in on our future plans. Birch again bubbled over with excitement, and had to show the house off, and so another tour was arranged with great excitement. I decided to sit it out, and as the girls happily headed into the garden, Birch turned at the door.

"Deads are you really alright, I mean it has been a lot for you to deal with, are we going too fast for you?" I spun round in my chair, and smiled, I could see the concern in her eyes.

"Honestly, I am okay, Birch, it has been a lot, last night and this morning, they are firsts for me. And yes, I wanted them, and I loved them, but I need a little space just to process and understand me. I have felt lost for so long, and it is just feeling found again that I need to adjust to, honestly, I may not look it, but I am so very happy." She smiled.

"Alright Sweetie, it probably does not help, but I am feeling the same, and for the record, no one has ever made me cum like that before, it has rattled me a little too."

They all finally left me in silence, and I sat back in my chair and closed my eyes, I had so many emotions swirling around in me. I had finally got what I wanted, and yet it felt way stronger than I had thought it would, it did feel a little scary.

I opened my eyes, and stared at the computer and the small blue icon on my task bar, and I knew what to do. I clicked it and the screen opened, I saw her name and hit the camera, it connected and suddenly she was sat smiling in front of me.

"It is funny, I expected this call." I gave a nod.

"Can I talk to you Roni?" She smiled.

"Bit of a daft question now isn't that, of course you can talk, she texted me, she is so happy, so how do you feel?" I gave a sigh.

"I may not look it, but I am actually happy, but I feel so emotional." Roni sat back in her seat.

"Abby sweetheart, this is huge, you have loved her for so long, and yet if I am honest, both of you have had an emotional hang up about Straight, Bi, Lesbian for so long, that your first time was always going to present challenges. I will ask you this, and you do not have to answer, but you both made love to each other, what did it feel like, and I mean actually feel like when you were in the midst of it all?" Wow talk about personal, Roni does not piss about. I took a deep breath and thought about it, I could not help smiling, and I blushed a little.

"I felt so loved Roni, I actually think it scared me, she was soft and gentle, honestly it is what I always thought it would be like, Roni I love her so much." She smiled.

"But?" I swallowed hard.

"It was so intense it frightened me." I watched her silently nod, her green eyes as intense as Birch's. Roni lifted her cup, and took a drink.

"Abby, love takes many different forms, as does love making. You are used to having sex, you know to a degree what to do and how that feels. If I am honest from the little Jemi has told me, for want of a better word, you have been sport fucking, which be honest, is pretty unemotional. With Jemi, I would imagine it was a completely different experience?" She was right, it wasn't like any of the others, I struggled for the words for a second.

"Roni I can only describe it as it felt loving and right." She understood and smiled.

"So, it was pretty bloody terrifying then?" She giggled. "Real connection is scary as hell Abby; it is a whole new league when it comes to relationships." She was right, I knew it last night.

"Will I get used to it?"

"Abby sweetheart I hope you do not."

"What?" She chuckled at me.

"When people get used to it, that is when the people think they have fallen out of love. We have too much one true love bullshit in this world, I have never bought into that clap trap. Abby listen to me when I say, when you first meet a person and you feel attracted, that is not love it is lust. Two people get to know each other, and through that process, that finding things in the other that draws them deeper in, that is when the love grows. Love is not found, it is built, and let's be honest, you two have been building it for a long time. If you ask me, last night cemented the foundations for something special, something lasting, and that can be really intimidating at first."

I understood that, but there was something else bothering me.

"Am I just a female Kev?" She smiled.

"Oh, you are so bright, I wondered if that would come up." I shrugged.

"I have to ask, I am sorry, but I have to."

"I take it that is worrying you most, will she still sleep with others and you, well I can certainly say this, there is no way she would ever live with Kev. Look Abby, firstly never compare yourself with others, because Jemi would never do that with you. Jemi has never felt involved deeply with anyone, not even Kev, if I am honest, for both of them it is convenient, they both had goals, and did not want holding back. Kev with his band and Jemi with her training, so Boyfriend/Girlfriend was a convenient label for both of them to hold others at arm's length."

"So she is not in love with him then?" Roni smiled.

"Oh, Abby you have no idea how deeply she has fallen, honestly these last few years she has been a nightmare, sulking around, and grumpy, and I may add very lonely. Kev has rung her several times, and she always gave him the brush off, she just never really understood its true value, until you had gone, which is why I wrote what I did on that card. It is also why I told her to leave here and go to you sooner. Abby do not let all that confidence of hers fool you, she can be very insecure at times." I nodded at her.

"I have seen that, she has never told me what was on the card, she has kept it sealed in her bag." Roni gave a sigh.

"You see that is typical Jemi, carrying it everywhere she goes. All I wrote was 'in love for the first time, and afraid.' It was true then, and is as true now. I hate to tell you this, but what you did with her this morning, blew her mind, she never expected it. The truth is, she always thought any sex would be one sided, and I thought she was right, and yet once again you showed her how much she means to you, simply by doing it, and that I think should tell you everything." I gave a smile.

"I thought it was just me." She shook her head.

"Abby, both of you need a night alone to just sit and talk, there is another word for relationship, it is 'Honest Negotiation' and you two need to talk more, and be honest about everything, I mean come on, you are so close, an open conversation will not bring the roof down."

I really got that, and I also knew Roni knew her better than anyone, and I felt a little more relaxed, I had done the right thing talking to her. I gave a long sigh and smiled.

"Thanks Roni, I actually feel so much better, you know when she first got here, I was so down, I had waited all the night before and she did not call, and I thought everything was over. Her text messages have slowly dwindled, and I thought she was over me, and honestly, I thought my life was over." Roni stared at the screen for a second, her eyes seem to glaze over, and I frowned. "Is everything alright."

"What.... Oh, I am so sorry Abby, what you just said suddenly opened a door I had not seen." She looked at me and became quite serious. "Abby, you did not think of doing anything stupid I hope?" I looked down at the desk, and felt embarrassed.

"I didn't do it, I was too drunk and passed out, Birch knows and she really screamed at me, I am sorry, but I thought I would never see her again." I looked up and she smiled.

"Abby you are an absolute treasure, thank you, I think I just found something that is very important to Jemi, regarding a case she had." I nodded.

"You mean Melody?" Roni looked really surprised.

"She has told you about that?" I gave a nod and she smiled. "Wow, I have spent a week trying to get her to open up, she is there a day with you and out it all comes. Now if that is not a sign, I have no idea what is, but you have been really helpful. I need to talk to her, but I need to look something up, will you be alright now?" I smiled.

"I feel tons better Roni, thanks, I knew you would know the right things to tell me." She smiled a loving smile.

"Abby I am always free to talk, don't be a stranger, and I think now you know what to do, you should do it soon. Alright sweetheart I have something important I need to check for her, but we will talk soon I promise." She blew me a kiss, and I smiled.

The call ended and I felt a huge relief, I know it sounds crazy, honestly at times my whole life has felt crazy, but something as silly as knowing Birch was going through the same thing I was, really helped me. I got up out of the chair, and felt exhausted, and walked into the bedroom, I looked at the bed and thought I better get on with things, I pulled the sheet and it came off the bed, it was time to do some laundry.

Most of the washing was done when they all returned, I still had one load in the dryer, but left it to put new sheets on the bed. They all came in laughing and joking, and I was putting new covers on the pillows, to finish the bed off, they all were talking excitedly. Chloe especially, was very loud and excited, she talked quickly of crashing at weekends and hanging out, and parties.

Birch had not told her yet. I understood what Birch was trying to do for them, and how massively important it would be to their lives, but I had realised that I had become more comfortable with silence in the last couple of years, and to be honest, I needed a little at the moment.

I finished the bed and did a quick tidy, and then made my way back for the last load of dry washing, mum smiled, as I folded everything neatly, and placed it in my laundry basket.

"Some big changes coming Abby, are you going to be okay with them?"

It is funny, I have always thought she did not understand me, and then at times she blew me away, by understanding me more than I thought possible. I looked up from the basket.

"I don't mind, I think it is good to embrace change, it's just...."

"You have become a writer, and a writer needs quiet contemplative focus?" I nodded at her, she smiled.

"It is no different for artists or therapists, we all need the peace to reflect. You know Abby if you look at things, Deb's will have her new book business, and there will be a lot involved in that. When she finds out, Chloe will hole up in her studio, just listening to her as she walked through here earlier, she sounded so like a young Hatty. Edwina codes, which takes great concentration, and you write, you are all perfectly suited to living together. I assume they will not know until the house is ready? To be honest, I think you will find it is really only wild at the weekends, through the week, even you, may find it a little too quiet."

I had never looked at it that way before, wow she made so much sense, and the more I thought about it, as I took the laundry back, and started putting it away, the more relaxed I felt.


Tomorrow was Monday, which meant back to work, everyone went home early. I had hung all my clothes, put the washed bedding back, and was sorting through towels when she came into the bedroom.

"Can I help with anything?" I stood up; my back was aching.

"I fancy a bath; do you want to join me?" She smiled.

"As long as you are okay with it, yes I would love to." I lifted up the towels.

"We have always bathed together here, why would now be different?" She shrugged.

"I feel I am rushing you too much, I guess I am not going to push my luck, the last thing I want is to be living alone across the street." I looked up from the towel pile.

"Why would you say that Birch, I want to live with you?" She came over and sat on the bed.

"You have been really quiet today, I feel so happy and I want to shout and scream, but Deads, it looked to me like you were not that comfortable with our new situation. Look if you are not, say so, we can take it back to the way it was, I did not come down here to mess up and lose you again. If I am honest, I am pretty terrified about it, and today has made me even more frightened." I gave a long sigh, and sat down beside her.

"It is not you it is me, I have grown quite solitary in the last few years, and with everything going on between us, a house full of noisy perverts was just too much for me today. I think we need to talk it through. I spoke to your mum today, I needed some advice, and she helped a lot." Birch understood.

"Okay, let's soak and talk in private, where there will be no one else lurking with strange sexual ideas."


Forty minutes later we were sat in the bath, soaking in hot water as Birch washed my hair again, there was no point in messing around, and so I asked out right.

"Am I a female Kev?" Her fingers stopped on my head.

"Absolutely not, why the hell would you think that Deads?"

"Well I take it we will not be sexually exclusive, or I am assuming not, so that is the same as Kev isn't it?" She started rubbing my scalp again.

"To be honest, I acted on impulse last night, I saw you with your hair done, and all I can say is I wanted you, I wanted to pleasure you, I wanted to know what it would be like to know you in a carnal way. I have not had time to think about it, all I can say is it felt right, and it was right for me, and I do not regret it Deads. This morning I did not expect it, I am still buzzing about it, because it had an impact on me like I have never felt before."

It made sense, had I not done the same thing too? I allowed her to touch me, because I wanted her to. I cannot deny, I did wonder if she would snap her legs together like she had done with Katie, but she did not, and that meant something to me.

"I wanted it too Birch, but we need to look at what we will become, I mean will we screw others, and by that, I mean men, I cannot sleep with any other woman?" She grabbed the shower head and started to rinse my hair.

"Honestly, I can take it or leave it. If you need men in your life, I can do that, we have done that in the past. I suppose what I am saying is, in the past we were none sexual for a reason, but there were times when I wanted you, and I had to ignore it. I am happy if we continue as we were, but on those times when we want each other, I want to be able to do it, because there are times when I want to touch you so badly, and not being able to drives me insane." It made sense.

"So, this is an open relationship sort of thing then?" She wrung my hair.

"Honestly, I spent four years alone without you, with just fleeting moments together, and that really opened my eyes to who I am. Deads you are the love of my life, I frigging adore you. I want this so badly, if we have casual sex on occasion with others then fine, but I am not putting any title to it, as far as I am concerned, we are simply being us. As far as Kev is concerned, he is gone, I texted him this morning, it was not unexpected, we have been drifting apart for some time." I turned and looked back at her.

"He is gone, why did you do that?" She looked me right in the eyes.

"He was always a temporary fix, awful as it sounds, telling people he was my boyfriend, put people off, I mean, it was the same for him too. Deads we were not in love, if anything we were friends with benefits, he will always be a special mate of mine, and I am very fond of him, but it was never love, this.... This here is, and again if I am honest, I never saw this coming, it just happened over time, but over the last couple of years, I knew it was right for me, it is the reason I am here." I smiled.

"So, you are my bitch, and I am your bitch?" She frowned.

"God No! I hate American terms, it is an awful word, especially for someone who means so much, and disrespectful. I like to think of it as, you are my super sweetie, and I am your super sweetie." She gave a giggle, and stood up. "Duck... it is your turn to do my hair." She slipped over me and sat down in front, as I slid back. "I am playing this by ear Deads, and I am not in a rush, let's just enjoy seeing where it goes."

"I can live with that.... Pass me the conditioner."


We ate after our bath with mum and dad, and mum handed Birch a form to fill in.

"Madge handles these now, I just thought it would be easier to give you a copy, rather than let her, let's just say it will give you some breathing space." Birch opened it up and I leaned over to see it and smiled, she looked up.

"Why do I have to be added to the Parish Register, I am not Christian?" I looked at mum.

"Yeah, the vicar has met her, and he knows she will not be attending." Mum shook her head.

"It is just a formality, it will help with parish news, not everything the council do is church related, you know we do a lot of other things, like the fete and such. It is probably pointless saying it, but it also allows you to run for a seat on the council." Birch's eyes sparkled.

"Really?" My mum chuckled.

"That does worry me I must admit, although you have to be resident for over a year to qualify, it should be handed to Madge, but if you want, I will do it for you?" Birch shook her head.

"No way, now that is a pleasure I want, I want to be looking her in the eyes when I tell her." I had to laugh, somehow, I knew I wanted to be there when she did it.

By the time we got back I was feeling tired, and I had spent the day busy with very little alcohol, which is a good thing. I went to bed early and curled up snug in clean sheets, Birch sat up for a bit, and then slipped in later and cuddled up to me.


I woke early feeling happy and fresh, and pottered around until Birch staggered out of the bedroom yawning.

"Hi Sweetie." She came over and hugged me. "I need coffee." I steered her to the desk seat, and went and put the kettle on. Several coffees later, both of us felt wide awake.

The day was much warmer than it had been, so we dressed, and headed into the village, our hair was back as it had been, and it was like stepping back in time, and I felt surprisingly good about it. Deb's was in the Tea Rooms, she saw us on the street and texted us, so we decided to join her.

Life in the village had changed a little, for starters, Anabel Jessop had burgundy red hair, two other girls on the street, had multi coloured hair, and instead of the usual red, white, and blue petunias, in the hanging baskets, hanging from the lamp posts, they were filled with a riot of colours, and all had been planted by Daisy, which was unheard of four years ago.

We entered the Tea Rooms, and were immediately mobbed by Lillian and Celia. Lillian appeared delighted to see my hair was back as it was, she made a point of stroking it as she told me how happy she was to see it back. My hair is longer than back then, and was hanging down the front, covering my bra less nipples, I noted how as she stroked, her hand lingered, and felt my nipple tingle and grow slightly, she became very flustered.

We ordered coffee and cake, as the two ladies flustered over Birch with her hair. I had to smile, Birch was such a flirt with them, and Celia appeared quite breathless as I paid her. She wafted herself with my ten pound note without realising it. I saw Deb's as she waved and I walked over to her, she was all smiles, fixing her long brown hair, yet another bobble had snapped.

Louise and Stacy, the two young waitresses were wiping tables and clearing pots, Deb's appeared interested in Louise, I looked back, she was sexy there was no doubt, and she did get a lot of attention from Lillian. Birch sat down and relaxed, as we chatted, Deb's had been in the bookshop, and bought several books before the sale started, I was a little envious to see her hard bound copy of the Time Machine by H.G. Wells, I had a tatty old paperback of it.

We were having a lovely time, and giggling, when the clouds arrived in the shape of Marjorie. I didn't notice her at first, but it became clear when she spoke.

"My god this place has slipping standards, I always said a leopard does not change its spots, and looking at the hair, I think that is quite apparent."

I looked up to see her scowling face, with her turned down lip, it was as if she was looking at utter filth. I am twenty four, and yet I have no idea why, but I am afraid of her. Birch looked at her.

"Hi Madge, if I had known you would be coming here, I would have worn my whore clothing to please you, although I should remind you, these days my work clothes are more a white coat, than whore boots and tight clothes." Her look was one of utter revulsion.

"You are as crude as you look, I am hoping your stay will be somewhat shorter than the last one?" Birch stood up, her eyes dancing with mischief.

"Why, will you be happy when I leave?"

Lillian scuttled about looking panicked, Marjorie stared at Birch, her lips pursed, and her eyes squinted, such was her distaste for her.

"If you ask me, I cannot see the back of you soon enough, you have done enough in the past to lower the tone of the village, I will be happy to be rid of you." Birch smiled and rummaged in her bag.

"Then you won't be interested in this then?" She lifted out a folded sheet of paper, and handed it to her, Marjorie looked at it, and snatched it out of her hand.

"And what exactly is this?"

Birch winked at Celia, who was hovering a few tables away looking concerned, the whole shop had gone quiet, and was watching, Birch just stood there watching every movement of Marjorie.

"It is a parish registration form, apparently I have to fill one in if I want to run for the council in a year's time." Marjorie did not even open it, and scoffed at her.

"Well Birch, I hardly think bunking up in a guest house, qualifies for this." She handed it back to Birch, but she refused to take it.

"I would hardly call four million pounds a guest house, oh and by the way, you address me as Dr Dixon." Debs coughed and choked on her coffee, she looked at me and gasped.

"Four Million?"

I was stunned as I looked at her, I could not believe she had paid that much, and she had said Bradley had negotiated the price down. Marjorie looked at her with utter hatred.

"What gibberish are you talking about now, Edwin's house has a good value, but his guest house is a minimal part of it?" Birch looked at the paper still held in her hand.

"I do not live in the guest house, I am just a guest there until Abby's and my house is ready, which should be in about two and a half weeks."

Marjorie looked at the paper, she lifted her other hand and unfolded it, and read the registration form, her eyes grew wider, as she read it, her head snapped up.

"It was you.... You who...." Birch smiled.

"Outbid you, yes it was, I told you I had money, didn't I?" Marjorie looked horrified.

"You have no right to that house, it was planned, and arranged, in advance with Gwenda, for it to be sold to us for Nigel. How dare you use your ill gotten money to soil this village, I won't stand for it." Birch smiled.

"I have four million rights to that house, compared to your two, and actually it was Gwenda's son that arranged the sale, her say was void the moment she died, and considering your sons deviant behaviour a few years back, I would say it is safer for Abby if he did not live there." She stepped back, waving the paper in her hand at Birch.

"I will not tolerate this, I won't, it is completely unacceptable, and I will stop this, to prevent your sort from destroying this village." Birch shrugged.

"I have time, and the money, and when I open the practice, I will have no shortage of extra income, so go for it Madge, I will see you in court, just make sure the paperwork reaches me. Dr Jemima Dixon, three, Waterside Lane, Wotton Dursley, I am sure you already know the post code."

Honestly, I sat there looking at Marjorie, as her face turned scarlet, I thought her head was going to explode. She wanted so much to say something, but she could not quite find the right words.

"This is unacceptable… Never, did I think this village would house two whores." Birch smiled and winked at her.

"Don't you mean eight, we all have a bedroom each to work out of." Marjorie gave a gasp of shock, turned, and marched towards the door waving the paper.

"You have not heard the end of this Birch… Doctor whatever the hell you call yourself these days."

Celia came up to the table as Birch sat down, Lillian scuttled up behind her.

"A word of warning Birch, she had her heart set on that house, and she is an unforgiving woman, be careful." Birch looked up and smiled.

"Thanks Celia Sweetie, I have done nothing wrong, I bought a house that was up for sale, and that is not a crime, not even in Wotton." I looked at her and could see the delight in her eyes, there was mischief brewing.

"Birch did you know Marjorie was after it?" She gave a titter.

"Not at first, I wanted to buy it, so you would be close to your mum. I thought it would be nice if she could pop in, and keep you company whilst I was at work, then Rupert said he had another bidder who was trying to outbid me. Bradley did some snooping, and got Rupert to tell him who and how much. When I found out it was Marjorie and she had offered two and a half, I simply upped it to four to ensure there was no bidding war." She reached across the table, and took my hand in hers.

"Deads, all I wanted was to get the deal done, and get down here as fast as I could, a bidding war would have meant waiting longer. I did nothing wrong; everything is legal and binding."

As with all news in Wotton, the fact that Birch had bought a house, which involved out bidding Marjorie, went round faster than the flu. The gossip hot lines exploded, and full details of every aspect of her conversation had hit town, before we even passed the bookshop. Birch's phone pinged; it was a message from Hatty.

'Well done you, and welcome to the neighbourhood.' Birch chuckled as she showed it to me.

"Well, we have one supporter at least." She smiled.

"I like Hatty, I want some of her art for the whore house."

Chapter 7

# Wildlife.

It was the last week of June, and things were getting a little hectic for us. The house was now a bright pastel yellow, with white trim, on the outside, Birch wanted it the same colour as the guest house, the decorators were busy inside. All the carpets had been measured and ordered, and were waiting for the decorators to finish. Birch had all the amenities set up and ready, and the gardeners were already in the property working under the supervision of Norman.

It had felt like we had both lived at the computer, choosing colours of paint, carpets and statues. Birch had some very erotic statues for the garden, and as she did inform me, as a sex therapist, it was expected. My concern was that it would give Chloe even more ideas, and her descent into perverted deviance would be complete.

We needed a break, and behind the scenes, we had been planning our camping trip, which had changed, when Birch found a new site, looking for investors. The site was a woodland/ meadow site, with yurts, that was being marketed toward the under thirty fives. The idea was that groups could book for outdoor parties, hen nights, and bachelor parties, as well as university frat parties.

Nudity was allowed, as was alcohol, at which point Birch rang them up, and asked what they needed, and her investment manager did the rest. As a result, we ended up, with us all getting a free four day trip away.

The yurt was the biggest on site, set in the heart of a woodland, had four double beds, and three singles. It had a wood fuelled stove, which we could cook on, and parking for three cars at the yurt, and three more on the private car park. The only drawback was, that there had been problems with the sewer lines and septic system, and the toilet block was out of commission, hence they were looking for more investors, they had arranged portable toilets in the car park.

If anyone has ever been to a festival, they will be aware of how bloody awful the toilets get, when young drunken people use them. We decided, if needs must, we would go in the woods, and so packed a spade and plenty of extra loo rolls.

We took Petal, in which Chloe and Edwina jumped in with all our stuff, and Deb's took her car, with Anthony and Brent, and we set the sat nav, and headed towards Hastings, which was the closest to a developed town that we could get. Although we noted that there was a lot of secluded beaches to be found, and a little seaside skinny dipping could be possible, if we needed it.

We arrived filled with joy, and Birch went in to announce our arrival, which saw us presented with VIP passes, to the bar and shop, all of which were discounted, being an investor had its perks. Armed with a map, we drove into the five acre site, and followed the directions to our yurt, which was named Acorn. It was right in the heart of the site, and a bloody long walk to the nearest portable toilet.

The yurt was far more spacious than I had thought it would be, to be honest it looked like a reinforced circus tent. There was plenty of wood stacked outside, which was graded in several different sizes. Brent pointed out it was for getting the stove started, which involved using the thin sticks to start it, and then the larger logs could be put in.

It was a big round room with beds and seats, a large dining table, and a few small cupboards, and no internal walls. I liked it, it was nice, and I headed for a bed near the window, and dropped my bag on it. Anthony claimed a double, as did Edwina, and Deb's opted for a single, which pretty much told me, she would probably slip in with me and Birch, leaving one double left for Chloe.

It is at this point I realised that Brent did not really know or understand us. It was mid afternoon, and we would need at some point to cook, so Brent showed Chloe, Birch and Deb's how to start the fire, and get the stove working.

It was already a warm day, although the evenings lately had been chilly. We all sat round with a beer chilling out and drinking, as the temperature inside began to rise, and because it is us, we did what we always do, the clothing started to come off. Brent had no real understanding of how liberated we were, we figured he is gay, so it does not really matter, after all, Anthony had been naked with us tons of times.

Chloe was cooking in a G-string, Birch and Edwina were completely naked, Deb's was topless as was I, as we both had shorts on, and we just got on with it. I suddenly realised he was sat on his bed facing the wall, and looked embarrassed. Anthony was helping Deb's set up the table. I pulled on a long top and walked over, and sat at his side, I could see his discomfort.

"Hey, are you alright, we forgot, you are new to us all?" He turned to me.

"I am not sure how to be, I do not want to be disrespectful, and I have not stared, but how should I be around naked women, I have never been in a situation like this before?" I smiled.

"Brent it is alright you know, you can look, it is not disrespectful. Tell me are you gay, or are you Bi?" He swallowed hard.

"No one has ever asked me that, everyone just assumed." I nodded.

"Alright then answer me this, will you be aroused looking at all of us naked?" He shook his head.

"Sorry, but I am not interested." I smiled.

"We don't mind, we believe each to their own, it is okay to be shy, and you do not have to be naked with us, this is just how we are. We love the freedom of it, so relax, trust me give it an hour and you won't even understand why you felt like this, just go with the flow, and you will be fine." He shook his head and smiled. I went to get up and he grabbed my hand.

"Abby, what if Ant gets naked?" I shrugged.

"To be honest he probably will, we all hang out and swim naked, it's not sexual you know? It's just confidence and freedom." He shook his head.

"You don't understand... I mean, Abby if he walks round naked, I will be aroused, and it will show." I gave a giggle.

"Brent in this group an erect penis is a normality, trust me, this lot have sucked em and screwed em, and done one hell of a lot more. If it stands up, they will probably admire it, although one word of warning, if it does, stay the hell away from Chloe, that girl is not to be trusted around anything long and thick." He looked over his shoulder, to where Chloe was busy cooking.

"Yeah, thanks for the heads up."

It wasn't the heads up I was worried about with Chloe; it was anything that would fit up. I patted his shoulder, and he turned round to watch Anthony, who was laying the table, I winked at him, and went to my bed and took my top back off.

I set my laptop up on my bedside cabinet, and put on a playlist, and we all sat down to eat. Anthony was now shirtless, and we were all pretty much naked, it was really warm and snug in the yurt.

Apparently, when Pemberton's did their oriental nights, Chloe and her mum did all the cooking, we sat down to Chow Mein, and it was delicious. Chloe and Edwina, had brought their own chop sticks, we all tucked in with forks, and trust me it pays to have the daughters of a restaurant owner with you, the meal was fabulous.

After the meal, and a few beers, as well as a wash up, which involved a hand pump to get cold water, Birch took my hand, and led me outside. She wanted to walk in the woodland, this was one of her favourite things in the world to do. She loved nature, and I could feel her joy, as we walked under the trees in the cool fresh air. I slipped my arm round her waist, and pulled her close, and she smiled.

The evening was still quite warm, but under the trees, it was a lot cooler. We walked together slowly along the sandy path, the grass was dark green and lush, birds were still singing in the trees, and the whole place, felt calm and serene. I breathed in the clean air, and just embraced the whole atmosphere, it felt calm, still, and so peaceful, and it felt right, like I was a part of it all, a part of everything. I looked up and watched as the breeze stirred through the trees.

"Isn't this place beautiful Deads?"

I glanced at Birch, she was looking up too at the thick canopy of leaves, and taking deep breaths of the air. It sounds strange, but as I watched her, with her patchy hair, flowing down to her round naked bum, and bright green eyes staring above at the patchy sky, and that soft smile, it was so clear how natural she was, and how this was a place she completely belonged.

"This is the perfect setting to see you in. I love the sound of the swaying tree tops; it reminds me of your breathing at night." She turned and smiled.

"It is called psithurism, the sound of the winds through the leaves. I feel more at one here, being naked in nature is the truth of who we really are, or at least that is how I see it. We belong in it; we are part of it." She lifted her hand to my face. "You belong in it too, you are also a natural creature, you just don't realise it."

"Psst... Guys come here!" Birch turned to see Chloe squatting on the path, she was waving at us, and grinning, her voice was low.

"Hurry up or you will miss it?"

Chloe seemed way too excited, and that bothered me, if it had her interest it had to be illegal or immoral. We walked towards her, and she frantically waved.

"Not stood up, crouch down." I had no idea what she was up to. I came up to her, and crouched.

"What are you up to?" Birch nodded, Chloe was all smiles, she turned and pointed.

"Look.... Brent is going to blow him."

"Huh?"

She pointed through the trees, maybe it was instinct, I am not sure, but I turned, and looked in the direction of her pointing finger. She was all smiles, it took me a few seconds and then I spotted Anthony against a tree, and Brent was on his knees, his head moving slowly, I turned to her.

"You are seriously frigging messed up you know that don't you?" She giggled.

"I have never seen live action gay sex, I was curious, and I tell you what, when Anthony gets up, hell it's worth looking at." Birch shook her head.

"When I open the practice come and see me, you can be Izzy's first client." I tapped her shoulder.

"Brent is a little shy... Come on Chloe, leave them to it, you should not be following them." She frowned.

"I wasn't, I came out for a piss and noticed them." Birch looked at her, looking alarmed.

"Jesus Chloe did you piss here, I have got bare feet, you don't piss on the path, you go in the grass?" She shook her head.

"I haven't pissed yet; I have been holding it in... Although?" Birch and I slid back, and spoke together.

"Not bloody here!" She rolled her eyes.

"Fucking nature lovers, dirt is dirt, alright I will go over there then."

She pointed to the grass. We both crept away and left her to it, as we walked the short distance back to the yurt, it was getting a little chilly, and I was starting to shiver.

We reached the yurt, and she turned to face me and smiled. Birch leaned in, and softly kissed me, it was a gentle caring kiss, and I lifted my arms and pulled her close, it felt like such a special, and precious romantic loving moment.

Suddenly there was a deafening scream behind us, my head snapped round, to see Chloe with her hands between her legs, running like a crazy person, screaming at the top of her voice.

"SOMETHING FUCKING BIT MY HOOCH!"

"Huh?" She flew passed us, and headed for the yurt.

"There is scary pervy animals, and snakes round here, attracted to the smell of fish, this place is fucking dangerous!" I looked round at Birch, feeling shocked, and a strong panic rising inside me.

"What the hell, are there snakes round here?" She frowned.

"Well, nothing that would attack her." I felt a little more panicked.

"Well what the frigging hell bit her?" She shook her head, and shrugged, I felt the panic build inside me, and snatched her hand into mine. Both of us turned and hurried as fast as we could, and headed back inside.


Chloe was running round the yurt, screeching, holding her parts, her face was red and she looked really in pain.

"Ow.... Ow... Ow it hurts!"

Deb's was chasing her round, as Edwina sat on the bed, pissing her sides laughing. I grabbed her, as she ran towards me, with her hands between her legs.

"Chloe, we need to see." She gritted her teeth.

"Fuck Abby, my piss flaps are on fire."

Birch snorted behind me, and I tried, but it was impossible not to smile, as Chloe hopped on the spot.

"Oh, Abby, for fuck sake, it's my Vag... I hope it's not poison, if it swells up, no bloke will ever get in again."

Birch sniggered even more; I was trying to be helpful; I could see the worry in her eyes, but I did smirk. Of the thousands of things, she could worry about, having it shut off to men was all she cared about.

"Look Chloe, come and lie down, I have to see it, we have a first aid kit in the car." She danced on the spot, and was red in the face, as she gritted her teeth.

"You are not putting a bloody plaster on it, what it if heals closed, you are fucked up Abby, you know that?" Birch gave a snort behind me.

I did my best to guide her to the bed, she lay down, but kept her hands between her legs.

"Chloe no matter what, you have to let go, I have to see if there is any damage." She was sweating.

"Okay... But no sodding touching, Deb's told me all about you, and there is no fucking way you are getting me wet with those soft hands, my lips stay dry around women." Birch sniggered again; Deb's looked down.

"Well, it wasn't my fault, her hands were soft, and no one had touched me like that before."

That was it, the mental flash back to shaving Deb's was more than enough for me, I stepped back, and looked at Birch.

"Screw that, you are the doctor, you frigging do it, I am out." Birch sniggered and leaned in.

"It is okay Sweetie; I have done this before." Chloe looked at Birch with a look of complete distrust.

"Yeah, I don't sodding trust you either, you were her fucking assistant." I looked at her.

"Chloe, you have to let someone look, what if it's poison, we need to see it?" She winced, it was obviously hurting, she nodded.

"Look only... No touching." She slowly slid her hand back, Deb's was impressed.

"WHOA!" Chloe sat bolt upright and looked down.

"WHAT... HOLY FUCK IS SOMETHING MISSING?"

I didn't want to laugh, honestly, but it just came out, Chloe looked terrified, Deb's had her eyes wide open.

"Holy Shit Chloe, your vagina is bloody massive!" She looked up.

"Do you think so?" Deb's nodded.

"It's bigger than mine." Birch looked at her.

"Actually...." Deb's gasped, and looked down.

"NO WAY!" I could see her quite clearly now, as she sat on the bed, I leaned in.

"What are all those white lumps, on her lips?" Chloe looked down. Birch leaned in.

"It looks like something stung you, those are definitely sting marks." Deb's appeared on the floor at the side of the bed, and was crouched down near Chloe's leg.

"Shouldn't we suck out the poison, you know, like you do with a bee sting, or a wasp?" Chloe's legs snapped shut.

"You can fuck off too Deb's, you got wet for a reason, nothing non male sucks my flaps." Birch looked at her.

"It is more than likely a nettle sting; you would be better rubbing it with dock." Chloe looked at her, and frowned.

"What, the fucking dwarf, what the fuck Birch?" Edwina burst out laughing, and shook her head.

"No Chloe the bloody leaf, it is a wild plant." She understood.

"Oh, yeah okay, I get it now, for a moment I thought she had been eating those wild mushrooms out there. I thought, where the fuck do I get a dwarf at this time of night?"

Birch turned to me, and rolled her eyes, I couldn't help sniggering.

"I will go find some leaves, I have seen a few around."

Chloe sat on the bed, with her legs crossed, with Deb's staring at her, she was clearly freaked out by her, she moved away from her, and Deb's looked back at me.

"It really is fascinating how nature has created chemical defences, I can see how it has attacked the tissue to cause irritation." Chloe looked at her cautiously.

"I bet you gave names to all the lab rats didn't you, just before you stuck the needle in?" Deb's looked up.

"Wow, how did you know?" Chloe looked up at me.

"Fucked up, and fucking scary, I trust this one the least." I started to giggle, as did Chloe.

It was not that long before Birch appeared, with a hand full of large green leaves, she handed them to Chloe. She looked at Birch.

"What the fuck do I do with these?" Birch gave a sigh.

"Look!"

She folded a leaf in half and twisted it, then opened it back up, Chloe uncrossed her legs, and Birch lay it on her palm then slapped it straight between her legs, Chloe jumped.

"Fuck, it's cold." Birch rubbed it up and down a couple of times, Chloe looked at her suspiciously.

"If that middle finger so much as moves inward, I am punching you." Birch chuckled.

"Okay you do it, rub it all around to make sure the sap is spread all over the rash." Chloe slid her hand between her legs, and started to rub, Birch shook her head. "Yeah, that looks way too unsettling for me." Chloe looked up at her, looking a little bit embarrassed.

"How do you think I feel, I normally only do this in front of guys." Deb's jaw dropped.

"Oh my god Chloe, you do that for men?" Chloe raised her eye brows, and smiled.

"Fuck yeah, it gets em hot, don't you?" Deb's went beetroot, and looked at me sat on the bed.

"Did you know you could do that?" Why was she asking me, I looked at her?

"I have never done it, but yeah, I would if the right person asked."

Birch turned to me and smiled a sexy smile, and suddenly I felt really hot around the cheeks. Deb's looked at Chloe with renewed admiration.

"Wow you are like a living book on sex." Chloe lay back rubbing herself a little bit too fast for my liking with the leaf.

"I know stuff, hell I have done enough... Oh this is soothing."

She lay back, closed her eyes and bit her lip, Deb's suddenly realised what Chloe was actually doing, she stood up quickly and stepped back.

"Oh shit!"

She turned, and scurried quickly off to her bed, where she would casually turn every so often and peep, as Chloe rubbed herself better. Deb's crossed her legs.

We all settled down and left her to it, it did look weird as hell, which was made a little weirder, as she started to smile and enjoy it. We opened beers, and relaxed on top of the bed. Chloe looked up with a smile.

"This is helping, thanks.... I got to ask... What if a dog has peed on it, it won't...? You know, have an effect?" Birch took a swig of her beer.

"Edwina, throw one of your chop sticks across the room, and if she runs after it, then we will know."

Edwina snorted, and then sprayed her beer all over the floor, and started violently coughing and choking. Deb's gave her a hard slap, and she coughed, and cleared her throat.

"Birch, you bitch."

There is only so much of watching Chloe with her leaf, you can stomach. We reached a point, where we felt, she had even perverted plant lore, and moved into masturbation. She lay back on the bed, spread her legs, and spent a good hour, rubbing herself with the leaf.

I was tired, it had been a long drive, and I slipped into bed, and faced away from Chloe. Birch slid in behind me and pulled me close, and ran her fingers along my arm, it was soft, and comforting and relaxing. I wriggled back into her, and felt the heat of her body, she leaned in, and whispered.

"This is torture, I get really turned on in the wild, and I want you, and cannot have you." I gave a soft giggle.

"Save it for tomorrow, we will find a secluded spot, I think sex outdoors will be awesome." She kissed my shoulder.

"That does not help... I think I might borrow a dock leaf off Chloe, just to bring the pressure down."

I started to giggle, she snuggled in, and took hold of my boob. I closed my eyes, and drifted. I wasn't asleep, but I wasn't awake either, I could feel Birch softly breathing behind me, and feel the warmth of her body against mine. I vaguely remember Brent and Anthony coming back in, and bits of conversation, from the others, but nothing really stuck, I was drifting calmly and peacefully, half in and half out of reality, and it was lovely.

Everyone had settled, and was in bed, the light faded into darkness, and it felt safe and tranquil. Birch was dreaming, and would occasionally tweak my boob, as I floated in space and time, lost to everything. The room was dark, and was filled with the sounds of soft breathing, outside the moon was high, and the stars were out, it was a cool clear perfect night.

"RAAARGH!" Deb's sat bolt upright in bed in the dark.

"What was that?"

The darkness was filled with soft breathing, she looked round the yurt nervously, it was total darkness apart from the glow of the red embers inside the stove. Her heart was thumping, she swallowed, and slid back down in her bed, and pulled up the blanket to her nose.

"RAAARGH!" Deb's sat up rapidly in her bed.

"OH HELL NO!" She looked round again in the almost total darkness. Her voice lowered. "I really am not sure I like this." She looked round.

"RAAARGH!"

"ABBY!" Deb's shot out of bed. "SCREW THIS SHIT!"

She came hurtling across the room, grabbed the blankets, and dived into bed behind Birch. Birch squealed and shot up in bed, in terror, her heart racing, and panic flooding into her system, a torch clicked on to reveal the terrified quaking figure of Deb's, clamped on to Birch, for dear life. Edwina looked at Birch who lifted her hand to shield her eyes.

"For fuck's sake Birch, if your gonna have a threesome keep the fucking noise down." Rapid muffled muttering came from under the blankets.

Outside there another blood curdling scream, that echoed round the yurt. The torch moved, hit the floor and went out, Edwina's terrified voice echoed through the darkness.

"WHAT THE HELL WAS THAT?"

I sat up and rubbed my eyes, the bed was shaking, as even faster muffled words came from below the blankets. Birch looked round at me, and gave a sigh. She lifted the blanket.

"Deb's Sweetie, you are gripping so hard, I cannot feel my legs."

"I am sorry... I think someone is being murdered outside, and I am terrified." Birch gave another sigh.

"Deb's it's a fox, they do that." Edwina's nervous voice came back through the darkness.

"Fuck off... Foxes are like dogs, they fuckin bark, that was definitely a woman's scream, Deb's is right, there is a fucking psychopath out there." Birch flopped back on the pillows.

"How the hell can you all live in the rural countryside, and not know what a fox sounds like? Trust me, I am a doctor, that was a fox, all the frigging psychopaths are locked in bloody here tonight." I lay back, and she turned and snuggled into me.

"Oh, the joys of triple glazing, how can anyone live in the countryside, and be so ignorant as to what is living with them?" The bed behind Birch twitched.

"Abby, Birch, I am staying here, so no funny stuff." Birch gave a long sigh.

"Fat chance of that happening, with you lot here. Go to sleep Deb's."

Chapter 8

# Our wild sides.

The sun rose, and the day warmed, and I slept. I woke, in what felt like a strange bed, to see Deb's soft brown eyes staring at me level with my pillow.

"Abby... It's late, are you getting up?" I yawned and blinked; I could feel Birch behind me, her arm round my waist.

"What time is it?" Deb's smiled.

"Nearly one, in the afternoon. I am making coffee; do you want some?" I nodded.

I turned to look round the room, Edwina was dressed and was boiling water, Chloe was sat on the bed, her legs wide open, stretching her lady parts, and examining them closely, I shuddered. Brent and Anthony were nowhere to be seen. I lay back on the pillow, and relaxed. Birch's hand moved, it slid slowly down, and rubbed, I gave a gasp, as a tingle ran up into my stomach.

Oh god, I really wanted to be alone right now with her, I parted my legs a little, she was moving really slowly, so no one would notice. I felt her finger exploring, and closed my eyes, God I was so turned on. I took a deep breath, and tried to remain calm and still, but her finger slipped inside, and my toes curled, I clenched my fists, and my legs stiffened. I tried to whisper.

"Oh god Birch, ooh."

Deb's walked over with two coffees. I smiled as she put them down.

"You should wake Birch." My whole body was tingling, Birch had stopped with her finger inside me, I tried to act calmly.

"I will in a minute, give her some time." Deb's narrowed her eyes, and looked at me shrewdly, and lowered her voice.

"She is fingering you, isn't she?" I nodded and smiled, she stepped back, her eyes wide, and looked guilty.

"Oh, god, I am so sorry."

She went beetroot, and walked quickly away. Birch's finger moved again, and I gave a little squirm, and gripped the mattress. I looked round to see if anyone else had noticed, Edwina appeared busy, Chloe was still stretching herself, and Deb's was sat on her bed trying not to watch, although she did keep turning and glancing my way. Birch hit the spot, and I instinctively gave a little jump.

"Ooh!" Deb's jumped on her bed, and turned scarlet. Birch gave a quiet chuckle below the covers.

It was getting harder, my insides were building, and I started to twitch, I could not believe how turned on I was. I was watching the others, as Birch explored me inside, and I found it erotic and hot. I was finding it hard not to buck my hips, and had to lie back and close my eyes, my legs started to tremble, oh shit, I was going to cum, and I knew it would be impossible to keep it quiet, silent panic started to engulf me.

I bit down on my lip, those little electric spasms were firing up into my stomach, and down my hips, I breathed in, and tried to hold my breath, it was unbearable, I wanted to scream, and then she stopped. I gasped as she came up smiling from above the blankets, I opened my eyes and looked at her, and whispered.

"Birch what the hell, I was almost there?" She gave me a big smile.

"Oh Sweetie, I was just getting you primed for later." I gasped, as I stared at her in utter disbelief.

"What the hell you rancid bitch, you need to finish me."

She started to laugh, and reached over me for her coffee, I leaned in and bit her nipple, she squealed, and almost knocked the cup off the dresser.

"DEADS WHAT THE FUCK?" Everyone turned to look, and I smiled.

"Oh, I am sorry SWEETIE, I was just getting you primed."

I lay back and laughed, as she rubbed it, she looked at me and gave a huge grin.

"I like it when you bite." She chuckled and lifted her coffee. "So, what are we doing today?" I glanced at her.

"Well not shagging…. At least not yet." She giggled.

"I like it when you are aggressive too."

We sat in bed drinking our coffee, and watching the others, well when I say others, not Chloe obviously. Edwina stood at the end of her bed and looked at her.

"Chloe leave it the hell alone, if you pull any harder, you will turn yourself inside out." She picked up a leaf off the bed, it had a hole in the middle, she held it up in front of Chloe.

"My god you are such a perverted slut." Chloe shrugged.

"The rubbing was getting to me." She shook her head, and dropped the leaf back on the bed.

"You are not safe to be left alone with anything, is it a skill, you know, the ability to turn everything into a perverted object?" She smiled.

"Sex is art, and I am an artist." Edwina screwed up her face.

"For god's sake, just leave it alone, and stop pulling at it, it looks like that monster from Stranger Things, cleaning its teeth." Both Birch and I snorted a laugh.

The day warmed, and we headed out into the great outdoors. We decided to go exploring, and get a really good look at the site. It was five acres, so there was plenty to see. We followed the trails marked on the map, and eventually came across a river, it was clear and deep, and it was getting hot. Birch slipped off her shorts.

"Come on." She dived straight in, and came up with a squeal.

"Oh, it is glorious."

I undid my button, and looked at the others, Chloe was already naked, and dived in, Edwina had her top off, Deb's looked unsure.

"Is it safe?" I frowned.

"It's water, how dangerous can it be?" She looked unsure.

"What if it has Pike, they have teeth, and bite you know?" I smiled.

"Deb's live a little, take the chance while you have it, come on."

I slipped out of my shorts, pulled off my top, and ran to the edge and jumped, I sailed through the air, and came splashing into the water, and it was freezing cold. I broke through the surface and screamed out with delight, to see Deb's legs spread wide, and her vagina, came hurtling at me like a big lipped fish.

Before I could do anything, it hit me straight in the face, and I was pushed back under the water, as it gripped my nose, and sent me sprawling backwards. My nose was up her hooch, and I was not happy about it.

I scrambled, half drowning, terrified of breathing out through my nose, as I felt an arm grip me, and yank me back to the surface. I came up gasping and choking as Birch held me close, Chloe and Edwina were pissing themselves laughing, as I coughed and retched. Deb's popped up in front of me, going red.

"Oh my god Abby, I am so sorry, are you alright?" I shook my head of the stars, and looked at her.

"I JUST SNORTED YOUR HOOCH JUICE, NO, I AM NOT FRIGGING ALRIGHT!"

Birch held me tight, as her tummy wobbled with her laughter, Deb's looked at me hurt.

"Honestly it was an accident, I am so sorry." I coughed and cleared my throat.

"I just got an underwater face fuck, and that frigging thing swallowed my nose." Birch's tummy wobbled even more, even Deb's sniggered.

I calmed down as I got more air, Birch held me until I was ready, and then let me swim, I relaxed and found some calmness inside. I snorted down my nose to clear it, and everyone giggled, it was not bloody funny. I was sure she was wet, but because we were in water it was hard to tell. I snorted again, and frothy juice sprayed out, I looked at Birch, who was watching me giggling.

"If that is cum, I am bloody drowning her." Giggles broke out all around.


Thirty minutes later we were lay on the bank, drying in the sun, and I was just loving the heat on my body, today was much warmer than yesterday, and it felt great. Chloe sat up, across the bank on the other side of the river, a group of guys were walking.

"Praise the lord, I see men."

She jumped up, and ran to the edge, and dived in. I lifted my head, and half sat up, and rested back on my arms, hell this girl wasted no time, one sniff of a penis, and she was off after it.

I watched as she swam across the river, and then walked casually out of the water and up the bank, the guys stopped. I mean obviously, Chloe was naked, had a great figure, and she was pretty good looking. She pointed back as she spoke to the group,

Birch lifted her hand and waved, when they looked up. Chloe was obviously stating the obvious, horny females were to be found locally. She nodded, and agreed something, and then with a big smile, she walked back to the water and swam back to us.

The group were all aged twenty to twenty five, they were mostly single, and had another yurt over near the pasture. They had booze, and were having a boy's weekend away. That basically meant they were horny as hell, and short on action, and asked Chloe if we would like to go round tonight and visit, for as she put it 'some fun.' She told them we would.

We headed back to the yurt, and showered outside, I kept blowing my nose, much to the amusement of everyone. Chloe was excited, so was Edwina, I sat on the bed drying my hair, Birch came over and pulled a pouch out of her bag, she slipped her hand in, and pulled out a large handful of condoms, she walked back to the table, and put them down.

"Girls, play safe." Edwina smiled. She came back, and sat on the bed next to me.

"Sweetie, we need to talk." I think I had expected it, I turned off the dryer.

"Okay... What is on your mind?" She smiled

"Are you okay with this...? Deads we do not have to go you know; I am happy as we are." I understood her, she was watching my every move, her eyes looked so beautiful.

"What do you want to do, I am going to go with your flow Birch?" She smiled, and lifted my hand.

"I don't want to lose you, if you cannot handle it, I am happy to avoid it." I nodded and understood her.

"Birch I have not slept with a guy in over a year, but saying that, I got involved with you thinking Kev would continue. I just figured when he stayed at the house, I would be sleeping alone, so if you need to sleep with a man, I can understand that. I mean I do not see me or you as lesbians, I suppose we are to a degree both Bi." She understood.

"It has been almost two years for me, as I said, I kept putting Kev off, and I was so busy, I did not have time. I will not deny, screwing a stranger will be nice, and I know it is messed up, but I remember watching you and Eric, and that really turned me on, I could do that again, but only if we are both cool with it?" I smiled.

"Why not go and see how we feel when we get there, let's call this a free pass weekend and see how it goes." She squeezed my hand.

"Okay Sweetie."

Birch cooked and we ate, and Deb's joined me washing the plates, she had something on her mind. I could see her glancing at me, as I washed the plates.

"What is on your mind Deb's?" She looked awkward, and uncomfortable.

"Are you and Birch going to sleep with others, I mean, will that be okay for you guys?" I turned her.

"We have an understanding, why are you so bothered, is this because of you and Jimmy?" She looked down.

"I know he is away, and we have talked about it before the wedding, I suppose what I am worried about is what if I go tonight and want to have sex?" I shrugged.

"You are not married yet, I mean, yes, you have promised to marry him, but honestly Deb's, do you think he is over there with the band, and not dipping into the groupie pool? I have to point it out, but you got together with him a year ago, and yet since then, Edwina stayed over in Cambridge, and you were banging each other in my toilet not that long ago. Do you think that because she is a woman it is different?" She stood there looking at the plate in her hand.

"I know he is sleeping with groupies, the last time we spoke, I could hear girls in the background." I stopped washing and looked at her.

"Are you okay with that, I mean it did not seem to bother you in the past, and if Kev's stories about life on the road are right, then this is something Jimmy is going to do after your married? I think you need to talk with him, and soon." She nodded, her head still down.

"I want to be a good wife Abby."

I really understood her, I had known her all my life, she was at heart a really kind, loving person, and I knew she wanted to live an honest life, but in a way, she was not street wise enough to really understand the world around her.

"Look Deb's, the way I see it, is out there are some amazing wives, but they are in relationships which are consensually none monogamous, and they are far more common than you think. There is also equally as many good wives in monogamous marriages, so I think that this is really something you need to look at, and then talk to Jimmy about it. At the end of the day, you do not have to have sex if you don't want to, that will always be your choice, so go, and see how you feel, that is what Birch and I are doing." She smiled.

"Thanks Abby, you always know what to say, you are the best."

I cannot deny, it really made me think, I had been for the last few years. I had watched my parents, and although things did appear to be looking fine between them, my dad was still in the spare room, which I had discovered on my first summer break home at Uni.

Living alone in my house, I had decided, that actually Hatty made the most sense. I had no intention of getting married until I really felt it was right, if ever. In the last week, I could not deny, Birch had made it possible for me to dodge that particular bullet, she to a degree, had become my Kev.

We all dressed and walked over, which was not a short walk, the pastures were on the far side of the property, Birch was in high spirits, and had her arm round my waist. Anthony and Brent came along with us, as we told them, they were together, but that should not prevent them having a good time.

The yurt was a little smaller than ours, and a lot more basic, but it had beds, and seats, and we all smiled and said hello, to what were a bunch of reasonably attractive guys. We grabbed drinks, I noted how Birch sniffed it first, and then dipped her finger in it, I frowned at her, she smiled.

"Special nail polish, my mum sent it me, it changes colour if the drink is spiked." She stuck her finger in my glass. "It never hurts to check."

The music was playing, and Chloe started dancing, and gyrating with a tall guy. Birch was getting a lot of looks, although I was having a good share of some of the views, Birch patted my leg.

"Come on let's dance." She downed her drink and gave a shudder.

"Christ, I have not done this in ages, I am really out of practice."

We had been up and dancing for a few minutes, when a guy came up with a drink in his hand, and started swaying in rhythm with me.

"Hi I am Colin." I nodded.

"I am Molly, where you from?" He smiled.

"Dover, we all are, how about you?"

"Manchester." He looked impressed.

"Your accent does not sound very northern." I shrugged.

"I pick up accents easily, just being down here has had its influences, I also work on phones talking to a lot of people down here, it has sort of rubbed off on me."

He bought it, Birch was at my side and sniggered, she was dancing with his friend. I had no intention of giving too much of my identity away, I had suffered too much in the past. The drinks flowed, and the night got rowdy, and over an hour later we were all having fun, laughing and joking.

I had danced with three guys, all of them pretty nice guys, even Deb's was having fun, she smiled at me from the other side of the room, as she danced in the arms of Colin, he had given up on me, but that was okay, I was not really that into him.

Birch was behind me, and kept bumping her bum into me, she leaned back towards my shoulder.

"I am getting really bloody horny; I want sex with either you or one of these. Honestly, I will do you here in front of everyone, same goes for these guys, what do you think?"

I was dancing with a guy called Mike, and he was not bad looking, he was clearly interested, I looked back.

"I could do this one or you, or do this one and you later." She giggled.

"Or we could both do him together."

I stopped dancing, turned, and was really surprised, I have never thought she would go threes up. I could not deny, I had seen Chloe with two men, and I had wondered what that would be like, but two girls with one guy, I had no idea how that would even work. Birch spun round and looked at Mike.

"Which do you like Mike, her or me, or both of us together?" He looked stunned.

"What you two at once?" Birch smiled.

"Choose quickly." His eyes widened and he nodded rapidly.

"Oh god, defo both." Birch giggled and winked at me.

"Come on."

She grabbed his hand, and mine, and made her way over towards a bed. I suddenly felt a little panicked, I looked at her as she walked us quickly towards the bed, I had not really considered this, and holy shit, she was going to do this.

"Whoa... Birch, are we not going outside, I mean everyone will be watching?"

She looked round, Chloe and Edwina were already naked and getting pounded, Deb's was still dressed, but on a bed with her hand down Colin's pants, Brent and Anthony were still dancing, and talking to another guy, the guy who Birch had just left, was stood alone watching everyone else.

"No one else is Sweetie."

We made it to the bed, and Birch stripped in seconds, she pushed Mike back, as I lifted my top, I could not believe I was going to do this, and yet weirdly, I had become ten times more aroused, it was absolutely insane. Birch grabbed a bottle, as Mike pulled his shirt over his head in a hurry, he had a good body, he looked like he worked out. Birch took a big swig of the vodka.

"I hope you have stamina Mike, because we are not easily pleased?"

She handed me the bottle, and grabbed his pants, he was looking more than excited, which became very apparent when his pants came off. I took a huge swig of the bottle, screwed my eyes up, and shuddered, as Birch leaned over and took him in her mouth, he closed his eyes and lay back, holy shit, I could not comprehend I was seeing this, but I had to admit, it was hot.

I could not believe watching her like this, would be such a huge turn on, I felt a throb lower down, she looked up, and smiled, and opened her hand, revealing a condom. I took it, opened it, and then leaned over, Mike was already breathing pretty deeply, I slipped it on and rolled it down. Birch smacked my ass.

"Up you get."

I climbed on the bed and straddled over him ready, holy shit, was a I really going to do this? I then lowered myself as Birch guided it in, he was big, and it had been some time, she smiled at me as I lowered.

"Is that nice Sweetie?"

I was still trying to compute that I was actually doing this, never in a million years did I think this would ever be the sort of thing I would consider, but hell, I was turned on more than I had ever been. Birch climbed up and faced me, she lowered herself onto his face, and gave a groan, he had obviously taken the bait. The lust in her eyes was as sexy as hell, she was enjoying it, and enjoying watching me grind.

Birch leaned over towards me, she grabbed my head and pulled it towards her, and then kissed me. It was crazy, I was grinding away, and kissing her, and she was being stimulated by his mouth, it was wild, and I could feel my insides running out of control.

Her kiss was long, passionate and sexy, her tongue explored my mouth, and I was getting completely lost in it. I started breathing really fast, and had to break free to breathe, I could feel an orgasm building, and my mind drifted down to my vagina on Mike. I started to grind harder, Birch slid down and started to kiss my breasts, the tingles were exploding everywhere inside me, I was getting way too excited, was this him or her that was making me feel this way? I simply did not know, but I thought I was seriously going to faint.

"Oh God, Birch, this is too much, I am going to cum." She patted my arm.

"Swap."

She got up off Mike's face, he looked red, as I slipped off, and Birch straddled round me, and slid on, my legs were trembling, as I manoeuvred round, I looked down at him. Is it weird, I felt a little sorry for him?

"Are you really alright with this?"

Birch was grinding at a fast pace, thrusting herself forward, he smiled.

"Are you fucking joking, I am bloody loving this?" He appeared to be really happy.

In all the activity, I had completely forgotten the rest of the room. I climbed onto Mike's face, and he was off working his mouth and tongue, and pressing all the right buttons. Birch had her eyes closed, and was feeling the buzz.

I looked round the room, Chloe had taken up the slack, and was knelt on the bed, with her first guy behind her, and the guy who been left alone was stood with his pants down in front of her, and she was taking good care of him with her mouth. Deb's was bent over the bed looking at me, as she rested on her arms, Colin was stood behind her pounding away, and she was watching Birch and me.

Birch gave a long moan, and I felt a huge tingle run through me, I could not believe I was this turned on. I could feel the power inside me building again, Birch gave another loud moan, and I felt myself throb, holy shit, watching her screw, was getting me off more than Mike's tongue.

I reached out to her breasts and played with them, she opened her eyes, and I was blown away. She looked so lustful, so sexy, she gasped as I tweaked harder, and moaned, I throbbed again, I leaned down and started to kiss them, Birch reacted by leaning back.

"OOOOOOOOOH!"

My orgasm was almost there I was throbbing like crazy, electric was shooting through me, I would not last much longer, I slid over to her other boob and bit down softly.

"OH Deads..... Deads.... Deads." She went faster, thrusting forward, and then stiffened.

"OOH GOD!" Her whole body shook, and my vagina exploded. I leaned back.

"OH GOD!"

I was cumming like crazy, as my whole body shook, Mike's hips bucked, and he stiffened below Birch, she gave another squeal, and leaned right back, I could see his hips jerking, we were not the only ones exploding. Deb's let out a long moan, and pushed her head into the bed covers, I could see her shaking, as Colin held her hips, the dirty bitch was getting off on watching us.

I flopped forward feeling light headed, I lifted my waist slightly to take the pressure off Mike, and leaned on Birch, gasping for air, her arms came round me, as she leaned onto my shoulder.

"Holy shit Deads, that was hot." My head was spinning, who was I becoming, oh Christ, had I really just done that?

She gasped for air. My legs felt like jelly, and I had to slide sideways, I could feel Mike gasping for air, and he was blowing out onto my very sensitive parts. I slid onto the bed at his side, as Birch tried to climb off him. Oh god, at some point, with these legs, I had to walk all the way back to our bloody yurt.

Birch sat on the end of the bed, Mike sat up smiling, his face and hair were soaked, he slipped the used condom off, and dropped it off the side of the bed, Birch shuddered.

She looked at me as I lay there, my legs were feeling broken, and she smiled. I gave a smile back, but honestly, I just needed air, and a long rest. Mike slipped off the bed and looked at us.

"Christ, you two are wild, I bloody loved that, I will never forget it." Birch looked at him.

"What can I say, we are every guy's wet dream." She turned and flopped on the bed at my side, she lay there looking into my eyes.

"Are you okay Sweetie?" I smiled and lifted my hand to her face, I had so many thoughts crashing through my mind.

"I am fine, tired, but fine.... Did we just do that?" She gave me a beautiful smile.

"So wild and so free, you are so amazing Deads, and I love you."

I closed my eyes and tried to breathe, and in my mind all I could think of was, holy shit, was this me, was this who I really was... Did I just do that?

Chapter 9

# Challenge's.

It was Sunday morning, and finally there was not a bell in ear shot. It had been a long bow legged walk back last night, and I had slept late, it was 12:15, and Birch was still fast asleep.

Chloe had seen my eyes open, and made me a coffee, Deb's and Edwina were still sound asleep, and so I lay back in the pillow, and watched Birch sleep, as my mind wandered through my life.

So much had changed, and yet nothing had changed. Birch was still Birch, and we were all older, although I am not certain if wiser. I thought of last night, and our adventure with Mike, did I regret it, no, but I could not deny, I had never thought that was me. Was this growing up or insanity?

I honestly had no idea, I had always had that ability to mentally file everything, and define what I thought was right for me. Yet, I was in a relationship with no definition, and I had not only received sexual gratification from Birch, I had also reciprocated it, and that did not fit the picture in my head of the me, I had grown up with.

I realised that maybe, mentally I was arranging everything in my mind, the way my mum did, with everything she owned. Everything had a place in her scheme of things, and I had to ask myself, was I like her in the way I had structured my life? The one thing I knew for certain, last night was most definitely not structured, it had been plain and simply motivated by instinct. I had not had time to think and gone with the flow.

Birch had asked, and I could have said no, but the crazy thing was, I did not want to, I wanted to know if I could do it. Could I honestly pleasure another guy in front of her, and could I watch her do the same? Well, the answer was yes, and the most shocking thing about it all, was it turned me on more than I had ever realised it could. Seeing her happy, seeing her having fun, excited me, was this the compersion she had talked about at Uni?

I had no idea really, I just knew it excited me, and it was quite a stark reality to face this morning. Birch groaned and moved in the bed, I looked down at her, and she opened her eyes and blinked, she gave a dreamy smile.

"Hi Sweetie." She licked her lips, sat up, and leaned her head on my shoulder. "I was sleepy." I slid my arm round her.

"It was a strenuous night, and a long walk back."

The guys had offered to let us stay, I think they were up for more action, but in all honesty, Chloe had three, Edwina took on two, and Deb's had Colin twice, and I did not want any more. Anthony and Brent had left early, and they were tucked up together when we got back. If I am honest, I did not want to hang around, all I wanted was to curl up in bed and be cuddled by Birch.

Once again, our life was nothing like the picture I had painted in my head, not only of myself, but also of all the others. There was no doubt we were liberated and empowered, I mean, hell, we literally were the ones in control last night, and yet the boys were all willing precipitants, and appeared to have enjoyed it equally as much as we did. The crazy thing about it all, was Mike appeared irrelevant in the scheme of things, my focus had been on watching Birch, and that had given me such joy, it contradicted everything I had believed I was, and I was trying to understand that.

I sat up and lifted my coffee, it was just warm, and took a mouthful, and offered some to Birch, she took it, and drank it all, and handed me back the empty cup.

"I feel like I need a shower, you want one with me?"

My problem with the shower was it was outside, it runs off a solar water heater, but it was lukewarm at best, but I must admit, I felt pretty sweaty. It was a warm day, but in order to cook or boil water, the stove had to be lit, and it heated the whole place up. I reached for my towel, as Birch looked for her wash things, and while I was waiting, I filled a pan with water, and put it on the stove.

The shower actually felt better than I thought it would, Birch lathered her hands and washed my back, and front, and between my legs, it felt like she was cleaning last night off me, she gave me the liquid soap, and it was my turn to do her. It felt nice to run my hands all over her, she had a soft happy smile on her face as I did it. I looked up at her, as I washed her legs.

"Do you regret last night, is that what this is about?" She looked down and smiled.

"No Sweetie, I really enjoyed watching you, it's shameful, but that guy was just a tool, I wanted to watch you enjoy yourself, and be a part of that, and honestly, it gave me a lot of joy to see you so happy."

I needed to know, and was glad to hear her answer. I ran my hands up over her breasts and she closed her eyes, as I washed them, she smiled, and opened her eyes.

"Can we spend the day in bed together?" Her eyes twinkled. "I don't mean sexually, I just mean sit, and cuddle and just be together, I want some alone time, I need it?" I nodded.

"Yeah, if that is what you want, I would love that." She smiled.

"It has been so busy lately, I need a little time to just stop, and take a moment for me, for us, before it all gets mad busy again."

I pushed her gently back under the water, and watched all the lather wash off her, and I smiled, there was that innocence, that lost little child again, and it was a part of her I loved.

"Come on, I will brush and dry your hair, and then we will just sit and chill out, and drink coffee."

She gave a soft smile, as I turned off the water, and wrapped her in a towel. Hand in hand, I led her back, made a coffee and then sat cross legged behind her on the bed, and brushed her hair and dried it.

The day passed, curled up in bed drifting in and out of sleep, warm and snug, and it was the best day of the weekend. Monday came, and it was time to pack up, and head home. We loaded up Petal, cleaned the yurt, and then took a picture of all of us stood outside, with bright smiling faces.

On the road home, we got a blow by blow account of the Sunday exploits of Chloe, Edwina and Deb's. They had met up with the boys at the river, where they had swum, drank a lot, laughed a lot, and screwed a lot, and all were happy.

We came back into Wotton happy and laughing, and dropped off Chloe and Edwina, and arrived home mid afternoon, parked

Petal in her spot, ready to unload. We headed into the guest house, and flopped down feeling calmer and happy, it was 14:12pm. I got up and filled the kettle.

"I say coffee, then empty Petal, then back to bed, what say you?"

There was no response, I leaned back to look, Birch was looking at her phone checking her emails, she looked worried, she read something and then dialled, and put the phone to her ear.

"Mum, what the hell is going on.... Yeah, sorry I turned it off, we were having a day off of peace and rest.... Look I am sorry, okay? I just forgot to turn it back on, I mean it's not like you have not done it a million times." She paced up the room and turned.

"Okay, I get that, but it was a legal deal."

She paced again, as I watched, her mind was focused and she had that look on her face, she shook her head.

"She cannot do that, can she.... Okay then what do we do?" She nodded, and turned again, and walked back across the room.

"I trust him, he is a good man, so is Ed.... Yes... No, I am coming, it is my project. I will be there, where do we meet you?"

She nodded and turned, and grabbed a sheet of paper out of my printer, she grabbed a pen out of my old mug, and started to write.

"Yeah, I got all that... I will be there, just wait for me." She ended the call and turned to me. I could feel the goosebumps up my arms.

"Is everything alright?" Her eyes blazed with defiance.

"You need to get dressed in something more appropriate, come on."

Birch marched into the bedroom, I have no idea why, but I felt panicked. I hurriedly followed her, Birch had the wardrobe open, and was looking at her business clothes, she pulled out a pale blue blouse, turned and held it up to me. She threw it on the bed.

"Put that on, and wear these." She threw a pair of black cotton pants on the bed. "And this." I felt the urgency but had no idea what was happening.

"Birch what the hell is going on?" She pulled a suit jacket out and held it against me as I unbuttoned my jeans.

"Wear that... We are going to court."

"What?"

She pulled off her top, and started unbuttoning her shorts, they dropped to the floor, and she stepped out of them.

"That bitch has tried to reverse the sale of the house, we are in court at four." I grabbed the blouse and pulled it on.

"How can she do that?" Birch pulled up her slacks.

"She can't, but that won't stop her trying, Bradley, your dad, and my mum are there, with our legal team, we need to get there... Brush your hair and tie it back."

I was going because I would stand by Birch, but honestly if her legal team was there, would she even need me? I pulled up my pants.

"I am not sure I will be much help, I will probably have to wait outside, but I will be there if you need me." She fastened her blouse and looked at me.

"You own half of it; you are going in, this is our fight Deads, we fight it together."

I stopped, and the pants slipped and fell down, as I stared at her, I found it hard to speak.

"What do you mean.... I own half of it?"

She slipped on her jacket, crouched down, grabbed my pants and pulled them up, she fastened the buttons, and straightened my blouse.

"I put it in both our names, it is half yours." She stood up and looked at me, her eyes shone bright green.

"Deads I love you; I want to share everything with you, I thought I told you that?" I swallowed hard; my brain was spinning.

"Birch... Yeah, I get that.... But... But... But I thought you meant life, like Saturday night, sharing experiences, having fun, travelling, getting drunk, you know, sharing everything?" She smiled.

"Sweetie, owning a home is an experience... Now come on get your jacket on, and I will do your hair."

"Birch... It's four million bloody quid." She nodded.

"I know Sweetie."

I was struggling for words, she spun me round, grabbed my hair, and began to brush it. I felt the snap of a bobble, and she turned me round to look at me. She lifted her hands and pulled her hair back, and then slipped another bobble off her wrist, and tied her own hair in a pony. She smiled.

"Wow you look quite the business woman." I just stared at her, I did not know what to say, I took a moment.

"You are not having me on are you, I mean this is not a prank, you are serious right?" Birch looked at me.

"I just told you Sweetie, it is half yours, I am just waiting for the final papers that show joint ownership."

She walked out of the bedroom towards the door, I followed her, as she went outside, and opened the back door of Petal. She pulled out some of our bags and handed them to me.

"Birch, it is four million bloody quid." I grabbed the bags, as she pushed them on to me, she gave a sigh.

"I know, I transferred the money, you know Deads I do wish you would stop saying it." She heaved up the food bag.

"Just put these in the middle of the living room, we will sort them out later." She walked back towards the house and I followed.

"Please Birch, can we talk about this, I am really uncomfortable with all this?" She gave a sigh and looked at me.

"Good, because money should make you uncomfortable. Look Deads, it's meaningless money, don't you see? I did nothing to earn it, I reached twenty one, and suddenly boom, I had eighteen million in the bank. It was just handed to me, and I did not want it really, all I want is a simple life, doing what I love, and snuggling up next to you. I would do that here, or over there across the street, hell, I would live in a frigging yurt with you. This... Me and you, and whatever the hell our relationship, friendship is, that means far more to me than money." I looked at her, she was so serious.

"You are sodding crazy, you know that?" She smiled.

"Yeah... But I am sodding crazy and rich... Look, we have a wonderful home base now, and Deads, it is so much more than that. Did you know Chloe cries at night in her flat, she is working all day and painting all night, just to get her name known in the art world? Or did you know that Edwina has spent her whole life savings on her business, and cannot afford an office in Wotton because they are too damned expensive, or that Goggles biggest fear is that she will lose touch with you, and she gets lonely and upset about it?" I had no idea, and it took my breath away to know it, Birch gave a nod.

"I did, and so I bought a house, and Chloe will have a nice place to live, with her dream studio, Edwina will have a home base to set up her office, and Goggles can come home to us whenever she wants, and will have her own room there for her. You keep saying four million, but it is not, it is the Curio's heartbeat, and we are the owners, so we can watch over them."

Boom, she exploded my brain! I was lost completely in how amazingly unbelievable she was.

"I never realised, I really didn't." She smiled and leaned in a kissed me on the cheek.

"We still need to stop that bitch from ruining it, so now, if we can, I would like to go and save our dream." She grabbed the paper off the desk, and handed it to me.

"You drive, we need to be there by at least 3:30."


It is a good thing Oxendale is only nine miles away, and I know all the back roads. At 15:10 we entered the lobby of the court building, Roni was waiting for us, she wasted no time, and turned.

"Follow me." She walked off down the long corridor of pale grey.

"Okay you two, we have a full legal team here, some of mine and some of Bradley's. We have arranged a meeting in the conference room at 15:30, so we have twenty minutes to prepare, Jemi these are the best, so listen to them, I want no rogue behaviour, do exactly as they say, that goes for you too Abby."

I was feeling really nervous, Roni had a sense of urgency, yet Birch looked really cool, and calm, as we marched down the hall. We arrived at a plain wooden door, and Roni swung in, we followed, and as I entered the room, I felt my breath catch in my chest.

Right down the middle of the room was a long wide polished wooden table, and all along one side, were various people, all dressed in business suits, all with papers on their desks. I recognised Bradley, my dad, Birch's dad, and my mum. She got up as I came into the room, and walked round the table to meet me.

"Abigail are you alright, you look white?" I gave a huge sigh; I was glad to see her.

"I am fine, we just had a brilliant few days, arrived home happy, and suddenly all this, what the hell is going on Mum, can she really do this?" My mum looked at the table filled with people.

"Roni, your dad, and Bradley, acted fast, the letter was delivered by courier to Bradley at eight o'clock Friday night, he came straight to us, and we contacted Roni, we worked until late. They drove down overnight, and on Saturday we all had a meeting at Bradley's house, we have been working on this all weekend, she is just being her usual vindictive self. Abigail, do not upset yourself, we will get this all sorted out."

Birch was stood with her mum, Bradley and a woman. Mum took me over as Bradley introduced her as Margret Stuart. She was about forty, impeccably dressed, and looked hard as stone, her face looked like chiselled granite. Just her gaze, scared the living shit out of me. She looked really hostile already, and we had not even started. I thought she was bloody scary. Margret looked at both of us, as Birch addressed her.

"Can she really do this and win?" I tried to slip back behind Birch's shoulder to hide. Margret gave a snort.

"She may well think she can, but leave her to me, she might think she has all the aces, but she has not done her homework properly. I need you to sit back, say nothing, and just allow me to work. I have eaten much bigger fish than this in the past, and as for that snivelling and witless idiot McDonald, he is in my pond now, and he is a minnow compared to all the other swimmers."

Yeah, I was right, she is bloody terrifying. I was so glad she was on our side, if Marjorie had hired her against Birch and me, I would have just handed her the keys, and ran off screaming.

We were sat at the head of the table, it was huge, I counted fifteen people, all sat down, reading through papers, the table was wide enough for four to sit, and Bradley and Roni sat next to Birch, my mum was sat at the top of our defence side, which I was glad about, and Margret, who in my head I nicknamed 'The Shredder.' Sat next to my mum.

I sat back and looked round, it was not that great a room, the paint was flaking on the corner of the old sash windows, which were greatly lacking a window cleaner. The carpet was reasonably new, although brown did match the grey of the walls. I thought it did have a bit of a remote dungeon feel to it, although maybe that was to get certain people used to their future dwelling, I mean this was a court after all.

I felt anxious, if I am honest, I had no idea why I was here, in my mind, I could not see how my presence would help. I mean, this was above my head, and there was a crowd of legal experts here to sort this house thing out, and not forgetting the Shredder. Crap, she was writing, and the pen looked like it would snap, I wondered if it will be engraved into the table when she lifts her pen?

There was a knock at the door, and I looked up, as my heart started beating faster, Birch slid her hand across the table, and grabbed mine, and squeezed it, she was looking at columns of numbers. None of any of this made sense to me, but I did recognise my dad's handwriting.

The door was opened by Bradley, Birch did not even look up. In walked an older man, two younger women, Marjorie, and my jaw dropped, as I saw Nigel. He looked right at me, and it was clear the idiot wanted to wave as he always did. It amazed me how he has hardly changed, apart from the most stupid looking moustache I have ever seen in my life, it was so thin, it made him look like he had a fungal infection on his top lip.

The group were seated at the end of the table, Nigel sat alone on the end of the long side facing some of our legal team. Marjorie sat staring at Birch and me, I thought she was trying to use some form a psychic mind hold to strangle me with.

I took a deep breath, I will not deny, I was feeling pretty nervous and scared, I was not used to any of this. I mean yes, I did business at Uni, but even so, all this was on a completely different level, and I felt a million miles out of place.

Bradley introduced everyone, and they nodded in turn, except for the Shredder, she did not even blink, she just stared down the table at Marjorie. I think this is the first time in my life I ever felt a little sorry for Marjorie, because the Shredder, bloody terrified me.

The old guy was Bennet McDonald, family solicitor to Marjorie. He had long wispy grey hair, and reminded me a little of Filch out of the Potter movies, he sort of looked like a slightly fatter version of him. Bradley walked past Nigel, with his lip fungus, and up the long table, he sat down. I felt clammy, and was starting to get really nervous. Bradley looked down the table.

"Right Bennet, I have seen your paper work, and my team, and Dr Dixon's team have had a look at it, so I will lay my cards out on the table. If you want to proceed to court in half an hour, we can do, but I feel this is a waste of court time, so let us know what you really want and we will talk." The young blonde at his side turned to face us.

"We want you to void the deal, we will arrange a return of the capital, and the house will then pass to its rightful owner, for the agreed price to our client, Mrs Wallace."

The Shredder stood up really quickly, and I jumped back in my seat. She is really bloody terrifying, she looked down the table and gave a laugh like shattering gravel. I swallowed hard as I thought, that is probably her hobby, destroying quarries with her laugh.

Marjorie scowled, I had to hand it to the old bag, I would have pulled a Rosie, and crapped in my pants if it had been me. The Shredder, lifted some papers from the table, and slowly walked round behind me, I instantly tensed up, and squeezed Birch's hand, as she passed. She was on my side, and I was still afraid of her. The Shredder walked slowly towards the young woman emitting vibes of prepare to die you bitch.

"Sorry I forgot your name, and you are whom exactly?"

The young woman looked intimidated, and I did not bleeding blame her at all, I was twenty feet away, and praying to my colon to behave, she stumbled a little on her words, whereas I would of screamed, and fled the scene.

"Gabriella... Pinkenhurst Bollocather, I am... Assistant Junior Partner to Mr McDonald."

I tried not to giggle, I put my head down, all I heard was 'Pinkie Bollocks Catcher.' Birch smirked, I knew it, she was playing the same game we played all the time at Uni, where we would try to find rude, and stupid nick names. Although, in regard to Margret, Shredder was a mark of total and absolute respect, on my part. The Shredder moved in closer, her voice was coarse, strong and powerful. I will not deny, I was utterly terrified of her.

"Could you please elaborate on your ridiculous statement

earlier, pertaining to a rightful owner, if you don't mind?"

I had to hand it to Pinkie, I would have just looked at the Shredder, and burned the paperwork, then legged it. Pinkie lifted a paper off the desk.

"If you note the date, which is fourteen months ago, you will find this is a private letter, which confirms a verbal arrangement for the sale of number three, Waterside Lane, Wotton Dursley. It is signed, and the signature has been authenticated, as belonging to Gwenda Perkins, current owner of the property at the time of signing. This as you will be well aware is a legal written contract of agreement to sell." The Shredder turned back towards us, and I shrank down in my seat.

"Dr Dixon, can you confirm this medical report for me please."

She handed a piece of paper to Pinkie. I looked round, holy shit, there were three of them, which one did she mean? William stood up, ah right, that cleared up things tremendously. He gave a cough and cleared his throat.

"The attached, is a medical report, dated nineteen months ago, that confirms substantial loss of mental capacity, carried out by Oxendale General Hospital, due to deterioration of the brain, and a progression towards dementia. It clearly confirms hallucinations, paranoia, and a reduction in cognitive function. It also recommends that the patient be offered accommodation at the Wotton Manor care facility, or home based nursing, and a care provider be placed. Having read through the whole assessment thoroughly, and as someone regarded as a specialist in this field, I have found the report to be correct, and would agree with the recommendation." He sat down.

So, good ole Gwenda, really was as bonkers as we all thought? The Shredder handed another sheet of paper over.

"I believe your client will recognise this, it is a letter from Mrs Perkin's son, dated two days after this mental capacity assessment, to your client, explaining that his mother would be relinquishing her post, at the local church flower group, due to her illness, and dwindling ability to remember."

I took a breath; holy shit, Marjorie knew all about her illness, the crooked bitch, she actually knew. I wanted to scream at her for putting Birch through this, and my allegiance towards the Shredder increased ten fold.

I sat there fantasizing, about the Shredder just walking up to Marjorie, and then ripping her head off, as she laughed and brought the building down on top of her. The Shredder moved in closer, and handed Pinkie another sheet.

"This is a court application for power of attorney made on behalf of Gwenda Perkins by her son Rupert, as you can see by the stamp, the court granted it, and as you can also see by the date, this was two months prior to the handwritten letter, that your client states, gives your client the rights to that property." The Shredder gave a terrifying smirk, and handed her another.

"A copy of Mrs Perkins will, which clearly shows her son Rupert as sole inheritor of the property and its contents, after her passing, you will note, there is no mention of your client."

Well, I mean it is all there, isn't it, the crazy old bat signed a legal paper to make her son Rupert responsible for her, and Gwenda gave him everything. I only met him a few times, the guy was an absolute moron, and as much as I hate to say it, he was a bigger bloody idiot than Nigel. In my mind this was a done deal, you could get no better evidence of Gwenda's oncoming insanity than that. The Shredder turned to walk back up the table.

"Mr Wheeler, I believe you have more?"

Marjorie snatched the papers and looked furious, as she looked at them. Pinkie sat down, Bradley rose from his seat, with yet more papers. I felt the chill of death walk past behind me, and cringed. I mean, I thought she was bloody amazing, I just felt the need to squeeze my butt cheeks together, to prevent a Rosie whenever she was near me. Bradley walked down and started placing papers on the table, in front of them.

"I have a letter from Mr Rupert Perkins confirming the sale of the house, another emailed this morning stating his intent to honour the sale. A bill of sale, and confirmation of the financial transaction, to Dr Jemima Dixon, and Miss Abigail Watson as co-owners, my solicitor's confirmation of the house being placed into the care of my holding company. Dr Dixons solicitor's letter of confirmation of the house being held until purchased, and the officially signed transfer of the property to Dr Jemima Dixon and Miss Abigail Watson. This deal is official and fully legally binding, the house is co owned under law, by the two above named."

Bradley walked back towards his seat, as Filch examined the

paperwork, he looked up the table.

"If you don't mind Wheeler, I see no approval of the parish, for the sale." Bradley looked to Margret, who shrugged, Pinkie gave a smug smile.

"Due to reasons of security, considering the high security nature of the residents of the parish, it is practice, as stated in the parish register, that all resident's need to be vetted and approved, before being allowed to purchase property, and live in the parish, something I believe has not been confirmed. The parish council have no knowledge of a Dr Dixon living in Wotton." Bradley looked stunned.

"I have never heard of it, I can assure you it is not standard practice, as I personally was never requested to make any application to the Parish." Filch looked up the table, and smirked, the twisted twat, he was enjoying this, and I hated him with a passion.

"That is an irrelevant fact, we are not discussing your residency, we are discussing that of Dr Dixon's, and the fact is, she does not have the approval of the parish, she can therefore not be resident." Bradley stumbled on his words, and looked at my mum.

"Is this true... Do you have to give consent to live in Wotton...? My God Felicity that is outrageous?" My mum sighed.

"Sadly, that actually is true, but I must admit it has always been seen as a formality, I am not sure it is legally enforceable."

I nodded at Bradley; I mean how the hell can a group of out of touch, and out of reality in most cases, old buzzards, have the right to say who can and cannot live here? God, it made me feel really angry. None of them really understood who Birch was, they had all assumed the worst, and it was not right. Filch smirked.

"Oh, but it is legal, I have the papers here to prove it, it was enacted by Oxendale and District Council as part of their heritage act in 1922. You may examine the documents if you like, but you will find it is well within my clients right to raise it, and enact it." He sat back and smirked, the slimy old bastard. Marjorie looked up the table, and gave a laugh.

"As you see Birch you need my authority to live in Wotton, and I will die before I consent to that. You may think you have won, but that house will stand empty, and you will have to take your trashy life back to where you belong in Manchester."

Roni stood up and banged her fists on the table as she leaned onto it.

"How dare you address my daughter with such disrespect, you conniving vicious old......"

I felt a burst of anger flash through me, I acted on instinct, and stood up and lifted my arm to Roni's shoulder. I could feel a huge wave of anger coursing up inside me, and I swallowed hard to force it back, I spoke through gritted teeth.

"Wait Roni, you are better than that."

I suddenly realised what I had done, and everyone was looking at me... Oh crap! My heart was beating like crazy, and I could feel real anger boiling inside me, I looked down at Birch, she had dropped her head. Holy shit if she cried because of Marjorie, not even the frigging Shredder would stop me jumping on the table, and running down it, and pasting the witch. I looked at Roni and smiled, I was still holding Birch's hand, and I squeezed it.

I swallowed hard and prayed I would not pull a Rosie. I was trembling, either from fear or pure anger. I really was not sure which, my throat went dry, and my hand shook slightly. I took a deep breath as I looked down the table, and directly into the eyes of Satan. My voice was quiet and shaky.

"I cannot deny, I do not understand a lot of this legal stuff, but I do know two things. Firstly, Mrs Wallace, you are not the parish, you are one vote as vice chair. I have sat through enough meetings, waiting for my mum in my life, to know how things work. The second thing I know is, I was born in this parish, and I have been in this parish all my life, apart from two years at university."

I swallowed hard, and silently prayed, please save her, don't let this fail, please save Birch, this is so wrong and she should not have to suffer. That house will be filled with nothing but love, and Chloe, so there will be some sex, actually, scratch that, it's Chloe, oh shit, it will be permanent sex.

"Therefore, could your solicitor confirm, I am a fully authorised legal resident of the parish, and if so, I am legally allowed to own the property am I not? Can I also ask if I am still allowed house guests without approval from the parish, because if I can, then even though I don't have to, I will inform Mrs Felicity Watson, the actual Chair of the Parish Council, That Dr Jemima Dixon will be my permanent guest for the foreseeable future."

My legs were shaking like hell, and I suddenly had a throat so dry that I was sure I could taste sand. My mother leaned forward.

"As Parish Council official chair, do I have a second?" My dad raised his hand.

"Seconded." Mum looked up at me and smiled a beautiful smile.

"Duly noted, it will be entered in the official notes of the next meeting, Dr Jemima Dixon will be an official guest of Miss Abigail Watson at number three Waterside Lane for the foreseeable future." Birch looked up at me with tears in her eyes and smiled, I squeezed her hand.

"All girls together." She smiled and wiped her eyes, and sniffled.

Bennet McDonald looked at Marjorie for guidance. The Shredder looked up at me, and gave one scary ass looking smile, she nodded, and I almost shat myself, and sat down fast. The Shredder looked at her watch.

"Well Bennet, the young lady asked a question, will you give her an answer?" My legs were shaking so much, I wanted to pee. Filch looked up the table at me.

"Well, I must say Miss Watson, you appear to have asked some very valid questions, and I cannot deny that you are quite right. As a resident of the village, who was indeed born there, you have every right to purchase property, in fact if memory serves me, you have a right to have precedence over those who live outside the parish borders. As a resident and a property owner, you also have the right to allow anyone you see fit to be a guest in your home, which as you have seen, has also been authorised by the Chair Woman herself, with a second. I believe it was a point we completely overlooked, and so therefore we have no choice but to withdraw our point in regard to the council mandate."

The Shredder stood up fast, and I crossed my legs, as I almost peed on the carpet. She looked down the table.

"It is almost time Bennet, are we to proceed into court or not?"

He looked at Marjorie, and gave a subtle shake of his head, it was clear by her face, she had no hope of winning, he turned and looked up the table.

"I believe considering the facts, to continue would serve no purpose, this would be a waste of precious court time."

Roni and Bradley both gave a long breath out of relief, Marjorie was furious, she stood up, and scowled up the table, and then Birch stood up really fast, and I jumped, seriously, my bladder was expanded, and it was not wise to shock me like that. I looked up at Birch, she looked so beautiful, her hair hung down her back right to the base of her bum, and I could see her long eyelashes silhouetted in the light. She took a breath, and raised her voice.

"BEFORE YOU LEAVE MRS WALLACE, MAY I HAVE A WORD PLEASE?"

Marjorie stared up the table at Birch with hate.

"What could you possibly say to me?"

Birch looked at her with her with beautiful bright green eyes, and I could almost see her thoughts, she was calm and collected, if not a little red from her tears.

"During the summer I spent living with Abby, you held a barbeque did you not?" She almost spat the words out of her mouth.

"What if I did, you know quite well I did, you were there?" Birch nodded.

"I was, and I will say you did a really wonderful job of organising it, us Manchester trash pride ourselves on a good barbie, but you even exceeded our expectations. My point is this, during that event, I made a donation of five hundred pounds in cash to the village fund. I believe I handed it to you in person, in front of Harriet Barker, your assistant Marion, and Mrs and Miss Watson who are present here?"

"So... What does that have to do with this?" Birch smiled.

"To be honest Mrs Wallace nothing, but I was curious, because you see I have a copy of the accounts for the Parish Council here mixed in with the council rule notes, and I was reading it whilst these proceedings were in progress, and yet I failed to see an entry in them for a five hundred pound donation, so I just wondered why that was?" My dad frowned.

"I have no recollection of that?" My mum nodded.

"Oh yes, I was there and saw it myself." Marjorie turned and headed for the door.

"I have no time for this foolishness, it is not even relevant to these proceedings. NIGEL!"

She stormed out through the door; he looked at me, then realised he was alone, and ran from the table.

"But mummy what about my house, I wanted it?" I gave a long sigh of relief, Birch turned and looked down at me, with red eyes.

"Deads you saved me, that was worth every penny I spent, now do you see why it does not matter?" I smiled, and yes, I did, I fully understood.

The room suddenly got busy. Filch, walked up the room and shook all our hands, I thought that was fair, he lost, but handled it like a true gent, and I liked that. Roni almost crushed me.

"I love you so much for that, if she had lost that house, it would have destroyed her. Thank you, Abby."

William shook my hand, so did Bradley with a wink, mum and dad both hugged me, it was weird, I turned to Birch and she smiled. She reached up and pulled out my bobble and let my hair fall, she arranged it round my face.

"Thank you, my dark little beastie."

She leaned in and gave me a short soft kiss on the lips. I felt a tap on my shoulder, and turned around, and there was definite leakage in my pants, well actually, they were Birch's pants, as I faced the Shredder. She made that ghastly smile, and I prayed I would not pull a Rosie, as my butt cheeks clenched tight. She grabbed my hand and shook it, she had a grip like a vice, and I winced.

"I missed it, and you spotted it, damned fine work Watson."

I nodded, my focus was on my bladder, and trying not to empty it. She lifted her phone.

"If you do not mind, I think your hair is pretty damned marvellous, could I have a picture to show my daughter?"

In all fairness I would give her anything she asked for, I would boot Birch out of her own house, and hand over the keys if she wanted it. I squeaked a quick and dry throated.

"Yeah... No problems." And then it suddenly hit me, did she say daughter?

Holy shit, who was brave enough to shag her? Christ, there must be one terrifying scary ass bloke walking round Oxendale. What the hell does the daughter look like? She took the picture and looked at it.

"If you don't mind me asking, who styled this?" I tried to relax, and failed.

"There is a fantastic stylist in Wotton called Antonio, he is the best for miles, well you can see, he does Birch... Jemi's hair as well."

She gave another grizzly smile, yep, there was leakage. Bradley walked up to talk to her, and I gave a huge sigh of relief, my bladder was fit to burst. I thought just one more encounter with the Shredder, and I am flooding the place. I felt an arm slide round my waist, and I smiled, I turned and looked at her.

"I really need the ladies or I am going to pee on the floor, I was so scared Birch."

She took my hand, and we walked down the room into the corridor, and looked for the sign. A minute later I was sat on the toilet enjoying the feel of a good long flow, Birch was next door and I could hear her wiping. I spoke more to myself than Birch.

"Holy Shit, I need to warn Anthony, if a female who looks like a cross between Quasimodo, and the Honey Monster, limps into his shop, dragging her arms on the floor, he should just give her whatever the hell she asks for, his life will depend on it." I heard Birch next door.

"Huh?"

Chapter 10

# Understanding.

I lay back on the bed, smiled, and closed my eyes, it had been an exhausting day, the long drive back from the camp, the courts, it was hard to focus, and yet all I could see was her face, as she stood in front of the window listening to her mum, and it was just beautiful.

"Jemi darling, I have some news about Melody, to be honest it was talking to Abby on video chat that helped me spot something important, you know that girl really has no idea how bright she is?"

Her face had clouded over, it had been a pretty emotional day at the court, her eyes still had a redness to them from her crying earlier, and her mum was now talking about Melody. I worried, as I stood there watching her, about if this was too soon, and her mum should have waited.

"Jemi, Abby told me about how broken hearted she was, because you did not call her the night before you arrived, and actually, I think I may have read a little more into that situation than she realised. But I knew you were there now, and so I did not concern myself, but she told me, how hard it was for her, and that struck a chord, and I asked myself, would it have been hard enough to do something stupid, something that would threaten her life?" Birch swallowed and her eyes teared up, Roni nodded.

"I thought so.... Jemi, what if Melody felt the same? It really bothered me, and so I did some digging, and I looked into her boyfriend. Apparently, there had been some issues, because he wanted her to come home, and obviously she wanted to stay at the University. He texted her less, and then just stopped completely. He was tired of trying to get Melody to see sense, Jemi, this is not unsimilar to you and Abby is it?"

Her face wrinkled, and she bit her lip, and tears rolled onto her cheeks, Birch knew how bad it had been for me, and so therefore she understood Melody better, she gave a small gasp, and her sob came up. Roni took her hand, and held it.

"Jemi you did everything right, this was not your mistake, it happened after your last session, there was absolutely no way you or I could have seen this. We are therapists, we do not predict the future, we handle what has been in the past, to help create new futures for those we work with, you are not to blame for her loss."

Birch looked down, and her shoulders shook, and she gave a desperate sob, I saw the tears hit the floor, Roni pulled her close and held her.

"You did everything you could Jemi, and you did it all right."

I hate seeing her cry, and yet at that moment she looked up at me, and the tears sparkled in her eyes, I have never seen anything as beautiful in my life, the depth and kindness behind those tears, were magnified, and it just blew me away.

I lay on the bed, my mind wandering through the day's events, it did not really surprise me that Marjorie would try to stop Birch living in Wotton, I just wish she hadn't. My mind wandered back to five years ago, and all the hate we had faced, and after all this time, it was clear, it had not gone away, some things had changed, but one thing that remained exactly the same, was Marjorie was as determined as ever, to claw back control, and destroy us.

Marjorie Wallace, had once again stalled in her tactics to combat as she put it, 'those whores.' She paced around Milton's office, her anger barely under control.

"That old windbag was useless, absolutely useless, poor Gabriella tried, but he did nothing, he just sat there and raised the white flag, and now Nigel has locked himself in his room, and is refusing to talk to either of us. Although watching her today, I think she is the right choice for Nigel, all we have to do now is find a way to get them to bond more." Milton appeared confused.

"Well, I must say, that is a little too much, what on earth did I do to the boy, this was your great scheme, I had nothing to do with it?" He clicked open his emails, and looked down the list.

"You know I have spoken to the girl, admittedly it was some time ago, she really is not that bad a person. I am sorry Madge, but I found her to be very bright, and caring. I do think you are going a little overboard, is there no way you can find it in you to be civil?" She looked horrified.

"She is a whore." He sighed, and sprayed spittle through his teeth on the desk.

"I hardly think she sleeps with men for money, I would say a girl of her openness, and her Wiccan background, would probably do it for nothing."

"What the hell is wrong with you, fornication is fornication, it does not matter whether money is involved or not, and don't forget, she admitted it, she actually handed me that money and told me, and I quote, 'I had to F word a lot of men for that.' I mean what more do you need to know about her?" Milton looked up from his screen.

"Madge I am sure it was just a jest; you know you did provoke her? No, I think that was just her way of evening the score." Marjorie stared at him like he was a complete idiot.

"Have you any idea how long it took me to wash and sterilise that money? I was washing my own hands for weeks, it made me feel so dirty." He gave a sigh.

"I am sure that was a tad of an overreaction, what became of it anyhow?"

"It is still sealed in an air tight bag in the safe, how could we use it, I had no idea what people would catch if they used it." He shook his head.

"Madge, the money is plastic, I am sure a good wash, ensured it was clean, you withholding it does not look very good, does it now?" She paced round the room.

"What other choice did I have? I cannot trust any aspect of that brazen whore, she is, and always has been trouble, and to be honest Milton, you need to watch yourself, if she ever finds out about your so called men's club activities, we will all be ruined. No, we have to strike while the iron is hot, and bring her, and that motley group of miscreants down with her."

Birch sat on the end of the bed and I opened my eyes, she held out a glass.

"Don't know about you, but I really need this, honestly, I hate thinking unkind things, but if that woman's vagina withered and healed up, I would celebrate." I gave a giggle.

"Do you think she would even notice? Let's be honest the

damage is done, she had Nigel." Birch shuddered.

"God, he creeps me out, did you see how he stared at you all day, it made my skin crawl?"

I placed my drink on the side and lay back, Birch slipped back and sat up against the head board, and put a pillow up her back.

"I am glad the others are busy tonight, I just want to be alone with you, it has felt a little bit too much for me today."

I understood, worrying about the house, and then having to deal with her mum bringing up Melody, it could not have been easy. In the living room the computer came to life and started to play the familiar ring tone, Birch sighed.

"What the hell could mum want now?"

She slipped off the bed, and went to see. I closed my eyes and lay back, even I had Melody in my thoughts. Roni had told me how alike we were, and I have seen how much the loss has affected her. I cannot deny, a part of me really hated myself, for even thinking about leaving her that way. I tried not to think about it, but it just kept haunting me, I could have destroyed her, and I had never once thought of that.

"Bev Sweetie." My eyes snapped open.

"Guard your vagina!" Birch walked into the bedroom with the laptop.

"Deads it's Bev, she is in France." She put the laptop on the bed, and I sat up against the pillows to see, Bev waved.

"Hey Deadly, or should I say 'Bond'your Mamma Gazelle.' I am getting proper good at this frog speak you know, its fucking blinding over here."

Birch sniggered. I looked at her, and her hair was green now, although she had even more face piercings than when I last saw her. I smiled.

"Honestly Bev, just for a moment I thought wow, I had no idea you were not French." Bev laughed and nodded at me.

"Aye, I bought one of them phase books, and I am doing proper good at it, I tell you, I am buried in frog biff, I tell ya, I eaten fuckin tonnes of frogs legs, and I ain't talking in a restaurant either, them folks are fucked up." She smiled. "I just look at em and go Park lee view, do ya fuck, and they are all over me. Hey guys, look I got an eye full tower in me brow, how cool is that?"

She pointed to yet another piercing in her eye brow, and yep, sure enough there it was, stuck right through the end of it, I gave a slight shudder, and smiled, Birch was doing her best not to giggle.

"That is pretty amazing that Bev, and I am glad you are enjoying your stay there." She nodded.

"Yeah, it's great, I am really getting into it, I eat them crossed ants at breakfast, although dipping them in chocolate is fucked up, I mean everyone knows that is a bed time drink, no wonder half of em look sleepy when I am trying to talk to em. But it's cool you know, and I am learning the lingo. To be honest, I want to ask you both something, you see there is this frog bloke called Enamel, and I think he wants to fuck me, but I have never done it with a bloke, and you and that Chloe, are the only straight people I know, so I thought I would call and ask."

I looked at Birch, she looked as equally as surprised as I did, I mean this was Bev, the legend of the lesbians, and she wanted advice on sex with men, holy shit, today was just getting weirder. I looked at her and tried to be delicate.

"Bev, has this Emmanuelle actually told you he wants to sleep with you?" She shrugged.

"Well sort of... He keeps giving me flowers, and he did buy me a clit stud with a diamond on it, so I am betting he wants to see it, and see if it works when he wiggles it."

I shuddered and got goosebumps; I was relieved to see the hairs on Birch's arms lifting up. Birch leaned in to the screen.

"Bev Sweetie, what is it you want to know, I mean, you know what you like, even with a dildo, so it's not like you are completely unaware of what it will be like?" She nodded, and smiled.

"This is sort of embarrassing you know, he sent me this pic."

She looked down, and tapped on her phone, both our phones pinged. I cannot deny I was hesitant opening it, and for good reason. I recoiled at the dick pick, with a huge golden ring through it. A cold shiver ran down my spine, Birch looked at it closely, I frowned at her, she looked up and smiled at Bev.

"He is quite fat Sweetie, so you will have good friction, it is hard to tell, but he does not look that long, but that is not always a bad thing."

I thought it was a fair appraisal, but I was still having problems coming to terms with this was Bev, and I could not resist the obvious.

"Bev... You know you don't have to sleep with this guy, he may have bought you gifts, but that still does not force you. If he gives you gifts, he should do it without expectation." She smiled and lifted her thumb up.

"You are a fucking good mate; you know that Deadly? And aye, I know I don't have to, but you know what they say, when in Italy, do what the Italyites do, and I wanna give this a go, you know just for shits and giggles. I mean he fucks men too, so it's not like a straight thing. Hey Jemi, yeah, I think it's quite fat, and if it doesn't go far in, well that is not bad eh! I mean it's probably longer than a tongue."

I cringed just at the thought, and went ice cold, and violently shuddered.

I began to realise just what Birch did for a living, and honestly, I know for definite, that was not something I could do. I watched her as she talked to Bev, she was so relaxed and calm, she listened so carefully, and considered all her answers before talking, was this the life of a sex therapist? I had no idea, my skin was crawling, I loved Bev to bits, she was really sweet and kind, but honestly, the less I knew about her vagina, and what went in it, the happier I was.

I understood that she did not get out and about much. I think here was the furthest she had ever travelled from home, and in a way, it was nice she was enjoying herself. Birch filled her in on the finer points of sex with a man, which honestly, freaked me out a little bit, and I wanted to change the subject.

"So, Bev what is it like being in Paris, have you enjoyed it there?" She gave a huge smile.

"Hey Deadly, it's fucking brill, as you know I went to the eye full tower, and it's fuckin massive, honestly I looked at it, and thought, how big was the fuckin ladder they used to carry all that shit up there? I tell you Deadly, it was fuckin mind blowing. I went to the Arc of Trump, and that is like boring, I mean it's just a fuckin posh bridge, I thought if they think that is fuckin good, they should come see our arches, I mean those fuckers are impressive."

Having been to Uppermill, I remembered the viaduct, I had to smile, but she was excited.

"I went to that Loo Ve gallery thing, fuckin loved the pointy greenhouse, but that moaning Lisa, it took a fuckin hour to see her, and it's just some miserable bitch with her arms folded, and sulking. I seen enough of them, I dated a few. I were proper let down, it's fuckin tiny, I thought it were this huge picture, but I am telling you, my Foo Fighters poster at home is bigger. Then I went on a boat on the river insane thing, and you know what... it fuckin reeks. I wanted to stand outside, but it stunk so bad, I almost tossed me dinner up, so I sat inside, and held me nose. I did like the 'Note red Van Dam', you know where that 'quashed his mojo' lived, I thought, no wonder he got the hump, some fucker burned it down."

It was really hard not to laugh, Birch was doing her best to stifle her giggles, and every now and again she snorted, I could see her tummy bouncing as she fought hard to quell the laughter, which did not help me. Bev smiled and looked at her watch.

"Look guys, I got this posh bird wants to fuck, she is called 'Shan Tell' so I am gonna go do her, but thanks for the advice. I want to see that posh house you bought Jemi, so I will show you all the pics when I come, Okay?" I smiled.

"Have fun over there Bev, it was lovely to see and hear from you, see you soon." Birch leaned into the screen.

"Bye Sweetie and I will see you soon." Bev waved and ended the call, I slid down the pillows.

"I love her to bits, but I wanted to piss myself laughing, bless her she really is something else." Birch smiled, as she got up to put the laptop back.

"She is one in a million Deads, she is also one of the kindest people I know, I am glad she is having fun, she deserves it." I lay back and closed my eyes.

"Quashed his mojo." I started to giggle, I heard Birch in the living room snigger.

Two vodkas, and three gins' later, and I was naked in bed lay on my back, Birch was lay on my shoulder, with her hand on my stomach, as I absentmindedly stroked her hair. I was drunk-ish, dreamy, and in a very reflective state of mind.

"Are you going to be okay Birch... You know, over what your

mum told you about Melody?" She stirred a little.

"I think so... What she told me made sense, but whether it was my fault or not, I didn't want her to die, and knowing she did with a broken heart, did not make it easier for me."

I could understand that, I know how hard it is to admit those deep hidden secrets, not only do I live in a village full of them, hadn't I also hidden mine, and eventually shared it with Birch? She moved slightly.

"This probably sounds wrong Deads... When mum was telling me, I really felt for Melody, I did, but honestly, all I could think of was you, how it could have been you, and I couldn't handle thinking I could have caused that, it tore me apart." I gave a sigh.

"Birch it wasn't, and you have to let go of that, because that will tear you up inside." She slid round and climbed on me, and sat on my waist, and looked down at me, her eyes looked filled with hurt.

"But Deads it could have been."

"But it wasn't." Tears flooded into her eyes.

"If I had not come back, it would have been." She gave a sob. I shook my head.

"No Birch, I told you, I passed out."

She gave a small gasp, and more tears flowed, and dripped onto my tummy.

"Okay not that night, but it could have been another, and I would have lost you forever." She shook slightly and breathed in; more tears dripped.

"I am so... So sorry Deads, and I do not know what to do, and it is eating me away inside." I sat up and pulled her close, she nuzzled into my neck and wept.

"I was so selfish, I put everything above you, and because of that you were alone and afraid. I hurt you Deads, I really hurt you, and I am so sorry." I held her as tight as I could.

"Birch I am here, and I am holding you, and that is all that matters, all these what ifs are meaningless." She gave a snort.

"I really want to make it up to you."

"Birch you just spent four million pounds on a house for us to live in, and gave me half of it, I mean who the hell does that?" She gave a snort.

"That is just stupid money, that does not count, I want to give you something that matters." She leaned back and wiped her eyes; I stroked the wet hair off her face.

"You are here, that counts, and honestly, you very unexpectedly went down on me, and gave me a massive orgasm, and that really counted, because I never in a million years expected that."

"But Deads that was just sex."

"No Birch... What we did with Mike was just sex, you were the reason I had such a big climax, because it was you. Do you understand that? You touched me like I have never been touched before. If it had been anyone else, just like you with Katie, I would have closed my legs, and stopped it. That only happened because it was you, I wanted that, but only with you, because that is how much you mean to me, can you honestly understand that? Birch I cannot do those things with another woman, I can only do them with you, that matters."

She nodded and gave a sniffle, I leaned over and grabbed the tissues, and handed her one, she gave another sniffle and dried her eyes, and then wiped her nose, her eyes still had small tears, and sparkled as she looked at me.

"I can only do that with you too, I feel the same way, I do not know why, I have tried to understand it, but all I come up with is because it is us."

"We do not have to understand it Birch, it does not need a label or tag, it is us, just us, we are curious about each other, and we are enjoying learning, and that is all it has to be. Stop putting all this added pressure on you, and just be you." She nodded.

"I can see you have talked to my mum." I gave a small chuckle.

"Not about us I haven't, if I need to know something, I talk to you and you alone." She swallowed back her remaining tears and smiled.

"Yeah, me too." I pulled her close and she slipped onto my shoulder, and nuzzled back into my neck.

"You make me so happy Deads, I love being with you." She kissed my neck.

We sat for a long time just holding each other, her warm slender frame was pressed tight into me, the smell of her hair was in my nostrils, and as crazy as it sounded, it made me happy too. For a while I had tried to understand it all, why her, out of all the females alive, she had something so special about her, I needed her close. Deep down inside I knew sleeping with Mike was a test for me, as I still wrestled with the notion of was this a gay relationship, was I gay, had I been gay all along?

I remembered my week in Uppermill, we had spent a lot of time at Birch's house talking, Bev was clear, she was a lesbian through and through, she had never slept with a man. I remembered laughing when she told me, her virginity was lost to Boris, a ten inch pink rubber dildo, she still had it, and was going to go and get it, but Birch and myself assured her it was fine. In Uppermill, she is so well known, and well liked, she is referred to as 'The Legend of the Lesbian's' and yet tonight, she had really made me think.

Bev was considering sex with a man for the first time, to her it was for shits and giggles, but I got the impression that for her, it took nothing away from who she already was. In Bev's mind, she was no less a lesbian, because she tried a man once, she was curious, and wasn't that what humans are really about?

Wasn't it out of curiosity, which took us from the cave to modern civilisation? In a strange way, tonight Bev showed me the true meaning of a Curio. She was living her life, experiencing what for her was a strange culture, eating strange food, and talking badly in a strange language, and she was even considering what for her would be a strange type of sexual experience. She was safe and secure in whom she was, but she was not afraid to expand her horizons, and I admired her for it.

Birch once borrowed my laptop, when hers was broken at Uni, and on it she wrote an article for an American magazine, that argued that love, real deep love, was a process of nature, and that fake love, or the idea of love, was a construct of society. I remember when she asked if she could have it on her memory stick, for her new laptop, I just copied it over, rather than move it completely, and that was because at that time it really struck a chord with me.

To Birch the feeling we have, that we name love, is a natural product of nature. She argued we had no say in the process, we just naturally grew towards a person, and feelings grew, until one day it hit us, and we realised. That made so much sense to me back then, and yet today it makes far more. I know when I look at her, I am in love with her, I have felt the anguish and the pain of being without her. I was at my lowest ebb when she returned, and from that second, I saw her drive round the village green, every ounce of that pain and anguish has disappeared.

I consider myself a straight girl. All the sex I have had has been driven by lust, and was massively arousing, and all of that was with men, and as I have seen in the last few days it has not gone away.

Deb's once jokingly asked me if I wanted to have sex with her, Katie constantly asked me to have sex with her, I know Edwina would if I asked, so would Bev. All of them have some of the qualities of Birch, Deb's, Katie, and Edwina, I would say all men would consider them as very sexy and hot. Bev has huge appeal to gay women, and yet, I feel no attraction at all to them, and if I ended up in a compromised situation with them, I know for a fact, my legs would be crossed.

It is a conundrum that is for sure, because I have fantasized about what it would be like to have sex with Birch. I had wet dreams about her when I was living alone, I would wake with my fingers inside myself calling out her name, and I honestly have no idea why. All I can say, is it is natural.

It just happened, I did not choose these feelings, as I sat in my dorm at Uni, they just appeared, and grew out of nowhere, and I have no idea why. Bev taught me tonight, not to question them, and sat here, with her wrapped around me, feeling her warmth radiate into me, I have decided I won't, I will simply enjoy what I have, and she is female, she is Birch, and I understand that now. I came out of my thoughts, and I heard her breathing softly in my ear.

"Seriously... You fell asleep on me?"

For the next ten minutes, I conducted what the SAS would consider to be tactical manoeuvres. I dragged back the duvet, and then slowly tilted to the side, using my arm to lower myself with Birch hugging me, down onto the pillow. Her legs were round my back, her arms round my neck, and she was gripping me tighter than a woolly monkey's child, on its mother.

It was no easy task wrestling free of her, but after some strange twists, which I am sure would be great yoga poses, I finally had her in the bed, lay on her side, with the duvet pulled over her.

I went into the kitchen and clicked on the kettle, suddenly from nowhere my mind was alive, and I needed coffee. While the water heated, I walked into the living room, and sat at my desk, for some time an idea had been bouncing around in my brain, I opened a new blank file, and rested my hands on the keyboard.

I looked at the blank white sheet on the screen, set on a grey background, and my mind became a sharp focus, and I started to type.

'Working title: The Seeds of Summer.

Chapter One.

Summer Approaching.

There comes a time during those hallowed days of university, when you sit up rather abruptly, and the seriousness of the moment hits you bang in the face....

The kettle clicked, but I was already in the red zone, hammering out the words, and this time it would not be gothic, it would not be fantasy, it would be real, and gritty, and a little shocking and naughty. It had to be, because it was going to be the truth, the truth of life, the truth of people, the confusion of sex and growing up. It was going to be their fears, their hopes and their dreams, and it was going to be all of that, because this was my summer, the summer Roni told her daughter, to make it Abigail's Summer.

Chapter 11

# Subtle Changes.

I cannot explain what it is like to be a writer, I think the best way of putting it is that it is like an illness that flares up, it comes and it goes. When it comes, time stops, there is nothing in your life, but a screen, and row after row of words, all strung together in a coherent manner. You laugh, you cry, you live, as you actually become so involved with the story in your head, you actually see the images in your mind, and they are as clear as if you were watching them on TV, or standing there as an observer.

Fantasy and reality become one, and that is all that matters, as you reach a level of focus, a Buddhist priest would be proud of. If you are as lucky as me, food and drinks just appear at your side, as your partner understands the process, and just reaches into your world at arm's length, to either deposit or remove the sustenance you need. I am really lucky; this is the first time Birch has ever seen me really work, and she just naturally understood, and got on with her work sat at the table, and did nothing to break my concentration.

The days slipped past, and Deb's watched through the window, and looked back at Birch and Felicity.

"How many days is it now?" Birch gave a titter.

"It has been six days, she writes, collapses and sleeps, wakes up, drinks coffee, and then sits and writes. She hardly speaks, unless it is muttering to herself, or she needs another word for her meaning. Apart from that, I am unnoticed."

Deb's frowned, as she watched through the glass fascinated. Birch had hung a sign on the door reading 'Writer at work, do not disturb.'

"Does it not bother you?" Birch nodded.

"No... That is who she is, and to be honest, it kind of turns me on. I mean look at her, look at the focus, look at the speed of her hands, the slight smile. I think she is at her most attractive when she is writing, that is a side of her few will ever see, and it just so happens I love it." Felicity looked at Birch and lowered her voice.

"Are you two sleeping together.... Well, I mean, I know you share the same bed, but do you.... Well, you know?" Birch smiled.

"Screw each other... Yes, we have done."

Felicity gave a slight smile, and leaned her head over to one side.

"Really... Well, I mean, to be honest I suspected it, so you two are les...."

"No Flick we are not, we screw guys too, but occasionally we have enjoyed each other, and we do love each other deeply." Felicity was very intrigued.

"I am a little surprised that Abby has not said anything to me, I always thought if you were, you know, she would have said so." Birch shook her head.

"Why would she, you have never told her about you and Hatty? To be honest, if you had, it would have helped her."

Felicity looked stunned, and a little pink around the cheeks.

"You know... How?" Birch, gave a smile of remembrance.

"I was at her big art show in Birmingham two years ago, my mum loves her work. We were staying at the same hotel, so sat in the bar talking, and getting very drunk, Hatty is no lightweight with whiskey. She asked me if I had been having sex with Abby. I told her no, I was very straight, and had struggled, because Abby was the only girl on the planet that gave me sexual thoughts, and that I really wanted to have sex with her, but I was afraid of losing her."

Felicity appeared to really understand. Birch patted her arm.

"Hatty never mentioned you, but she told me the story of a friend she grew up with, and how just like me, she was very straight, but had these thoughts. She told me she went on holiday with her camping, and was drunk and horny, and how one night she just lost control, and went for it. She said she was really surprised, because the other girl responded. Hatty said, they both had the most amazing night of their lives.... You have no idea how much that helped me, just knowing I was not alone, and other women had felt as I did at that time, made a huge difference to me." Felicity smiled.

"So, if she never mentioned me, how did you know?"

Birch looked at her bright blue eyes, and gave a soft smile.

"Abby has your eyes. Flick I look into those beautiful blue eyes of hers, and I cannot stop myself falling even more in love with her, they hold me captive. I have all sorts of wild thoughts, and I have this massive desire, which boils up inside me, and all I want is to be as close to her as I can get." Felicity gave a gasp.

"Wow... Oh dear... I am not sure what to say." Birch looked through the window.

"You cannot say anything they captivate you. I just connected the dots, if Abby's eyes do that to me, it made sense, they did the same to Hatty. I really did not know if I was right until two minutes ago."

Deb's was fascinated and completely oblivious to Felicity and Birch, Felicity looked through the glass and smiled.

"I understand what you mean Birch, when her eyes fill with tears, just seeing them that way, destroys me. I have always thought she talks with her eyes. I take it Abby does not know?"

"Nope... Flick it is not my place to tell her, it is yours if you ever do, but it appears to me that you have something else in common with her."

Felicity stood back on the lawn next to Birch, as Deb's peered through the window several feet away, and watched her daughter at work.

"You know over the last couple of years, I have spent hours out here watching her do that. I look at her face, and I see me when I paint. It is the same certainty, the same focus, the same dedication to her art, I find her inspiring." Birch nodded.

"Then paint it... Paint the picture of her sat there, paint the picture of Abby, as seen through the window, writing her stories, and when it is done, show her, show her the truth of how your love for her inspires you, because if you are as good as Hatty says you are, Abby will see it."

"I have not picked up a brush since I did your car, and it was ages before that." Birch shrugged.

"So, go get one." Felicity looked at her.

"You really are serious, aren't you?" Birch watched Abby.

"I cannot deny Flick, nothing would give me greater pleasure, than sitting back there, and watching a mother and daughter create, two works of art at the same time, it would be a rare moment worth seeing." She sighed.

"I admire your belief in her, her books have not sold well." Birch shook her head.

"I have both her books, and I have read them many times in the last few years, those books were good imaginative stories, they just lacked a connection to life. This one, she is more connected now, than she has ever been, trust me Flick, I can feel the power of this one already, this will get the name of Abigail Jennifer Watson noticed."

With Abby busy, Birch tagged along with Deb's. The bookshop was in its final week of the sale, and a large chunk of the stock had gone. Deb's had arranged to call in, and get a better look at things, and take some pictures for the builder who would be refitting out the shop, and making some changes.

It had been a busy time; Birch was dealing with the clean up ready for the carpet fitters at the house. Abby was working herself into the floor, and Debs was liaising with her father, to decide what the new shop would look like.

They arrived at the shop, and it was very clear why Agatha Willington was selling; she was struggling with a pile of books to be boxed. Birch took them off her, and helped pack them, Deb's made her a cup of tea, and sat her on the seat at the counter.

"You girls are so good; I must say I am quite tired now. I appreciate this, I really do, and I must say, I am so happy that you Debbie, will be keeping the tradition of a bookshop going. It has not been easy these last few years, but I will rest happy, knowing you and Abigail, and your lovely friend here, will be taking this on. It has to be a labour of love, and I think with the two best customers I have ever had in here, she will be in good hands." Birch smiled as she moved the box.

"So, all book shops are female, are they?" Agatha chuckled.

"They are indeed. You see, a good bookshop like a good woman, does not show everything at once. You have to get to know her, understand her, before she reveals all her secrets. If you get inside the mind of a good woman, then that is like the inside of the shop. You have to wander around, get familiar, even flirt a little, and then, only then will she reveal the best of her." Birch put the box down, and noticed the shelf at her side.

"Oh wow, the complete works of Conan Doyle, I am having this." Agatha gave a bright smile.

"You see... You helped her, and now she is rewarding you." Birch looked up with a beaming smile holding the book.

"I love the way you see this shop; it is just perfectly right." Birch walked to the till, and pulled out her money, Agatha waved her hand.

"No, take it, you have helped out a lot today." Birch looked a little uneasy.

"Agatha, I have just moved in here, this village is going to be my home, my practice will be next door, but I have not spent a penny in the village yet. I am grateful for your offer, but I would really love it, if the first time I bought something as a resident here, it was a book, and it was from here whilst you are still the owner. It would make the book a lot more precious." Agatha smiled.

"What a lovely sentiment, well Dr Dixon, we must do this right, I seldom use the receipts, but I think one today is in order, you can use it as a book mark, and as proof it was your first Wotton Dursley purchase."

She typed in the numbers, and the till beeped, Birch paid, and the till gave the change and receipt. Birch looked at the receipt with delight, and slipped it inside the book.

"Thanks Agatha, that does make it so much more precious, I will treasure this." Deb's snapped a picture of them as Birch held the book.


There was work to be done, Deb's took Birch through to the back, and explained what she had in mind.

"There is an extension on the back, which is a store room, that needs a little work, but not so much, and I am going to have heating put in to keep the stock warm and dry. This back room here, will become part of the shop, the till will be moved, and the wall is going to be knocked out. There is a kitchen upstairs, and a toilet, those will stay, as will the downstairs toilet. The other rooms will be remodelled, to give better access, for rare and collectable books. Edwina is working on a new web site design, and that is where those books will mainly be sold." Birch was impressed.

"It looks like you have most of it pretty much planned out, I must admit, I am really excited about seeing it." They walked back through into the main shop.

"Most of the window is obscured by large bookcases, opening up the back, means I can move them back there, and put smaller shelves here, and that will allow a lot more light in, and people outside will have a clearer view of how the shop looks inside." It made complete sense, Deb's had really thought everything through, and it was clear how excited she was about it.

More changes were coming to Wotton, it was another sign of how change could not be halted, as the young stepped up to replace the older generations, and Marjorie did not like it. She stood with Marion at the top of the street, as Deb's and Birch came out of the bookshop.

"More modernisation, first the charity shop, which has gone to that whore, and another one of her delinquent friends is about to take a hammer to Agatha's place, is there no stopping them? They are like a virus, slowly infecting this village with their strange and obscene notions. I am telling you Marion, it will not be long before they seize control of the Parish Council, and they will be suggesting one of those new age, female, beatnik type vicars, God knows what will happen to us all then?" Marion was not completely convinced.

"Marjorie, we have to accept, no one wanted to keep the bookshop going. The Wheeler girl, is a real book fan, she is the only one who wanted to keep it. I understand your resentment of them, but even you have to face facts, you may not like her, but she is actually helping to keep a tradition alive, there has always been a book shop in Wotton, and now thanks to her, there still will be." Marjorie scowled at her.

"Whose side are you on? Those types will not have the sort of books you read, they will have smut and porn, and the likes, you know, books on lesbians, and filthy man sex books, it will be a disgrace." Marion looked down the street at where the bookshop was.

"Oh really, and you know this for a fact do you?" There was a strange new glint in Marion's eyes.

I finished the chapter and clicked save. I flopped back in the seat, and yawned. Suddenly I felt drained, not more than a minute ago, my mind had been alive and exploding, but with the last full stop, it felt like suddenly, the final curtain had come down, and the exhaustion just crashed into me.

I lifted my cup, the coffee was cold, but my mouth was dry, I just drank it. My back ached like hell, and my legs felt numb. I stood up and stretched, it felt strange, and I was a little unstable. I staggered into the bedroom, Birch was not there, I had not seen her get up or go out, I looked at my watch. Shit, it was almost 17:00, how long had I been writing for?

The truth was I did not care, I was simply too tired, I saw the bed and slipped off my pants, and top, and then flopped onto the cool duvet cover, it felt wonderful and soft, and it smelt of Birch. I closed my eyes, my mind was so tired, and yet there in the background beyond the haze, the book still lived, writing itself in my brain, and getting ready to feel the keys on the tips of my fingers again, and then I would have another surge, and like an exorcism, it would all pour out. That was then, and this was now, and for now, I needed to ease my aches and sleep.

I do not know how long I slept for, it was dark when I woke up, Birch sat at my side, sipping a gin and reading a book. I rolled over, and she turned and smiled.

"Hi Sweetie, feel better?" I stretched as I smiled, and it became a yawn.

"Hmm yes, I was really tired."

"I am not surprised, you have not stopped in over six days, I take it that it is going well?" I lay back, and looked up at her.

"I have neglected you, haven't I?" Birch closed the book.

"Not at all, it has been a joy watching you write, I am fascinated by the process, it reminds me very much of Uni. I suppose it has felt familiar, just like those days when I would sit on my bed in the dorm, and watch you write your essays. It probably sounds strange, but I like the sound of the keys, as they click. I lay here the other evening, listening to them in there as you wrote, and it was like listening to the rain. The rhythm would change as you reached a point that excited you, and it was like, when the winds get up, and suddenly, the patter of the rain changes and speeds up, it is strangely comforting."

I lay there listening, and in my mind, I could almost hear it, the pitter patter of the drops, the softness of her voice behind it, it was a beautiful way to see it, and I smiled, she had such a wonderful way of seeing the world around her, and it fed my creativity.

"I couldn't write like this when you were gone, I struggled a lot. I would get frustrated and delete it all, and start again, some days it felt like torture." She understood me, but I knew she would.

"Deads, you had forgotten to live, you were locked in here pounding away, but you were not fully alive inside, if you are going to write, you have to live."

That interested me, I watched her carefully, her eyes were so green, soft, and gentle, her long white and patched hair hung down, following the shape of her body, gently resting in on it her like fresh snow, she reached out as she noticed me, and smiled as she brushed the hair from my face.

"If you do not live Deads, you starve the source of your writing, trust me, I grew up in a house with a writer of professional papers, and a writer of self help books, and both of those, depended heavily on observations from life." It made sense as I lay there thinking about it.

"So, because I was not out and about, talking to people, and interacting, I was robbing myself of experiences, that I could use?" She gave a nod.

"Hmm, yes, look at Dracula, yes it was a dark and scary book for many at the time, but it was set in an era of discovery, which gave richness to the surroundings, but at its heart, even though it appeared like a book about the survival of a race, it was really an epic love story. I have always thought, the reason he chose vampires to feed on blood, was because it is blood that fuelled the heart, without blood they die, and maybe that was because the heart died, and they lost what love they had, which if you think about it, was their last connection to life and humanity."

I lay back, she had just completely blown my mind, I had never once, even remotely thought of it that way, and it was one of my all time favourite books, I looked up at her.

"I just got completely mind blown by you, I have been reading it wrong all these years." She giggled.

"Oh, Sweetie stick around me, and I will destroy your thoughts on every book you have ever read." I sat up and slid down the bed, I needed a pee, I looked back at her.

"We are never talking about Pullman."

"Oh, that is a shame, I have a really good theory about Lyra." I jumped up, and put my fingers in my ears.

"La, la, la, la, la, la, la, la, la."

I ran to the toilet to pee, I sat down, and could hear her laughing in the bedroom, I smiled, as I let the flow go. I loved the sound of her laughter.

I sat there thinking, and had not even realised I had stopped peeing. Birch was right, I had lived here alone, and shut myself away, I disconnected from everything, let myself go, when I should have been getting out of the house, and been talking to people, having adventures and living my life.

I was writing again in a way I had never written before, and this was something I had never expected to write. The story was bright and full of life, it was not gothic, not death, it was about us, and the life we had lived, every painful experience, every moment of joy. This story had a life of its own, and that was why it was coming so fast, I had lived it. It was me, all of me, hidden behind secret doors. which were my characters, everything I had seen, or heard, every feeling and emotion I had experienced, it was almost as if this story had my pulse, and they were beating as one. I came out of the toilet and Birch was in the kitchen, I leaned in on the door frame.

"What are you doing?" She turned and smiled.

"You need to eat, you have hardly eaten properly in days, it will be pointless trying to finish this book, if you die of hunger or malnutrition, so I am making you a cheese salad, it has everything you need in it to recharge your batteries, there is also beer in the fridge." My stomach gave a loud groan, she gave a chuckle. "See what I mean? Good grief, you writers put yourself through it for your work."

What would I do without her, to be honest I had no idea? I walked into the kitchen, opened the fridge, and took out two beers. I popped off the lids, and placed one next to her. I stood behind her, and watched the gentle shake of her hips as she cut the salad, she really was amazing. I put down the beer and walked behind her, and then slipped my arms around her, and snuggled into her back.

"Thank you, just for being here."

Her skin was soft and smooth, I felt her buttocks pressed into my hips, and they were so warm, and firm, yet soft. My hands were on her hips, and I could feel her hip bones, and the little indentation that ran down between her legs, I felt my hands slip, and glide across her skin, over her flat tummy, and down. She gave a quiet sigh.

"Deads Sweetie, I am trying to make you food."

I ran my hands up, feeling her warm flesh, the arch of her ribs, and the little crease under her breasts. I felt her leg tremble, as I moved up over the soft round mounds, I turned my head and kissed her spine below her neck, she leaned forward and pressed her buttocks into me, she put down the knife, and leaned onto the counter, and gave a soft moan as I ran my fingers over her nipples.

"Oh... OH.... Deads, Sweetie you really need to eat... OH!"

I kissed her back, my hands freely exploring, I felt the vibrations in her body, I kissed a little lower, working my way down her back. Her hips moved back, pushing her tighter against me. I reached the nape of her spine, she was trembling, and I was loving the reaction I was getting from her. I moved lower, and on to her right buttock, she gasped.

"Oh god Deads, this is driving me wild... Oh... Oh you are cruel."

My hands slipped down to her hips, and I pushed the tips of my fingers into the crease, and softly stroked down, as I kissed her buttock, and then slid across the gap to the other one. Her head fell forward, I stroked slowly down, hardly touching her skin.

"MMM! OH, oh god.... Deads, please Sweetie don't tease me, touch me, this is sending me crazy, and I can't stand it.... Hah!... Oh."

I could see her trying to grip the counter top, this was awesome, and I was making the most of it. She gasped out, her breathing was becoming rapid, I could not believe the effect it was having on her, her legs were shaking, and her toes curled as she leaned further forward. I knew what I was going to do, my fingertips were there right above her entrance, and I knew she was begging me in her head to go in, but I had something better planned.

This was all so new to me, I had never thought of what it was that actually turns me on, I had never thought of sex in this way, or how my body reacted to others, it was strange and yet amazing. This was a whole brand new level of intimacy and arousal, and feeling her react to my touch, was incredible.

I reached the centre of her buttock, then quickly pulled my hands to her hips, and then opening my mouth wide, I bit down on the soft flesh, and she squealed. I pulled on her hips as she jumped in surprise, and she spun round with a yelp!

I wasted no time, and pushed myself up, pushing her left leg with my hand, her legs separated, and I dived straight in with my tongue. The shock hit her hard, and her hands clenched onto the back of my head, and she threw back her own head.

"OOOOOH MY GOD!" She was shaking so hard, I kept losing my grip on her legs, I knew she could not last much longer.

"OH GOD DEADS, I AM GOING TO CUM."

I laughed inside, it was a perfect strike, unexpected, and it had caught her off guard, I could feel the massive vibrations running down her legs, and she was reacting to each and every one, as she twitched constantly. Her fingers curled in my hair, she was almost there, she gasped out above me.

"OH...OH....OH." Here it comes.

Her legs suddenly locked tight and went rigid, her hands pushed into my head, I could feel her whole body tighten, and she leaned back on the unit thrusting into my mouth hard and...

"oooooOOOOOOOOOOH MY GOD, AARRGHhhhh!" She exploded, and shook violently.

I pulled back with a smile, and softly kissed her tummy, and looked up, she was still leaning back quivering, she let go of my head, and gripped the counter tight, her breasts were heaving forward and back, as she swallowed in more air. I stood up, her chest, neck and throat were bright red, as she gasped, and lifted her head forward, her eyes were bright, as she smiled, still breathing rapidly. I slipped my arms round her, and she came forward, and leant on to me, she gasped out her first words.

"I don't think I can stand Deads." She slouched, her legs were really weak, I chuckled.

"Good, that means I did everything right." Her head was on my shoulder, as she breathed in heavily.

"That was beyond right, Christ Deads, you broke me."

She just hung from my shoulder, as her climax subsided slowly, it took a lot longer than I expected. She moved, and lifted her head.

"Deads Sweetie, can you finish the food, I think I need to sit down?"

It is amazing to me, how we can make someone else feel so amazing, simply by touch, I had wanted this so much, I had dreamed of it since leaving Uni, but here and now in this moment, I could feel something stronger, something more wonderful than I had ever dreamed of. I thought back to that wonderful summer five years ago, and how I had worried and panicked that I was turning gay, and yet here I was with a woman, making love to her, it was so new and so unexpected, and yet deep down inside I was so happy, and felt so much closer to her. Deb's was right, it just flows and happens, almost as if it was a part of my primal self, I just instinctively knew this was right, and that was a really powerful thing. I smiled, and gave her a soft kiss.

"Do you want me to help you?" I could see her legs were still trembling, she nodded.

"Yeah, you completely buggered my legs up, I can barely stand."

I helped her out of the kitchen, and guided her towards the sofa with a smile, she was walking like a toddler, taking her first steps. I giggled as I lowered her down, she sat back and looked up at me and smiled.

"Holy shit Deads, next time warn me, honestly, I thought I was going to faint."

Chapter 12

# Strange Happenings.

Having a night off alone with Birch, and having the joy of pleasuring her unexpectedly, was like a tonic, I had been writing for over six days straight, and my brain was tired, but more alive than it had been for years. I woke the next morning, made a coffee, and left Birch in bed, poor girl, I wore her out, and I sat at my computer, and read through the last five chapters, and then opened a new page, and started hammering at the keys at high speed, I only realised Birch was up, when a delivery arrived, and she placed the oversized mug of fresh coffee, on my desk.

I did feel a little guilty, Birch was handling all the new house renovations and refits alone, and the carpets had been measured and selected, and as I began to write all my memories of that summer into another chapter, she oversaw the fitting of the carpets, to the upstairs rooms, landings and halls. Downstairs would be another day's work, and the day past with my typing, and darkness descended, and I was three more chapters in.

When I saved the last file, Birch was already asleep, and I slid into bed, mentally tired, and with an aching back. Birch was flat out, spread eagled under the duvet, on her back, and breathing softly, and yet as soon as I slipped in, she instinctively, rolled on her side and cuddled into me.

The following day was a repeat performance, I drank coffee from my oversized mug, that had a little vampire motif on it, and wrote, and she headed out alone, to once again oversee the carpet fitting for downstairs, and have beds delivered for every room.

There were two guest rooms, one double, and one twin, everything was taken into account. Once the library was done, Deb's helped her move four large desks into it, on which four brand new computers were set up. They were arranged in a square, and in the gap in the middle, all the powerlines, plugged into floor based sockets, she really had thought of everything.

During the remodelling of the house, internet cables were channelled into the walls, and every room in the house had wall sockets, that computers could be plugged into, no minor detail was ignored, and little did I realise as I typed at high speed, how much the house across the road would change, before I was done.

The end of the week arrived, as more items were delivered to the new house, and in the village, it was being noted, how I was absent, as Birch and Deb's were seen together, more and more.

The Bookshop finally closed on Friday at 5pm, and Agatha retired for good. It was marked with a bottle of wine, and three paper cups, as Deb's and Birch, toasted her future, and wished her well, and with a smile and tears in her eyes, Agatha hugged them, and wished Deb's the best. I was sorry I missed it, but I was home, reliving a summer from five years ago, and heading towards the final chapters.


It was evening, and Birch was sat at the table, reading emails on her laptop, when I finished yet another chapter, and pushed on the floor, and my chair wheeled back. I leaned back in my chair, my back ached, and I felt exhausted.

"Another one done?" I turned and smiled.

"I am almost there, I think two more, at the most three, but I think I have written something good, or at least I hope so." She smiled.

"Take a break Deads, you look exhausted, relax a little, I have a meal cooking, sit with me and eat, I am missing you." I nodded, and gave her a smile.

"Yeah, I miss you too."

Birch had cooked spaghetti bolognaise, and we sat at the table together with a gin, and talked as we ate. I had not realised how hungry I was, after not eating a full meal for over a week. She filled me in on Deb's, and Agatha's farewell, and then told me all about the house, and I listened as her excitement grew, she looked so happy, sat there describing the carpets, and the wall deco, and all the work Norman had done to make the garden nicer.

I had missed this, I had been writing about it, but I missed sitting and listening to it, she happily chatted through the whole meal, and when she had finally finished, I smiled, and told her how excited I was. She got up to clear the plates and I grabbed her wrist, she stopped and looked at me.

"The house has beds and lights and everything, yes?" She nodded.

"Yeah, once we move your stuff, and I get all mine unpacked, pretty much most of it is in the garage being stored, but yeah, I have been waiting for you to finish, and once you have written the final chapter, we can move in." I stood up, and pulled her close.

"So, it has a bed…. I need a rest, I am really tired, so how about we grab some booze, and a blanket, head over there while it is empty, and you rip off my clothes, throw me on the bed and make love to me?" Her eyes sparkled with devilish delight.

"We can honestly do that?"

I moved in and kissed her slowly and seductively, she gasped as I pulled away and winked.

"You own it, that is our home, we can do whatever we want in it, so why don't we christen it alone, before we let anyone know it is ready?" She looked really excited.

"Sweetie yeah, let's do it."

Ten minutes later with blankets, and bottles, Birch opened the door, and my jaw dropped. "Holy Shit!"

Decorated, with carpets down, it looked like a completely different house, Birch closed the door behind me, as I stepped into the entrance hall. At the base of the central grand staircase, there were two marble statues of Venus in different poses. Along the hall, there were small antique looking tables, and large ornate white pots, that contained huge indoor palms, and other assorted plants, I was blown away, and this was just the entrance. I turned to look at her as she smiled.

"Birch, this is unbelievable, I mean, honestly I am blown away, I cannot believe I will live here." She took my hand, and her eyes danced, and she let out a cackle of a laugh.

"That is nothing, come and see what Goggles has done."

She hurried across the entrance towards the double doors almost dragging me off my feet, she stopped at the doors, and turned to me, her eyes sparkled with utter joy.

"We have more to do, but this will be the heart of the house."

She put her hands behind her back, and I heard the lock click, she pushed with a chuckle and the doors swung open into the room, I could not believe my eyes.

"Ta da!"

I walked in and felt my breath catch. The room was all bookcases, which I had seen before, but they were empty, and now half the room was filled. Birch turned.

"These are just mine and Deb's, and a load I bought in the sale at the shop." She turned and giggled.

"Deb's has spent all day working on it, look, we have fantasy, there is sci fi, over there is steampunk and robot, she calls it mecha, that there is a mix of pagan, religion, witchcraft, herblore, plant lore, and anything in that sort of genre. These here are encyclopaedia's dictionary's thesaurus's, anything writing or word related and so on, we have it half filled already, and you have not added your books yet, and we want an arts and crafts section as well."

Once again, I was lost for words, I looked round the room with the four desks, with modern computers, and a long table along the window. I walked towards the desks, and looked at the computer screen facing the door.

"Why four computers?" She came up at my side, and slipped her arm round my waist.

"One of them is yours, you have to pick which one." I looked at them carefully.

"Birch this is overwhelming me, I do not know what to say, I am happy and terrified at the same time... Although, if I was to work in here, I would want the one facing the window, so I can stare outside when I am thinking."

She took my hand, and walked me round to it, pulled out the comfy padded office chair.

"Take your seat and claim this realm as yours."

I smiled; I cannot deny I was a little excited. I slid in front of the seat and sat down, and grabbed the key board, and lifted the legs on the underside, and then rested my hands on it. The seat was a little too low, so I pushed the lever and the chair rose. When the height was right, I tapped the keyboard, it felt good, and made a really nice clicking sound.

"This is nice, the seat is good, yeah I really like this."

Birch bent down and pushed the button on the pc sat under the desk to one side, and the monitor, which was the biggest I have ever used at 24 inches, came to life. The screen opened up and there was a password box, Birch leaned down.

"I set it for now, as Deadly37, you know, your name and your number?"

I loved it and I typed it in, and the screen opened to a desktop image of all of us stood with Petal outside the salon. It sounds stupid, but as soon as I saw it, my eyes filled with tears. Birch came up with a box in her hand, and smiled as I looked up at her. She lifted out a pot, with a little vampire on it, filled with pens, and placed it on my desk.

"Birch, this is the nicest thing that has ever happened to me." My tears exploded out of me. I shook my head.

"I know it is silly, but it really is amazingly wonderful." She put the box down, and swung my chair round to face her, and on her knees, she embraced me.

"This is a new start, no isolation, no loneliness, and a life worth living. We came back to this village side by side, and they hated us, some of them hate us more. This is where you and I will live, and we will show them, we will show all of them, that having us here is the best thing this village has ever known, and all that starts, with having a house which is the envy of them all. It is also a house filled with love and friendship, I hope that now, you can see why I have done all this. Deads, just by living a good happy life, we will prove all of them wrong."

I understood, it was all making sense slowly to me. Birch leaned over the desk and grabbed the mouse, she clicked the icon, and shut it down. She took my hand, and pulled me out of the chair, and lifted a small pot with birch trees on it, out of the box. We walked to the computer at the side, and she placed her pot down on the desk.

"I will sit here, where I will have the best view of you as you write." I gave her a smile, and she winked.

"I can also hold your hand across the desk if you need me too." She gave a giggle.

Birch led me by the hand out into the entrance, picked up the bedding, and onto the stairs holding my hand, she walked just in front, and I followed, we reached the top, and walked to the door I knew was her room, she pushed it open and walked in. The room had changed little apart from the fact that there were lots of stacked boxes, and a large king sized bed, on the wall opposite the partition doors that led through to what I knew would be my room.

She walked to the bed, turned, grabbed my shoulders, and manoeuvred me round, I felt my calves touch the base of the bed, she smiled.

"I love you Sweetie."

She grabbed my top, and pulled it up over my head, and I was about to reply when she lifted her hand and pushed me. I landed feet still on the floor, with my back on the soft springy bed, I started to giggle, she pulled off her top, dropped her skirt, and then leaned forward over me, and dropped to my breasts, and started to devour them, I gave a happy contented gasp, as she nibbled, and I felt her undo my jeans, and start to slide them down, I was instantly turned on.

My bum was on the edge of the bed, as the jeans slipped passed, and fell to my ankles, and Birch who was exploring my nipples, then slid down to my tummy with her tongue. I felt the heat flow into me, I looked down along my chest to see her kissing and licking as she slowly made her way lower, I clenched my fists, oh god after a week of writing, I really wanted this.

Say hello to the night, from the Lost Boys, suddenly started to play loudly. It was my phone ring tone, and Birch was already between my thighs about to plunge into me, I gave a frustrated sigh.

"Oh god Birch, ignore it."

It was too late, it had lit up in my jeans pocket, and she had picked it up and hit answer, she was an inch from my vagina.

"Hello."

She jumped and pulled the phone away from her ear, she hit the speaker phone button. Anthony was talking in a very high squeaky voice, at high speed, and he was garbled. I looked at her with a what the hell sort of look, she shrugged, but we could not understand a word. I reached out and took the phone, and lay back on the bed with a frustrated sigh, Birch moved closer, and I felt her warm breath.

"Anthony... I am sorry but we cannot understand a word you

are saying, you need to take a deep breath and just calm yourself a little."

Birch moved in and I closed my eyes, oh god, she was in there. I placed the phone near my head and gripped the plastic cover. She was swirling her tongue, and it was driving me insane. On the phone we could hear deep breaths being taken.

"Abby... Abby.... Abby, I need help."

He sounded really distressed, I lifted my head, but oh god she was right on the spot.

"Anthony what is wrong?"

"Oh Abby, I came round to see Peter, because Brent is working away, and I was lonely, and it's stuck up his bum."

I sat up instantly, Birch pulled out and stared at me in shock.

"Christ Anthony, how the hell did it get stuck... I mean, will it come out at all?"

Birch rose from my vagina like a periscope, and stared at me, with a slight smile.

"Oh god Abby it is in there, and it won't come out, and poor Peter is having orgasm after orgasm, and it looks like it's killing him." Birch gasped.

"I am not bloody surprised, poor bastard." She leaned in from between my legs.

"Anthony, why did you put it in there, I thought it was only for Brent?" He gave a shriek, and we jumped.

"I think he is having a fit... I didn't put it in, he did." Birch frowned.

"Well, why did you let him?"

"What... What, oh god he his jerking about, oh please Abby, Birch, I need you."

He was very panicked and sounded terrified. I leaned over the phone.

"Anthony where are you, where does this Peter live?"

"His house is 26, Garden Road, it's past the station, Oh Abby please hurry... Oh... Oh.... I think I am going to faint."

CRASH! The phone went dead. Birch was up on her feet.

"OH SHIT... How far is this place?" I stood up, and pulled up my jeans.

"It is not far, it's past the nursery on the way towards Pilkington's, it is about four minutes in Petal, three if you drive.

Birch how the hell did he get his cock stuck up another guy's bum?" She pulled on her top.

"It can happen, what I want to know is why is he even screwing Peter, and how sodding big is Anthony, if he got the bugger stuck?"

I pulled my top over my head and looked at her.

"That is what is on your mind, how big?" She shrugged.

"Deads, it has to be big to get wedged like that."

I shook my head, feeling a sense of urgency, as weird pictures of what was happening flooded into my brain, which totally freaked me out, my sense of urgency and panic was increasing at a rapid rate.

"Come on, we need to get there."


We came belting down the stairs, Birch snatched her keys, from the table near the door, and we shot out of the house onto the drive, where Petal sat waiting. We jumped in, I grabbed the driver's seat, and slipped in the keys. The engine fired up as Birch lifted the small fob off the console, and pressed the button, the gates started to swing open, as I put Petal in gear.

We drove through the village, and turned onto Station Road, after the nursery it was fields, so I put my foot down.

"I cannot believe Anthony would screw around behind Brent's back, honestly Birch, I just never saw him that way." She watched out of the window.

"I got to tell you Deads, it has surprised me too, I mean, I would not put it past Brent, but I never pegged Anthony for it."

I saw the turning, and indicated, and slowed Petal down a little, we turned right, and entered Garden Road, Birch watched the houses. It was a tree lined road, with wide grass verges, the houses had small neat gardens, and low garden walls, Birch opened her window and leaned out.

"The evens are on this side, up a bit further, there... Red door." I hit the brakes hard, and came to a screeching stop next to the curb.

"We jumped out of Petal, like we were on a police raid, and ran down the garden path, Birch grabbed the door handle, and pushed it down, the door opened.

"Who the hell leaves the door unlocked when they are

screwing?" I looked at Birch and smiled.

"Well we did, does that count?" She smiled.

"I was in a hurry, and you were gagging for it."

We stepped in, and looked down the hall.

"Anthony Sweetie, where are you?" A feeble voice sounded out.

"OH Birch, we are up here."

She turned toward the opening, where the stairs ran up, and I suddenly felt panicked. It sounds crazy, but, okay so about guys and the kind of sex they have, or at least as I understand the logistics, but in truth I had never actually seen it. I mean, it is not something you do is it, you know ask a couple, if they mind if you watch?

I was about to be confronted with it head on, and for some bizarre reason all I could think of was that time I caught Bev going down on Edwina. I mean, I knew about that kind of sex, but seeing Bev chomp at Edwina's hooch, like she was gnawing a tree down, freaked the shit out of me. I grabbed Birch's arm.

"Birch I am getting freaked out." She looked at me and smiled.

"Sweetie it is fine, it's just a penis in a hole."

I shook my head, as just hearing that panicked me even more, I swallowed hard and tried to whisper.

"It's not just a hole, Birch this is a butt hole, and it's not just a penis, it's Anthony's. I am not sure I want to see this; I mean, I know we have seen him naked and all, but this will be different, it will be all swollen and fat... And stuck!"

I could feel my heart rate increasing, and I felt all hot and panicked. She giggled.

"Sweetie, just calm yourself down, it's no different to watching Mike's slip in and out of me, it's like a pig in a blanket, except the piggy bit is Anthony, and the blanket will be Pete." I felt my breathing increase as I freaked out more.

"HOLY FUCK IS THAT WHAT IT LOOKS LIKE?" She gave a snigger.

"Wow your eyes are so huge right now, I am getting wet looking at them."

I shook my head trying to breathe. No frigging shit, I was freaking out big time. I took deep breaths and lent on the wall, I was sweating like crazy, she stroked the hair from my face.

"Deads Sweetie, it will be fine, we will go up there, and get him relaxed, and as he does, it will shrink and flop out." I took deep breaths as I looked at her.

"Relaxed... Yeah, all we need is nice music and a cigarette. For Christ's sake Birch, how the hell is he going to relax with his cock stuck up the ass of his mate, have you never tried to separate dogs?"

Her face changed, and she suddenly looked very serious, her voice had elements of alarm to it.

"You don't think it will be like that do you?" I stared at her feeling even more panicked.

"I DON'T FRIGGING KNOW, YOU ARE THE FRIGGING SEX DOCTOR, I THOUGHT YOU KNEW ABOUT THIS SHIT?" She looked up the stairs and back to me, and shook her head.

"I've read about it, but I have never actually seen it. Holy shit I hope they have vodka." I gave a nod.

"Does that help, will that relax him." She looked back at me.

"Relax who?" I pointed up the stairs.

"Anthony, will the vodka relax him?" She frowned, and sounded alarmed.

"It's not for frigging him, I bloody well need it."

Upstairs there was a squeal. I looked at Birch, it was now or never, both of us charged up them, like a police raiding party, the bedroom door was open, and Anthony was sat on the bed... Fully dressed, and as soon as he saw us, he burst into tears. The side of his face looked swollen.

It took me a few minutes to fully understand the scenario, Birch instinctively knew what to do. Peter lay on the bed face down jerking, like he was having a fit. I walked in and looked at Anthony who was crying his eyes out, and pulled him into a hug.

"Hey come on, we are here." My heart was racing, I held him tight, as he shook in my arms.

"Abby it is stuck up there, and it won't come out."

I could see Peter lay on the bed, he was jerking and twitching, and flopping about. Birch looked at Peter and patted his face.

"Peter, can you hear me, I am a doctor, and I am going to help you, alright?" He stared blankly at her, she reached over and opened his eyes wide.

"He looks like he is going into shock, Deads we need to get him to a hospital, how far is the nearest one?"

"It's Oxendale A&E, I am not sure the local clinic can deal with this." I pulled Anthony off my shoulder, and stood him up in front of me.

"Anthony, you need your big boy pants on for this, we have to get him to hospital, and we will need your help, so come on, we are here, and we will do our best for Peter, what has he got inside himself?" Anthony gave a snort, and pulled a hankie out, and wiped his eyes and nose.

"I think it is a vibrator."

"Yep, I can hear it, and it's running like a bleeding saw mill." I turned to see Birch, with her ear on his hip. I was stunned.

"Bugger off Birch, there is no way you would hear that." She looked at me.

"Listen for yourself, it's as clear as day."

Do you remember that morbid curiosity I had at Uni? Yep, it was back, and suddenly my fear and panic were gone. I went round the bed, and pushed Birch out of the way, and leaned down and put my head on his thigh.

"HOLY SHIT, IT'S RUNNING LIKE A TRACTION ENGINE!" My mind was blown, I looked up at Anthony.

"Have you frigging heard this?" He looked upset, and started to cry again.

"When you two have finished, can you both get your head out of my friend's butt, and can we go?"

I suddenly felt guilty, Birch smirked. We stood up like two naughty school kids, and I saw a pair of jogging pants hanging on the back of the chair. Birch leaned in, and sniggered quietly.

"Hey Deads, when I lifted his leg, the tone changed, it was frigging awesome." I sniggered; Anthony passed me the pants.

It was a bit of a fight getting the pants on, but finally we managed it, and sat Peter up, the moment he did, his eyes opened wide and he began to shake violently. Birch grabbed a t shirt and rammed it over his head quickly.

"Shit, stand him the hell up, I think sitting has pushed it up more." I panicked and dithered.

"What.... Holy shit, can that happen, holy shit Birch, what do I do?" She shrugged.

"Not sure to be honest, but looking at his eyes, he got a freaking big surprise he never expected, and he already knew he had a vibrator jammed up his ass."

Walking him to the car took some time, he was heavy, and with each step he jerked around like he was being tasered. Anthony had one of Peter's arms over his shoulder, and I had another one over mine. Birch held him at the waist as we walked him to the back of Petal, we thought he would be best served lying down.

Once again, I drove, and took the fastest route I knew to the hospital, Birch questioned a slightly calmer Anthony. He sat looking very upset.

"Peter and Craig, are two of Brent's good friends, they have been in a relationship for years, and the way it appears, Craig was having extras with a young Italian boy, and Peter found out. They broke up a few months ago, but Peter has suffered terribly, and we have been looking out for him. Brent asked me to check on him whilst he was working away, and when I got there, he was like this."

Birch nodded; she was starting to understand everything that had happened.

"So how did you know what he had done Anthony?"

Anthony fanned himself with his hand he looked very pale, it was clear how traumatic it was for him.

"He was not this bad when I arrived, he told me Craig had taken the other toys, and just left this, he said he used too much lube, and it slipped out of his hand, and when he looked it was gone."

It was not funny, and yet I was smirking.

We approached the hospital and Birch opened the dash box. She pulled out a lanyard with a white plastic ID card on it, and pulled it over her head, I was a little surprised, it read. 'Dr Jemima Dixon, Consultant Sexual Therapist. It even had an NHS logo on it. She saw me look at it as I pulled up and parked the car.

"Part of mum's practice, we help out at the local hospitals." She jumped out, and looked at one of the ambulance drivers.

"I need a gurney, I have a patient with a woman's stimulator lodged in his rectal passage." He shook his head.

"Not another bloody one?" I was a little more than surprised, holy shit, was this normal?

Peter was taken up the long corridor into the consultancy room, where there were several beds, all with differing cases of casualties, who were being taken care of. Some of them looked pretty grizzly and I shuddered. Staff were running around as people sat with bloody bandages, and arms in slings, some were out cold on the beds, it looked like bedlam

Anthony looked white faced, and a little lost, as they pulled the curtains round the bed. I grabbed his hand and squeezed it, as we stood back out of the way, a nurse, looked at a clip board, and started to fill out a form, and another attended to Peter. He looked at me and shook his head.

"I am not sure I can do this Abby." He was shaking. I squeezed his hand tighter.

"Anthony we will need his details, and we do not know them, I know you, trust me you can do this, because you are helping your friend."

He swallowed and looked terrified, and very pale, but he gave a nod and twitched. The second nurse, was pulling Peter's pants down talking to Birch.

"I tell you what, if I never see another one of these I won't complain, this is the third this week, two nights ago I had a guy in with his wife, and it had snapped off inside him, that was an eye opener." She looked up at Birch.

"I know you; I saw you and your mum a few years back at that talk she did in Wotton. I worked at the clinic at the time, I thought you were all up north?" Birch shook her head.

"We are about to open a second practice in Wotton, my mum is still handling the northern side of things, and I am running the operation down here." She finally got his pants off, and looked at Anthony and me.

"We could use a lift, we are short staffed tonight, you don't mind helping do you?" Anthony took a step back, I looked at him.

"You do the paper work, I will help the nurse." He looked eternally grateful.

Peter was out of it, so we helped lift his buttocks, and packed underneath him with pillows. Birch was stood at the end of the bed, the nurse returned with a tray of something covered in a cloth. I moved back to the side of Birch, and she went to work.

I cannot deny, I had no idea how they were going to do this.

Remember that morbid curiosity, well yeah... Well one day, it will be the death of me. I was suddenly really interested, and I regretted that pretty bloody fast.

The nurse whipped out the shiny metal tool from under the cloth, squirted a lube like substance on it, and just jammed it into Peter's ass. I was going to ask Birch what it was called, but having seen its use, I knew dammed well, I never wanted to know. I felt my own tiny little rose bud tighten between my butt cheeks, and my legs felt the sudden need to tighten and cross.

What came next, scared the living shit out of me, I don't care who you are, there is nothing I know of that can prepare you for what happened next.

The nurse just grabbed at the handles, and whipped the thing apart, and WHOMP! There was a frigging big hole where Peter's rose bud had lived. I recoiled, it was like that Predator movie, where that thing looks at Arnie and then WHOMP! It's whole frigging face opened. I looked at Birch.

"HOLY SHIT, DID YOU KNOW IT COULD DO THAT?"

The nurse giggled, as I stared down into the void that was Peter's ass. The really messed up thing was, as soon as his ass opened, I could hear the buzz of the vibrator, it was like plugging your ear phones in, and suddenly it was loud.

Out from under the cloth came a pair of forceps, and the nurse just reached in, and pulled out the vibrator. The sudden buzzing alerted Anthony, who looked at it, and saw his friend's ass hole wide enough to hide a football in, and it was just too much for him.

"OH MY GOD......." CRASH!

We turned to see just his feet sticking through the bottom of the curtain. Poor sod, it had been a very challenging night for him. I went out to help, and Birch stayed back to handle everything else.

With the help of a porter, we lifted Anthony's limp body, and sat him down, he was whiter than white, and he was shaking like a leaf, and taking deep breaths. I felt really sorry for him, he was sensitive, and this was just all too much for him. I went and grabbed a shit coffee, out of the machine. It took a while for him to come round properly. He was still very pale, he looked at me.

"Did you know they could do that?" I looked at him.

"What, go wide enough to shove your head up... To be honest

Anthony, Christ no, and if I am honest, I frigging wish I didn't now I have seen it?"

I took a deep breath and shook my head, no one's ass hole should be so big you could wear them as a hat.

With some time, care, and attention, Peter came round, and was able to walk out of the hospital unaided, albeit slowly, and carefully, that alone impressed me. The drive home was a quiet one, Peter was very ashamed, and Anthony was traumatised forever, I think.

We dropped them off, and Anthony told us he would stay to comfort him, and he thanked us for all we had done. I felt so sorry for him, he did not need to be put through that, he was a gentle caring boy, but those are the bumps in the road we all have to go over.

By the time we arrived home, at number three and parked Petal, I was too tired, but I did want to stay in the house. Birch went into the garage and came out with a box, we carried it upstairs, and made her bed with her sheets and duvet cover. We could not find the pillows yet, so we took all the cushions out of Petal. I lay back, with her curled into me, her head resting on my shoulder.

"What an insane night, have you seen a lot of things like that?"

She was quiet, and I got the impression, she was remembering events, she looked at me, with those green eyes that twinkled.

"I have seen and heard some weird bloody things Deads, but it fascinates me, because it still amazes me what some people will do for that buzz, and the thrill they get from it. I do feel sorry for Peter, he was lonely and hurting, and just wanted some relief from it all, but sadly it went wrong. You know the odd thing is, most people think my job is all about screwing, but it is not, I would say, in the last few years, most of the people who have had sessions with me, have been like Peter, they were heartbroken and terribly lonely, and missed the connection and intimacy of having someone there."

I could hear the sadness in her voice, she really cared about people, and that was the crazy thing about living here, Marjorie hated her, but why, Birch cared deeply for people, it made no sense to hate her?

"You know Birch, the thing I don't get is you are opposed to marriage, and yet you see so much loneliness, is that not a contradiction, because surely marriage is the cure?" She looked at me, her eyes looked sad.

"It is not a cure Deads, most marriages force other people to be who they are not, and that is done through enforced monogamy, and I do not agree with it. I have seen so many where one person sets the terms, and the other has to comply, and feel a loss to some aspect of themselves. Look it does work for some, but we see it as the only way as a society, and that is simply not true. There are many ways people can raise their young, or share a life. If you look at the whole of this planet, you will find the western ideals of marriage, are but just one way, many cultures, remove shame from sex and marriage, and it works. I am not against marriage; I am against the ideal that society says, monogamous marriage is the only way, because it is not."

She fascinates me, each day with her, is a learning curve, and a window into a wider world, not just into her, but also into me. I lay there drifting as I headed into sleep, thinking about tonight, and all the things Birch and I had done together. She was a million times different from anyone raised here, her whole outlook on life was challenging to many, and yet in a strange way, as I looked at who I was, and who I was supposed to be, Birch's idea of life, made far more sense to me, than anything this village believed in.

Chapter 13

# New Home.

When I woke, the sun was streaming in through the large windows, and it was blinding. I rolled over, and the bed was empty, I lay staring at the empty cushions. It was a little strange to be here, I was so used to my dark little room in the guest house. Here, the room was large, spacious, smelt of fresh paint, and it had a completely different feel to it. I sat up, and was greeted with a huge stack of boxes, all labelled in the neat hand writing of Birch.

I slid over to her side of the bed, and slid my legs over the edge, my feet landed in a soft deep carpet, and it felt delightful. My head felt a little groggy, but my body was rested, so I made my way out of the door onto the top of the stairs, and looked out over the rail, and down into the huge hallway, as the bright light streamed in from the windows above the door.

Everything about this house is bright, there are no dark shady corners, even now it is hard to take it all in. To me this place is like a mansion, and I guess after living in such a small space for so long, it felt a little too big, and in an odd sort of way intimidating.

When I walked down the stairs, I had a feeling that this must be what the royal family feel like, especially with two naked marble statues of Venus at the bottom. I wandered round them, and through the hallway, lined with lush green plants towards the kitchen, which was looking fuller, now it had a long polished table surrounded by chairs at one end of it.

Birch was behind the central island with her back to me humming, at her side a filter machine hissed. She was making toast, I walked up to the island and sat on a stool.

"Why didn't you wake me?" Birched turned.

"Hi Sweetie, oh you got up.... I was making you breakfast in bed."

I rubbed my eyes. I liked the idea of a naked wife making food, but I was here now. She turned and placed a large plate of toast down, and poured me a freshly ground coffee. I lifted it gratefully, and held it with two hands, as I sipped it, then realised it was my large mug from the guest house, she smiled, when she saw me look at it.

"I went over earlier to collect a few things, and brought it here for your morning coffee." I was not yet awake, but was holding the solution.

"This is nice Birch, you know just us having breakfast in our house, I like it." She sat on the other side of the island with her drink.

"I have a busy day; will you be writing again today?" I looked at her.

"Will it be a problem if I do? I mean, I am doing really well on it, and I am not far away from the last chapter, if I have to, I could leave it, if you need help."

She leaned forward, her eyes green, glinting, and her hair as white as snow with those black patches, illuminated from the light through the patio doors, and she smiled.

"It is not a problem, but can I ask you something special, and would you do it for me?" I frowned.

"Well, we are naked and this is the kitchen, are we talking on the dining table, or are we doing each other here?" She giggled as she looked at the long table, and bit her lip.

"Oh god I wish I had thought of that.... Damn... No sweetie, we have a large furniture company coming, and they will be here soon to deliver the furniture." She looked back at the table.

"Shit Deads, I really want to do it on the table now, I really wish I had got you up sooner." She looked back at me, and sighed.

"Deads Sweetie, can I ask you to finish your book here... I know it sounds crazy, but if you wrote your last words on your computer here, and it became the first book you wrote here, it would mean the world to me, just knowing it was in our home." She smiled a beautiful smile, and I must admit I liked the idea of it.

"It would be nice to do it here, the problem is it is all on my computer back at home." She grinned that devilish smile.

"Well not exactly... Yeah, about that... You see... I needed bread and milk, and a few other things, so I nipped over earlier, and well... Well to be honest, you had left your computer on, and I just so happened to have a memory stick in my bag, and so.... I hope you don't mind; I didn't read any of it I promise, but I copied it onto the stick... It is on your desk in front of your com." I gave a chuckle and shook my head.

"Why does your sneaky side bother me?" She giggled and her eyes sparkled.

"I am going to put some clothes on, I want to look the part when the furniture arrives, I will keep the library doors closed, so you can either dress or stay naked, it is up to you, the heating is on, so it will be nice and warm."

To be honest, I did not really care, I walked with my coffee to the library, and sat at my desk, I turned on the computer and it booted up, as I sipped my drink, and then I plugged in the memory stick, copied the files over into my documents folder, and opened a new empty clean page, placed my keyboard in the right place, dragged the mouse closer, and started to write.

As I hammered away on my keyboard, the house slowly filled with furniture, as Birch in loose dungarees and a vest, directed each item of furniture, to its allotted spot with Deb's, who had arrived with yet more books, but had placed them neatly outside so as not to disturb me. My mug refilled without me noticing, and I powered through two chapters before I sat back, and felt really excited. I had just written a great chapter, and was idly scrolling through it checking each line, when Birch came in and sat in her desk seat.

She logged in on her computer, and clicked with the mouse, I rested back in my chair, and watched, as her eyes moved across the screen, as she read the lines of her emails, she gave a slight smile.

"I can feel you watching me, stop it, as it is unsettling." I grinned.

"Now you know how I feel." She gave a giggle.

"How is the writing going?" I stretched my arms out to the sides, and arched my back.

"It is one chapter away from finished. I just want to write an ending conclusion, and then it is done." She smiled.

"I am so happy that you finished it here, and it is the first thing you used your com for here, I cannot wait to read it. Edwina and Chloe are coming over later to see the house, they still do not know, and so I want to ask them after they have seen the place, again I know I am pestering you Deads...."

"I want to be there Birch; I want to be a part of that, I want to see their faces, especially when Chloe sees the studio, I really want to be a part of it all, they mean the world to me." Birch turned and gave a small nod.

"I really am so excited, this is going to be so great, and it will make such a huge difference to their lives. Sweetie I am so glad you are letting me do this." I frowned.

"I am not letting you do this, we both agreed it was a good idea, this is us honouring the Curio's, you know, we stand together and we fight together, well soon it will also be, we live together."

My cup was empty, and I was in between chapters, so I wandered into the kitchen for a top up. I walked up to the filter machine and poured out my cup, two guys in grey work overalls were installing what looked like a huge double doored fridge, I smiled and raised my cup.

"There is plenty of coffee if you want one guys."

They stared at me as if I was a lunatic. Deb's stood in the doorway holding a box, she giggled, I looked back at the workers who were still staring at me.

"What is their problem, I thought I was being nice?" Deb's giggled.

"Oh, you were being very nice Abby, I mean how many times a day do they see a writer filling their cup, and especially a completely naked one?" It took a moment for her words to sink in, I looked down.

"Holy shit, I completely forgot." Deb's giggled even more.

"You know, you have been around Birch way too long, there is no saving you now?"

I hurried down the hall back to the library with my refilled cup. Oh hell, Deb's was right, Birch has influenced me in ways I had never even noticed. I sat in my chair and smiled, hell, it probably made their day, and it was time to make it mine, and start the final chapter.

I took a drink, and put down the cup and began, and the clicks echoed from below my fingers, and minutes blurred, as I lost myself in those final moments of farewell. The tears rolled into my eyes, as I wrote, and also remembered, and as Birch has already said, it was a very bitter sweet moment, one strangely enough, that was the picture that was now my desk top background.

Finally, the story of that summer, that Roni had told Birch to make Abigail's Summer, came to a close. All the names of the people and places had changed, and I had the story I should have written five years ago, well in a way I had, but it was a diary piece. The story I had written involved Willow and Bram, but it was our story, and all of it was true, even though I knew it would be listed as fiction.

It did not really matter to me; I knew the truth, and my circle of Curio's knew the truth; I had no idea if it would have appeal, I really didn't, but I did not really care. I sat back and looked at the last page, there was laughing in the house, and I assumed, Chloe and Edwina had arrived, and were getting the tour.

I stared at my last page, and it felt good, it felt like I had achieved something, and that is part of the joy of writing. You slave over an idea, and expand it into a format, others will understand, and hopefully enjoy. You have no idea who will love it and who will hate it, it is just good to know that deep within yourself, you found the time to do the work. It could stay on my computer forever, and never get published, the joy for me is in the creation, and to be honest, that is all that really matters to me.

Sat in my chair as it saved and closed, I saw the list in the file of 33 single chapters, and it looked as good as any painting would to an artist that had just finished their picture, because this was my art. I drew pictures with words, and all a person had to do, was read the words, and a picture would be painted in their mind, and the greatest thing in all that, was every person would paint a different picture, and for me that was magical.

I felt the aftershock of writing, which basically is your brain has been drained for the hours you have focused on the chapter, it is where your mind for a short time becomes numb. I logged off and walked out into the hall, and headed for the kitchen, I could hear voices upstairs, and wandered into the kitchen where the counter had several bottles on it. I grabbed the mixed fruit flavoured gin, and poured a glass, and then walked back towards the library, and the room opposite, which I supposed would be the main living room. I was really surprised when I walked in.

The room was really large, and in the centre, were what I can only describe as two really colourful Moroccan style sofas, both were huge and L shaped, and they faced each other in a way that created a large square arena. In the middle was a low very wide mahogany coffee table, and the sofas were covered in large cushions, and brightly coloured throws. They really looked comfortable and inviting. I sat back, and they were so wide and deep, my legs did not touch the floor. I slid into a corner and curled into it, and I cannot deny, I love it, yes, I could see myself snuggling up here in the winter and reading.

I relaxed and sipped my drink, and closed my eyes just to rest them, and it was not long before they all came talking excitedly down the stairs. Birch noticed the open doors and came in. I didn't so much as see her, as felt her, she slipped on the sofa at the side of me and kissed my cheek, I nodded fully awake and smiled.

"Hi Sweetie, is that it, is it done?" She giggled excitedly, I leaned onto her shoulder.

"It is, I am yours again... Although it is just the first draft, I will have editing and cutting it together to do, but the basics are there."

She slipped her arm round me and smiled. Deb's Chloe and Edwina plopped down and settled into the huge sofa's; Chloe looked round the room.

"This place is awesome; I cannot wait until my day off to visit, and swim in the pool."

Birch looked at me and her eyes twinkled, I could see she was getting very excited, I smiled and gave a nod, and she gave a little squeal of joy, she turned to face them, but Chloe pointed at me.

"Abby you are naked, can anyone be naked here?" I looked at Birch.

"I have no issue with it, do you?" She shook her head.

"I am always naked at home, I am only wearing clothes because unlike you, I was not going to flash the delivery men, that could be one of our first house rules, if you want to be naked, be naked." Chloe was up on her feet.

"Fuck yeah, these clothes stink of turps." She stripped on the spot, and relaxed back on the chair, Birch looked at her clothes on the floor.

"Should I wash those with ours, and then put them in your room?"

Chloe blinked not quite understanding at first, and then she froze staring at us. Birch smiled, and I leaned forward to pick up my drink, Deb's gave a titter.

"We were assuming you two would be moving in, we are right, aren't we?" Chloe swallowed hard.

"Don't be cruel, don't fuck with me Abby, it is not nice, I would give my art for a place like this." Birch smiled.

"Chloe, we are not joking, we meant it, we know things are not great for you in Oxendale, so we want you here, where you will always be safe." Two tears appeared in her eyes, and her voice went squeaky.

"I can live here with you guys.... Honestly?" I smiled.

"All girls together, we stand and we fight together, well if you want, we can all live together?"

She burst into heavy tears, Edwina slid over to her and pulled her into a hug, and she had tears in her own eyes, she smiled at us and mouthed, 'thanks guys.' Chloe took a deep breath and sniffled. She looked at us both.

"I am good at cooking, and I can clean, I will pull my weight and earn my place. I am trying to sell paintings, so if I do, I will pay my way, I have always paid my way, even when I lived at home." Birch smiled.

"I am really surprised that you did not notice the sign on your room, it was the one with the paint easel on it, and your room Edwina if you want it, is the one with the little computer on it." She had tears in her eyes too, and smiled a huge smile.

"You know what, you two really are something, you know that, and yes, I would love to live here, it really is a beautiful house." I nodded at her.

"It is more than a house Edwina, it is a home, your home, our home." She swallowed hard.

"I really love you guys; I have never met anyone like you two." Birch stood up.

"There is a little more to show, we have another place you have not seen."

She offered her hand to Chloe, she stood, and then suddenly leapt on Birch dragging her into a tight hug.

"This means so much to me, I have no idea what words to use, there is so much I want to say." Birch slipped back and smiled.

"You just said it perfectly, now stop it, or you will make me cry too."

Chloe gave a giggle and wiped her eyes; she smiled the biggest smile I have ever seen. Deb's wiped her eyes and looked at me, she gave a nod, as if to say nice one. Birch took Chloe by the hand and led her down the hall, and back to the kitchen.

Edwina walked with me, Deb's was on her other side, Edwina took my hand in hers, and I slowed a little and turned to her, she wiped her eyes.

"You guys have no idea how much this means. My parents are so worried about her, the landlord keeps putting up the rent on that shit hole she lives in, and she has really struggled. My mum has been so worried that she is not eating properly, and they have begged her to come home, but she is hell bent on living the artisan life. Honestly Abby, I am so relieved, you guys are like her guardian angels, I will owe you forever for this."

I understood, I have no idea how Birch found out about Chloe, but just seeing the look on Edwina's face told me, Birch had done it again.

"Edwina, we are all girls together, you stood by us, and we will return the favour by standing by you." She gave a smile, and we continued into the kitchen.


The kitchen pretty much ran the whole length of the back of the house, which was why it was so big. Both outdoor sides, had a large bank of patio doors, and the wall in between them was where the kitchen had been built. As we turned to the left, and looked down the room, there were two doors, and between those was the washer and dryer, and a work top to sort everything out on. The door to the left went through to the garage, the door at the end to the right was closed, Birch stopped with Chloe until we caught up. Birch looked at the door.

"Right Chloe, if you are going to live here, then you can solve a problem for us." Chloe gave a nod. "Through that door Chloe is a space, it is a good enough space, but it has no purpose, and we need someone, or something that will give it a purpose. So, to solve the dilemma between Deads and I, you can look at it, and tell us what you honestly think it should be used for, because we have no idea what to do with it, is that okay with you?" Chloe shrugged.

"I will look at it, but to be honest I am not really good at stuff like this." Birch gave an understanding nod.

"Okay.... Open the door and tell us what you think, and we will see how it goes."

Chloe looked serious, she turned, opened the door and we heard her catch her breath, Edwina craned her neck to try and get a better look.

The room was empty, it was three plain walls painted white, and the fourth was all sliding patio doors like Hatty's studio. In the centre of the room stood a brand new easel.

Chloe stepped in and looked round, looking as if she was in shock, she walked up to the easel and touched it, then ran her fingers down its side, she looked back and me I smiled at her, and then her face wrinkled.

Chloe suddenly fell to her knees and burst into tears, her shoulders shook, as she shook her head, and tears rained everywhere across the floor. I felt the tears in my eyes cloud them, as Chloe just broke down, and broke her heart, and tried to talk.

"You guys are too much..." She gave a massive sob, she looked up as the tears streamed from her eyes.

"I cannot take this; it is too much for me to handle."

She gave another sob and shook harder, it was killing me, and was so heart breaking to watch it, and I walked through the door as she wept, and knelt beside her. Chloe threw her arms round me and wept on my shoulder.

"Abby this is my dream.... Just an empty room to paint in, it is all I have ever wanted." She shook in my arms, and wept even more. Birch crouched down and hugged her with me.

"Well, it is an empty room Chloe, so the rent is cheap."

Chloe tried to manage a laugh, she slipped off me and pulled Birch into a hug. I looked back to see Edwina still in the kitchen, breaking her heart on Deb's shoulder, she smiled.

It took quite some time, for Chloe to calm down enough, and she walked round the room touching everything, which was just four walls really. She ran her hands along them; it was clear to see how important it was to her. Finally, we just left her to it, and came back into the hall. Birch walked to the library, there were still books piled outside. Edwina looked round.

"Wow this is impressive, is this where you work Abby?"

"This is where we all work Edwina; all you have to do is pick a desk without a jar on it."

She saw the computers, and walked over, to the desk on the side opposite Birch's and at the side on mine. She leaned forward to take a better look, then crouched to look at the PC under the desk.

"Wow you got some serious kit here guys, what are the specs?" I shrugged.

"It is your computer, so you tell me?" She looked at me like I was an idiot.

"Don't Abby, I would kill for one of these."

Birch walked up and placed a small jar with pens in it on the desk. It had a small picture of a laptop on it.

"It looks to me like this is your desk Edwina, so that is your computer, because you live here, so it must be your home base, what do you think Deads and Debs?" She stood up and pulled out the chair, and jumped in.

"No way, I would screw you guys, if you weren't together, I would sleep with both of you, and you too Deb's just for being here." The computer booted up; Birch leaned in.

"I believe your flower arrangement was called, it's a Birch thing, and your number was 77, that is all lower case, no spaces."

"FUCK YEAH!"

She typed in the password and the desktop came to life, within seconds she was clicking the mouse, and windows were opening all over the screen to show all the specs.

"I will boost your security, it is good but not good enough to keep someone like me out, so I will fix that on your system, and

I can boost that download speed easily. Do not worry about any issues, I will keep these babies running at their best, anything in this house that is tech, I will keep all of it in top notch, hell guys, I have no idea how I can thank you, especially for Chloe, but I will find a way."

Deb's Birch and myself retired, and left her to play, we topped up our drinks and went back into the living room and chilled out on the sofa, Deb's just sat smiling at us.

"Chloe was right, you two really are something special." Birch leaned back and took a deep breath.

"This village will die if the young leave Deb's. Villages all over are seeing their children growing up and leaving, someone has to show them they do not have to. You have saved the bookshop; Anthony has slowly slipped in more modern styles for his customers. I will soon have a practice, Deads will be a famous author, Chloe will emulate Hatty, and Edwina, will base her company here. Once we show the village, we are serious about this place, they will fully embrace us, and one day we will be the ones maintaining it to its traditional standards. Marjorie's biggest mistake has always been, that she thinks we should not embrace modern living, she thinks change will destroy the village. I say changes can be made that will enhance the village, and keep it the rural beauty it is, and the only way we can do that, is to appeal to the young, and show them the way." Deb's sat back and took a sip of her drink.

"That is a big task Birch, she will fight to the death to keep things her way." Birch nodded.

"That is okay, I am young, we all are, we have more time than her, trust me, one day, we will be the ones the villagers rally around, and this house will be the centre of everything." It was easy to say, I was not convinced.

"You do know she will make the next few years of our life a living hell, don't you?" Birch smiled.

"I hope so.... It will speed up her demise."


Chloe came marching into the room, and stood in the doorway, her eyes had makeup streaking down from her crying, and they were still red. She looked really serious, we looked at her, as she took a deep breath, and composed herself, she clenched her fists.

"Abby... Birch?" She sounded very forthright, and business like, she had a fixed stare.

"Guys I have been thinking... I think I need to show some gesture of my appreciation, but I have hardly any cash and nothing of value, to be honest my greatest asset is sex, it's sad, but that is a fact."

We all nodded, we knew this to be true, we had witnessed her in action. She took another deep breath.

"Guys.... I am so fucking straight; I mean you have no fucking idea how so fucking straight I am.... But..." She stumbled a little and took a massive deep breath.

"As a token of my gratitude, I am prepared.... Prepared.... Prepared to screw you both... Not at once, that is just too fucked up for me, but I will do it... As a token of thanks." Deb's sniggered, Birch stood up.

"Wow Chloe that is a really mighty gesture, and I know how hard it must have been to decide that, you know, you being all straight and that, I mean that is life changing."

Birch walked to the end of the coffee table and grabbed a pillow. I nearly gasped out loud, as her dungarees hit the floor. She stepped out of them, and kicked them hard across the floor, Chloe blinked and swallowed hard. Birch slid up her vest, and pulled it over her head and smiled at Chloe, as she tossed it at me.

Holding the pillow, she sat on the edge of the table, put the pillow behind her head, and held it in place whilst she leaned back on the table. Debs' looked shocked, Chloe went white and looked terrified, Birch smiled.

"Is here okay Sweetie?" Her legs snapped apart so fast, we all jumped. I looked at her lay on the table, Birch put her head on her chest, and looked at Chloe.

"Whenever you are ready Sweetie, take your time, I really want to make the most of this... Oh, and be gentle with me." Deb's looked at Chloe, who looked absolutely petrified.

"Holy shit Chloe, are you sure you can do this?"

Chloe was now whiter than the walls, and clenching her fists so hard I thought she would cut herself, and she nervously nodded, and her voice was three octaves higher.

"I keep my word."

I watched, lost for words as she took very nervous steps

forward, she looked really unstable. Slowly she went down on her knees, and moved towards Birch's open legs, where Birch was watching from her chest. Chloe slowly leaned in, and I have got to say, it was the single most unerotic thing I have ever seen.

She leaned forward towards Birch's vagina, talk about hesitant, if she was any slower, she would stop. Birch watched as Chloe got closer.

"Wet your lips, no girl likes a dry tongue." Chloe looked absolutely appalled.

"Huh?"

She started to breathe in and out, taking deeper and deeper breaths, as she got closer, and tried to lick her lips, but her mouth was dry. Birch gave a soft moan.

"Oh god, I am so excited, I am getting really wet." Chloe shuddered violently.

She pushed out her tongue, gave it a wiggle, and breathed rapidly through her nose. Birch was watching between her legs.

"Oh god, you look hot tonight Chloe."

Chloe looked more panicked than I had ever seen her, I sort of felt sorry for her, and as much as I tried not to, I had to stifle my giggles.

Her clenched fists were on the floor, and her arms were shaking like crazy, as we all watched, holding our breath. She slightly closed her eyes, and leaned closer. Birch gave another soft moan.

"Oh yeah, do me good bitch."

Her breathing became more rapid, and she sounded like a charging Rhino, her tongue wiggled up and down, like an angry lizard, and she moved a little closer. She was two inches from Birch's vagina, and breathing faster than a charging bull, she moved another inch closer, and closed her eyes, as her tongue wiggled up and down.

"YEAH, FUCK ME CHLOE!"

We all jumped out of our skin, as Birch screamed out, and Chloe nearly had a heart attack. Birch rolled backwards on the table, and landed kneeling on it, and screamed with her cackling laughter, as Chloe shot backwards, and fell on the floor, panting and looking terrified.

Deb's was in fits screaming with laughter, and holding her sides, rolling on the sofa. It was hysterical, I was almost crying, I was laughing so hard, Chloe looked stunned, and a little relieved, Birch pointed at her as she howled with laughter.

"Your bloody face was priceless." She smiled.

"You bitch, that scared the crap out of me." Birch was hysterical, as Chloe looked at me. "I would have done it, I would."

I wiped my eyes and tried to settle down a little, God that was the funniest thing I have seen in years, the giggle fits kept erupting back up in me, I tried not to laugh.

"Chloe, you do not have to go that far, we know you are grateful, honestly, do something else, I mean paint us a picture, we could use some decoration on the walls." She gave a massive sigh of relief, and flopped back on the carpet.

"Well, if you would rather I did that? Well yeah, I would love too." I smiled.

"I saw your tongue technique, trust me, Birch would have died of old age before you made her cum."

Birch slipped off the table and snuggled up to me, for the rest of the night, we would all randomly break out in fits of giggles, even Chloe saw the funny side eventually.

Edwina sat in the library, her eyes glued to the screen, and a fixed smile on her face. Her fingers typing at speed, and the sound of clicking softly wafted into the living room, I smiled, it looked like we had a family, and also a new family home.


As I slipped into bed beside Birch, I felt a glow inside me, Chloe was so happy, that she decided to sleep over, even though we had still not found all the bedding. She wanted to sleep in her room for the first night, Edwina was in the library, with a small lamp on, clicking away until the early hours, and because we had less bedding, Deb's jumped in with us, and was already fast asleep.

I lay on my side looking out of the window, the moon was out and bright. I stared at it, thinking of the words of Birch, she was right, we were the future, is it strange that I had not realised that?

Marjorie could not rule forever, something had to come after her, it was a natural progression, and one day we would have to step up to the plate. Actually, I just realised something, she was talking about us, holy shit, would we be running things one day? I mean, just thinking about tonight, was a little unsettling, who the hell would be stupid enough to put us in charge? There again, as

Birch has always said, it will not be boring. Wotton Dursley, the craziest place in the south of England, it sort of has a ring to it, don't you think?

Chapter 14

# Moving On.

It was Sunday morning, yeah, I know, she is already up and about somewhere. I slipped out of bed and wandered down to the kitchen, and it was noisy, and in various stages of dress, which pretty much involved panties, thongs, and boxer shorts, except Birch and myself, who had just risen and walked around as we always did. Everyone was gathered round the island, drinking coffee and eating toast, Birch was eating what looked like a bowl of seeds.

I walked up yawning and sat down, Birch smiled as she put my coffee down in front of me.

"Morning Sweetie." I looked at her suspiciously.

"Why are you so happy?" She tried to look innocent.

"I don't know what you mean Sweetie." I frowned.

"Birch it's Bell Twats' Day, and yet you are smiling, normally you are stomping round yelling at the sky about it's a bloody liberty?" She giggled.

"I sound proofed the house, high quality triple glazing, sound proof wall insulation, the works, those twats cannot reach me here, it will remain forever a Bell Twat free zone." Deb's gave a giggle; Birch was too smart for her own good.

Today was packing and moving day, but before all that, Birch had yet one more surprise. On the table was a large box, she walked over to it with a huge smile on her face, which I knew meant mischief, I looked across the room at her.

"What are you up to?" She gave a giggle, as she pulled the tape off the box.

"Do you remember my friend in Uppermill, you know the Wiccan?" I nodded.

"Vaguely... She used to dance naked, and rub herself up against trees in the woods?" Birch nodded.

"Yeah... Raven Moon, she is such a Sweetie."

Honestly, I thought she was not all there, and had come to the point of view that if her life's mission was to just rub her vagina up trees to climax, she was safe enough to be free in the community.

"What about her?"

"She is such a Sweetie, I emailed her and asked her if she would make these."

She lifted out a clear bag, that contained something dark purple, she threw it at me. I caught it, and it was surprisingly heavy.

"Goggles catch."

Deb's got a bright red one, Edwina's was blue, and Chloe's was bright yellow. The fabric was a very heavy cotton and looked familiar, I opened the bag and slipped out the garment, it was a hooded robe like Birch's black one, except it was deep purple with small opened books and quills embroidered on the fluted cuffs. I held it up and looked at it, and having seen mine, the others excitedly opened theirs.

It was a few minutes later that we all stood in the kitchen in robes of various colours, with pointed hoods, looking at each other. Chloe sniggered, Edwina's pointed hood shook slightly, Birch was bubbling away with joy, with her hands together, against her heart.

"Oh, they look so amazing, I cannot believe we all look like sisters together now." I looked at her with her bright happy eyes, and her smiling face.

"Birch, we look like a coven of gay garden gnomes, about to set off on an expedition, to return the one true cock ring."

Chloe sniggered again, and her hood shook. Deb's held out her arms, her red cuffs had little cogs on them.

"I love it, and I think we look awesome." I stared at her.

"Why does that not surprise me at all, although, it will be fun when the vicar comes?" Birch looked suddenly alarmed.

"Why would the Bell Twat come here?"

Edwina started to chuckle, and her hood began shaking, I was just glad it did not have a bell on it.

"Birch you are a new resident, he always visits, and sound proofing won't stop him."

"Crap... I don't want him in here, I frigging hate them." I smiled.

"Well we are the future after all, and as the new leaders of our generation, we should welcome him, and be respectful." She seethed and pulled her hood up.

"I am not playing anymore, it sucks."

We had unpacking to do, and so it was decided, the first job would be the garage, all the boxes had to be sorted, and then distributed to whichever rooms they belonged in. We walked in a long line behind Birch towards the garage door, and I started to whistle 'it's off to work we go.' Chloe was behind me and hit me in the back, as she sniggered.

"Pack it in Abby, I will pee."

It was a little later, when I came out of Birch's room, as Edwina walked towards me, we met at the top of the stairs and looked down, to see gnomes carrying boxes into each of the rooms, I gave a sigh.

"It looks like moving day at Willie Wonker's down there." She laughed.

"To be honest Abby, they are pretty comfy to wear, especially if naked, I must admit I like the feel on my skin."

I noticed the keyboard keys round her cuffs, Birch had actually put a lot of thought into the design of each robe.

It took several hours for us to sort all the boxes out, but once it was done, and with a few of the boxes we had empty, Chloe and Edwina headed home to pack. We decided the kitchen was the best place to start, we began unpacking, and allotting a space for everything to go, I reached up and stopped, in front of the top corner cupboard, and looked at Birch.

"It is safe to open this isn't it?" She gave a chuckle.

"It is empty, why were you worried?" I giggled.

"With you I never know." Deb's gave a squeal at the other end of the kitchen, and Birch smiled.

"For Christ's sake Birch... I mean why would you.... Why would you, it's a kitchen?" Birch shrugged.

"This is the one room we all use, I thought if any of you need one, well, you know, you could just help yourself, I mean the library or the living room would just be weird right?" Deb's looked astounded; her voice went weak.

"But it's a kitchen!" I shrugged.

"Well, as we have seen, Chloe has no issue with a kitchen." Deb's shuddered and screwed up her eyes.

"Please Abby, I have tried so hard to unsee that."

Birch and I giggled, it was to say the least, memorable, I doubt any of us would ever cleanse our mind of that moment. It was a sobering thought to realise, she would be living here soon, and expecting the unexpected, would probably be a huge part of our life.

With everything Birch had unpacked, we worked on the bedding, each room had a wardrobe, and two chests of drawers, Birch decided that one of hers would be used for all the extra bedding she had. We finally found all her pillows, and some more cushions, which she threw on the bed. Next was her clothing, and after some time with all three of us trying stuff on, she sat on the bed and gave a gasp of relief.

"Finally, we are done." Our next job was my place.


Packing up my little home in the guest house was hard, we backed Petal up to the door, and boxed my books and DVD's. As Birch and Deb's carefully packed up my things, I took apart my computer, and boxed it, with my laptop. My desk was small, and so with some careful loading of Petal, it fitted in perfectly. Birch stripped the bed, and threw it in a wash bag, as Debs neatly folded my clothes, we put them on the front seat, Birch drove and we walked across the road to the house.

Chloe and Edwina had borrowed their dads van, and I was really surprised to see how little Chloe actually owned. As we arrived, she was helping Edwina up the stairs with a long computer desk, they had it at the top of the stairs, and were taking a breather, it was heavy. We emptied Petal, my desk was tiny by comparison, and soon my room looked like Birch's that first night we stayed.

My desk was against the wall opposite my bed, and along the wall that backed onto the hall I had my wardrobe and drawers, and all I needed now was my sofa from the guest house, and I would have pretty much everything I needed.

There were things still in my old bedroom from when I moved into the guest house, but I thought I could get those as I needed them. We returned and got the sofa, and brought it over, and after a lot of grunting and giggling, we made it into the room, where I set it next to my desk. My final task was to put all my posters back, I put Avril above my desk, and filled the walls, mainly with Avril, I hung the framed picture of my first book advert, and then hung Hatty's picture above my bed, and then hung my small green rosette at the side, and suddenly it felt like home.

It is a strange thing how we connect with inanimate objects. The empty room had felt a little overwhelming for me, but seeing all my things in it, changed the feel of the room completely. I felt calmer and more relaxed, and a little more at home. Birch and Deb's mucked in helping Edwina and Chloe, then headed off to Deb's for her stuff, and so I walked back to do one last check of the guest house.

I stood in the bedroom, looking at the empty stripped bed, and everything I had owned gone, and I felt sad. I had no idea why. I mean, I was now living in this fantastic and amazing house, and yet stood in the doorway, looking at the bedroom and the living room stripped bare, with empty shelves, and no desk, it felt almost painful.

The little house had seen so much, we had met here, sat naked and got drunk as a group, and laughed until the early hours. Here Birch had cried over Melody, comforted me after I told her of Martin, she had danced in her robes flashing her nakedness, as I panicked over the vicar, and this was the place I sat on the video chat, every week for four years, talking to her in Manchester.

It was such a special place, a huge part of who I was, and a central place for all the Curio's. Most importantly, this was the place, where Birch did the one thing, I had never expected, and she told me how much I meant to her, and made love to me for the first time. I stared at the bed, with tears in my eyes, how could I leave this place, this centre of my world?

The door creaked and my mum walked in, I turned to her and gave a sniffle.

"I am so happy mum, I really am, we are all going to live and work together, and it is amazing and awesome, but leaving here is breaking my heart."

She walked over with a sad smile, and pulled me into a hug, her voice was soft and filled with her care for me.

"I remember when I left home, and just like you now, it tore me apart. This place is so small, but the space it has in your heart is so big. If you think about it, this is where you hid from the world, when you were lost and alone. I remember back when you were young, and this was just one big room and my art studio, you would sneak in, and hide when your dad shouted at you. I suppose Abby, this has always been your safe haven, but you know what, it always will be. No matter what happens Abby, you will always have here to come back to." She kissed the top of my head.

"First my mum, and now you, it has seen some happy times." I dried my eyes on the cuff of my robe.

"Thanks mum... Thanks for everything you have ever done, I loved growing up here with you, I really have had a great time here in this house." She smiled.

"You are only across the lane, but I will miss you, both of you, it has been wonderful having all of you round again. So, when can I finally see the house?" I gave a grin.

"Not yet, but very soon, it's a Birch thing, she wants everything in place, and looking perfect, and then she want's Dad and you to come for a meal to celebrate. I think she wants to show you we will both be fine, and she wants you to know I will be safe." Mum understood, she looked round the room.

"This place used to be so big when it was a studio, I remember drawing the plans up to frame it out for a house for your grandmother, and then we did it all again after we lost her, it has seen some changes, and if the walls could talk, it would probably tell some stories." She looked at me and gave a soft smile.

"This was where you fell in love with Birch, that alone will always keep this place in your heart." She smiled. "You are both wonderful together, and before you ask, no, he does not know, he just thinks you are all friends living together." She took my hand in hers.

"Abigail, today you leave here, and so the reason I came down here when I saw you alone was to tell you something important." I looked at her, she looked really serious.

"Abigail... Go and live your life, it is good you shed tears for this place, but leaving it is the best thing you have done. Listen to me carefully…. Do not become me."

I was shocked, how could she say that, I mean I loved her, I watched how she ran everything so well, and how she managed to handle anything that was thrown at her, I could not believe what I was hearing.

"Mum you are a huge inspiration, how can you even say that?" She squeezed my hand.

"When I was nineteen Abby, I looked just like you did, the day you came home. I had the long black hair and the black canvas pants, I was wild and free, and…. I was also in love with a woman." I gasped.

"Holy shit, you were… Oops sorry, you were, why have you never told me?"

"Well to be honest, I never thought you would understand, and I was also a coward who was afraid of the village. I had a secret relationship, hidden from sight, it was not a long one, but it was enough. I broke her heart, and met a guy and married him, and then pretended it did not matter, but it did Abby and I regret what I did. Honestly when you came back looking just like me, I freaked out. But seeing you with Birch, it brought back so many happy memories, and it made me realise that you were much stronger than I was. So, I am telling you this now, so that you know, whatever you face in this world, I will always be here to listen and understand." She leaned forward and kissed me softly on the cheek.

"I love you Abigail, do not sell out yourself to fit in, carve your own path, and create a place you belong, I didn't, and I regret it." I smiled.

"I love you so much mum."

She smiled as I pulled her into a tight hug. It is hard to think back, and remember that day when she did not recognise me, and thought I was a peg selling gypsy. So much has happened since then, and we both have changed. Back then I felt I had nothing in common with her, but now, I feel so close to her, it's crazy.

We walked out of the door together and up towards the patio, both of us turned back and looked at the small stone house, with textured yellow walls, and it's one big window, it was beautiful.

"It feels strange seeing it empty mum." She gave a sigh.

"It does, maybe it is time to unpack my paints, and put

something inside there that is living again." I loved the idea.

"That would be wonderful, I wrote my first two books there, I think you should paint a masterpiece in there to match." She gave a chuckle.

"I am not sure I am that good, but it would be nice to have a quiet place to try again, yes, I think tonight I will have a look in the garage, and see what I have left."


It was weird to walk across the road and home, and see a set of gates open, that had always been my neighbours, and now they were mine. My life changed so much at Uni, as I befriended Birch, and that change kept me going through a tough Summer here. As I returned to Uni for a second year, it changed again as I studied for my degree, and then I came home, and my life crashed without her.

As I walked through the gates, I had no idea what the rest of my life would be like, but Birch was back, she was to a degree my lover, and my life had changed yet again, and now the ultimate change was upon me. I was living in a house I owned half of, with my crazy friends, it could be a lot of change, but the one thing I knew, as I put my key in the door, it was not going to be boring from now on.

I had not been through the door a second, when I heard screams, and the thumping of feet on the upstairs hall, and looked up, to see the partially naked, billowing red robe of Deb's fly across the top landing, she was followed in hot pursuit by a very naked Chloe.

There were more screams, and then Deb's reappeared at the top of the stairs, hugging a teddy bear, she looked behind her, and gave another loud scream, then seeing me at the bottom of the stairs, she bolted down towards me, Chloe appeared laughing, and charged down behind her.

"Give it me I want it." Deb's came flying down and grabbed my robes.

"Abby... Abby save me, save Phileas."

She ducked behind me, and grabbed onto my waist, as Chloe came hurtling towards me laughing wildly. Deb's watched from behind me, dragging me from the left to right, as Chloe tried to reach over me.

"I want it, it's so cute, I have got to have it." I raised my hands.

"Enough, enough, for frigg's sake guys." Deb's peeped out from behind me, as Chloe giggled.

"Abby stop her, she tried to steal Phileas, tell her how important he is."

Honestly, how the hell did I become the mum figure? Birch leaned on the door frame of the library and chuckled, I gave her the for god's sake, help me look, it failed, as she giggled. I looked at Chloe.

"Phileas is off limits Chloe; he is a very special bear. He is the very first present she ever got from Bradley, and he really is very precious to her." Chloe giggled.

"Okay, I will leave him, but only if she lets me cuddle him for a minute." I looked at her, she was twenty four years old for god's sake.

"Seriously, I never pegged you as a teddy lover." Deb's was still hiding behind me.

"She has a room full, and she is trying to bear-nap Phileas, don't trust her Abby." Chloe giggled.

"He is so cute, I saw him, and just had to hug him, he has a monocle and a top hat, oh god, I really want to sleep with him." Okay that worried me.

"I hope you mean closed eyes, and snoring, and nothing untoward and perverse?" She gave me a stern look.

"I am not that sort of a girl, although I do a have one teddy with a strap on, you know, for those minor emergencies, I call him Percy, Percy the ....!"

"Yeah, I get you, and the less you say about Percy the happier I am, god you are seriously messed up Chloe." Deb's came out from behind me hugging Phileas.

"You can give him a hug in the living room only, and then you hand him right back." Chloe nodded, and agreed.

"Deal."

She gave an excited squeak and ran into the living room, and stood there with her arms out waiting. Deb's cautiously approached her, and held Phileas out, Chloe snatched him out of her hands and then pulled him close to her face, and gave him a huge hug, it was strange to watch, as Chloe went all lovey dovey and dreamy. Birch came up at my side.

"You should see her room, she has hundreds of teddy bears, it is weird, I never thought she would be the one to have so many, Deb's I totally get, that makes complete sense, but Chloe, nope, never saw that one. I have seen Percy, wow that girl is screwed up, he has a twelve inch penis." I shuddered.

"Let's just avoid all talk of Percy, the less I know about what happens in her room, when she is alone, the better I will sleep." Birch gave a giggle.

"I think we have seen a small view of our life here tonight, and is it weird, that for some reason, I feel we are being seen as the parents?" I shuddered.

"Jesus we are all screwed, I think I am mom, and you are daddy." Birch gave a laugh, as she walked towards the kitchen.

"I better get a strap on then." I turned feeling worried, and followed, after all that, I needed alcohol.


We sat at the island, drinking gin. Quiet had descended on the house, as peace was made. Edwina was upstairs in her room, setting up her own computer from home, Chloe joined Deb's in her room to help her unpack, it had been a hard day shifting boxes and desks, and everything else. My room was trashed, but all my stuff was finally here, and I was officially moved in. Birch sat at my side and leaned onto me.

"So, do you like the robe?"

The fact was, I had worn it all day, and it was really comfortable to wear, I had been naked under it, and warm, even walking across the street to my old house.

"Yes, I like it, it is much more comfortable than I thought it would be, thank you, it is a very sweet gift." She smiled, and I kissed her. She slid her hand into mine.

"You want to see something amazing?"

The thing is, this is Birch, and so whenever she says that I worry, because she is capable of anything. I was suspicious, which I have found is the right attitude when faced with that question. She smiled and pulled me away from the island. We walked to what was now the studio, leading me, holding my hand, she opened the door and I was blown away.

Chloe had been busy, she had stands filled with every different type of paint, jars filled with brushes, and stacks of sketch pads, all filled with her drawings. Part of the wall had a couple of nails hammered in and a wire stretched across, and she had a stack of fabrics to hang from it. Just like Hatty, she had a digital camera on a tri pod, and several spotlights on adjustable stands, but what blew my mind was her work. I looked at Birch, and she smiled.

"I think Chloe has a bit of a crush on you."

There was a picture that was easily five feet high, and at least four feet across, and it was me, with my red fringe, and my red tipped hair. I could hardly breathe looking at it, it was so real, so life like, my head spun. Birch stood at my side.

"It is beautiful, I am going to buy it off her for my room, Deads, it is everything you are."

I was lost for words, I could tell by the red tips, she must have painted this five years ago.

She had several canvasses stacked up against the wall, just like Hatty had, and there was a wide mix of pictures, some of them very erotic, and quite a few of Edwina, she was really talented. I looked at Birch.

"Why the hell is she struggling to sell these, she is brilliant?" Birch smiled as she looked at the pictures around the room.

"We really did the right thing Deads, she is wasted in that art supplier in Oxendale, she should be home doing this for a living."

I had to agree, but Chloe needed money to live, and until her art sold, she had no choice. Chloe and Deb's came down for a drink, Chloe saw us and walked over.

"It is not ready yet, I have more to do." I looked at her.

"Chloe this stuff is amazing." She gave a shy smile.

"You think so?" I nodded.

"You need to get this stuff higher profile, and make out a price list. Hatty sells hers online, you need to talk to her, and find out how she does it, this stuff should be seen by the world." Birch turned, and pointed at the picture of me.

"How much is this one?" She looked at it a little embarrassed.

"I did that when you first came back, it is sort of a favourite, I have never shown it anyone before, I have never put a price on it." Birch stared at it.

"I will give you ten thousand for it tonight." Deb's slurped her drink, and choked, Chloe's eyes bulged.

"WHAT... Fuck Birch don't say shit like that?" Birch turned

back to her.

"Chloe I am serious, if it is not enough, I will understand, just name your price and I will buy it." She looked her right in the eyes.

"I aim to own this picture, I love it, I want it, and I will buy it, so stop frigging dithering and name your price."

Deb's was still coughing and red in the face. Chloe took a deep breath.

"Birch I was only going to sell it for a couple of hundred, and that is only if I had to." Birch nodded.

"You bloody well have to sell it me, because I am going to make your life a living hell until you sell it me." She swallowed hard, and raised her hand.

"Okay, I hear you." Birch picked it up.

"Jesus Chloe, you may be good at painting, but you know bugger all about art, ten thousand it is, follow me and bring your bank card so I know where to pay."

She walked past me and out of the studio, Chloe looked at me shocked, and pointed behind her with her thumb.

"Is she being fucking serious?" I shrugged and shook my head.

"Birch is an art collector like her mum, I am assuming she is serious, I mean she really loves that picture, you heard her, she aims to buy it." She looked mind blown.

"Oh shit!" She turned and ran after Birch. "Hey hold up Birch."

Once Chloe had found her card, she took it to Birch.

"You are really serious about this aren't you, I mean I will take less, I am just glad to have a sale?"

Birch took her card off her, and opened her online bank account, and opened a new payment, she filled in the details.

"With that sort of attitude Chloe, you will never make it in the art world. The people who buy art, buy it as an investment, which is also a tax write off, if you are going to sell art for a living, I will be setting your price list, no one is getting the better of a Curio." She clicked her mouse.

"Right, you have been paid, the picture is mine. Tomorrow you go into work and quit, leave me your laptop, I will be setting up your accounts, and invoicing for you. I will talk to your sister and get her to speed up your web site, all you have to do from now on is paint. That money will see you over for a while, and then when everything is set up, I will show you who to pitch your art to, I already know a collector of erotic art, I want all your pictures photographing, so I can show them around." Chloe took her card back.

"You're not really a human are you, are you like some sort of alien, you know, an advanced race or something?" Birch gave a chuckle.

"Chloe, have you any idea how good that picture of Deads is? I don't actually think you do, but trust me, I have seen and bought a lot of art in my time, and that is by far the best painting I have ever bought." Chloe looked at it leaning against the book case.

"Birch it is good, but if I had the time, I can do way better than that." Birch winked at her.

"Well you now have ten thousand reasons to make time, don't you?"

I sat with Deb's in the kitchen, just chilling out, when I heard a chime, I looked at Deb's.

"Do we have a door bell?" She looked confused.

"It's your house, don't you know?" I got off my seat.

"Honestly, no."

I walked down the hall and heard Chloe and Birch talking in the Library, I looked in through the door.

"Is that our doorbell?" Birch looked up.

"Not sure, do we even have one?"

I walked across the entrance hall, and grabbed the handle, I opened the door to be confronted, with a slightly taller woman, she had long flowing curly red hair, a pale complexion, and red round glasses. She wore what looked like a black velvet top that had been splattered with bleach, and long purple boot cut pants and boots. Round her neck was a long flowing, flowery silk scarf. She gave me a smile.

"Well the robes have to be her, and by the look of that hair, I would say you have to be Deadly, so I finally found the right house, by the way, you do know you left the gates open?" I leaned out and had a look, she was right, I looked at her,

"Who are you exactly?" She put out her hand.

"Isabella Johnson, sexual relationships and dysfunction

counsellor, but call me Izzy." In the library there was a loud wild scream.

"IZZY?"

Birch came belting past me out of the door and into her arms, she clung to her like a crazy groupie, and both of them screamed together as they hugged each other, Chloe leaned round the door to see what was happening. Izzy released her, and Birch slipped her arm round Izzy's waist and looked at me.

"Izzy, this is Deads... See, isn't she just as scrumptious as I told you she was?" Izzy gave a smile.

"I hope you two are screwing each other, because if you are not already, Christ you need me here. Right drinks, I believe it is time."

I stepped back, and she walked in pulling a large suitcase she had been holding behind her, she looked at Chloe standing naked.

"Well you are not screwing this one that's for sure, you have the wrong equipment for this one." I blinked.

Holy shit, she knew Chloe was straight just by looking at her. I looked at Izzy like she was the goddess and fountain of all sexual knowledge, no wonder Birch was so good.

Chapter 15

# IZZY.

It was a rowdy night, but I was really tired, and struggling to stay awake, I have found the day hard work, but also emotional. I had been writing flat out, and had finally finished my book, and then moving everything out of my small home here, there was a lot of emotions that rose to the surface.

Writing, and the more reclusive side of me yearned for some quiet. I slipped away quietly, went upstairs and made my bed, and finally I slipped in, still surrounded by boxes, and closed my eyes, sleep was not that far away. At some point in the night, I am not sure when, Birch slid into my bed, and snuggled up to me.

By the time I got up, Birch and Izzy were sat at the kitchen counter, Birch smiled as I flopped into the kitchen.

"Hi Sweetie."

I sat down, and Birch poured me a coffee, Izzy smiled, by the look on her face, her night had been heavy, and she needed the coffee as much as I did. Birch sat down in front of me.

"I'm going to take Izzy into the village and show her the shop, are you going to join us?" I yawned, and looked round the empty kitchen.

"Yeah probably, what is everyone else doing?" Birch sipped her drink.

"Chloe has gone to quit, she looked really happy this morning, Edwina is in her room working on a project, Deb's is at the bookshop with the builders, and hopefully, we should be able to get inside the Charity Shop, as it is empty, plus I want to familiarise Izzy with the village." I nodded.

"Let me get dressed, I feel like I have been sat down for weeks, a walk will do me good."

It took me some time to get ready, and another two large coffees, but feeling alive and in black jeans, and a long top, we all left the house, and walked towards the village. Izzy was more alert as she looked round the place.

"Wow there is a lot of money here, so that is good." I glanced at her.

"Why is that good?" She had a sly looking grin on her face.

"Deadly my dear, everyone seeks money, but what I have found in my life, is that those who get everything they want in life, end up screwed up by it. You see money creates a false sense of security, and you believe that you can get away with anything, and that usually leads to chaos and instability, and for someone like me, that means clients." It made some sense to me.

"I get that, I do, but doesn't poverty also create chaos and instability?" She nodded.

"Yes, it does, and that is why the practice is registered as an NHS facility, but you have to understand, for us to be able to offer that service, and supply good staff, we need wealthy clients, people who are prepared to pay for good therapy. They will provide the lion's share of the cash, for the practice to run at its best." It made sense.

"So, what you are basically saying, is you rob the rich to heal the poor?" Izzy gave a deep wheezy laugh, and looked at Birch.

"I like how she thinks, I see what you mean about her, she is funny."

Birch beamed a huge smile, and grabbed my hand. We reached the village, the bookshop had all the windows papered over, and inside there was the sound of hammering, and drilling.

The charity shop was empty, and I looked through the window, it looked huge. A young girl was stood outside waiting. She looked about nineteen, early twenties, and was a little familiar, but I could not place her. She had shoulder length mousey hair, a red woolly jumper and jeans on. Birch smiled as she saw her.

"Everyone, this is Gillian, she will work the front desk."

She smiled as Birch introduced us, I nodded, I was not really a part of the staff, so felt a little out of place. Gillian handed the keys to Birch, and she unlocked the doors and walked in, we followed.

The shop was basically a huge rectangular room, that was two single shops wide, with tatty green carpet, it smelt a little musty. We walked through a large wide, rectangular archway, to the back, which was just another huge room, over double the size of the front shop, which had two large windows and a door into a yard at the back. In the corner was a dirty looking sink, next to a small walled area, I took to be a toilet. On the wall that ran along the inner shop wall, was a set of open plan stairs, that led up to several upstairs rooms. The whole place was dusty and grubby, it really needed a dammed good clean.

Birch explained how upstairs, there would be counselling rooms, and here in the back room, a proper kitchen and toilet would be fitted in. One section would be used as a councillor's lounge, and extra counselling room, for those not good on stairs. The larger space would be used for group therapy sessions.

Each counsellor would have their own room upstairs for sessions. In the front part of the shop there would be a large waiting area, and the main desk, from which most of the admin would be done, that would be Gillian's role.

Birch did say she was looking for another receptionist, who like Gillian, she hoped to employ from the village. Counselling would take place in person at the practice, and would also be done by video call, Izzy had one or two clients in Manchester she wanted to keep up sessions with.

The place looked a dump, but I had learned with Petal, that Birch already had a picture in her mind of what the place would look like.

A shop fitter had been hired from Oxendale, and would commence the refit as of tomorrow, with the goal of having the place open from August first, it was a short timeline. Gillian asked a lot of questions, she appeared quite stiff at first glance, but as she walked round talking to Birch and Izzy, I warmed to her, she was actually bright and quite cheerful, but very thorough, as she talked through her role at the front desk.

The strange thing was I got to see another side of Birch, here she was the boss, and a doctor, and Gillian showed her a lot of respect. She had a different quality to her, a more serious and less flaky side to her, she talked with great authority, and it was clear she had memorised every detail of how this operation would run. I actually thought she was setting a high bar from the start, and I have no idea why it surprised me, I had seen how serious she was at Uni, but to me, she somehow came across as being more grown up, and very like Roni.

Deb's came out of the bookshop wearing a hard hat, which looked a little comical with her fox tail like pony tail hanging down the back, she stood by the open door and I walked over to her. She looked happy.

"The bookshop is going to look so cool Abby; I am so excited." She looked inside as Birch walked round talking to the others.

"Is that Gillian Barker Tomlinson, wow Birch knows how to pick them doesn't she?" I looked back into the shop.

"Yeah... Why does Birch know how to pick them?" Deb's looked at me.

"Don't you remember her, she was a year down from us, she was a mathematical genius? I heard she went to business college, but they could not keep up with her, apparently, she really knows her stuff. Your dad knows her, he offered her a job out of high school, she was so good, she is related to Hatty. I think she is her dad's brothers, daughter's, daughter, so she is her cousin once removed, if I am right. I heard she was quiet and shy." I stared at Deb's.

"Deb's, firstly, too much information, and secondly, you have successfully mind blown me. A relative of Hatty's would have served the purpose wonderfully." Deb's giggled.

"Sorry, I cannot help it. Look I am going to the tea rooms for a coffee, how about you all join us when you are done... Oh and by the way Hatty is back, she walked past a few minutes ago, she was with a tall looking guy with a goatee."

"That must be the elusive artist she is seeing, I heard she had taken a week off on holiday to stay with him, it will be nice to see her, I hope she comes to the house. I will talk to Birch, we probably will meet you, keep a table free." She nodded.

"I will do." Her hard hat wobbled, and I giggled. She waved as she walked off, and I leant on the frame and waited for Birch.


Deb's found a corner space and let Lillian know, that Abby and Birch would be joining her. She noticed Marjorie sat in her usual seat, with Bethany Goodwaters, another of her infamous supporters, and organiser of the fete's grand prize draw each year. Deb's had no love of Bethany; she had been a prominent figure in the victimisation of her mother, when she married

Bradley. Deb's sat quietly, trying to stay low profile.

Marjorie watched through the window, and spotted Daisy Merryweather, as she dropped in some parcels to the post office.

"Good God! She is pregnant again, is there no end to their reproduction? It's bad enough they have destroyed that beautiful heritage site, and now they are popping out offspring like they want to over populate the village. Didn't I tell you, letting those beatnik's loose on the village would be its downfall?" Bethany, looked out of the window.

"Well that is what happens when you marry trash, they bring you down to their level, the poor old group captain must be turning in his grave."

Deb's bit her lip and gripped the chair, they were not even quiet about their views. Marjorie craned her neck.

"Speaking of trash.... Good God, what the hell is that with her?"

Birch walked up the street with Izzy, who today was dressed in a bright pink blouse, purple velvet boot cut pants, and 2 inch, wedged heeled boots. She had on her round red glasses, which I had learned were prescription, and around her neck she had a long floral yellow scarf, that flapped in the breeze behind her. To be quite frank, for a forty year old woman, I thought she looked pretty bloody cool. Bethany looked appalled.

"Bad seeds gather, I am afraid they are far too dangerous to be allowed to run free, it is a bad advert for us when the tourists flood in. We must unseat Felicity and take control back; it is the only way to root out all the weeds Marjorie." She scowled as they approached the tea rooms laughing.

Gillian had said she would return home, but I convinced her she should hang out with us, so she could get to know everyone a little better, she appeared afraid to enter the Tea Rooms, no doubt like I had, she had spotted Marjorie. I leaned into her as we approached.

"The down side to working at the practice is there are some who hate Birch, but if you want to last, it is something you will have to get used to." She looked worried, but gave an agreeable nod.

"Dr Dixon has warned me it could be rough, Harriet talked to me too, she told me how rough it had been on all of you, and I might get some flack, but this is such a good job, and it's local.

I have encountered nothing but nice people since I got the job, Rodger and Pat were really lovely when I met them in London. I really wanted this job Abigail, this practice will help so many people, and I want to be a part of that."

I was not sure she really understood the job, I mean, we are talking perverts and kinks, and all manner of strange, and just from the little Birch has told me about working for her mum was quite freaky.

"Gillian, the one thing I know about Birch, is if you stand your ground, she will stand right by your side with you, no matter what they throw at you. I can assure you, that you will not be alone." She smiled.

"Thanks Abigail, that actually helps."

"It's Abby... Alright here we go, what we do is this, Birch will go and chat up Lillian and Celia, we will make a dash for Deb's who has a table saved, and Marjorie will no doubt say something loud and vile. So just stay calm, and keep your head down, Birch will handle it."

We walked in through the door, I gripped Gillian's arm, and swung her left, and we headed for Deb's in the corner. I smiled politely as I passed Marjorie, who sneered as I went by.

"God this place is going downhill fast."

I let it go, and carried onto the table, Gillian gasped as she sat down, Deb's gave a wide smile.

"Hi Gill, long time no see?"

I found out that Gillian and Deb's were in the chess club at high school, which was something I had never known about. To be honest, if I had known there was a chess club, I probably would have joined it, although as they talked, it turned out Nigel was the club leader, so scratch that, there is no way I would have joined the chess club, which is probably why Deb's never mentioned it.

Birch introduced Izzy, and told them she would be working at the practice. Lillian flustered over Birch as she flirted with her, whilst placing her order.

"You know ladies, we are thinking of having a naked house warming party, would either of you two lovelies' like to come, and show off your goods, whilst admiring mine, and Abby's?"

Lillian was way too excited, and she spluttered and gasped, as she fanned herself with a dinner plate. Celia looked more than interested.

"Will your friend from the north be there?" Birch winked.

"Would you like her there? I mean if she comes, she will have the spare room all to herself." Celia suddenly looked very keen.

"Let me know the dates." Birch smiled and turned with Izzy.

They walked from the counter, I could tell by Lillian's red face, and her fanning, Birch had been extra naughty. They approached Marjorie and I prepared, I sat in my seat hoping it would not get out of hand. Marjorie scowled, and her nose wrinkled up.

"Good grief, do you deliberately go looking under rocks for them?" Birch gave a smile.

"Marjorie, you are looking healthy, I take it you drained a few innocent virgins in the night? This is Isabella, I found her under the most professional therapist in the UK rock, and head hunted her for the practice." She turned to Izzy. "I would like to meet our head village vamp, Marjorie, it's okay Sweetie, you are far too soiled for her tastes, you are safe." Izzy smiled.

"I am hoping it's nice to meet you, and your friend, although feeling the aura around this table I am certain, I will maybe regret it."

I watched holding my breath, Birch left Izzy and walked to us smiling, I was not sure it was safe to leave her alone with them, I cannot deny it worried me. I watched holding my breath. Bethany and Marjorie suddenly stood up.

"GOOD GOD.... WHAT KIND OF A THERAPIST ARE YOU... THAT IS DISGUSTING!?" Birch sat down with a smile, as she noticed my concern.

"Oh, trust me Sweetie, let her deal with it, she has seen it all, nothing rattles Izzy."

I was starting to see that. Bethany and Marjorie made a sharp exit, and I was sure they actually looked terrified.

Izzy walked calmly back to the table, and sat down, as Stacy arrived with a tray of coffees and cakes. I could just about see Marjorie hurrying across the road, she looked back several times, looking horrified. Stacy smiled, as she put my cup down.

"She is taken, feast your eyes elsewhere." Stacy stepped back quick, and I looked at Izzy, she smiled.

"That one you should watch." I looked at Stacy as she hurried away. I could not quite get my head round it.

"No way, Stacy is not like that, I have seen her around for years." Izzy shrugged.

"It is up to you Deadly, but I am not wrong."

I craned my neck to see out of the window, Marjorie and Bethany were nowhere in sight.

"Izzy I am sure you have some sort of built in deviant detector, and what the hell did you say to Madge, she looked terrified?"

Birch gave a knowing smile. Izzy took out a hip flask, unscrewed it and poured a good measure of its contents into her coffee, she looked at me over her red glasses.

"I sized them up, worked them out, and then asked if they would be interested in joining my open masturbation circle."

Deb's choked with a huge cough, spluttered, and sprayed coffee all over the table, she sat back red faced and choking, as Izzy gave her a good sound pat on the back.

"You can join too if you want Debbie?"

Deb's coughed and retched, her eyes watered as she coughed and breathed in new air, as Gillian sat back turning purple, and looking concerned.

"Christ Abby, you lot should come with trigger warnings."

She coughed again. I cannot deny, I found it fascinating, seriously messed up, but fascinating.

"Were you joking Izzy, or were you serious, I mean will you be doing that in the practice?" She let her arm slide to Deb's cup, and just held it down a moment.

"It is a standard part of my work; in Manchester it was the first Tuesday of every month. I provided a safe space, lit some candles and incense to calm the mood, and then just let them all have at it. It is a good therapy that allows them to release all their inner frustrations, they have a good well, you know, yell out their pain, and leave happy and smiling."

Deb's looked at her with a horrified look on her face, Izzy took her hand off her cup.

"You have a wank class, are they all in the same room, or do they have a cubicle or something?" Izzy shook her head.

"No, they are all sat in a circle." Deb's looked at me. Birch giggled; Deb's looked terrified.

"I really could not do that, I mean, I would do it for Jimmy, but in front of a group, I would dry up with fear." Izzy shrugged.

"Maybe we should all get pissed one night and try it?" Deb's looked at her.

"Please never ever tell Chloe, she will bloody well do it, and I am never going to be ready for that." Izzy smiled.

"And that is why you should come to a class." I winked at Deb's.

"Hey guess who will be next door when it happens, you can put a glass to the wall, and listen?" Birch gave a cackle of a laugh; Deb's gave a big shudder.

"I am wearing ear plugs those days."

Gillian started to look really worried, I smiled at her, she really had no idea what she was getting into, but somehow, I thought it would be good for her. We spent the afternoon, talking and laughing, Gillian even relaxed and joined in, and as we left the shop, she looked really happy as she said goodbye.

Walking back, Birch took my hand and leaned into me.

"Sorry, I have ignored you a bit today." I smiled at her.

"You have a lot to do, and a lot to sort out, I understand Birch, look how you have tolerated my grumpy silence when I am writing, this is our life now, it is not a problem honestly. Look I really want this practice to flourish, I want you to have that dream that you have had since I met you. Every day you will come home to me, let's be honest I have not had that for the last four years, I get to be with you every day."

"We will have less time though Deads." I agreed.

"We are not students any more Birch, we work for a living, it is part of growing up." I stopped. "Oh shit!" She looked at me.

"What?" I pointed.

"That car outside the house, it's the vicars." She gave a sigh.

"Oh bollocks, what does that Bell Twat want now?" Izzy leaned in.

"Our souls... Leave him to me."

We opened the door as quietly as possible, and tipped toed in, I could see Chloe sat at the island through the kitchen doorway, she looked hopeful as she saw us, and gave a pleading look of 'please save me.' I heard Edwina speak, he had both of them trapped, I looked at Birch, and wagged a finger.

"Be nice." She looked offended.

"Sweetie I am always nice, even to unwanted Bell Twats in my home."

I panicked, I knew her so well, and I had not forgotten that day when she told me no more Bell Twats, she would not be that nice again.

The vicar sat happily chatting and spraying his words over everything, Chloe kept slipping a pot towel off her lap, and wiping the top. Edwina looked bored to death, and gasped with relief when she saw us. I must admit, I wanted to know if he would actually see us, or did Birch have her cloaking device fully activated. He turned, and I think smiled, I mean his teeth moved, but his expression did not change that much.

"Oh, and there you all are?"

Yep, it was us, of that there was no doubt, and this time we had been spotted.

"I was just telling the delightful Edwina; how much I love what you have done with the house. I must say, I think it is a credit to you, and so bohemian, but tastefully done, it is much nicer than it was, it was so dark and gloomy. Yes, yes, it is an extraordinary renovation, and quite beautiful."

Birch smiled through gritted teeth, I was just glad she was not wearing her robe, with those tight jeans, she had no possible place to hide a weapon.

"I would like you to meet our new working councillor for the practice Bell... Vicar, this is Isabella." Izzy leaned in to me, and lowered her voice.

"This is the anal kink vicar, yes?" I almost laughed, and nodded.

"Yep." She gave a nod and walked towards him with her hand out.

"So nice to meet you Vicar, I am the counselling advisor for those who have issues around sexual kink, you know leather, whips, chains and anal probing, I help people come to terms with it, and assure them it's fine."

He looked far too excited for my comfort, his eyes sparkled, and I felt cold shivers run down my spine. Chloe saw her opening, and legged it, she shot past me and headed for her room, I thought, Percy is probably going to help her calm down. Edwina shot through the other door and disappeared, and Deb's was already nowhere to be seen. Birch stepped back and grabbed my hand.

"Let's scarper while we have an opening."

We both turned, and bolted for the stairs, I heard the vicar say, as we headed up them.

"Oh really, well there are clubs for that you know?"

I shuddered, I had no idea what the club was, but the fact he knew about it, gave me the creeps. God knows what he got up to, all I knew was, I never ever wanted to see pictures of it, not ever!

Two hours later I was lay back in bed with Birch, having made the most of our alone time, and I was hot and sweating, as I lay back in the pillows breathing heavily. Birch lay at my side gasping the same. We were learning about each other all the time, and to be honest, it was a fun way to learn, although being quiet, was really hard. I had at one point, covered my face with a pillow so I could make a little more noise. The door opened, and Izzy leaned in, she smiled.

"Good for you two, there is something cathartic about screwing around members of the church, I should know, I once screwed a nun." I sat up.

"Holy shit Izzy." She grinned.

"Oh, it was, I had her legs akimbo over the font." I was mightily impressed. She smiled.

"He is gone now, it is safe for you to come out, to be honest, I really enjoyed that, he is quite fascinating, and really knowledgeable on kink. I rarely meet people these days with such wide ranging tastes for things, and he is very experienced."

Why did that bother me? I mean, I get everyone is sexual, and wants to feel wonderful, well maybe not Bethany and Marjorie, but I just found out, I had a mental block over the vicar.

I suppose they are people just like us, but we all see them as different. In a strange sort of way, they are above us, better than us, so trying to associate that doddering old badger, with any kind of sex, just created a mental blockage I could not get past. I suppose simply put, I really did not want to know, in fact the less I knew the happier I felt.

Izzy interested me; she really was accepting of everything. I suppose after working in her line of work, you uncovered so much, that you reached a point where nothing really shocked you, and I was curious about her. Birch had told me a little about her, but I really wanted to know more.

"Can I ask you Izzy, because I am kind of curious, but why did you decide to leave Manchester and come down here? I get the impression you had a thriving client list, and this is a new practice, it will take time to get back to that."

She smiled and walked into the room, and sat on the end of the bed, Birch and myself were naked, sweaty and smelling heavily of sex, and yet she did not appear to mind at all.

"Deadly, the simple truth is, I needed change, I have talked to Roni a few times about leaving, because my case load was high. Roni has replaced me with two counsellors, which sort of shows the size of my case load. Jemi has offered me the chance at a lighter load, and some more time off for me, and that is appealing. I am to be in a more managerial role down here, because I will be involved in the day to day running of the practice, and that for me is a new challenge. To be honest, I am also a huge fan of Jemi and her approach, which is slightly more modern than her mothers. Then of course there is Rodney." I looked at her and then to Birch.

"Who the hell is Rodney?" Birch giggled.

"He is Izzy's equivalent of Nigel, but much worse." I gasped and looked at Izzy.

"You have a stalker?" She raised her eyebrows.

"He has become much worse than that. It is a long story, I will not bore you with, but he was a nice guy, open to many different aspects of sex. I was young and crazy and loved screwing, in as many different ways as possible, and we did get on fine. He constantly asked me to marry him, and I was enjoying the wild life I had outside of the therapy rooms, he did help me lose the stress, it was a good all around relationship." She paused as if remembering.

"The thing was it went on and on, and we stayed as we were, nothing changed, and it got boring. Spicing up a relationship that has been all spice is not that easy, and he started to want to take dangerous risks, and that was where I drew the line. We went away to Wales for a weekend, and I guess everything I was feeling just came out, talk about a holiday from hell, he really lost his shit and hit me, so I pushed him out of the window." I gasped, and my mouth fell open.

"Holy shit Izzy!" Birch giggled; Izzy flapped her hand.

"It was only the first floor, I knew he would live, we had done worse screwing. He broke a leg and got pissed off at me, so when we got back, I left him, and moved into my own place, and he shot me."

I could not believe what I was hearing, Birch smirked as I stared at her, absolutely captivated, my voice dropped to one of whispered astonishment.

"No frigging way!"

To Izzy, this appeared to be no big deal, I could see Birch watching me, she knew this story, so it was no surprise for her, but I got the impression she was really enjoying my reaction. I cannot deny I was captivated, Izzy shrugged it off.

"He thought he was being cute." I gasped hanging on every word.

"CUTE! Izzy, he frigging shot you?" She smiled.

"He liked hunting with a bow and made his own arrows, the daft prick made one with a heart shaped point, and clipped the feathers in a heart shape, silly fucker thought he was Cupid." I could not believe how cool she was being.

"Jesus Izzy, what did you do?" Birch watched me carefully.

"I did what any other girl would do, when my leg healed, I tracked him down, and shot him in the ass with his own arrow. It got weird after that, he poisoned my cat, set my car on fire, and then burned my flat down, and offered me a chance to crash at his place."

Okay, so my head was mashed, she was just so relaxed about it all, I would have fallen apart or killed Nigel and gone to prison, she smiled.

"We had some fun times, it wasn't all bad, coming here takes me where he will never find me, and I can live with that. It is no fun looking over your shoulder for a sex crazed lunatic." I had no idea what to say, I flopped back on the bed with a gasp.

"Oh man you are like the ultimate in totally awesome Izzy, you have blown my mind." She patted my leg.

"We all have our adventures Deadly; I am sure you will too. Right, I need whiskey, so I will leave you two for another much louder round of sex, and I will head down for drinks." I watched her leave, and looked at Birch, she smiled at me.

"I told you she was awesome Sweetie." I looked up into her green eyes as they twinkled.

"You would never hurt me like that would you, because I could never hurt you?" She smiled a soft smile.

"Oh Sweetie, no, I could never do that, I would kill you in a fast and painless manner, you would not even know what hit you." She grinned and I started to giggle, she slid over on top of me and looked down at me.

"You know Izzy had a point, I am feeling much more rested, do you want to make some noise?"

I smiled; I liked the idea of that.

Chapter 16

# Spirits.

The following day, Birch left early, and I returned to my computer, to copy my manuscript to a memory stick, so I could work upstairs in my room. Edwina was busy on her computer building Deb's website, and Birch with Izzy, had gone to meet the shop fitters.

In my room I started to unpack the boxes, and hang up my clothes, it took up most of the morning, and once done, I returned to the kitchen to make a coffee, the door to the studio was slightly open, and I secretly peeped in.

The radio was on, and Chloe was sat naked and cross legged in front of a canvass on the floor, and was painting, she was quietly humming along, and carefully moving her hand, stroking the paint. It was fascinating to watch, it was like she was a completely different person, I had to wonder, if that was how others saw me, when I was working?

I finally tore myself away, and headed back to my room, and copied the files from my stick back to my computer, and then I opened up chapter one, and began to read, making changes as I read it. This would be the long process of editing, and it would take quite some time. The day was warm and sunny, and I had the window open a jar, and the fresh air was blowing in. I could hear the birds outside singing, I was sat naked and cross legged, on my chair and lost in my manuscript, it felt perfect.

Like pretty much most of my life in the last few weeks, Birch appeared, and it was nine o'clock at night. She brought in a cooked meal, and two tall tumblers of what I assumed were gin.

"I made you some food, come on take a break Sweetie."

I sat back and stretched, and gave a shudder, the window was still open, and the night had cooled. I got up and closed the window, Birch sat on the bed, with our food, and I walked over and sat down, suddenly I was hungry. She looked round the room.

"It looks good in here now you have unpacked; it does have a feel of the guest house, it feels familiar, and homely." She was right, now everything was away, I felt more at ease in here than I had.

"I suppose that the house is so big, I felt it was too big to take in all at once. I am not complaining Birch, I really do love the place, but it felt a little overwhelming at first." She understood, she sliced the beef on her plate and looked at me.

"I get that, it was the same for me, don't forget, the guest house was like home to me too, I missed it. That first night we stayed together, I was uneasy, I only really settled down because I could snuggle into you. Once we were in bed, I felt more relaxed, so I do understand. I am getting used to the place now, I think more people in it helps, but I must admit, I do love the kitchen, especially when we are all in it, I think it is my favourite place, apart from this room, here I feel normal again."

She had felt the same and said nothing, but somehow, I felt relieved by that, we ate our meal and sat on the bed and had our drinks, and she told me about her day, and what the fitters were doing, and how she was going to arrange everything in the practice, and it was nice.

It was just like our days at Uni, we would sit together on one of the beds, and talk about our lectures. If this was what my future was going to be like living here, I was okay with it, I stretched my legs and yawned, she smiled.

"I will go and wash up, you are tired, get into bed."

"Leave them, put them on the desk and I will do them in the morning, cuddle me until I fall asleep."

She picked up the plates, and carried them across the room as I slipped into bed, and then she undressed, and slid in beside me, and snuggled up. I relaxed feeling her warmth against me, and closed my eyes, and the words of the chapter I was editing, bounced around in my mind. I had written about how I questioned myself, my identity, and my feelings five years ago, I wanted so badly to tell her how I felt, and had wrestled so much with it, riddled with doubt.

Yet look at me now, relaxed and calm, living in our own home together, and warm and safe in her embrace, how silly I was back then, and I could see that I too had changed. I suppose we all had, it was inevitable, we all had to grow up eventually.

Deb's sat on the studio floor on a flowery cushion watching Chloe paint, they had spent the night talking and drinking.

"You know Chloe, I find it so strange at times, because I was really afraid of you at school, and yet here I am sat watching you paint, and you are nothing like I thought you were, and you are one of my best friends now, do you know that?" Chloe lifted her brush from the canvas and turned to her.

"We were stupid as kids; I am really glad you gave me another chance. To be honest Deb's, I did not deserve it, you were a better person than I was, but I am really glad we did make it up, because I see all of you like part of my family. I really mean that, you guys are the coolest, and I love all of you."

"Whoo...Woow... Whooooooooooo!" Debs turned looking alarmed.

"What was that?" Chloe looked at her and frowned.

"What was what?" It was pitch dark outside; Deb's looked round at the windows nervously, she felt an icy shudder run down her spine.

"I heard a really freaky sound, don't tell me you didn't hear it, because that will freak the hell out of me." Chloe shook her head.

"Honest Deb's, I didn't hea...."

"Whoo...Woow... Whooooooooooo!" Chloe shot up on her feet.

"Okay, I fucking heard that." Chloe looked at Deb's, her face had paled a little.

"What the fuck makes that kind of sound?" She looked really pale, and her dark eyes were opened really wide, Deb's stood up.

"I am going to really hate myself for saying this, but I thought it came out of the wall." Chloe stepped back quickly.

"Fuck off Deb's, don't say fucked upped shit like that, I am shitting myself here." She looked at her.

"What do we know of that makes fucked sounds like that?" Deb's was white and trembling, her voice quaked a little.

"Walls should not make noises, but there has to be some rational explanation."

"Whoo...Woow... Whooooooooooo!"

Chloe moved closer to Deb's, who swallowed hard and gripped

her arm, goose bumps ran up her arms, as her hairs stood on end.

"Oh, fuck no... No... No, I am not doing this right now, Debs' there is fucked up shit in this house, and we are alone." Deb's looked terrified, her voice was squeaky as she swallowed hard.

"What do you mean... In this house?" Chloe shook her head, and closed her eyes.

"I fucking knew I should have asked the vicar to bless the house."

Deb's swallowed really hard, feeling more than a little panicked, her voice was quiet.

"Why?"

Chloe looked at her real close, Deb's heart was already pounding, and she was starting to sweat, Chloe leaned in close, her eyes were really wide, Deb's watched her and swallowed hard, Chloe lowered her voice to an almost whisper.

"Let's be honest, Gwenda was fucking weird, and into some strange fucking stuff. Her son was hanging out with voodoo warriors, and all kinds of fucking weird in Africa, and she fucking hated us. What if she never actually left?" Deb's felt a jolt of panic run through her, and her heart rate increased.

"Stop it! I mean it Chloe, shut the hell up, I don't want Gwenda in the walls, I am already scared shitless."

"Whoo...Woow... Whooooooooooo!"

Chloe jumped, and snatched Deb's into her arms, and shook like crazy, her voice trembled.

"If it's Gwenda, just so you know, I love you Deb's." Deb's pushed her off.

"Sod bloody that, if it is Gwenda, she is not bloody well having me, I am getting Abby and Birch, it is their bloody house."

"Whoo...Woow... Whooooooooooo!" Chloe turned.

"Oh, fuck this shit!"

She grabbed Deb's hand, and headed for the door, the kitchen was pitch black, and she slid to a halt.

"Crap!"

Deb's was breathing really hard at her side. In the complete darkness the kitchen looked really eerie and weird. The light from the moon as the clouds swept across it, cast moving shadows against all the walls, as it came in through the patio doors.

The large glass doors reflected strange shapes, in the triple glazed panes, and throughout the kitchen, dark shadows loomed in the blackness. The only sound was their breathing, as it was swallowed in the darkness. Chloe swallowed really hard, her voice was quiet and a little shaky.

"Ghosts like glow in the dark and shit yes?" Deb's voice was higher than normal.

"I don't frigging know, and I never want to find out."

Chloe grabbed Deb's hand, and slowly they tip toed forward up the kitchen, both of them were shaking, and trying to hold their breath. Their eyes strained for the slightest movement in the heavy and oppressive darkness. They reached the kitchen door, Chloe peered round into the hall, and jumped back quick, Deb's almost had heart failure, she gave a terrified whisper.

"Don't bloody do that, I almost joined Gwenda."

Chloe swallowed something hard in her throat, her heart was beating really fast, and she took long deep breaths to try and calm down. In the darkness she turned slightly to look at Deb's.

"I am really going to hate myself, but Deb's there is something glowing fucking white up there." Deb's panicked.

"Just stop it, I am freaked out enough." Chloe took a really deep breath.

"I am not shitting you Deb's, fucking look for yourself."

Deb's took a huge breath, and swallowed the air, and then slipped slowly passed Chloe, and took a step forward. The hallway was filled with tall plants, and as the small amount of light came in through the windows above the door, they cast eerie shadows all over the hallway.

Long black fingers hung in the air, cast by the large dark palms, and there in the midst of it all, was the glow of something white. She jumped back quick feeling terrified, she sounded way more than a little panicked, as she leaned against the wall at the side of Chloe, breathing rapidly.

"Oh shit, it's Gwenda. What the hell do we do, I am supposed to get married in a month? Jimmy is expecting a human, not the ruddy corpse bride?" Chloe took long deep breaths.

"Okay, look, I have seen the Potter movies loads of times, and they run through Nick and give him the shudders. Ghosts have no solid form; so, we can run through Gwenda and get to Birch."

Deb's shook her head rapidly.

"I am not running through Gwenda; you can just sod right off Chloe." Chloe gave a shrug in the darkness.

"Deb's, she has not got hands, so she cannot grab us." Deb's terror level increased.

"What the hell Chloe, why has she got no frigging hands?"

Deb's shook her head, she had read enough ghost stories to know, it was the ones without hands that could suck your soul into their being, and torture you for eternity. Chloe shrugged her eyes glinting in the dark.

"She hasn't, have another look."

Nervously, Deb's looked round the corner of the door, and peered out from the kitchen, and stared at the hallway, she gave a gasp and turned and slapped Chloe on the arm.

"Christ Chloe, you daft twit, that's not Gwenda, it's sodding Venus, it's a marble bloody statue. You had me scared stupid." Chloe leaned round the door to look.

"Oh yeah, I forgot about them."

"Whoo...Woow... Whoooooooooooo!"

They both jumped, Chloe looked behind her, into the darkness that was where the noise had started, was it behind them, around them, or in front of them, she had no way of knowing?

"Fuck this shit, I am legging it,"

She suddenly turned, and legged it for the stairs. Realising she was all alone, or possibly with Gwenda, Deb's panicked like mad, and ran after Chloe.

"Don't bloody leave me!"

Chloe had a head start, but Deb's was first to the top of the stairs, both of them charged into Birch room's, the bed was unmade and empty. They stopped gasping for air, and looked round in the darkness. Chloe looked at Deb's.

"Holy fuck did Gwenda get her already?"

Deb's was whiter than Gwenda, and was shaking like a leaf.

"You need to shut the hell up Chloe, I am freaking the hell out already."

Deb's was sweating heavily, she looked round the room and saw the adjoining door.

"Abby's room, oh please don't let Gwenda have her already?"

I was relaxed and peaceful, drifting through my dreams, where somewhere in my dream Birch was softly breathing, and it was tranquil and calm, then suddenly, everything went loud as I was tossed around in my dream world.

"ABBY... WAKE THE FUCK UP, GWENDA IS BACK TO GET HER REVENGE!" I sat bolt upright in bed.

"What.... What.... What the hell Deb's... Holy shit are you alright, you look like shit?" She burst into tears.

"Abby, Oh Abby. It's been horrible, I think Gwenda has come back to get us all for stealing her house, and she aims to drag us into the walls." Chloe nodded vigorously behind her, equally as white and sweating like crazy.

"Huh?" Chloe took a deep breath.

"This place is haunted, Gwenda is hiding in the fucking walls, and trying to get out, and when she does, we are all fucked."

"Huh?"

I was looking at two really completely mental lunatics. The door swung open, and a white figure appeared. Deb's screamed and dived under the duvet, my heart almost stopped. Chloe ran round the side of the bed, and was pressed against the wall. Edwina rubbed her eyes, she stood naked in the doorway lit by the moonlight, as the clouds revealed the moon, and illuminated her in a white shimmering light.

"What is with the bloody screaming guys, I was sleeping really peacefully?" Chloe was holding her heart.

"Fucking hell Edwina, don't just walk in glowing like a ghost, fucking knock you bitch, you almost gave me a fucking heart attack." Birch suddenly sat bolt upright in bed, and everyone jumped with a squeal.

"Ghosts... I love ghosts."

She turned her head slowly, and even I shit myself; she was already snow white skinned, but with that hair, she looked like a scary ass ghost. She smiled.

"Hi Sweetie, did you say ghost?" Chloe nodded rapidly.

"Gwenda is back and haunting the walls."

Birch looked at her and frowned. Deb's popped out from under the duvet.

"No shit Birch, you can hear her moaning behind the plaster, it is as messed up as it gets, and bloody terrifying." Birch slipped off the bed.

"Awesome, show me." Deb's slid back under the duvet.

"Screw you Birch, I ain't going back down there."

Birch leaned over the bed, she spoke really softly, and slowly.

"Okay Sweetie… Stay here alone… With no protection… Defenceless then, with just you and Gwenda." Deb's lifted the duvet and looked at me.

"I bloody hate her at times, you know that?" I giggled.


We all came out of the room in the darkness, Birch turned on the light, Deb's realised and slapped Chloe.

"Why didn't you do that?" Chloe looked at her blankly.

"I don't fucking know, I was panicked and scared, why didn't you do it?"

Edwina tutted, and followed Birch. We all came downstairs, and quietly stood in the kitchen, Birch looked round.

"So where is Gwenda?" Deb's still looked very pale.

"Honestly guys we are not messing, there was this really freaky moaning sound in the walls."

Edwina was walking round looking at all the walls, so was Birch, there was nothing. Birch looked at the other two.

"Are you sure you heard this; you weren't just really pissed?" Chloe shrugged.

"I was really pissed, but I can tell you straight out, I am fucking sober now."

"Whoo…Woow… Whoooooooooooo!" I jumped and looked behind me.

"What the hell was that?" Deb's nodded looking terrified.

"See, it's bloody Gwenda."

I have got to admit, my heart had started beating really fast, I looked at Birch, I won't deny, that was a scary ass creepy noise.

"If that is really Gwenda, you are on your own, I am sleeping back in the guest house tonight." Edwina looked down the kitchen.

"Guys, it is louder behind this door."

We all walked up cautiously, and looked at Birch. Chloe looked puzzled.

"Why the hell when you own a big house like this, would you haunt the fucking broom cupboard?"

I must admit, I had never even noticed the door before, there was another door a little further up, I had no idea they were there. Birch grabbed the handle, and turned the lock, Chloe panicked.

"What the hell are you doing Birch, don't let her out?" Birch sniggered, and looked at her terrified face.

"Chloe she is a ghost, she does not use doors, she can float through the wall." Debs swallowed hard, and gripped my arm as she trembled.

"I so wish, you had not said that."

Birch opened the door, and to all our surprise, it was a staircase, under the hall staircase, and it headed down under the house. Chloe stepped quickly away from the door, shaking her head, and pointing at it.

"Oh, fuck this, I wanted a broom cupboard, not a fucking crypt." Birch appeared excited.

"Guys this is awesome, there could be a wine cellar, and old things." Chloe nodded.

"Yeah, old things, like corpses and Gwenda, and things of an unnatural state, like fucking dead Birch, but still walking about." I leaned over to have a look.

"I have got to admit Birch, it looks creepy as hell down there, I am not in a rush to find out if Gwenda is down there." Deb's pulled back on my arm.

"I'm with Abby, she seems the most sensible at the moment." Chloe nodded in agreement.

The steps descended into darkness, I noticed the light switch, and leaned over and flicked it on, nothing happened. Chloe swallowed hard.

"Yeah, fuck that, you see, that is how they fucking get you, they remove your strengths, like seeing them clearly, this is so fucked up guys, we need to call an exorcist." Birch looked round.

"Who has their phone on them?" I looked at her in disbelief.

"Birch we are all naked, where the frig would we put our phones?" She gave a long sigh.

"We have some tea lights in the drawer, we will have to use them."

Edwina hurried across the kitchen, and opened the drawer,

she pulled out a hand full and a box of matches, she lit one, and carried it over, and handed it to Birch. She held it up and the flame flickered.

Okay so at this point, I was hoping Birch would see reason and chicken out, but once again smelling adventure, even if it was a scary ass adventure, she was off. Birch did not hesitate and walked straight down the steps; Chloe stepped back.

"What the fuck Birch, are you fucking mental?"

Edwina followed, and even though I was actually quite scared, I stepped onto the first step, with Deb's gripping my arm. Okay so my reasoning here was simple, I was scared shitless and did not want to be alone.

"Whoo...Woow... Whoooooooooooo!"

We all stopped, it was a lot louder than we expected, and I felt my legs shaking. Chloe dithered and danced at the top of the stairs.

"Do we really have to do this?" Birch looked back up the stairs.

"All girls together Chloe, or you can stay there, alone, in a house where everyone else is down here, possibly being murdered. It is up to you Sweetie." I looked back and smiled, Chloe gritted her teeth and whispered through them.

"I fucking hate her at times, Abby she is going to get us all fucking corpsed by Gwenda. I am too young to die, I have only shagged sixty guys, I was hoping to at least make it one hundred."

Slowly we all made our descent, as the flickering lights swayed in the breeze of the draft down here. At the bottom was a large room filled with wine racks, sadly they were empty, I could have used a bottle about now.

Edwina passed me a candle, and lit it from hers, and I held it up, to try and light the room more. Strange shadows were cast on the red walls and floor, and they moved with the flickering of our candles. Chloe shook her head.

"We are so fucking going to get soul sucked, I feel it guys, unnatural things have happened down here."

Down the side of the large wine rack, there was a passage, made out of red brick, Birch walked towards it, I could hear Chloe behind reciting psalms from church. I will not deny I was really nervous, Birch stopped, and pointed down the tunnel, there was a flickering light on the wall ahead. Her eyes sparkled in the candle light, yeah she was too stupid to be as afraid as we were.

Debs saw it, and gripped me even tighter, I could feel her shaking, I looked to see if she was alright, she had her eyes closed tight. Chloe was a few paces behind me; she saw the light ahead.

"Oh fuck, there she is, that has to be Gwenda, we should have left a Ouija board in the kitchen, so my mum could still talk to me."

My heart was beating really fast, as I tip toed into the tunnel. Birch was a little way ahead. Now I know it sounds silly, but I did not want the gap between us, so I sped up to catch up. Chloe panicked, and looked behind her, she hurried forward. I came up behind Birch, as the tunnel turned into a larger room, I was almost at Birch's side, as we turned, and.......

Edwina dropped her candle, her light went out, Chloe screamed, I gasped in shock, and then Chloe looked down.

"I am so sorry guys; it just came out."

She had pissed all over the floor. Deb's eyes flicked open and she gasped.

"OH MY GOD, IS THAT THE FUCKING VICAR?"

I have to admit, that was a pretty good description of what I was looking at. It was indeed the vicar and.... At the end of the room, was a leather covered bed, with chains and shackles on it, in which our rubber covered vicar, was held captive on his knees. Behind him, completely naked, but wearing a very large strap on, was Izzy, and she was banging away like a jack hammer. She looked up and saw us and smiled.

"Sorry about the noise, he does get very excited."

The vicar looked up and saw us, five completely naked women, and moaned.

"Whoo...Woow... Whoooooooooooo!"

That was enough for me, Debs had already fled, Chloe was stood in a pool of piss, and I just wanted to disinfect my eyes, and walked backwards away from the room, feeling utterly freaked out. Birch looked at Izzy.

"Sweetie, keep the noise down, its freaking the girls out."

She smiled, still banging away, Birch turned as Edwina just stared at her in disbelief.

"What that's it, she is fucking the shit out of the vicar, and you tell her to keep the fucking noise down, Birch she is fucking the vicar?" Birch looked at Edwina.

"It is not my place to tell anyone who she can or cannot screw, is it now?"

Edwina looked gobsmacked. Birch walked back up the tunnel towards the stairs to the kitchen. Edwina followed, and she was really angry.

"Are you fucking serious Birch, Izzy is fucking the bloody vicar, in our fucking house at three in the morning, are you so fucked up, you do not see what is wrong with that fucking picture?"

It was three in the morning and we all sat at the kitchen island, having a stiff drink. Deb's was sat trembling, looking into her glass. I put my arm on her shoulder.

"Are you alright Deb's?" She shook her head.

"How can I stand in church on my wedding day, and look at him marrying me, as I swear an oath, after seeing him with Izzy screwing him with a bloody big dildo?"

Birch came up the stairs, followed by Edwina, she closed the door, and I could see the fire in her eyes, she turned, Edwina was not backing down.

"Edwina, please.... I WILL FUCKING DEAL WITH IT; NOW LEAVE ME THE FUCK ALONE, DO YOU HEAR ME EDWINA, FUCK OFF!?"

Edwina backed off and held up her hands.

"Whoa Birch, I am sorry, honestly, I am sorry."

Birch looked at her and bit her lip, she took a really deep breath, and I could see the fire in her eyes, but also the hurt.

"I am sorry Sweetie, I am, please give me time, and I will sort this all out."

I could see the tears well up in her eyes, Birch turned, and leaned her head against the door. I walked over to her.

"Girls, go to bed, it's late, and some of us have had a real scare, we will sort all this out in the morning."

Edwina gave a nod. Chloe took Deb's by the arm, they quietly all walked out. I slipped my arms round her.

"Are you okay?" Birch gave a long breath out.

"Why Deads, why the hell did she have to pick him?"

I could hear the hurt and sadness in her voice, she was

trembling and her voice was a little shaky, I held her tight and kissed her softly on her shoulder, I really had no idea what to do.

"I really don't know; you know her better than any of us. Look leave this until tomorrow, and then talk to her."

She turned and pulled me into her arms, and then buried her head in my neck, and gave a big sob.

"Deb's will never forgive me for this." I kissed the side of her face.

"Birch you gave Izzy a place to live, but her conduct is not your responsibility, she is forty for god's sake, she is old enough to make her own mistakes." Birch gave a sniffle.

"Maybe so, but does Deb's know that, I heard her as I came up the stairs, and she has a good point, how can she look at him in church?"

I pulled her back and looked at her, her eyes were damp with tears.

"You know what Birch; this is not on you. Deb's is no angel, and neither is Jimmy It is easy for her to call the vicar, but she did not mind Colin banging her brains out at the campsite. I bet Jimmy has had more than his fair share of groupies on tour. Well, if they can have a free pass whenever they are apart, why the hell can't the vicar? If you ask me, they all have a lot in common." She gave a sigh and smiled.

"I really love you; do you know that?" I smiled.

"We both need some sleep, come on, all this will still be here in the morning, why don't we just curl up, and wait until tomorrow?" She gave me a nod; she knew I was right.

"Okay Sweetie."


I lay in bed for some time, I was tired, but I did not want to sleep. Birch was curled behind me, I could hear her breathing, but was not sure she was asleep. Tonight, I saw yet another side to her, and it hurt to see it, somehow everyone in the house had made it Birch's responsibility, and it wasn't.

We are no longer children, we are young adults, and when a crisis hit, they all looked to her, and she shouldered everything, but to me that was wrong, surely all of us had equal responsibility?

I did not even know we had a cellar, and yet I half own this

house, so why was I not responsible, why had Edwina looked to
Birch? I felt unsettled, somehow it did not feel fair, she was not
our parent here, and they had no right to look to her that way.

I will not deny I was really freaked out when I saw him there
in his gimp suit, but the way I saw it, this was Izzy's doing, not
Birch's, and I felt that all of the girls had to understand that.
None of us were angels, and I was again reminded of that night
sat in the guest house, when I told all of them, that we were no
better than Madge.

Is it okay to sit in judgement of the vicar or even Birch, when in
this village, our own wild and free lifestyle was seen as equally as
shameful, and resort to Madge like behaviour and shaming?

I for was one was not going to sit in judgement, and play judge
and jury, especially with Birch.

This had to be sorted out, and I was not going to let Birch do
it alone, we needed some rules if we were all going to live here,
and the others needed to step up to the plate and take some
responsibility.

Chapter 17

# House Meet.

I woke to the sound of voices, and rolled over, the door to Birch's bedroom was closed, but I could still hear them.

"I trusted you Izzy, when everyone was giving up on you after the fire, I was the one that reached out to you, it was me remember? Everyone said you were broken and through, but not me, I was the one that pulled you out of all that shit, and helped you get through it. I have had your back, and brought you down here, and have given you the fresh start you wanted, and now look. Of all the people, you had to pick him, you live with them, you know what his family has done to them, how could you frigging betray them like that?"

"Jemi, I have said I am sorry; I didn't want that, I had no idea there were air vents down there, and the sound carried up, how the hell was I to know? You didn't even know you had a cellar, and you own the bloody place. I didn't want all of you traipsing down there in the dark, and seeing that, and I do understand what his wife is like, and what she has done. Milton is not like that, honestly, he has nothing bad to say about you, it's all her not him. Jemi for fuck's sake, you have worked with how many like him, lost and alone and living in shame, fuck me, how many of the girls in this house have been made to feel that way?"

"I get it, I bloody well do, I have been studying this shit for years, but that does not change the fact that at some point today, I have to look Deb's in the eye. I have to explain to her, why on the most sacred day of her life, she will be stood in front of a man, who last night she saw getting anal, with a bloody huge dildo, by her house mate. Seriously Izzy, how the fuck do I explain that to her?"

"You won't have to Jemi, I have told you, I am sorry, this is my screw up, and I will fix it. When they are all home, I will stand in front of them all, and I will be the one to apologise, and I will try to fix this and make it right with Debbie. You know I hate to say this, but you are not their mum, they are all grownups, and they are responsible for themselves. Look Jemi, this is my kink, it is my way of being sexual, it is who I am, and always has been, and I have never hidden that from you or anyone else. Okay so maybe the vicar was a poor choice in the eyes of this house, but he and his friends are my kind of people, and we share the same vice. It is sad we have to hide it, because as you know I hate that, but they are making plans to move the club. You know Jemi I hate to point out the obvious, but you are not much different, none of you are here."

"How do you mean? No offence Izzy, but we were not in the cellar at three in the morning screwing the bloody vicar."

"No, you weren't, but what about sitting on a guy's face watching the love of your life screw a guy, is that any better in the eyes of this village than me, is that fine, because it's you? You forget, I was there too when you broke down, and almost quit your mum's practice, because you missed her so much it was destroying you. I really fucking hate pointing it out, but wasn't that what Melody was really all about, you saw her as Deadly, and you fell apart because you feared she would do the same thing, because you had even thought of it yourself? Sweeties Retreat, really, why don't you name it what it really is, Deadly's and Jemi's Retreat, because that is why you are here, and have done all of this. Look at this place, this is not you, this was your way of protecting her, this was your way of showing her how God dammed much you love her. You can wrap this up any which way you bloody well want to, but this was all for her, because I remember when she left to come home, and the fucking mess you were in. Have you told her you wanted to cancel your doctorate, and come here, have you? Yeah, you can point the finger at me for being sexually deviant, and being seduced by my kink, but tell me this is different Jemi, because from where I am standing it looks to me like you did exactly the same as I did last night, just to be close to something you love, tell me she is not your kink?"

I swallowed hard, holy shit, was all of this just for me? The bedroom door opened and Edwina walked in with a coffee, she came quickly over to the bed and sat down, and whispered.

"You just heard that then? Abby I really am sorry, I should not have flown off the handle with her last night."

I was struggling for words, and took the cup to drink. In the other room Birch gave a long sigh.

"Izzy, I am sorry, I really am, you're right, you came here to escape a life, I came here because I lost a life, but you know what, I don't regret a second of it."

"I know kid, I have never seen you happier, and I am really glad for you, honestly, I am. Look, I will talk to the girls and sort this out, and then I will talk to Milton. You know for what it is worth, they do not actually screw each other, well not with their own, it really is just a play space, and they are building another one. Gwenda and Patrick set it up here, it has been here for over twenty years, Milton just wanted one more time for old time's sake, before it was taken apart, that is all, I will explain everything to the girls."

"Alright Izzy, we will group it out, and see what happens." Edwina grabbed my cup.

"Abby, lie down and pretend you are asleep." I looked at her.

"Why?"

"Just trust me, please just do it."

I had no idea what was going on any more, I lay back and closed my eyes. Edwina watched the door, she heard Birch's bedroom door open and then close, and the sound of Birch. She sat on the edge of the bed, holding my cup, and as the partition door opened, she gently shook me.

"Abby... Abby... Come on it's time to wake up." I opened my eyes, and stretched, Edwina smiled.

"Come on sleepy, I have made you a coffee."

I rolled over to see Birch standing in the door, I smiled at her, she looked upset, but she smiled back.

"Hi Sweetie."

I sat up and Edwina handed me the coffee, I took it and yawned, then took a sip, Edwina gave a small wink and then left us, Birch came over and lay on the bed at the side of me.

"Are you Okay?" I smiled.

"I am fine, how are you this morning, last night was pretty surreal?" She gave a sigh.

"Deb's left first thing, she spent the night in Chloe's room, apparently she cried a lot."

I looked at her, and could see her concern.

"I meant what I said last night, this is not all on you, all of us have a responsibility to the group, leave Deb's to me, I know her better than anyone."

It was three hours later, I tracked down Deb's, she was at home with her mum and dad. Well, she was in their house, in her part of the complex, this was where she would live with Jimmy once they were married. I leaned on the door frame, and watched as she folded bedding, not even aware I was there. I knocked on the frame, and she turned, saw me and looked down.

"I am assuming I am welcome, if not just say so?" She looked up at me.

"Don't be silly, you are my best friend, you will always be welcome wherever I am."

I walked in and looked round, it was a nice place, she had redecorated and refitted the whole place out.

"This is nice, you have really made it feel homely." Deb's just stood there holding the sheets.

"Look I know why you are here, just say what you have to say Abby, and get this done."

I took the sheet out of her hands, and then sat on the sofa and patted it, she moved and sat down at my side.

"I have got to tell you Deb's; you are shit at folding sheets." She tried to smile, I took her hand in mine and patted it.

"Deb's last night was a really big shock for all of us, and today all of us are trying to come to terms with it, not just you. I mean honestly, seeing the vicar get ploughed by Izzy, Jesus I wish I had a recycle bin in my brain, because that would defo be going right in it." She wriggled in her seat.

"Oh, please don't say it Abby, I nearly died when I saw that, I am not sure I can handle just knowing it happened."

"Deb's it happened, and hiding here folding sheets badly, will not change that. You know this is not school, we are both twenty four years old. Deb's life is changing for all of us, and this is the real world now, and we have to learn to navigate it." She turned and looked at me.

"Abby, she was screwing him with that thing, I mean how can I look him in the eyes at my wedding?" I nodded and sighed.

"This may sound cruel, and I really don't want it to, but honestly, that is what you are bothered about? Deb's, I think I am more freaked out knowing he put his actual cock in Marjorie, I mean look at it this way, he would rather have a big rubber dildo up his ass than screw her these days." She shuddered.

"I wish you would stop saying dildo." I smiled.

"Deb's do you remember that crazy night when we helped you shave your vagina for the first time?" She looked at me and frowned.

"Why does that matter?" I shrugged as I looked at her.

"You think it doesn't? Deb's that was the first time you ever got turned on, because a girl touched you there, which at that time, was really taboo for you. Birch gave you a vibrator, and you took it into the shower. Do you remember how that felt?" She turned slightly red.

"Abby, I don't want to answer that, it was private." I giggled.

"Wow your orgasm was that good?" She went beetroot, and put her head down.

"I am ashamed of myself for that.... Abby, I closed my eyes and pretended it was you screwing me with it... I am sorry, I really am, I was so turned on by you, and I knew you wanted Birch, but I wanted you too." I gave a sigh.

"Jesus Deb's, talk about hit me out of nowhere."

"I am sorry, I didn't mean to make you cheat on her." I looked at her with disbelief.

"I didn't cheat on anyone, I was not with her at the time, and for god's sake, don't blame me for your messed up thoughts. I don't have a problem with you letting me screw you in your head, just keep it the hell out of mine." She gave a little giggle.

"Am I messed up?"

"Oh Christ yeah! Look Deb's can you see what I mean, how is it okay for you to bang yourself and think of someone else, and yet when the vicar did it, you hold it against him? Think about it, did you care what the vicar thought, when Colin was banging the shit out of you at the camp, or were you lost in the moment enjoying yourself?" She bit her lip.

"I get what you are saying, I am being a hypocrite aren't I?" I gave a long sigh.

"Deb's whether we like it or not, everyone is sexual, you know it will not go away when we are older, a lot of people are lonely, they want all those glorious feelings we have, and they are deprived of it. The vicar is lonely, he has a strange kink, and we may not understand it, but that is what makes him happy, he is human after all, and let's be honest, do you think Marjorie still wants sex? Last night, just like you in the shower was private, if we had all been in bed, we would never have found out about it, and you would still be married by him without a care in the world, can you understand that?" She gave a long sigh, and nodded.

"I know you are right, Chloe said something similar, but honestly Abby, I was so freaked out when I saw those teeth sticking out of his mask, I almost fainted."

"Yeah, me too, hell Chloe pissed herself. I do understand, I do, it does seem completely messed up to me too, but he has a right to be happy. We all do, hell that is the bloody point of living together, but I will say something else also. Deb's, Birch is not a mother figure either, everyone turned on her last night, and they forgot, I own half that house too. She took it all and it stressed her out, and hurt her more than you realise, and I hate seeing her like that. We are all grownups, it is not her place to fix everything, not even me." She looked at me and gave a nod.

"I have been stupid haven't I, I am so sorry?" I smiled.

"You are just being you. Look Izzy wants to apologise to all of us together, it will be hard for her, but she will do it. So how about I help you finish these sheets, because honestly you suck, and then we go back together and hear her out?" She smiled at me and gave a nod.

"Yeah, we should do that."

By the time everyone was home and settled, we met in the living room, and gathered together on the large sofas. Birch leaned onto me, as I took what was becoming my favourite part of the sofa, the corner. I felt her arm slide behind me, as she snuggled up.

Izzy appeared in the doorway, in a long green robe, it appeared Birch had purchased her one too. She looked at us all, as we sat there, but focused more on Deb's.

"Look guys, I wanted to face you all and make an apology for distressing you all last night. I have thought about it, and I should have given all of you the heads up, and for that I am sorry." Chloe frowned.

"So, you are not sorry you fucked the vicar with a dildo?" She looked at her.

"I am into that sort of sexual play, so firstly I will add that I will never apologise for being me, and secondly, I should have no need to apologise to anyone for my sex play, let me ask you Chloe, will you apologise for fucking Percy?" Chloe looked offended.

"It is nowhere near the same, why should I apologise, I only use Percy when men are scarce?" Izzy gave a nod of recognition.

"It is your right to screw whomever or whatever you want, I will never condemn you for it, but it is not fair that I do not have the same right." Deb's looked up.

"Izzy, I get that, I honestly do, but why of all people the vicar?"

Izzy walked to the drinks table and poured a triple whiskey, and walked to the coffee table, and stood up on it, then lowered, and sat cross legged facing us all.

"Look guys, there is a history behind all this you do not know, so let me tell you, as it is the reason why. BDSM is still shamed in a lot of the places, hell straight sex is shamed here. Just over twenty years ago, Patrick Perkins placed an advert in a local magazine looking for like minded people. It was answered by a small group of eight people, two of which it appeared lived local." She took a swig of her drink.

"Patrick and Gwenda met them all in a bar in Oxendale, and as a result, a very secret and private club was set up, of which Patrick was the principal leader of the club. He converted part of the wine cellar into a dungeon themed playground, that catered to their particular sexual need, and it has been running once a month ever since."

She took another big swig, and all of us sat there just watching her, she flicked back her long red hair.

"When he died, Gwenda kept the club running, but when she got ill, she started to suffer memory loss, and she simply forgot all about it, and the club had no choice but to look for another venue. Think about it, how easy would that be around here, especially if you wanted to keep it secret? One of the members is working on it, and it is being built as we speak, and it is not that far away, but the biggest problem is, because it was so secret,

Gwenda's son was not aware that below the house, was all of the club's equipment. The vicar told me this, and so I arranged for him to come along in the night and remove it." I frowned at her.

"So why did you end up banging him?" She gave a sigh.

"Deadly, do you know what it is like to get so turned on, and not be able to act?"

I suddenly felt on the spot, and felt my face glow, Birch pulled her hand tighter round my waist, she knew, I looked at Izzy.

"I can understand that, yes." Izzy smiled.

"I allowed him in through the side tunnel, there is a door at the side of the garage, that leads down the steps and into the cellar. It used to be used for wine deliveries, there is a door that can only be opened from inside down there, so I went down and opened it, and let Milton in. He was telling me how sad it was that the club would lose its place, as he had some very fond memories of it. You know he is not a bad guy, and actually, he really likes all of you, he does not agree with everything his wife does. He told me the reason she tried to take the house off you, was because she does know about his deviant hobby, and she knew it was here. His wife did not want the truth to come out, and embarrass her." Edwina flopped back in her seat.

"Well hell yeah, if that little morsel hit the news network, she would be destroyed, especially after all of the people she has shamed." Izzy raised her glass.

"Look, I understand, not all of you get it, not everyone does, but you have to understand that it really is my only way of finding my sexual relief, it is my kink too. Milton told me about the club, as he gathered his things, and... Well to cut a long story short, when he picked up his rubber suit, he got a little excited, so I told him to try it on for me, and I got a little more turned on than I thought I would. The next thing I knew I was doing... Well, you know what, and you all walked in naked, and honestly, looking at you guys naked watching me do that, really fucking did it for me, I have not felt like that in over a year. It was the same for Milton, it has been almost a year since the club has met." Deb's looked at Izzy.

"Abby said he is very lonely." Izzy nodded.

"His wife is cold to him, Gwenda was a really good friend to him, and he does miss her, he is very lonely Debbie, and I know that feeling. His kink can be the most amazing thing, but at times because of society, it can feel like a cage." Deb's looked sad and put her head down.

"I feel really bad now, I know that feeling, before Abby and Birch came back here five years ago, I was so lonely." Chloe gave a nod.

"I think we all were Deb's; it was Abby and Birch that changed that for all of us." Edwina gave a nod of agreement. Izzy looked round the room.

"Deb's I really was not thinking, he told me the club never had physical intercourse with each other, it was just the toys and play. For him it is a fine line, but he and his wife do not regard it as a betrayal of their vows. He did say, when she was younger, she was very understanding, but it did not appeal to her, and they formed an agreement between them. At the end of the day, they are almost finished with their new dungeon, all they really want is to move their equipment without any one knowing about it, and then the cellar will be clear, he also told me, he wanted to protect Gwenda's reputation, now she has passed on."

I cannot speak for the others, but I was starting to feel a little guilty, it looked like Edwina did too.

"I think they should be allowed their stuff back, and I also think that we should honour Gwenda's legacy. I say we keep this quiet, and live here where we will live the same sort of private life, and at times engage in what makes us feel good, even if that involves a messed up teddy called Percy." Deb's giggled.

"I cannot believe you screw your teddy Chloe." She gave a prideful grin.

"If Phileas had Percy's moves, you would fuck him too." Birch gave a snigger, and looked at Izzy.

"I have and always will defend sexual freedom, I agree with Deads, we let them take their things and move their club, and we will protect them, and live our lives in honour of who we are too." Edwina and Chloe nodded.

"Yeah, we are in." Izzy looked at Deb's.

"What about you, this has had the biggest impact on you Debbie?" She looked up at Izzy.

"I have no right to call others, Jimmy and me have an arrangement, that others would see as shameful, I am in agreement with this. I am still nervous about the wedding, but I will not hold it against him." Izzy smiled.

"Thanks Debbie, I will let Milton know, and will keep you all up to date, I will make sure there is no more awkward moments again for you all."

It was agreed by all of us, and we gave a long sigh of relief, Chloe put her hand up, Birch frowned.

"What the hell Chloe, this is not frigging school, if you want to say something, just say it." She smiled.

"I like this, actually what is it, a house meet? Anyway, I wanted to ask, can we actually bring people back here, because to be honest, I have been screwing Carter, actually Michael, Stefan, George, and I think he is called Robert, I cannot quite remember. He makes me cum so much, I lose my memory of him, anyway, it is a bloody nightmare running all over the place, trying to fit them all in, so can they come here, I mean, is that alright because mum never let us at home?" I stared at her.

"How the hell do you even walk?" She grinned and raised her eyebrows.

"With a spring in my step." Deb's giggled. Birch gave another long frustrated sigh.

"Guys this is your home, you can come and go as you please, and live as you please, that is the whole bloody point of living here. This is our safe house, all we ask is you contribute whatever you can, pull your weight with the chores to keep the house clean, and respect those living here with you."

Chloe smiled, and they all started to move, I wanted to say something.

"Everyone I want to also add something important. This is our house, all girls together, we are supposed to be grownups, so the next time the shit hits the fan, we deal with it as a group. Birch is not mother, and you are not children, we do this, we sit, we talk, and we deal with it, okay?"

Everyone nodded and agreed and I felt happy, Birch snuggled into me.

"Thank you, Sweetie, although I like playing mummy with you." Deb's frowned.

"Okay that is really messed up, I never want to know why. Oh, and just so you know, last Sunday lying in bed moaning and groaning and yelling Oh God many times, is not going to get you into heaven." Birch giggled.

"You know Deb's, the clitoris serves only one function, and that is pleasure, so answer me this, if sex on Sunday is so wrong, why did God give me one, and Deads fingers to play with it?" Deb's got up, and smirked.

"Your idea of church Birch, is so messed up, and yet I would defo be in the congregation." She beamed a smile, and Birch chuckled.

The evening went on with drinks and jokes, and after an hour Carter appeared, Chloe snook him off to her room. We talked and joked, and finally headed to bed with the sound of Chloe's headboard making a dull thud on the wall. I slipped into bed and waited for Birch, she arrived with drinks, and had a sparkle in her eye, it had been a great relief to deal with it all. She slipped into bed and moved onto me, she sat on my waist, and looked down at me.

"How did you know the vicar was lonely?" I should have known better; she never missed a trick. I had no choice, I had to confess.

"I heard everything you and Izzy said, Edwina thought it best to pretend I didn't. I never realised you were suffering as much as me, and I am really sorry for that." She gave a sad smile.

"It's in the past Deads, we do not have to think about it, we are happy, isn't that all that should matter?" I stared at her, sat there on my waist, like an alabaster amazon.

"Birch if you had quit, I would have put you on the first train back to finish, I could not live with that. I would rather suffer the loss of you, than know you gave up your dream for me, it would destroy me." She smiled.

"Yeah, Izzy said that to me, I was so unhappy, I guess I was not thinking straight. Izzy helped me see the light again, and that is when I decided to qualify and come here, I started planning it that week. I am sorry you heard that, it must have hurt?" I nodded.

"It did a little, but it also helped me understand you better." She narrowed her eyes.

"How so?"

"It showed me you were terrified of loving me, as much as I was you, and also how stupid we were for not talking sooner about it. You know Birch I can write anywhere; I would have come to Manchester if you asked me." She smiled a soft smile.

"I knew that Deads, but honestly, mum needed you more here, she had a rough time, and having you home helped heal her, in my mind, that was more important, because let's be honest, we both need her."

She was always right, but I sort of like that about her.

Chapter 18

# Parents, vampires.

With the dust settled over the vicar and his club friends, we all settled back into life. The weather was warming as we crept through July, it was not as warm as previous years, but the forecast was good. Deb's was busy, as opening time came closer, and Birch and myself settled down to plan what was to be our first big challenge. Parents Day.

Yep, we were stupid enough to invite our parents for lunch, on the upcoming Sunday, and finally open the house for inspection. Yep, we would have my mother, Ellen Wheeler, and Margret Pemberton, around to eat, they were probably three of the greatest cooks in the district, and in the words of Chloe, 'Fuck, I am shitting myself!' we planned the menu.

Dressed in sawn off shorts, and white t shirts, and all wearing red aprons with our names embroidered on them, supplied by Birch, we hit the kitchen. We made full use of our range cooker, and double oven, to cook a full on roast beef dinner, supervised by Chloe and Edwina, the two best cooks we had. This was high pressure stakes, as Birch, and Izzy, danced round to full blast Led Zeppelin, with the hoover, and duster, in the living room and library.

Deb's handled the long table, which when pulled out was the size of a small yacht, and used four table cloths to cover it. We bought place mats, new glasses, and three sets of new cutleries, and drafted in Anthony, Brent, Hatty and Clive, to mix up the numbers and serve as distractions.

The patio doors were open, the pool was full and clean, the grass was cut by Izzy on the drive on mower, although she was insane at driving, and we did have one garden statue missing an arm. Chloe even opened up her studio, anything to keep the women away from the stove, and allow us to work without comment.

I spent most of the day getting bumped on the hip, as Edwina or Chloe would observe my work, and then bump me with their hips saying.

"Here let me do it, it's quicker."

I was starting to think I had drawn the short straw. With the table laid, Deb's did room inspection, to ensure nothing untoward was on display, we went with the rule, that if it made Deb's blush, our parents would not approve.

By three o'clock the pressure was on, I was feeling fried, as the first of our guests arrived, it was the Pemberton's, my greatest fear. Birch was excellent, in the way she stewarded them into the living room, and held them captive until the others arrived. And so, the tour began, and we all held our breath, as each upstairs room was displayed by Deb's and Birch. In each room Birch gave a rundown of each of us, Percy was hidden in a wardrobe, and she walked from room to room, and kept up the banter, and answered all questions with great diplomacy.

Downstairs, I was red in the face, panicked, and scrambling around, checking items off our exhaustive list. Chloe and Edwina were watching everything, making sure everything was cooked to perfection. At some point, I am not sure when, Edwina had become head chef, and barked her orders, we did not argue, we just did what she said.

Anthony and Brent appeared, and opened the wine to breathe, which was pretty much my most positive contribution. I somehow knew more about wine than the others, and it was red meat, so I chose the nearest alternative, after a quick internet search, to find out what my dad would buy.

The noise on the stairs, informed us they were heading our way, so after the library, they would be in here, and the pressure ratcheted up. Plates were laid out on the island, Edwina checked the beef, the roasts were almost perfect, I mean they looked done to me, but Chloe assured me, not quite yet. And as the army of the most critical guests, we would ever have approached, we were almost ready. Birch walked in, and in a bright and cheery voice announced.

"And this is the kitchen."

It felt hotter than a submarines boiler room, and I was losing body fluids by the rate of a pint a second, as I wiped my brow, and prepared for service. Birch waved her hand, like she was Queen Victoria.

"The table is ready, if you would all care to be seated."

Anthony and Brent were on hand in white shirts, to guide them to their seats. I was two steps away from a heart attack, as I felt those eyes of critical women upon me, as they walked past taking account of the three of us working our asses off.

Chloe and me stood back, Edwina stepped up to carve, and the moment she sliced, we sprang into action with piping hot potatoes, mashed and roasted, veg, and gravy. We served with speed, and the boys whipped them off as we named each recipient. The service was as smooth as Deb's vagina, and I finally flopped into my seat exhausted, as Anthony poured the wine before sitting down to join us.

I was so nervous as everyone started to eat, and the silence was killing me, when suddenly, Margret Pemberton looked up, and she looked right at me. I shit myself.

"Abigail, you and the girls have done an excellent job, this is beautiful."

I gasped a sigh of relief, and reached for my wine. The table exploded with conversation, and I tucked in, I think I needed the carbs, just to overcome the stress.

With the meal over, team two kicked into gear, Deb's, Birch, and Izzy, cleared the table, and started the washing up, and I took everyone out into the garden, for coffee or drinks on the patio, and breathed in the fresh air, as I tried to cool down, because I would rather have been naked.

The garden here is vast, because it backs onto the property of the manor, there is more land available. Most of it lawned, with trees, and large ornate shrubs, although there are some nice long flower beds that are covered in bark, and Norman has assured us they are low maintenance. There is the pool, which is three times bigger than the one I had in my home, the long pool house, a massive patio, with full outdoor kitchen, and lawned areas which had concealed statues, of which some were pretty erotic. The sun was out, we had plenty of chairs and tables, and to be honest, the whole back area was perfect for entertaining.

It did not take Hatty and Clive long to find the studio, as Chloe asked loads of questions, and got great advice from the pair, even her parents were impressed. Edwina talked to the Wheelers, and I smiled at mum, as she sat with my dad who was having a large whiskey and soda. He lifted his glass.

"Today has been a credit to all of you girls, and I think your house is very lovely, I am really quite proud of all of you." It was high praise indeed. Mum got up, took my hand, and walked onto the grass.

"You have a lovely home Abby, I am actually very surprised, it is not what I expected. I take it there was a massive clean up operation prior to our arrival? I remember the first time my mother came to my flat, I was terrified, that woman could find fault with anything." I gave a chuckle.

"To be honest, we did not need to clean up as much as you would think, everyone here is pretty tidy, I hid all my dirty clothes in my wardrobe though, you know, to clear the floor." She smiled.

"It is very beautiful out here, this is a nice space for you all, Birch has arranged everything very nicely. How is she Abby, she looks tired, how has she handled Melody?" I was really surprised.

"So, you did know, I did wonder that day in the guest house? She is better mum, she is not fully over it, and this house has taken a lot out of her, but she is happier." She gave a sigh of relief.

"I am happy to hear it, Abby can I ask you a really private question?"

I was unsure, it was not what I expected from her. We stood well away from the patio, and out of earshot.

"Okay.... I suppose so, what is this about?" She looked me straight in the eyes.

"Did you... Were you so unhappy without her, you honestly thought of doing it, you know, like Melody... Abby was Birch right, would you have killed yourself?"

I felt my world crash. How do you answer that, how do you admit to a parent you thought about it, hell you were ready to do it? I struggled for a good answer.

"I was at a very low ebb; it crossed my mind. I felt like a failure, the books were not selling, I was missing her, I felt lonely without

Deb's. I could not write, the village hated me, and I thought Birch had gone forever. Things got to me mum, so yeah, it crossed my mind, I honestly thought what is the point of living like this." She gave a sigh and nodded.

"I understand, I really do. Oh god Abby, you have no idea how much I understand. Abby promise me, if you ever get that way again, just come to me, never sit alone like that and feel that way, just come to me." I felt really guilty, my stomach squirmed.

"I am sorry mum, I am fine, I promise."

She smiled at me, and her eyes twinkled, she lifted her hand to my cheek.

"I once considered it Abby, I was there, you were eighteen, out of college, and leaving me for Uni. It felt like a thousand miles away, and I couldn't bear the thought of it. I stood in your bedroom doorway, and watched you sleep; I must have been there for an hour. I felt at that time I had lost you forever, and had nothing left, absolutely nothing. Yet as I looked at you, I knew, that I could not leave you, even though I thought you hated me at the time. I realised, I would rather be hated by you, than never see you again. Abby I am so proud of the woman you are becoming, I truly am."

It was nice to hear it, I pulled her into a hug. Birch walked down the grass with fresh drinks and a beaming smile, she hugged mum.

"So mum, Ed appears happy, he is talking shop with Bradley and Derek." Mum looked right at her.

"Birch I am not known for mincing my words, you have proved your point, now talk to her, she is really missing you." Birch gave a sigh, I looked at Birch and frowned.

"Why are you and your mum not talking, why didn't you tell me?" She looked awkward.

"It's a long story, mum did not think I was ready, so I set up Sweeties Retreat without her consent. She is still pissed at me, because I wanted to quit to come here." I didn't understand, Birch and her mum were solid, she was there in the courts.

"Birch she was fine in the courts, what has happened?" She looked even more awkward.

"Bradley did not know my mum was out of the loop, so when he contacted her, they both blew a fuse. Mum played along, and acted like she was in on it, but she sent me some pretty pissed off texts. She managed to get the paperwork done, and brought the company into her operation, but it was a close call, and yes, I blew my lid at her, because I wanted independence, we have not spoken that much since. I am sorry."

It all made sense, and why she had been so stressed out, and buried herself in the house, I looked at her.

"I am inviting her here Birch, you two need to sort this out, she is your mum, she has stood by you no matter what. Birch you have to talk to her and make things right, even if that means backing down a little." She could see I was angry, and she gave me a nod.

"I know... Honestly, I meant to, I have just been so busy with the house and the practice, I wanted it all perfect before she saw it. I wanted her to see I am not a little girl Deads, I am a woman, and I am good at this." My mum took her hand.

"Do you honestly think she is not aware of that Birch, she knows, you have shown her, and actually she is really proud of you. Abby is right, you need to talk to her."

Birch understood.


It is easy to look back and see the solution to a problem, and I suppose that is the point of getting older, we can look back. Having spent weeks working on my book, which is about a very important time in my life, I am reminded of that night before I was leaving to go back to Uni, and how I sat in my living room with my friends, and regretted that I had not gotten to know them sooner. I thought of all the wonderful moments I had missed, and all the doubts I had about the future, and the fact was, I really should not have worried about it all. Birch had been right, when she told me, be you, and everyone would get used to it.

Over the last three years, the relationship with my mother has improved, we have talked more, and I was more open with her than I ever had been about many things, and yet with her, I had still hidden the truth of my weakness, and not told her I had in fact thought of suicide twice.

Today I discovered that Birch had also hidden her weakness, or as it now appeared, her perceived weakness. Not only had she felt deep pain because of our separation, she had risked ending her career, and that had driven a wedge between her and her mother. I suppose what shocked me, was she hid it from me, even Birch who appeared so strong to me, could not live up to everyone's expectations, and had crumbled a little. It really bothered me to know she had kept something secret from me, after all, she had always appeared so open about everything.

We all think we can cope and deal with life, and we all plan far into the future, and yet life has the strange way of altering things. Birch reached her goal, and was about to set up her practice here, but in order to do that, she had been forced to confront the truth of whom she was. I suppose in a way, I had achieved mine, after all I was a published author, a failed one, but an author all the same.

I had confronted my own truths, I had been forced to face them, and the hardest one of all, was I needed to improve as a writer. I had learned from it, my stories lacked life, and that happened because I had lost touch with life, I was not living at the time I wrote them.

The coming months, would ultimately reveal if I had learned enough to continue. Having faced my truth, I had written something completely different, I had written about life, about actual living, the naked truth of the life of myself, and those around me. It was real, and it was gritty, and I already knew that the likes of Marjorie, would hate it, because the simple truth was, it was real, and life is not all political correctness and good manners. Life can be brutal, and painful, it is the lows we all go through, and I had learned because of it, to appreciate the highs so much more.

My first summer home from Uni, had been painful, and heart breaking. I had felt shamed and afraid, and I had even hated myself, for simply being me, that is real life, people are rude and cruel, even grownups bully.

The strange thing was, that as I looked back to write my story, I saw there was balance, because that summer also had the wonder of dancing at a festival, the relief of being able to finally talk more openly with mum, and I had the joy of seeing my friends work hard and win prizes in the fete, and most of all, I discovered I had an abundance of love around me.

The love of my mum, and my friends, but most of all, the love of

Birch. For all her crazy and strange little ways, I had gone against everything I believed in, and fallen in love with this amazing, wonderful, liberated lunatic, she had become the centre of my universe, and the centre of my soul.

Without understanding why, or how, I had started to grow up and mature, and it all began during the heat of that glorious summer. So much has changed since that time, I can see that now. I suppose that is the point, we cannot see what is around the corner, we really do not know what comes next. We can jump on the road of life, and run at high speed with the pack, or we can slow down and admire the scenery. I guess for myself, I had opted for the river of life, and I had chosen through understanding, to lower the sail, and drift along, and simply go with the flow, and that was right for me.

We walked round the garden and enjoyed the day, then headed back to the others, everyone was sat relaxed, chatting, and getting on well. Hatty smiled as I hugged her, I had missed her. Clive was nice, a bit weird, but he seemed kind, and he was very into Hatty, that was very obvious, she looked at us sat side by side.

"So, you two, the word on the manner is you two are after seats on the council, Madge is already at work to make sure that never happens. I hope you are planning to make your debut at some point next year?" She laughed. Birch leaned back in her chair.

"I am too busy at the moment, but we have considered it, the council needs younger blood, and we are aware that one day we will need to step up, and prepare this village to survive in the future. The way I see it Hatty, if it keeps her on her toes, then for now I am happy." Hatty gave a bright smile.

"So that's a yes then?" We all giggled.

The day turned out to be a big success, but we did put a mammoth amount of effort into it, and as a group all of us played our part perfectly. Once everyone had left, and after many hugs, we gathered in the kitchen for fresh drinks. Birch raised her glass.

"To the Curio's, Wotton's unstoppable force." We all cheered with joy as we raised our glasses.

As everyone chatted away excitedly, I noticed Birch quietly slipped out of the door, into the hallway. I walked slowly over and peeped round the doorway; she went in the library. I walked softly up the hallway, and stood by the door, and listened, Birch was on her computer, I heard the ringtone of the video call.

"Hi Mum, I am sorry it is late, look we need to talk… I need to talk, is that okay?" I smiled, and walked back to the kitchen.

In Wotton, the only thing faster than email, is gossip. Hatty and Margret Pemberton, moved quickly, and the word was out about how stylish, and beautiful the house was. It was spread across the whole village, how clean it was, and how the girls worked as a really good team, and what amazing cooks they were. None of this pleased Marjorie, Henrietta and Bethany, who had no idea where it was all coming from, but as the summer program kicked in, and the Marquees were erected on the village green, it appeared to be all people could talk about.

Hatty was teaching an art class as part of the four week long, summer activities, and she invited Chloe to join her as an assistant, she was absolutely crazy with excitement, and proudly walked into the tent with her art equipment.

For Deb's the big day finally came, and we all stood outside the newly remodelled shop, with a much bigger crowd than expected. The shop had a beautiful Edwardian looking sign, painted by Chloe, that read 'Cogs and Wheelers Books.' It had little cogs and wheels painted around it, and it looked so wonderful. At ten on the dot, the shop was officially opened by Dr Jemima Dixon, in fits of giggles, she cut the tape, and we all walked in for the first time.

I was blown away, the change was incredible, the shop looked huge, as it ran right to the back of the property, and it had thousands of books. The walls were vinyl boarded, and had large pictures of old book covers scattered across them, all the sections were clearly marked, and labelled. My favourite thing of all, was that the window was clear and the light flooded in, and at the base, were two really old restored Edwardian chairs, and an antique table. The till was computer operated, with a scanner, and there was even a coffee machine, and some seats at the back.

I eyed the fantasy and sci fi section carefully, she had it all. Her steam punk section was filled with some of the greatest classics ever written, and on the top of the book shelf, in a glass case was

Jimmy's top hat with the goggles on it.

The self help section, had copies of all of Roni's books, and the sex section was very well stacked, and true to her word, there were books on potions, spells and witchcraft. The whole place had a new life. I was delighted to see Agatha walk in and hug Deb's, she had tears in her eyes, as she saw the improvements. I hugged her with joy, and it was clear to her, she had sold it to the perfect person to keep up her legacy. Marjorie scowled across the road stood by the antique shop, with Bethany and Marion.

"That lot knows no limits, defiling a classic shop and turning it into that vulgar, tasteless, display of modern capitalism, it looks more like a sex shop, than a book shop." Felicity walked up behind them.

"Ladies... I am happy to see we still have a bookshop, you can call it all you like Madge, but you saw who the other bidders were. There was a betting shop, a competitive local shop, A cabby company, and I believe Hatty and Birch even considered opening a brothel in it. Be honest Madge, if Debbie had not taken it, we would have much worse. Agatha told me, she sold to Debbie for no other reason than Debbie talked about saving the heritage of the village. Now who would have expected that?" She walked onto the road and headed for the shop.

"You like crime thrillers Madge, and I believe Debbie has doubled the stock, and brought in a lot of new exciting titles, you should check it out, after all you are Vice of the Parish Council." Felicity smiled as she crossed the road. "Wow Debbie, you have outdone yourself."


I sat in the chair by the shop window, and looked at the book in my hand. 'Handed Death by Abigail Jennifer Watson. It felt strange, as I looked up at the young girl, of about sixteen.

"What is your name?" She gave me a big smile.

"My name is Jennifer too, Jenifer Fletcher." I opened the book to the title page.

"Jennifer, this is the first book I have ever signed for a fan in my home village."

I looked at the page, and started to write. 'To Jennifer, my first fan from home. Thanks, Abigail Jennifer Watson.' I closed the book and handed it back to her, she looked so thrilled.

"I don't want to be rude Miss Watson, but could I have a picture with you, with this book please?" Birch stood back and smiled as she watched.

"Here let me take it, sit in the seat next to her Jenny."

Jennifer sat down all smiles, and we both leaned in, she held up the book between us, and Birch took a picture using Jenny's phone, she then lifted her own, and took another. Jennifer looked at her phone and was delighted. She thanked me, and I watched as she walked to her friends, and showed them the picture, she was so happy, and I felt happy too. Birch sat down in the other chair.

"That was really nice to watch Deads, you know, you get down about your books not selling, and maybe they have only been in low numbers, but you are missing the point. That girl, Jennifer, she will treasure that book for the rest of her life, she does not care if you sell ten or a million, because she owns one that is worth far more than them to her, she owns the memory of meeting you, and watching you sign it."

It was an interesting point, and I knew she was right, but that's her, it was a Birch thing, and I wondered if I would ever get used to it. I sat back against the window watching the shop, filled with people all buying books, Deb's was at the till with her mum, and Bradley was walking round smiling.

"I love book shops Birch, I have always loved this one, this shop is the reason I became a writer. I am really glad Deb's took the plunge and bought it; she is perfect for this place."

We stayed for a few hours, and then made our excuses and left, as we walked back towards home, Birch looked at me.

"Do you fancy a walk on the canal, we have never really walked down it have we?" I shrugged.

"Yeah, if you want, that would be really nice."

We walked along a little way, it was cool under the trees, and the still water felt soothing, she looked at me again.

"Can we visit your archway; I mean the last time I was there it was pretty traumatic; I would like to see it under better circumstances?"

We walked along a little further, and I took her up into the trees, on a less steep bank, and came out on the path that ran from my gate. It was nice to be back up here, it had been a really long time since I had walked here, the path was almost over grown, from lack of use.

Birch took my hand, enjoying the walk, as she looked round at the trees. We came up to the arch and I stopped. The floor had been swept, and the large tartan rug from Petal had been laid out, and in the middle was a picnic hamper. I looked at her and she smiled.

"I wanted us to be truly alone for a while, I wanted it to be just us, and what better place than where no one would ever find you?"

I was so happy, I looked at her bright smiling face, and those dancing green eyes, she was so special and beautiful.

"I wanted to thank you Deads, I spoke to my mum last night. She told me how you two had been talking, and how you were worried about me, but were watching over me, my mum was so relieved Deads. This is my way of saying thanks, I believe in the hand of death, a young maiden sits below the arches and eats her bread, where she is attacked and seduced by a vampire, so?"

She dropped to her knees, and started to unbutton my pants; I felt my heart rate increase.

"Birch, this is a pretty public place."

She pulled them down and I felt the cooler air rush, across my legs, she stood up and grabbed my top and pulled it up, I stepped out of my pants.

"Do you honestly think vampires care, my dark little beastie?"

My top came off, and she stood back and admired the view, as she lifted her top. I was scared stiff, and suddenly so turned on, she dropped her top, and unbuttoned her pants, and slipped them down, and never once took her eyes of me.

"First we eat, and then comes the food." It was a line from my book.

She lowered herself, and pulled my arm, pulling me down to the floor with her, I was filled with a sudden raging lust for her. It was almost as if my book was coming to life, as I pulled her close and then kissed her, with a passion like I had never known, she smiled.

"Yes, my dark little beastie, seduce me!"

Our bodies met, and writhed together, I felt wild, free, and untamed, it was the most amazing thing I had ever felt. She rolled me over, and I looked up at the sky, and the archway above me, she was kissing me, ravishing me, and my body was alive, and reacting to her. I gave a sharp intake of breath and closed my eyes, as my back arched, and my body contorted with electricity.

"Oh God!"

Was this it? Is this what it really feels like, to be truly a vampire? My body was burning, and screaming with lust and desire, and I really wanted to bite something.

Chapter 19

# Tarts.

The one certainty you have in this village, is repetition, and like all things, the annual meet up of the Parish Council, to present their summer agenda was tonight. I hated them, but as mum constantly reminded me, everyone goes, it is expected. Birch was unusually happy about it, and smiled as I bitched at my computer, sat in the library with her and Edwina.

"Deads, if we want to get anywhere in this village, we have to be seen to be involved, look at how well Deb's is doing in the bookshop. People are saying some lovely things about her, it has been very positive not just for her, but for all of us." I sighed.

"You are boring when you are always right." Edwina giggled, and winked at me.

The truth was, I loved the village, I loved the row of stone houses converted to shops, the village green, the stately building that was the Hunters. It was a beautiful place, but the fact remained that Marjorie still had a firm grip on opinion. I was one of two of her targets, and even now, I still got snide remarks whilst walking round the place.

"Do I have to go... You go, and take notes for me, I have almost finished my editing and want to do a final cut?" Birch smiled at me.

"Deads Sweetie, what will happen if your mum loses her seat on the council?" I frowned at her, to be honest I could not believe she asked.

"That won't happen.... Will it?" Birch looked at me, with those big bright green eyes.

"Marjorie is gaining momentum again, it could just happen, and if she does, we will be in for a nightmare of a time. We need to be behind your mum, she needs our support now more than ever, and that is why all of us have to be there." She looked at her screen, and I felt something was not quite right, call it a writer's hunch.

"You are up to something, I know it, I don't know how I know it, I just do, so Dr Dixon, what exactly are you cooking up in that crazy head of yours?" She gave a giggle.

"You are getting too good, I need to change tact with you, for the record I do have something in mind, but for now, it is something I am working on alone, in good time Miss Watson, you will find out." I sat back hoping my hard stare would penetrate her defences, she smiled.

"I am immune to that now Sweetie, save it for Deb's it works on her."

We had a meal at the kitchen island, and then got ready, Birch walked into my room in her business suit, I was instantly suspicious, and pointed at her.

"You are... I frigging knew it; you are plotting something big." She smirked.

"Deads I open the practice soon, and I still need a receptionist, it is a new business, and so I will be given a spot tonight to introduce it, that is all, I want to look professional, nothing more." I narrowed my eyes at her.

"I don't trust you; I know you Birch, and any chance you get to have a pop in public at Marjorie, you take it." She started to giggle nervously.

"Sweetie, I have always been restrained around Marjorie, I promise, I am just making an announcement, nothing more."

I accepted it, but I still felt I should have my shields up. I have seen in the past, how Birch is at her more dangerous when she is at her nicest. I remembered her niceness, during her gnome adventures with the vicar in my garden, and so naturally, I did not trust her.

Just like every year, because this village does feel like Groundhog Day most days, Marion was on the door, and I expected her usual derogatory remarks. She handed me a program, and then grabbed my wrist, I panicked a little. Marion leaned into me and lowered her voice.

"Abby, some of us love the bookshop, we know you all helped, and we do like what you have done, but be warned, forces are working against you."

She let go of my hand, and I did not know quite what to say, I cannot believe I did it, but I actually did, I smiled. I mean holy shit I smiled at Marion, and meant it.

"Thanks Marion, thanks for the heads up."

She nodded and lifted a program, and handed it to Chloe. We walked in, and as always, the back row contained all the familiar faces, I sat down and Chloe sat at my side.

"Okay that was fucking creepy, what do you think she meant?" I shook my head.

"I am not sure Chloe, but it has really bothered me, if Marion is switching sides, what the hell is coming?"

The hall filled up as I looked back, and remembered five years ago, and the hard stares, and the silent conversations about me. I had sat almost in the same spot, feeling nervous and afraid, tonight things had moved on, more people said hello, and nodded as they entered, and yet I still felt as nervous as I had then. Was this the writer's instinct I had read so much about? I did not know, but as far as I was concerned, I was taking note of it.

The committee filed on stage, and little had changed. Lillian had stepped down this year, and been replaced by Marion. An additional place had been created for Phillip Morrison the Butcher, but apart from that, it was the usual long drawn out drone of items, events, and the summer festivities. I almost knew it word for word, and was day dreaming when my mother stood up, and announced a presentation by 'Doctor Jemima Dixon.' I bloody knew it, she stood up with some papers in her hand and I scowled at her.

"See... I knew you intended to stir the pot." She gave a giggle, and winked.

"I really love that you know me so well, I knew sleeping with you would be good for us both." I laughed.

"Okay flattery is good, keep it up Doctor."

Birch walked down the centre of the room in her business suit, her ass looked great in those pants, as was noted by a few, who leaned out to look, after she passed them.

There was applause, as she walked onto the stage, Marjorie looked as dark as thunder, as Birch passed the long table, and stood at the podium. She adjusted the mic, as those clapping for her, slowly died down, she smiled, God she reminded me of Roni from that night of her talk here.

"Ladies and gentlemen, members of the Parish Council, I am delighted to stand here tonight, before you as a member of this village, because as some of you may or may not know, I recently took up residency here. Tonight, I would like with your indulgence to talk a little about the future of village life."

She was so like Roni, clear and precise, and I leant forward in my chair to watch her.

"I grew up in a place not unsimilar to this in the North of England, on the outskirts of Manchester, it had a slightly larger population, and was on a major transport route, so it was busier, but in many ways, the two places are very similar. There is one thing both places share, which is a trend throughout all villages in the UK, and that is the very real problem that children are growing up, and leaving the village to find work. The impact of this is having a major detrimental effect on what will be the future of village life, and it needs to be curbed." Chloe leaned into me.

"Oh fuck, she is about to go on a crusade, and why do I suddenly feel we will need helmets and shields?" I gave her a nod.

"You know Birch, she gets an idea, and we all end up involved, one way or the other."

"I have been a frequent visitor to Wotton. Five years ago, I spent the whole of the summer here, and I cannot deny I was very impressed, at just how much this community does with its young people's initiative, to help keep them entertained and happy, over the summer. Even today, you had a wonderful set up of games and crafts, supervised by Marjorie Wallace, and Marion Butler Davis, and by the look of it, most of the young people aged eighteen and under have had a wonderful day. It is a glowing example of how this village can support every generation, and yet I feel there is one area that is not being addressed, and I wish to bring it to your attention." Deb's leaned forward next to Chloe, and looked at me.

"Oh, shit Abby, she is going to pick on us, isn't she?"

I had no idea, but I was glued to her, waiting and watching. Birch looked round the room at everyone, who was giving her their undivided attention.

"In recent weeks I have been involved in a series of talks with Felicity Watson, Chair Person of the council, and have aired my thoughts, and sought her approval. Because while there are many events for people under eighteen, and a lot of events that attract our older residents, there is however, a short fall in opportunities for those aged eighteen to thirty years old. That is the bracket, most at risk of leaving the village to seek employment." Chloe nodded.

"Yep, she is on a crusade, oh fuck what has she got us into now?"

"I am here tonight to ask you all to consider this problem, because I feel with support from this community, we really could do some good. Think of it this way, do any of you want your sons and daughters to leave the village? If you do not, then please try and help out. There is another way, and that is currently being highlighted by those younger adults in the heart of this community, and is probably going unnoticed." Deb's nodded.

"Yep, we are about to be put in the spotlight guys, here comes Joan of Wotton, on her white horse, brandishing her sword of the totally insane, and guess who is going to get to run alongside her?"

Chloe and I giggled, Debs was right, Birch did look like a conquering heroine, and I was actually very drawn to her, as she stood on the stage.

"For the last few years Antonio, has made brave changes to the salon with his business partner Delphine, and as a result of that approach, they now employ two young people from this village as stylists. One is qualified, and one currently training, that is two people who have not left this village. Last week Miss Debbie Ford Wheeler, reopened the bookshop, after a complete remodelling, and that has allowed her to expand her range of books offering a far bigger selection, than previously. All the old favourites and genres are still available, because she worked very closely with Agatha Willington, to ensure none of her old customers were excluded. The fact is, as even Agatha admitted, without Debbie, the shop would have closed forever. She is twenty four years old, and will be part of the future of this village, that is one more young adult who is not lost to the wider world." Deb's put her head down and went beetroot.

"Oh, I really wish she would not do this shit without a trigger warning."

Birch smiled as she saw me watching her, even from the back I saw the twinkle in her eyes.

"I stood in the bookshop the day it opened, and I saw something really touching. Our very own local author, was approached and asked by a young teenager, if she would sign the copy of her book, that she had just purchased from Debbie. It was a delight to see Abigail Jennifer Watson, village resident and Author, meet her first home fan. Why are we not supporting her creative work more, she is twenty four years old?"

I love her, I really do, and in a weird way that really hit me hard in the chest. People turned round to look at me and smiled, but I was really smiling at Birch, she always managed to surprise me when I least expected it. Birch looked round the room.

"Only last week another local talent took her first steps into village life, when she joined our resident artist Harriet Barker, and acted as her assistant during the two day series of art classes. Chloe Pemberton is twenty four years old, and is a very talented artist, who is just setting up her web site, so that she can remain a resident in this village, and work in her newly created studio. Her sister Edwina Pemberton, now runs a rapidly growing home based business based in this village, using her graphic design and computer qualifications, and exceptional skills, to supply modern fast running ecommerce web sites, and contract work for large companies such as K.O. Productions, a global promotions agency, she will be twenty six in just two months." Edwina leaned forward and shrugged.

"I can use the plug, it all helps towards the rent, and sexy knickers." I smirked.

"You never wear any from what I see." She winked.

"I am not trying to entice you into my bed, so I don't need them." Birch continued.

"This week I will finally get into the new business venture I have set up, which will fill the large space that used to be the Charity Shop. Sweetie's Retreat will offer help and support, and therapies to the whole community. I am twenty five, and a qualified Doctor in Forensic and Clinical Psychology, and I have also completed all my stages of counselling qualifications. When I open the practice, one of my first employees will be Gillian Barker Tomlinson, she is a local girl, and is twenty three years old, she will head up my front team at reception, and handle most of the administration duties of my practice."

I looked at Hatty sat not that far away, and she smiled and winked, she was enjoying this. Birch continued.

"Sweeties Retreat is also looking to fill two vacancies for reception work, and Miss Wheeler has asked if I would also inform you that she will be advertising for a shop assistant for the bookshop. Ladies and gentlemen, that is ten jobs saved, and ten less young adults leaving this village. Felicity and myself want to do more, because young adults now are vital to the preservation of the future of this village. I have seen Molly and Sophia, and Nigel, all volunteering to help out at all village events, but it is not enough, we need your daughters and sons, to join in and get involved more in village life. We have some very capable council members, and their skills need to be passed on and shared, so that a whole new generation can benefit from their experience. They need you to support them, and if you are a local employer, look to bringing them into your business, and keeping them employed here, not in other parts of the country." Norman stood up and raised his hand, Birch smiled.

"Yes Mr Merryweather." He smiled.

"I will have four vacancies at the nursery come September, as we expand into new lines, young people can come and see me at the nursery if they are interested." Birch held out her hand.

"Thank you, Mr Merryweather, that will be fourteen people contributing to this village. See ladies and gentlemen, we can have a future and we can keep our traditions, but we need to keep our young adults employed to do it. In regard to that and with encouragement and support from Felicity Watson, your Parish Council Chair, I am looking for some young volunteers to join me in setting up The Adult Recognition, Training Support program. It will run through Sweeties Retreat, and help find new ways to not only involve, but retain our young adults in village life. It does not matter what your politics in this village are, be they young or old, traditional or modern, all of us have the same agenda, which is to keep this village alive, and looking as perfectly picturesque as it is today. Next Friday I will introduce my new staff in an open day as the retreat prepares to open, I would like all of you to please come along and have a look at the operation, we plan to do so much more than mental health, and we would love to see you there. Ladies and gentlemen, members of the Parish Council, I give you my thanks for your kind attention, thank you."

She walked with a smile, as the whole room applauded, Hatty slid along the seats close to me with a big smile.

"And that Abby, is a future council leader, I hope you will be sat at her side... Look at Madge, talk about the most public fuck you Birch has ever done, I just think she has saved your mums seat on the council for another year, Christ she is good." Deb's leaned in.

"Did Birch just announce a new council program, named T.A.R.T.S, you know what, I bloody love her?"

I had not even realised, we all started laughing, and I could not help but wonder, if Madge had even noticed. People stopped her, to shake her hand as she passed, it appeared the Tarts program was a big hit. Marjorie turned at the table and looked at Felicity.

"Why was I not aware of any of this, I should have been consulted?" Felicity smiled.

"Madge, Birch has been working on this for some time, but with the house and the practice, she was not sure she would be ready in time, so I waited for her. This afternoon, I was meeting in the Tea Rooms with Celia, Peter and Phillip, when she called me, so I put her on speaker phone, and she spoke to all of us, and the four of us all agreed it was a wonderful idea. To be honest, we all thought you would be on board with it, after all, maintaining this village to a high standard, has always been your biggest concern, and with this program, it may well ensure your legacy continues for many more years."

Marjorie knew when she had been skilfully out manoeuvred, and she was well aware that to oppose it would not go down well in the village, she had been backed into a corner, and she knew it.

"There is no doubt I will support everything that maintains the highs standards of this village, all I was asking was why was I not informed of something of this importance? Felicity I am the Vice Chair, a little prior warning is all I seek, but I will commend all of you for allowing such a program to move forward." She turned back to the table and banged the gavel.

"Can we please settle down; we have much to do. Right, now, on to the summer list of upcoming events, may I remind all of you, that just as Dr Dixon has already implied, if any of us want a village for our young, we must support all the organised events. We still have tickets remaining for all events, please do your part and support them." Birch sat down with a huge smile.

"That was fun." I looked at her.

"I am assuming this is a Curio's driven thing?" She gave a giggle.

"You know, all of you are inspirational, and I think the village needed to know just how much. You know guys there is a serious aspect to all this, if we win over the younger adults, we all gain more acceptance, and the more of that we have, the harder it will be for the parents of those young adults, to side with Marjorie. Come on guys, what parent who has their child close is going to fight us, look how happy your mum is Chloe that you moved back closer to her, and Deads, look at the change in your mum having you home. This is good for everyone not just us."

She was right, I could not argue with her, but there was one flaw that I had spotted.

"What about your Mum Birch, do you not think she feels the same?" She patted my leg.

"I am going home for a couple of weeks in September, to spend some time with her."

"You are?" She smiled.

"Sorry, we are." She winked. "Once the practice is running and Izzy has found her feet, I thought I would drive us up there to see the moors, and walk with her on them. It will also be nice to see Bev." Deb's leaned forward and looked round.

"Guard your vagina's." I burst out laughing.

Finally, the meeting came to a close, and everyone, as tradition dictates, hung back to talk and have refreshments. As Curio tradition dictates, it was time for a fast exit, and alcohol, Hatty stood up.

"And just where do all of you think you are going?" I looked at her feeling confused.

"Home, to get pissed." She shook her head.

"I do not think so girls, Flick warned me you would do this... Oh no, you do not drop a youth bomb on Madge, and then bugger off, nope, you stay to face it, so all of you can park those asses right back where you lifted them from, you are our new inspirational youth, so bloody act like it."

There was only one thing we could do, she was using her teacher voice, so we took the usual route, we sulked and sat down.

It was not long before we were spotted, the five females and one male, all sat in an orderly row, and once spied, we faced the onslaught. Hands were shaken questions were asked, and I stood at the side of Birch trying to look inspirational. Chloe was approached by a young seventeen year old, who she recognised from the art sessions when she assisted Hatty, he gave a nervous smile.

"Hi… I wondered if I could talk to you… Sort of privately, it's about my drawings?" Chloe smiled.

"How can I help you; I saw you working with Hatty at the summer event didn't I, don't you want to speak to her?" He gave a nervous cough.

"It's a little bit… I don't know, delicate, and she being my teacher from college, you know, she can be a bit scary, which is why I wanted to talk with you." Chloe shrugged.

"Okay, so what do you need to know?"

He looked at Deb's, Edwina and Anthony, and then me, he pinked up a little, and I could not resist.

"You want to paint naughty pictures don't you, it's okay we have modelled nude for Hatty, and Chloe does amazing erotic art, chill out we get it." He went beetroot and Chloe smiled.

"The human form presents a lot of challenges for an artist, but with the right connections, you can have the advantage of good models to work with."

The poor lad he looked so embarrassed, and yet Chloe was completely at ease with it, she smiled.

"Have you ever posed for an artist, dressed or otherwise?" He looked surprised.

"Well no… I mean, I am supposed to be the one doing the drawing, I use porn clips and pause them, but my drawings lack something." Chloe understood.

"Been there and done that, what you need is to pose yourself, that is the only way you will understand the model, and what you ask of them, and then with some help, you will be able to access good models. I tell you what, call round tomorrow, and I will show you some of my work, I am at three Waterside Lane, not too early mind, we are planning on a few drinks later." She smiled and he looked delighted.

"Thanks... I really do appreciate this, I really do." She smiled at him.

"Good, so what is your name?" He gave a gasp.

"Fuck... Oh sorry.... It's Gavin." Chloe smiled.

"Okay Gavin... See you tomorrow, bring your sketches." He gave a big beetroot smile and walked off; Deb's looked at Chloe.

"My god, you are going to bang him, aren't you?" Chloe smiled, and shrugged.

"That is up to him, but we are getting our kit off, are you going to join us?" Deb's gave a shy smile and went beetroot.


Anthony ended up surrounded by girls, which he loved, and was his usual dramatic self, he stood pawing the different girl's hair, making comments.

"Oh darling, you have bleached it to straw... Oh deary dear, what on earth have you been putting on this? Well girl I have to admit, you are brave to be seen in public with this thatch, oh I have no idea what you girls have been thinking, you all must come, and let me work my magic on you as soon as possible."

Edwina was sat with three men talking about web sites, and Birch was very busy talking to a lot of very happy parents. I stood watching and thinking, what has she started, when a young boy and his girlfriend came up to me. He smiled at me.

"Miss Watson." I feel so weird when they call me that. He pulled a book out of his pocket.

"Would you mind signing our books, we love your works, and we have been told you are preparing another one?"

It is such a weird thing to happen, it is like embarrassing, and yet thrilling at the same time. I took the book, and a hand came out holding a pen, it was Birch, she did not look at me, but carried on talking. I chuckled; God was there nothing she was not prepared for? I slipped through the chairs in front, to get closer, and sat down on the one that had been in front of me.

"I am actually working on two, I have my third vampire book ready, but I have been doing a read through, and making some adjustments, and I have written something more personal, about the life of a gang of girls. I am hoping to get one of them out soon, I am just polishing them up at the moment. Okay what name do I put in it?" He leaned forward, and he was definitely looking down my top.

"It is Mark."

I looked up, and smiled, then opened the book and signed the page, a flash alerted me to the fact Hatty had her camera out, and I looked up, and handed the book back.

"Thanks for reading it Mark, I appreciate it." I looked at the girl, who blushed as she handed me hers, she looked familiar.

"I know you right?" She went really beetroot.

"I am Stacy's younger sister Angelina; my sister works in the Tea Rooms. It is her book, she is a massive fan, she asked me to get it signed. I think your friend scared her a little." I understood, Izzy thought she was into me sexually, she wasn't she was a fan of my writing.

"Is she here Angelina?" She turned, and pointed.

"She is over there with my parents."

I looked up and saw her peering from her father's shoulder, she saw me looking, and jumped back out of sight, I giggled and signed the book.

"I will hand it back to her personally, if that is alright with you?" Angelina gave a huge smile.

"That would mean so much to her, it really would, she never stops talking about your stories, she is dying to read the next one."

I got up and walked down the hall towards where she had disappeared behind her father. I walked right up holding the book, and held it out to her.

"Ignore Izzy, her bark is far greater than her bite... Thank you Stacy for reading my story, I will make sure you get advanced copies of the next ones." Stacy turned scarlet, she smiled, and her mum looked at her.

"What do you say Stace?" She opened the book and looked at the signature, she smiled a huge smile and looked at me.

"I am so grateful for this, thank you Miss Watson, I love your books, I cannot wait for more.”

Her mum smiled at me, and I nodded, I looked at Stacy, she was holding the book like it was her greatest prize staring at the inscription.

“Call me Abby, we live in the same village.” She looked up, and her eyes sparkled, she nodded.

“Thank you, Abby, thank you so much.” I smiled.

“My pleasure, and nice to meet a fan who cares.”

I walked back and felt really good, Birch had been watching me, and she smiled as I walked towards her. Mum was talking to her, and she turned as I approached.

“I should have known, only you can make Birch smile like that. I was just saying how wonderful her presentation was, it has really struck a chord in the community, I hope you will be joining us and helping?” I gave a chuckle as Deb’s joined us.

“Do any of us really have a choice? It’s a Birch thing, we will get dragged kicking and screaming into this no matter whether we want to or not.” Mum gave a chuckle.

“Birch was right about all of you, she told the truth Abigail, all of you should be recognised for your efforts, and you are inspiring to the others around here. This village needs to see that, because one day Marjorie and myself will be too old and too tired to continue, do you honestly want this village handed to Molly and Sophia?”

Now that was a chilling thought, Molly with her fire and brimstone, spouting from the stage, made me an instant fan of Tarts.

“I am in, anything but Molly, my god she would bore god himself to death.”


Hatty was becoming as annoying as a tourist, as she ran round taking pictures of everyone and everything, I was afraid she would follow us into the toilet to prove we were healthy, fit and strong. I raised a finger as she aimed, and shot the picture anyway, she grinned.

“That is definitely going on the web site…. Edwin, say cheese, it’s for the Parish Paper.”

I laughed as my dad looked angry, and turned his back on her, some things never change in this village. Hatty walked off giggling.

It was finally over, and we all walked together home, we all had one thing in mind, get naked, and get drunk, after all it was Friday night, and under the Uni rules, that is what Fridays are for, it's a girl's thing.

We all flopped back on the sofas, armed with drinks and released from our clothing, and relaxed. Chloe put on some music, and we all slouched, she danced next to the coffee table shaking her hips and giggling, and then she turned round and looked at all of us.

"Who wants to model naked for a virgin school boy?" Deb's looked up from her drink.

"He is seventeen and a college student, and how do you know he is a virgin?" Chloe gave a knowing smile.

"You were there Deb's did you not see it?" She frowned.

"No... What was I supposed to see?" Chloe giggled.

"His junk... He was fully up, and holy shit, if he was not just fucking huge, honestly, I am on first, but if you guys want to share, you are all my sisters and I love you, that dick, needs to be screwed, and all of you should go for it."

Deb's looked shocked, and Birch and myself burst out laughing, Chloe danced round and round, wiggling her hips, with a huge saucy smile on her face. Deb's blushed, but I could tell, she was definitely thinking about it.

Chapter 20

# Artisans.

By midday, Birch and I sat outside on the grass at the side of the pool, nursing really bad headaches. We had the tartan rug out, and lay back, the day was heating up, and this had been our first day since moving in, that we had enjoyed the garden. Edwina was in the pool doing lengths.

Gavin arrived with a stack of pads, and was met at the door by Chloe in her long robe, she led him through to the studio, and he had a good look round, and was blown away by her work, he asked a thousand questions, I leaned up on my elbows.

"Chloe has her fresh meat." Birch looked up and smiled.

"Poor bugger, she looks so frail and feminine, he has no idea of the predator that is lurking in her crotch. I bet you ten, she has her vagina out in less than ten minutes." I looked at her.

"I bet you she has his dick out first, she really wants that monster." Birch giggled.

Chloe plugged in her tablet to the cable, and walked over to Gavin, she felt his chest, and smiled.

"Good you have a defined chest, take your top off." She knelt down, and felt his calve muscles, she looked at him. "You are wearing underwear, right?" He blushed, and swallowed hard.

"Yes." She stood up.

"Okay take your pants off, and turn sideways on to me, then twist your waist, so I can see your torso, and watch the screen."

She walked to the large screen mounted on the wall, and switched it on, she picked up her light pen. Gavin was beetroot, stood in just his underpants. He posed as Chloe had told him, she stepped back and examined him, she walked back to him, and gently moved his shoulders. She smiled, knelt down and inched his front leg forward to reveal the other leg.

"Yeah, these don't work."

She suddenly gripped the waist of his underpants, and pulled them straight down, he let out a squeal. I looked at Birch.

"Told ya, you owe me ten quid." She giggled. Chloe stepped back and admired Gavin's body.

"Oh Gav, you have a body worth drawing, now watch the screen." She lifted her light pen and started to sketch.

"See how I work from the centre out, that way my first aspect of the drawing sets the perspective, and the ratio."

Her hand moved like lightning, she looked at him, as he stood frozen, and she drew his pectoral muscles. She stopped, and pulled off her robe and it fell down revealing her naked body, and carried on sketching. Birch sat up.

"Oh dear, I do believe we have growth."

"Holy shit she was not kidding. How old is he?" Edwina had stopped swimming, and was resting on the side of the pool, watching.

"He is old enough to jump on, is he going to stop growing?"

Chloe was in her element as she sketched lower. Gavin was beetroot staring at the screen, watching as Chloe drew him, well actually his penis. He apologised, but she shook her head.

"I fucking love sex, and sex is art, this is brilliant, I will paint this body in hundreds of different ways, now can you see how the model inspires the artist?"

He was slightly overcoming his embarrassment as he watched himself appear on the screen, and it was fascinating to see. She had his enlarged penis, legs and torso, and sketched in his arms.

"You should not expect a model to do something you have not. You have a wonderful body Gav; I am sure the ladies at college love it?" He looked at her.

"They do not understand my art, they are not interested in me." Chloe looked up from her sketch.

"What... That is insane, you have a fantastic body, so I take it, a lack of a girlfriend is why you have no model to draw, because most artist's sketch those they are around?" He looked saddened, she looked up, and studied his shoulder.

"So, sketching porn cannot be easy, all those hormones running round inside, you need to release that. I draw a hundred times better after I have had my brains screwed out, and honestly, I can only paint after several good orgasms, it sort of clears my mind and helps me focus."

She leaned slightly to the side, and sketched in some detail, he was really blown away by the way she was drawing, layer by layer, she looked up.

"Would you like to sketch my naked form, looking at the size of your expansion, I am taking it you like what you see?" He took a deep breath.

"I am not used to seeing naked women, but yes, honestly Chloe, you have a really beautiful body." She smiled.

"Aw, thank you Gav…. So, do you want to shag it?" He looked panicked; Chloe gave a giggle.

"Chill out it is okay to find someone you work with desirable, if you are going to work with models you need to be very open and honest. Getting the right picture is all that matters, but it is okay to bang your models if they want to as well, that is the point of an artisan life, it is open and free, so are we screwing when I finish or not?" He gave a slight nod.

"I have never done it before." Chloe smiled and gave him a wink; her hand was working quicker.

"Do not worry about a little thing like that Gav, I have more than enough experience, for the both of us…. Okay done, what do you think?" He stared at it with wonder.

"Wow that is really amazing."

Chloe walked over and took him by the hand, and moved him to the small bed, she lay him back, and then went to work. Birch turned to me.

"You have got to admit, it is a privilege watching her work, I mean she does not disappoint?" I looked at her straddling, him and writhing around on him.

"Well she does not piss about, that is for sure." Edwina gave a sigh.

"I want a cock now, I have been all girls recently, I need some man action. For the first time in my life, I am actually jealous of Chloe. We need a party guys, with men here, or we need to go somewhere, like the lake."

I have not thought about the lake in years, wow those were really wild days that summer. I lay back as Chloe approached orgasm, and I wondered if the new kids still did that. Were the new younger generation as wild as we were? It was hard to work out, here in the village it felt like no one had sex. I mean, I assumed they did, after all the village had kids, but compared to the kids that were around our age back then, today's kids appeared less interested and more uptight, I somehow found it hard to imagine them being as free as we had been. Chloe came very vocally, and Edwina slipped off the side.

"Shit I am depressed." She slipped under the water out of sight, Birch giggled and looked at me.

"What do you think, do you feel the need to have a man, you know I do not want you to turn it down; we are us; we can screw others, I have never put limits on you, just like at the campsite?" I lay back and slipped my glasses over my face.

"I am fine with what we have, but if the opportunity arose like it did at the camp, I would probably take it up if I liked them enough. I hope you would too Birch, I cannot deny I have often wondered, because back in Uni, you could not get enough." She lay back in the sun.

"We were all different at Uni Deads, that feels like a life time away. I think if it presented itself and I wanted to I would, but as for every night of the week, I don't really need that these days."

I could really understand that, I felt exactly the same, I stretched out, and just let the time slip past, enjoying relaxing in the garden. Chloe walked down with an arm full of cold beers, she was sweating pretty hard. She placed one each, down at the side of us.

"Fuck that thing is a monster, I am shagged out." I chuckled.

"We saw."

"Gav wants to sketch nudes; do you mind if he does you guys whilst I coach him?" Birch lifted her head.

"I am easy with it, but be warned, if that thing comes up again, Edwina is on the hunt, and you owe her for a drummer." Chloe shivered.

"Fuck Birch, I told you, never mention Zac again, I am dreading the wedding, he will be there, and I will have to look at him in the daylight." Birch sniggered.

"And he is five years older, and more worn out, I pity you Chloe, but look on the bright side, you got him when he was good looking." She gave a huge shudder, I burst out laughing.

Gavin walked down the grass looking sheepish, he was still naked, and had been fine with Chloe, but around us he became very self conscious. Edwina surfaced and swam to the edge, where she leaned on the stone, and watched his groin for movement.

Deb's came out in her robe and walked down to us, she dropped her robe, and then sat down, and that was when she noticed Gavin, she looked suddenly shy, as she stared between his legs, I giggled, and handed her my spare mirrored sun glasses, and lay back in the sun. Gavin was happily drawing as Chloe sat at his side, and gave him instruction, when mum and Hatty appeared round the side of the garage, with towels.

"Abby can we borrow the pool, it's hot, and your dad is being annoying, and has decided to drain ours and clean it?" I lifted my hand to wave, Gavin looked terrified, Chloe patted his leg.

"Get used to this, I told you about the life of an artisan, well those two are the best bloody artists for miles."

He looked at them, they rested their towels on the chair, slipped off their pants and tops, and dived in. My mum had on her bikini, Hatty as always wore nothing, this was more than a little eye opening for him, he continued to sketch. Chloe watched over his shoulder, making points and encouraging him, I actually thought she was pretty cool, in the way she was patient, and gave him good tips. We moved a lot so he had to sketch fast.

I also liked that Chloe gave him canned drinks and no alcohol, it is so easy to see her as irresponsible, but she wasn't, she was actually really level headed with him, and very nurturing. I mean she had screwed his brains out not long back, but watching her and the way she took care of him, was actually quite sweet.

Edwina came out of the pool and stretched out on the grass to dry, this was the most relaxed day we had seen in ages. She turned to Birch.

"There is a group of IT advisors I was helping train last week, down from Cambridge, they are attending a seminar in Oxendale. I texted them, and asked if they are up for a visit, I told them to bring plenty of booze. They say it will be about eight to nine when they get here, they are a fun lot, and decent people. If they all come, it will be about six women and nine guys, so we need to get ready later. I have said nothing to Flick or Hatty, so we will talk after they leave." We both nodded and she lay back.

Mum and Hatty came out of the pool, saw a sketch pad, and zoned in on it, Gavin became nervous. Hatty sat down and went through his sketches, she showed them my mum.

"These are pretty good, this one of Deb's is really nice." She sat up.

"What, he has drawn me?" Hatty looked at her.

"Yeah, and it is really good, see."

She handed it over, and Deb's looked at it, she seemed really pleased.

"Can I have this, I mean if it is for your course work or anything I will understand, but Gavin this is really amazing." He smiled at her.

"You had just the right pose, I could not help drawing it, but yes if you want it, I would love you to have it. Thanks for liking it so much, that means a lot to me."

A new artist was born, under the direction of Chloe, sat naked in the garden, Gavin had realised his dream, and having given the picture away, he had become officially a nude artist.

It is the strange thing about living with artists, you get quite use to looking up from a book or a computer, and seeing Chloe, or Edwina with a pad, sketching you. Edwina converts hers into digital characters, whereas Chloe paints them, the house is filled with them, so lying in the garden, being sketched by Gavin, just felt normal. It was getting really hot, but I was so calm and relaxed, and enjoying being laid back with my eyes closed, listening to the conversation, I was happy to let the day drift by.

He left at four, dressed, happy, and very relaxed, and grinning from ear to ear. He swapped numbers with Chloe, and promised to keep her up to date, and she printed him out a copy of her sketch of him to take with him, she even signed it, and in a way, that was our first Tart project completed, another young person wanted to live in the village and become an artist.

It had been a hot day, so we swam in the pool and talked, and drank more beer, I showered around six to freshen up. Hatty pointed out we had loungers in the pool house, none of us had actually been in there, so we carried them out and set them up on the patio. The back garden faced south, so the sun beat down onto the patio all day.

Birch fired up the hot tub, and filled the fridge with extra booze from our stock pile. With new bulbs in the cellar, it provided us the perfect store for the booze, so we had stocked up big, and all of it was stored out of sight, and kept really cool. Chilling it in the fridge took half the time. We were outside on the loungers enjoying the cooler sun, when the party arrived, and we had all forgotten to dress.

Our guests piled outside, saw we were naked, and loved it, and they all stripped on the spot, and Debs had them place their folded clothes on the kitchen table. A couple of the women went down to their underwear, but that did not last long, it was amazing. They piled up their booze, which was a huge pile, music went on in the background, they swam in the pool or jumped in the hot tub, and generally lazed around hitting on each other.

Edwina beat Chloe, and scored first. She was talking to a couple, and explained how she had built a site for unicorns, I really need to look that up. They appeared very interested to find out she had led the way on the site, and shortly after, she excused herself with them both, and disappeared upstairs. Chloe took a few guys to see her art, and less came back, so I assumed she too had scored.

I was sat with Birch, and was getting plenty of attention from John and Daniel, especially Daniel, who was supplying the drinks on a regular basis. Both of them were good looking guys, and reasonably hung, until I noticed Daniel had a white patch of skin round his finger. He was married, and had removed his ring, Birch had already spotted it, she saw me look at it, and leaned in and whispered.

"Sweetie, I have no idea how you feel, but that for me is a no go zone, shame really I would have had him if you didn't. There is no judgement, it is up to you." I already knew he was off the table for me, I looked at John.

"Fancy a swim?" He smiled.

"I would love too." I grabbed his hand, and walked towards the pool; I was feeling happy and giddy, and very relaxed and calm. Birch looked at Daniel.

"So where is the ring, how long have you been married?" He

looked embarrassed.

"It is at the hotel, and two years." She gave a sigh.

"When a woman sees a ring, she has a choice, personally it is a no go for me, but I know other girls who are not as picky. When you try to hide it, you remove that choice, and that is how people get badly hurt."

She got up and walked into the kitchen; Barry followed her. He leaned on the fridge, as she opened a bottle of vodka, and poured out a measure, then topped it with cola. She offered him the bottle, he waved his hand, and she put it on the unit, he smiled.

"I like what you said, Danny is having problems at home." Birch leaned on the unit, and took a drink.

"I am not frigging surprised, he has been married only two years, and he is trying to screw around. I bet his wife is not out sleeping with other men, maybe she is not happy about that, what about you, are you married?" He gave a laugh.

"No, that is not for me, I spend too much time on the road, it is a life that suits me. I have seen a lot of marriage's crumble because of this job, I am not walking into that pain any time soon." Birch nodded.

"Good answer, so why did you follow me in, was it to tell me what an awesome guy you are, or was it just to see if you could screw me?" He smirked.

"Well, I did not intend on coming here just to screw all of you, no, all I wanted was just to explain Danny, he is not a bad guy, his life is not good." Birch shrugged.

"Okay so Danny is wonderful, I still meant what I said, he should never hide the ring, a woman has the right to choose, not me, I don't go there, but others will. So, you wanna see my room?" He looked at her.

"You are pretty direct you know?" She gave a chuckle.

"I like direct, it cuts out all the lame flirting bullshit, you never asked me if I want to screw you?" Barry looked surprised.

"I never thought to ask?" She smiled.

"Good answer... I mean it's a lie, you have been watching me for forty minutes, you entered, eyed up Deads and me, could not choose, and waited. When Deads walked off with John, and I rebuked dear Danny, you knew I was the one for you, so you followed me in here, and played nice guy Barry. I think that is about right, am I wrong?" He started to laugh.

"I really do like you, I find you a tad intimidating, but I do love your straight talk." She grinned.

"Hell, if you think this is intimidating, wait until you are in my bed, it's this way, you coming?" She walked off, and he followed, quietly laughing to himself.


Feeling warm, very relaxed, buzzed from the alcohol, and happy, laughing in the pool having had a few minutes of fooling around, I opened my legs, as John swam towards me. As he got closer, I locked them behind him, and pulled him in, he wasted no time. I stretched my arms out along the side of the pool, and he started to kiss me, I could feel his hands sliding over my wet warm body, as he explored me. It felt strange, I felt the hands of John on my skin, they were rougher, and more aggressive than the soft touch of Birch, and yet I liked it.

I slid one arm off the side and slipped it into the water, he was getting hard, and I gripped it and stroked, as his hand slipped between my opened legs, I leaned back with my head on the edge, and gave a long soft moan, he was rough, but he was doing the job nicely. He was getting a lot harder, I let go, and put my arm back on the side, and then lifted myself out of the water slightly, I could feel it stroking my entrance, and I felt that strong yearning to lower down on it.

I gasped as he suddenly lurched up. "OH SHIT!!!"

His hands gripped my waist, and he held me, as he slowly slid up and down. It had felt like an age, and I was drowning in desire, and then I remembered. I pushed on the side and slipped off him, gasping.

"Oh god John, I need this I really do, but you cannot cum in me, you need a condom." He looked a little pissed off, but backed up and nodded, I smiled.

"It is okay you know; I have plenty in my room." He smiled, then looked down.

"I cannot exactly walk up there like this."

I giggled. I pointed across the grass were two of the group were screwing on the grass in front of everyone else. I reached for his hand and pulled him on to the steps.

"Come on and hurry, I need you back on the job very quickly."

We ran across the grass laughing, John's swollen manhood, bouncing around in front of him, we hit the kitchen with smiles, and I took him up the stairs. Some woman was screaming for God, I assumed it was Edwina's female member of the couple. We entered my room, to the sounds of a man moaning and groaning in Birch's room, whatever she was doing it was working.

Still dripping from the pool, I dropped down to my knees, and took him into my mouth, it was not long before my magic tongue had the desired effect, and he leaned back moaning. One last long slurp and he was ready, I grabbed the condom out of the bedside unit drawer, tore it open with my teeth, and slipped it on. I jumped back on the bed, and he followed, he wasted no time and slid in, then leaned forward and kissed my boobs, oh wow, I chose right, this guy was good.

I reached up and gripped the head board, and arched my back, then pushed my hips at him hard, and he slammed into me. Birch gave a long low moan next door, and a tingle shot through my system, listening to her screwing was turning me on more. John grabbed my legs and lifted them up, he shuffled close, and began to thrust hard, I thought I would die, and my whole body exploded with tingles.

He pounded into me, and my head bobbed with each thrust, but oh the sensations, I had shots of tingles in every direction from my vagina. I could feel it building, he started to pant and moan, and I gripped the head board tighter.

"Oh... oh... oh... oh... Oh John yes, keep going I am going to cum." He pounded harder and then lifted me slightly higher off the bed, my head exploded as he hit my spot, and I was flooded with electric shocks.

"HOLY SHIT!!!!" In the other room Birch screamed out.

"OH GOD.... OH GOD.... OH GOD!!!!!"

I think it was getting John even hotter. I was going to cum, I was so close as my body burned.

"OH, OH, OH, OH, OH, OH, I AM CUMMING!" My head suddenly exploded, in the other room Birch gave a loud squeal of joy.

John went upright and stiffened, his whole body shook, and my vagina throbbed and exploded again, I thought my stomach was going to explode. I let out a long loud moan to mask his. He sagged and I fell limp on to the bed, my whole body trembling, he rolled off me gasping for air, and lay on his back

"Christ girl, that was amazing."

I lay there looking up at the ceiling gasping for air, I did not want to talk, all I wanted to do was just lie there, feeling the ripples that were running wild through my body.

I drifted in bliss, I was so relaxed and mellow, John was in the bathroom that joined the two rooms pissing, I heard the flush, and hoped that was the condom, I hated finding those cold buggers on the floor, guys can be really disgusting. He walked back in and sat on the bed, and smiled.

"Thanks for that, it was wonderful, I really needed it."

I smiled; the ass could not even remember my name. I patted his back, but I felt dreamy, light headed and happy.

"You were amazing John, you can head back down if you want, and grab a drink, I need a few more moments, I will be down in a bit."


He left the room and I relaxed, and took a breath, wow my head was buzzing, sex had never done that before. I felt the calmness swirling over me, it was glorious, like I was floating, and I slowly regulated my breathing. I swallowed in the calm, and just drifted along nice and relaxed, and I have no idea how long for, it was longer than normal, but it was a glorious and relaxed feeling I had, it was almost like floating.

"What the fuck do you think you are doing?" I twitched, and jerked and opened my eyes.

"Birch is that you?" The ceiling looked misty, and filled with little twinkling lights.

"GET THE FUCK OFF HER, YOU FUCKING CREEP!" I smiled a big smile.

"Chloe, baby where is you, I want to see you paint me?"

"FUCKING WANKER.... BIRCH... BIRCH, I NEED YOU, IT'S ABBY!"

"What the hell is going on, what are you doing here, get the hell out Daniel?"

"Birch he was stood in front of her wanking, I think he was going to fuck her, Birch, Abby is out for the count, do you think he drugged her?"

Birch appeared over me, she was floating and glowing like an angel, I smiled.

"Hey sweetie pie, where ya been, don't hang up there you will drop sweetie?" My face knocked, and I blinked.

"Deads... Deads Sweetie come back to me, come on Sweetie wake up, IZZY GET HIM THE HELL OUT OF HERE, THE PARTY IS OVER, DEADS HAS BEEN SPIKED!"

"Is she alright, she was fine when I left her honestly, we just had great sex, nothing else." I laughed out loud.

"Johnny you screw ace mate, I frigging loved it."

"Deads Sweetie, come on baby wake up, John who got the drinks, was it you?"

"No, I was talking to you guys, I am not sure, someone was handing out beers."

"Izzy take Chloe, find that piece of shit Daniel, frisk the bastard, if he has any on him, you go full frigging BDSM on his ass, then throw him the hell out."

The room was getting louder, and the clouds were moving away, I didn't want that, they were lovely, I loved floating, it was so relaxing and peaceful. I felt my face being patted.

"Please baby wake up." I heard Birch sob.

"No... No cry... No cry it's not nice."

I saw her again and smiled, then frowned. Her eyes were filled with tears. I lifted my hand to her face.

"Birch your eyes are wet." She smiled, and gave a gasp of a sob.

"I know baby, I was missing you."

She lifted me close, and held me tight, it felt warm and delightful as we drifted and floated around together.

"Here I made her some coffee, sit her up and let her drink it. Birch, is it? I really am so sorry, and never thought he was like that, if I had known for one minute, I would have thrown him out myself."

The picture was clearing, the lights had gone, and I could see the room through Birch's hair, it looked sort of pretty. Birch pulled me up and held me.

"Deads Sweetie, I need you to drink this." I smelt the coffee and retched violently.

"Quick let me."

I was whisked up into the air, as I retched again, and suddenly I was in the bathroom, over a toilet, I gave a huge heaving retch, and whoosh, up it all came, and burned the back of my throat, as it poured into the loo.

I came back to reality with a bang, and gasped in air slightly panicked, what the hell was happening to me? I retched, oh god not again. Whoosh, another load came thrusting up my throat and out into the toilet, I came back to greater reality in a flash. Birch stroked my hair back from my face.

"It is okay Sweetie, you are fine, I am here."

"Jesus Birch how much have I drank?" I retched violently.

"Oh god, I frigging hate this, that is for sure."

I retched again, and whoosh up came another load. I gave a slightly panicked gasp.

"Oh god!"

"Get it all out Deads, the more up the better."

I gasped for air, the taste in my mouth was vile. I licked my lips.

"What the hell was I drinking, it tastes like shit."

"We are not sure, how do you feel Deads, is your mind clear? We think Daniel spiked you."

I sat back and looked at her through the blur of the tears, she leaned in and checked my eyes. I could see her beautiful big green eyes, and they were filled with concern.

"What do you remember Sweetie?" I blinked, it hurt to think.

"I asked John to swim with me, we both got turned on, I wanted to screw him so started, then realised we had no protection, so I brought him up here, we had great sex, I think, then I felt tired so rested, and the next thing I know I am puking my frigging guts out." She smiled, and gave a sigh of relief.

"Okay Sweetie, that is fine. You should be fine now, wash your face, you will feel better."

It took me a few minutes to wash up, I rinsed my mouth out several times. When I walked into the room, I still felt a little vague and woozy, John was sat with Birch on the bed, he was dressed. Chloe, Edwina and Debs were stood by the window, looking really upset, Izzy was by the door. John smiled and got up; he came over to me.

"How are you feeling?"

"I am fine, how are you?" He smiled, and nodded his head.

"I am fine now knowing you are okay. Barry has gone after him, he will be leaving the project, that kind of behaviour is not acceptable to any of us. I just want you to know how sorry we all are."

I was not completely sure what was going on, but I nodded to him, he seemed like a decent guy, and he was great between the sheets, I think?

"Thanks, no bloody idea what you are talking about, but you sound pretty cool."

I looked at Birch. She patted the bed at her side, I moved over, and sat down with her, I looked at her, her eyes were a little red around the edges.

"Have you been crying?"

"Deads Sweetie, tonight just before you went off with John, it looks like Daniel tried to spike you, it took a while to kick in, after John left, and you passed out. Luckily Chloe saw Daniel creep into your room, and followed him in here, you were out for the count, and he was getting himself primed ready, she stopped him, before he did anything, and Izzy chased him off."

I understood, I had heard of it happening, but in truth I don't remember any of it, I was enjoying the feeling of just relaxing. I nodded and turned to look back, Chloe looked really worried, I think I knew what she was thinking of.

"Thanks Chloe, I owe you one." She smiled.

"I kicked him in the bollocks, I am good." She laughed, and I smiled back.


It was a few hours before I came properly around, and could fully understand everything. By eleven o'clock the party had ended, and we all sat in the living room. Deb's looked really upset still, and curled into me. John had the car, and left to go and collect Barry and the others, who helped him look, apparently Daniel had made it to Oxendale and legged it.

I remembered Edwina, telling us about the lake, and how to always take our own drinks, and keep our thumbs in the top of our bottles. We all dropped our guard because we were at home, and yet, we were still at risk, and that was a good lesson to have learned for all of us. It is a sad fact of life, that many unreported assaults happen, and many of those are from people they know, not all assaults are by strangers, a great number are so called friends.

Daniel had been warm, funny and friendly; I would never have thought that could happen. What put me off was he was married, had he not been, I might have slept with him of my own free will. He had not seen it that way, and had already acted, Birch was right, women have the choice, it is up to them to choose, and whether men like it or not, that is how it should be.

I went to bed earlier than the others, my stomach felt off, although puking had not helped, and I was so tired. Birch told me it was probably some of whatever he had given me, that had leeched in to my system. I lay in the dark with the blinds down, feeling shaken. It had been such a nice day, I was having such fun, chilling out with everyone. John had been nice, and I had loved having sex, it was a shame, he was a good looking guy, and his other friends had been really nice.

They had great senses of humour, and the evening had been filled with laughter, and one guy had spoiled it all, and brought chaos to everything. Why is it some people are like that, why do they feel the need to control everything to their way? The simple fact was had he been honest, I am sure Chloe would have slept with him, or possibly Deb's, she had not noticed his hand.

Birch was right, we should have been able to choose for ourselves, we were not children, we were young adults, and even though we believe in a free open lifestyle, that did not mean we had no responsibility for what we did. The difference was, it was up to us to decide, not Daniel.

Chapter 21

# Family.

Sunday arrived, and I was up, and weirdly enough decided to wear some panties. I cannot explain it, I just felt a little vulnerable, and they helped me feels safe. I know it is irrational, I am in a house filled with naked women, there is not a man in sight, but everyone keeps looking at me, with those sad frigging eyes, and it is driving me bonkers. I do not want to be a victim, I have done enough of that, and I felt I wanted to try to be simply my normal self. I will not allow it, not for them or anyone, yes, I screwed up, I let my guard down, and maybe I am a little too trusting with people, but isn't it a shame, that it had been in my own home?

I went up to my room, with coffee and toast, I thought I would work on my books, and enjoy the peace. Edwina had connected my computers for me, it was great because I no longer had to keep sticking files from one to the other, and it made my life so much easier. With the large window's open, and the warm air of the day flowing in, I relaxed and started to read my continuing vamp story, and made some pretty major changes, and it was already tons better.

The day slipped past, and people started smiling again, and I lost the panties, took a break, and sat on my balcony, watching Anthony and Brent, splashing around in the pool with Deb's, and Chloe. Edwina was sat on the grass on her laptop doing updates to her own sites. Birch was nowhere to be seen, so I assumed she would be in the library on her computer, working, the open day was this Friday coming, and her practice was almost ready to open the following Monday.

I came down to eat dinner with everyone. Dinner being the southern version of a Manchester tea, and we all sat around talking as we ate. Like all things in a group of girls, talk soon turned to sex and vaginas, as Edwina mentioned losing her virginity, and how it felt like so long ago.

"God he was useless, I am surprised he actually got it in me, he kept missing, it would slip south, I almost thought I would lose my anal virginity first." We all giggled, Deb's beamed with delight.

"I was so happy I gave mine to Jimmy, to be honest I was pretty drunk, and so although it hurt a bit, I was too pissed to remember, but I do remember the second time, and that felt so amazing." Chloe was leaning on the doorframe.

"It must have been, because once we hit the lake, you really enjoyed it a lot." Giggles broke out as Deb's gave a big smile; Chloe looked puzzled.

"All I remember was it hurt like hell, to be honest I never really did the dildo masturbation thing, I wish I had now, he started to pump, and it was so painful I told him to fuck off." She looked at me. "What about your first time Abby, how was it for you?" Birch got up as I smiled.

"Pretty boring to be honest." She frowned at me.

"What, is that it? Fuck Abby, I want to know details, come on what was it really like?"

Birch walked to the door with her empty glass, and smiled at Chloe, then leaned in to her and whispered quietly.

"Chloe drop it... Just let this one slide, because I really love you, I do Sweetie, I think you are an amazing person, which is why I really do not want to have to kill you, and seal you up in the wall with Gwenda... Thanks Sweetie."

She walked into the kitchen, and headed for the vodka bottle, Chloe looked at me, and then back at Birch, she shuddered.

"So what was it like for you Birch, come on, yours must have been epic?" Birch came out a few minutes later smiling.

"Not really, I lost it by accident."

She walked to her chair, and sat back and winked at me, I smiled, I had no idea what she said, but I was glad she had, that was a night I had tried to forget. Deb's looked at Birch.

"That makes no sense, how the hell can you lose your virginity by accident, it is not possible?" Birch shrugged.

"I did, I was fourteen, and my mum had a load of new spare toys, and I liked how one of them buzzed, so I went to the bedroom and took off my knickers, and stood next to my bed. I started the thing up, I mean, it's ridiculous, but I wanted to save my virginity for my wedding day back then. Anyhow, I was just putting it in, you know just through the lips, and it was really buzzing my clit, and oh my god it felt great. The problem was it made me feel giddy, and my legs shook, so without thinking I sat down on the bed, to save me from falling over, and ta da, I was a woman!"

Edwina sprayed her drink across the patio, I burst into laughter, Chloe fell into the kitchen, she was laughing so hard, and Deb's stared at Birch with a really serious face.

"Oh, Christ, Birch, did you ever get it back?" Birch leaned forward and patted her knee.

"No Sweetie, it is still in there, buzzing away, that is why I am always so happy." There was another massive explosion of more laughter, Deb's looked at us all laughing, and smiled.

"No it isn't, the battery would have run out by now."

I laughed so hard, I cried, Birch let out a huge cackle of a laugh, and leaned forward and hugged Deb's.

"I do love you Sweetie."

Anthony and Brent sat back observing, I am not sure if any talk of vibrators was still a sensitive subject, I cannot deny, I had no wish to ask how Peter was doing.

It was a fun night, and I got the impression, that they were all trying to normalise life for me, but it was not needed, I was honestly fine. I had been given a stark reminder of today's world, but Daniel had not done anything other than try to stiffen himself in front of me, and I was out of it and saw nothing.

It was nice to finally reach the end of the day and the weekend, and I slipped into bed, and curled up, and when Birch arrived, I looked at her.

"Will you face the other way tonight?" She looked instantly upset.

"Can I not cuddle up to you, Deads if you are feeling uncomfortable, I can sleep in my bed?" She misunderstood me.

"Birch, I want to cuddle into you... Just for tonight, I just feel..."

"Sweetie, I would love that."

She climbed in and lay down, and I turned to face her back, I cuddled up, and put my arm round her waist, she snuggled back, and then placed her hand on mine, and I pushed my face into her lower neck, she was so warm, and so soft, and it felt really nice.

"Will you be alright Deads?" I kissed the back of her neck.

"Honestly I am fine, I just wanted to do this tonight."

"Okay Sweetie.... Actually, this is really nice."

The new day started at a crazy pace, most of the fitting work at Sweetie's Retreat was almost done. Carpets were down, units and desks fitted, computers were going in, and the long front window, had a slatted vertical blind the whole length of it, which was closed to hide the ongoing work. Painters were outside, freshening up the look, and the new sign was put in place. Birch was living on her mobile, talking to staff, and people applying to work for her, she was also liaising with the fitters, and decorators.

By the time Wednesday arrived, I drove Petal, and parked her outside the Practice, Birch was stressed but excited, as she opened the doors, her new counsellors were in town, and planned to arrive. With Izzy at our side, Birch swung open the door, and I took a huge gasp, the transformation was mind blowing.

The whole place was bright, as light streamed in through the pale blinds, along the window there were padded seats in a dark blue for those waiting, the carpet was the same blue. Down the centre of the shop was a long pale wooden reception station, I walked up to it and looked over, there were three computers, pads pens, assorted stationary, a computer telephone console, and really comfy seats for the staff.

On the door end of the station, there was a pair of waist high swinging doors to walk through, I pushed, and they separated to let me through. The walls had motivational, framed pictures, and along the back wall, a long neon sign reading Sweetie's Retreat was lit up in blue. Birch looked really nervous, as she watched me biting her lip.

"Is it alright Deads, you know, it looks professional, doesn't it?"

I looked round at the large plants and the whole layout; in my mind it was a lot nicer than the doctor's clinic. I was really impressed.

"Birch it is amazing, how can you doubt it? This place is mind blowing." She gave a gasp.

"You think so, you really think so?" I smiled.

"It's perfect, honestly I am so proud of you at the moment, this place was a shit hole, and you have absolutely transformed it." Izzy stood in the archway that led through to the back.

"See I told you, if she loves it, your mum will, come on I have put the kettle on, let's have a brew before she arrives." I looked at Birch.

"Roni is coming, she is here?" I smiled. Birch nodded, and looked panicked.

"Mum will be here shortly, honest Deads, I am really shitting myself."

We walked through into the back, the doors had gone, and it was a neat square archway, through which, was now a wide clear space, with the stairs going up to the counsellor's offices. There were a few chairs and plants, and more pictures, two of which I recognised as Hatty's. Right in front was an office, with a large window, and next to that was a long corridor with doors, all which had silver signs on. There was a disabled toilet, Staff toilets, public toilet, Kitchen, Conference/Group Therapy room, Therapist's lounge, and a meetings room. I noticed the door to the main office had Practice Manager on it.

There was a door at the far end, that led out into a yard, which had planters and seating, so sessions could even be conducted outside, it was inspiring to say the least. Every aspect was clean, neat, and very tastefully done; I didn't think she had anything at all to be concerned about.

Izzy took me into the Conference Room, this was where group therapy and staff briefings would be done. Gillian arrived and smiled as she walked in.

"Doesn't it look great?" I gave her a big smile, she looked at Izzy.

"I will man reception, and send everyone through as they show up." She gave a wave, and then disappeared. Birch kept looking at her watch, and Izzy gave a sigh.

"Relax Jemi, she will love the place."

I had never seen her look so nervous, the door opened and she jumped. A short white haired man walked in, he had bright blue eyes, a round face and a big smile. He wore an open collared shirt with a deep red cravat, he looked really happy and jolly, and was clearly gay. Birch smiled and walked over.

"Rodger, good to see you."

Rodger Bancroft, was the gender counsellor, he was very jolly as he waved at me in a giddy fashion.

"Hi... I am Rodger." I liked him straight away, he looked at me and then pointed, as he looked at Birch.

"Oh my, Jemi, if that is Deadly, she is way cuter than you said, oh she is gorgeous, you naughty girl." I giggled and he winked. "Oh, she has dimples, how divine."

Behind him a woman appeared, she had on a long flowing pale green skirt, a loose long top secured with a chain belt, about six long golden chains round her neck, one of which had a huge white stone on it. Long flowing wavy brown hair and dark sensual eyes, she smiled, and she looked so sweet and kind, Birch gave a sigh of relief seeing her.

"Oh, you found us Pat?" She smiled, as she looked round the room, looking impressed.

"Well the road here could be better sign posted, but it was a short drive from Oxendale, not too far. Hi Rodger, hi Izzy, and you I am assuming are the infamous Deadly we have heard so much about, it is nice to meet you finally?"

I smiled as I took her hand, which had shit loads of pretty expensive rings on it. Birch looked at Izzy.

"I think it is best done out front, then we can walk her through. Can we all gather in reception; she will be here shortly?"

In reception Gillian, who everyone else called Gill, was already on the phone, Birch had rerouted all calls to her mobile, and I was really surprised to hear, she was already booking new appointments. Her screen showed the diaries of all the counsellors, and their free spots, and as she spoke on her head set, she imputed the data.

"Good morning, Sweetie's Retreat, how may I help you? Yes, that is right, it is on the main street, you would, yes, with Isabella, yes, she is our specialist in that field. I can offer you ten am, or four pm Thursday, would that be convenient? Wonderful, and your name is... Okay that is fine... Yes, we will see you then, enjoy your day."

She sounded so good, and her manner was lovely, Birch smiled as she saw me looking at her, she understood I approved. All the staff lined up as Birch looked at her watch, it was almost time. I walked up and looked at her, she looked panicked.

"Should I leave, or do you need me here?" She gave a nervous gasp.

"Don't leave me, you will have to wait here whilst I do the tour, but please Deads, just be in the building with me." I smiled, and shook my head

"Honestly, you would think it was Madge, and all her relatives coming. Come on Birch, this is your mum, relax a bit. Birch, this place is amazing, she will love what you have done." Rodger leaned over.

"Listen to her Jemi dear, the girl is right, I mean it's not like she is possibly the single most respected therapist in the western hemisphere is it now?"

Izzy gave a titter, Birch blanched white, and I thought she was already pretty white, this went beyond even that. She took a deep breath and smiled, the clatter of leather shoes sounded outside, Birch swallowed hard, and looked freaked out.

"Here goes." I stepped back and the door opened, I smiled.

"Hey Roni." The phone bleeped.

"Sweeties Retreat, how may I help you?"

Roni smiled as she looked round, and William came in behind her. Birch walked towards her mum.

"Good morning, Doctor Dixon." William looked up.

"Hi Jemi."

I sniggered, this was going to be really confusing, there were three Doctor Dixon's, and they were all in the same room. Roni smirked.

"Jemi darling, this is your establishment, why be so formal?" Birch gave a sigh of relief.

"I want this all to be right." Roni looked round smiling, she winked at me. Birch raised her hand, and gestured towards the line of staff.

"Mum, I would like you to meet my staff."

It was really nice to watch Birch introduce her mother to the people she would be working with. I had seen just how much she had put into this, the long nights sat with a pad and calculator, or reading all the fine print on every aspect of the practice, and she had filled in endless amounts of paperwork to ensure everything met the rigorous safety standards. The result of all those long hours, either at the guest house or in our new house, her mother was now walking round, and although I really am not qualified in this field, I personally thought she had done an outstanding job.

She was tired, it was obvious, and clearly very nervous, because even though the practice had been brought under the umbrella of her mother's business, all of this was solely Birch. Roni shook hands with the new counsellors, Izzy she already knew, and for the whole time Gill was busy on the phone, booking appointments, and giving out information, I was sat listening, and I was quietly thrilled for Birch, and I knew that William was listening intently. Birch finally took her mum through for a tour of the rest of the facility, and Gill looked up.

"Do you want a coffee whilst you wait?"

I nodded at her, I was dry, I was as nervous as Birch was. I got up and came behind the front desk, Gill got up and clicked on the kettle on a small wooden unit behind her, I noticed the small fridge for the milk. She spooned out the coffee, into the cups, and turned back as she waited for the kettle to boil.

I noticed that the phone was less busy, she smiled, and slipped her hand in her pocket, and pulled out a mobile. She gave a little giggle, and pressed the screen, the phone in the surgery rang, she tapped her head set.

"Good morning, Sweetie's Retreat." My mouth fell open.

"No way?" Gill chuckled.

"Jemi needs to make sure her mum thinks this place is a success, she is getting appointments, so there are dates already on the books, and it is looking good, I just thought I would present a good impression for her mother."

She gave a little giggle, and turned as the kettle clicked off. I really liked that, Deb's was right, she is a very clever girl.

In the back, I could hear Birch or Izzy, talking about the many uses of the facility, Gill handed me my drink, and we sat talking for a good thirty minutes, occasionally the phone would ring, and she would stop to answer with a touch of her head set, people were asking a lot of questions, and making booking consultations. Gill handled them all like a pro, I could see why Birch had chosen her. I was lazing around, when I heard them all walking down the stairs talking, moments later, the group appeared, Birch seemed a lot calmer. I stood up, initially to go to Birch, Roni smiled at me.

"Abby, would you care to walk with me, I am going to meet Flick?"

I felt a little wrong footed, I wanted to talk to Birch, but I think she knew that, I looked at Birch, she gave a slight nod, and then to Roni.

"If you want me to, I can do, yes." She smiled, and turned to Birch.

"I will see you later, I will leave you to get on, you have a lot to do before Friday."

I didn't even get a chance to say goodbye, as Roni grabbed my arm and linked it, and walked me to the door, I felt I was being kidnapped. As I left the shop, the last thing I saw was Birch watching, there was nothing I could do. I was flanked on both sides as Will walked opposite Roni. Out in the fresh air she slowed her pace, still linking my arm.

"So, what do you think Abby, after all you have been there by her side, are you pleased with her set up?" I felt trapped.

"I have no understanding of a practice Roni; all I know is she worked day and night. To be honest, she has worked too many hours, but you know her, you have no need to ask me, you know how much effort she has put in." Roni gave a small chuckle.

"Nice answer, I admire your loyalty to her." I stopped and pulled my arm free.

"I am not being loyal, I am being honest, she has killed herself to impress you. To be honest Roni, you could have cut her some slack, she was terrified this morning, and it's not fair, she does not deserve that, she has worked her ass off... You know what, go to my mums on your own, I am going back to her."

Roni gave a tremendous burst of laughter, it pissed me off more, she stood there in the street laughing, and I felt my blood boil.

"Screw you Roni." I turned, and felt a tug on my arm, Roni was trying not to smile.

"Abby, I truly am sorry, please walk with me, I will try my hardest to be fair, and not offend you." William was smirking, I looked at them both.

"Look I know about her wanting to quit and come here, when I found out and she admitted it, I told her, I would have put her right back on the train, and sent her back. Roni, Will, can you not see this is her dream, this is what she wanted, be proud of her, and give her the support of you both, she really needs it, she has given everything for this." Roni gave a nod and smiled.

"Abby, no one is prouder of her today more than I am, and yes you are right, the evidence of her work is there. I had her counsellors checked out, and to be honest I was envious that she has head hunted such good people. The practice is modern and sharp looking, her organisation is a good match between her and Izzy. I think she will have tremendous success here." I was finding it hard to understand.

"Then why have you been so hard on her, Roni she was so scared this morning, it was upsetting me seeing her that way, it makes no sense?" Roni took my arm and started to walk towards Manor Road.

"Abby she is my daughter, and I hate to say it, she is very like me, and that is not always an easy thing. Jemi did this on her own, but I was not as in the dark as you may have thought. I was aware of what she was doing, and I kept a careful watch. The thing is Abby, when it comes to Jemi, I know how strong willed she is, and I knew if she thought for one second, I could shut her down, she would work harder and pull off a miracle. When that awful Wallace woman pulled her stunt on the house, I took my chance, you see Jemi was so angry at me for trying to steal her prize, she did not quite read the small print. Between you and me, Sweetie's Retreat is a fully independent company." It made no sense to me, I looked at her unsure.

"How can that be, I was there at court, it was made clear, that the practice was under the umbrella of your main operation. Bradley was very clear about it, and all your legal people were there, how can it be all hers?" Roni winked.

"We were not in court Abby, we were in a court meeting room, there was no oath, and no judge present. My legal people were there just in case, the paperwork was done, and it was there, and had it gone into a court room, all I would have had to do is sign ten sheets of paper, and it would have been absorbed into my organisation. Abby, because she thought she would lose it, she fought like hell to make it work. I will let you into a secret, Jemi has no fear of failure, none at all, she will just get right back up, brush herself off, and do something else. She does however, fear failing me and her father, and because she thought we could be liable, she thought everything through perfectly, do you now understand?" I looked at her and then William, and furrowed my brow.

"That is a bit bloody underhanded, I mean talk about a setup, wow you two are a bit sinister when you work together." William gave a hearty laugh.

"There was nothing sinister Abby, I feel, all we did was provide extra motivation." I narrowed my eyes.

"Yeah, sinister." He chuckled.

We walked up to the gates of our house, and I went to cross over, Roni looked at me. "Where are you going?" I pointed.

"My mum's house." Roni shook her head.

"I am not meeting her for another two hours; I was hoping you would invite us in for coffee." I felt awkward.

"Birch is not here." William winked at me.

"Precisely, we have had one tour today, where she tried to flannel us, we thought it would be nicer if you showed us round."

Crap! I knew it, caught in a trap again, God these two were impossible. I opened the box and key padded us in, the gate opened, and we walked up to the front door, I took out my key and opened the door, and stepped in.

"I am home, where are you girls?"

Edwina shouted from the library, Chloe yelled from her studio, I knew Deb's was at the book store, she was interviewing for a shop assistant. Roni and William followed me, and looked around the place. I felt nervous.

Roni looked in the living room, whilst William went in the library, shit, they split up, crap! I didn't trust either of them. Roni turned in the centre of the massive living room.

"Wow it really is a big place, and so clean and tidy, I love the décor, although it does need some art." I walked in and looked round.

"Yeah, Chloe is working on some, and now Hatty is back, Birch wants a couple off her. You know Roni, there are six of us here, and we are pretty serious about the place, we want it nice." She smiled.

"I am sorry, I was not disrespecting any of you, I really love the place, it has character, and it is really well decorated, your home is beautiful Abby." I felt happy, I loved that people liked it.

"Yeah, we are lucky as it keeps us all together."

Roni walked across the hall into the library, she looked at the four computers, and I saw her little smirk.

"She once mentioned how nice it would be to all work in the same room, she has such vision. Hi Edwina, I won't interrupt you, just carry on."

William was stood behind her watching; Edwina was coding Deb's bookshop pages for her web site. Roni looked at the pots on the desks and smiled, she could see who worked where. The book cases with the addition of my books were looking pretty full, but there was room for more, Roni gave a happy chuckle.

"I see the organisation skills of a bookshop owner; little Debbie has been busy."

"Have a good look, I will put the kettle on."

I breathed a sigh of relief as I walked down the hall, I put the kettle on, and then opened the patio doors. I waited, sat at the island for them to appear. I felt it was easier to let them look for themselves, after all, Roni could see right through me, Birch was much better at this stuff than I was.

They finally arrived and Roni sat down, she loved the kitchen, William looked out over the garden, I poured the fresh coffee and sat with her. She gave me a happy smile.

"I have wanted to see the house since she bought it, I think you both have invested wisely, it is very homely, and warm, I like it a great deal." I lifted my cup.

"I still struggle with the fact it is half mine, honestly, I would have been happier if it was all hers." Roni understood that.

"Abby, you two have something very special and unique, Jemi knew it, I knew it, and your friends know it. In all my years of work, I have never met a female who is only sexually attracted to one woman, and yet both of you are, it has fascinated me since you both first met. Whatever you have has not been defined yet, but it is strong, and that really is all that matters. Jemi wanted so badly to show you that she had not deserted you, and that you really were so very important to her, and this was her way of doing it. You know the silly thing is, if she had not inherited all those shares, she would be living in the guest house still, and building Sweetie's Retreat, with my money. No matter what, the result would have been the same."

I understood all that, I really did, but to just give away half of a house worth so much, it made no sense to me.

"It is just so much money Roni, it makes me uncomfortable." Roni shrugged.

"That is where you are going wrong Abby, Jemi hates money, to her this is many things far more important than capital. Look Abby, to Jemi, firstly this provides a level of status, that forces the villagers to accept you both. In a way, it removes some of the shaming, just like it did for Bradley and Ellen. It has also created a creative hub, for her young friends starting out, and I may add, it has removed some of the pressure from all of you to do that. Look at Edwina, she is based here working from home, so is Chloe, Debbie has a safe haven, and you can write from here, and Jemi is working and uses this as her sanctuary, whilst seeing all of you safe and secure. This is far more than money, it's a family, and that is what it means to her. This family is her support as well, because she will not admit it, but she misses Will and me, and all you guys, you are her replacements for us."

"So, what are you saying, I am some sort of mother figure to her, because Roni, that is a little messed up?" Roni burst out laughing.

"Oh, Abby you are funny, no, Abby she loves you, oh you have no idea what I went through because of it, you know what, I will say this, if Jemi had to pick between you and me, I would lose... I already did."

Talk about a slap to the face, that came out of nowhere and just slammed me into the floor, it really shocked me. I stared into those same green eyes, and my voice lowered, and I shook my head slowly.

"Please don't say that Roni, it really hurts to hear it. I don't want that, I really don't. I never want her to choose, I could not handle that at all." I felt my words stick in my throat, she smiled, and her eyes filled with tears.

"And that is why you are so special, and why she loves you Abby." I felt a tear run down my cheek.

"She means the same, she does, but I cannot have that at the expense of you. I love the bond you have; it drove me to find that with my mum, and we are getting there, Roni you must never allow that, not ever, it would destroy me to see it." She smiled.

"It won't Abby, I promise, I learned my lesson, and I have worked hard to fix things between us, and we too are getting there." I gave a sniffle, and nodded.

"That is a good thing Roni, I am so happy to hear it, because she suffered you know, she missed you like crazy." Roni gave a nod of appreciation.

"Thanks Abby, I needed to hear that."

"Abby, I need to run into…… Holy fuck parents!"

Chloe stood naked, and covered in paint at the end of the kitchen, Roni turned and smiled.

"Hi Chloe, I see you carried the theme of your hair onto your tits?"

Chloe looked down at the paint all over her, she smiled, turned, and ran back to her studio with a squeal. A few moments later she reappeared wearing her robe, she smiled coyly.

"Sorry about that, I thought Birch was back, you know, you guys really look alike. Hi Mr D, sorry." He gave a giggle.

"Birch is my daughter Chloe, naked people pop up wherever she is, I am quite used to it." She nodded.

"Yeah, I totally get that, she is pretty natural." Roni leaned back to see through the door.

"Your studio I take it, would it be alright for me to have a look?" Chloe looked a little awkward.

"I am not as good as Hatty yet, as long as you do not expect that sort of standard, I am getting there, I just need more time." Roni slipped off the seat.

"Good grief girl, you cannot be Harriet, you can only be you. I am interested in your heart when it comes to art, not Harriet's. I want to see your idea of love and beauty, come on don't be shy, show me yourself." Chloe gave a giggle.

"I pretty much think I just did that."

She followed Roni into the studio, and I sipped my coffee thinking of what Roni had told me. A hub of creativity echoed in my thoughts. William stepped out, and went for a walk round the garden.

I stared at the wall, so much made sense, the Curio's were all working hard to make a name for themselves, the practice would help the young understand themselves, as well as be a centre for the Tarts program. Roni was right, the house was a status symbol, was that why Hatty and Margret had worked so hard, to make it known how lovely the house was, did the vicar confirm that to Marjorie?

In a way having grown up here I should have seen it, I mean after all look at my dad, how many questions I have had to endure on the value of the property, and how much Birch is worth?

It is exactly how this village works, everything is about status and money, and the more you have, the more credible you are. Birch had done that in one swift move, by purchasing this place, and bringing us all under its roof. By giving me half, it undid a lot of the shaming I had suffered, because a good percentage now treated me more respectfully, for no other reason than I owned half a house.

How sad it is that the world is like this, where your bank balance is more credible than your good intentions? I really understood Birch now, rather than fight the system, she had joined it, and it was from the inside, she had a better chance of changing it. That was what her speech to the village was really about, she planned to attack from within.

Chapter 22

# Storms Approaching.

Marjorie sat in the Vicarage with Walter Parkinson, Conservative Member of Parliament for the Metropolitan Borough of Oxendale. She had business in mind.

"Well Walter, I cannot deny I am looking forward to it, closing the library was a massive mistake as you know, so I think a new mobile library in the village is a wonderful idea, and I know just the spot for it, where everyone will have easy access." Walter looked very pleased with himself.

"I am delighted to see that once again, I have yours and the villages support. I have no idea Marjorie how I would manage without the assistance you provide in this community, your support is greatly appreciated, now on to the other matter." Marjorie smiled.

"Yes, it is in regard to the church hall, and the latest certification of the wiring." He gave a frown.

"The wiring, I was under the impression all was fine, if memory serves me right, there is nothing at fault?" Marjorie looked at him.

"I will be candid Walter, I have a problem, an annoyance if you like, I need it to go away." He leaned forward in his chair.

"Really... Do tell, what is this annoyance?" She smirked.

"We need the hall until after the fete, which is Saturday 24th through to Monday 26th, after that I need you to pull a string or two for me. I want the hall closed on Sat 31st, I thought maybe a fault in the wiring would suffice? I mean if the electrics for the lights and the sound system were deemed unsafe, the hall would have to close, wouldn't it? I would think it would take at least fourteen days to rectify it?" He understood and considered it.

"That is a big ask Marjorie, the inspector is not an easy man to convince, that would involve... Well to be honest it could be costly."

Now he was talking her way of doing things. Marjorie reached into her handbag, and pulled out a plastic bag containing five hundred pounds, in twenty pound notes.

"I believe this will suffice, I would think if the hall is closed from, let's say Wednesday the 28th until at least September 10th, that should give me more than enough time to deal with my little problem."

She handed the cash in the bag over to him, and he smirked, and slipped it into his pocket.

"I am sure we will find some small problem, if we look hard enough. As always Marjorie, you understand the workings of life, and it is a pleasure doing business with you." Marjorie smiled.

"As you know Walter, I have always been a loyal supporter of the party, and of your dedication to your office. I am sure our contributions to the party fund will flow for a very long time." He smirked smugly, and enjoyed the power he was feeling.

It was early evening, and Roni and Will were back, as was Bradley and Ellen. They sat in the living room, with Anthony and Brent, whilst upstairs was chaos. Marie Jenkins was a specialist designer of bridal wear, who had been hired by Bradley and Ellen, and finally all the dresses were ready. It was fitting time, and we gathered in Birch's bedroom, and squeezed ourselves into the dresses supervised by Jane, a young art student, who was working as an assistant to Marie.

Chloe looked at herself in the mirror, and saw the short skirt of copper coloured tulle, with the cream satin corset, trimmed with a bronze band of embroidered wheels, flowers. and cogs. She really did look amazing; it suited her figure perfectly. She turned as I pulled up the corset a little, I had small boobs and felt there was a little too much space. Jane slid her hand in, cupped my left boob and pulled it up. I looked down.

"Holy shit, I have a cleavage!"

Okay, admittedly it was small, I could probably only wedge a biro in there, whereas Chloe could probably get the whole pack in, but I was chuffed, as my two orange sized balls of pink, met in the middle. Chloe leaned over.

"It looks like a babies bum." Birch gave a giggle.

"Ignore her Sweetie, I think it's very sexy."

I smiled, and felt my confidence rise until I saw Birch's slightly bigger, and more rounded mounds perched on the top of her corset. Chloe looked back at the mirror; she was swinging her hips from side to side.

"Yeah, I like this, my legs are free to dance, and I can screw in it, I like easy access should the need arise." Birch looked at her.

"You do know Zac is the best man, don't you?" Chloe turned and looked at Birch.

"Fuck right off, there is no way that ugly twat would be best man?" Birch gave a titter.

"I am sorry to say, Floyd is playing the lead in on his guitar, so the job has gone to Zac. Shame really, Floyd really is the only good looking one, so if you think of it Chloe, the best man gets first dibs on the bridesmaids, it could be your second lucky night." She gave a big shudder.

"Oh, fuck, that is depressing, the sad thing is he is great with his dick, it is just looking at him that is the problem, fuck he is ugly." Edwina gave a giggle.

"I don't know Chloe, you could always turn the lights out, I mean he was pretty good looking in the dark." I started to laugh, as she cringed.

"Honestly guys I can't... Oh god no I just can't, not again, once was enough, even in the dark I would see it in my head... Oh god no.... Oh, God, I am depressed."

The dress felt a little strange at first, but there again, when you live pretty much naked all the time, any clothing you wear starts to feel strange. Jane was finally happy with us, I loved the fact we all had the same dresses on, as we looked like sisters. Happy and giggling, we headed down stairs, to show off, and walked into the living room. Roni stood up with Ellen, and both looked all sort of weird and motherly, it freaked me out a little. Roni looked at Birch and me stood together.

"Oh girls, you look so beautiful."

Her eyes filled up, and it made me feel a little warm round my cheeks. William smiled from his seat.

"You do look stunning, although may I just add, possibly underwear would complete the ensemble?" Birch frowned.

"But I never wear any. God Dad do I have to?" Ellen gave a

giggle.

"I think for church girls, it may be a sacrifice worth paying, just for this one day." Birch looked unhappy.

"Okay I will get something to match, but just for one day." Roni gave a happy smile, she walked up for a closer look.

"I must admit when I was told it was a steam punk themed wedding, I was a little unsure, but honestly girls, I have never seen you looking more elegant and feminine. I really got taken aback when I saw you."

Deb's voice sounded upstairs, and we all moved into the room, and waited in a line for her. Jane stood by the side of the door, and smiled as she watched her come down the staircase, we all waited, and then she appeared with giggles.

Her dress was stunning. She had a matching corset, and short front skirt, with a heavily embroidered intricate floral design. It was an under the boob corset, and her breasts were covered in a heavy satin top piece, decorated with ribbons and fabric roses. It had two inch thick straps, that were slipped off her shoulder, decorated with silk flowers, it was so elegant. Her underskirt was frilly layers of tule, in a rich cream, and was short at the front, halfway down her thighs, and then from her hips, and all round the back, her tule frilly skirt reached to the floor.

It looked sort of Victorian, meets the Wild West, I could imagine her hiding a small pistol in her cleavage, but I have to confess, she looked stunning. She stood there looking bashful and awkward.

"How does it look guys?"

Ellen burst into tears, so did Roni, what was this weird and strange phenomenon? Bradley rose from his seat.

"Oh, Debbie sweetheart, I am at a loss for words, you look absolutely stunning."

He smiled, and she gave him the most beautiful smile I think I have ever seen, the love between them was amazing, and I felt the tears form in my eyes. Oh crap it's catching, I wiped my eye quickly.

"Well Jimmy will love it, I mean, you can stay dressed on the wedding night. All he will have to do is shove you back on the bed. and he will have access to everything." We all turned together.

"Chloe!!" She smiled, and shrugged.

"I am not wrong, fuck, I am straight, and even I want to screw her in that." Ellen wiped her eyes and giggled.

"Not what I want to think looking at my daughter in her wedding dress, but you may have a point." Chloe chuckled; Ellen looked at Deb's.

"Debbie you look so beautiful, I cannot tell you how happy I am for you, I am blown away, I really am." She gave a big smile.

"Thanks mum."


Everyone appeared happy, and Marie clapped her hands, they had to come off, so we all traipsed back up the stairs to change, well I say change we were all naked when this lot arrived, and now we had to dress. Putting these things on is one thing, and I was starting to think Chloe had a point, getting out of these things was a nightmare. I had to wonder, how the hell did cowboy town prostitutes, spend all day, screwing when they had to wear stuff like this, I was exhausted just undressing.

I finally wrestled my way out with the help of Jane, you know she was very keen on cupping my breasts to free them, I was starting to wonder about her. Finally, in shorts and a vest, I made my way with the girls back down stairs for drinks. The talk was all weddings, but we expected that. I was maid of honour, so had the big task of ensuring the hen party, and the day went smoothly.

I headed to the kitchen, and heard Birch, she was stood by the island with a drink in her hand, looking towards the cooker.

"It makes no sense, we have two spare rooms, why lay out the money? Mum that is like me and Deads coming home, and staying in rooms at the Church Inn, it's stupid, you should be here with Deads and me." I stopped in the hall holding my empty glass.

"Jemi considering the way things have been, we did not want to create waves, that is all. Look you have done an amazing job, you really have, the house and the practice are beautiful, can you not see that I do not want a repeat of when you were younger? Jemi, I hate it, but my reputation has a habit of getting in the way of things."

"Not here, this is my bloody home, and here you are not some famous superstar, you are my mum. I mean it mum, I want you here, and I am not going to take no for an answer, my home is your home.”

"But Jemi, it is not just your home is it, there are others to consider?”

"Honestly, I do not give a shit what they think, I am not having my mum and dad, stay in a hotel, when there is a perfectly good house here, and actually, I think the others would agree with me." I walked into the kitchen, and they both turned and looked at me.

"She is right Roni, Will and you should be here, my mum comes over and has coffee with me most days, Ellen is a regular visitor. You have come four hundred miles, how can you two sort things out if you are not here? This place has enough space for both of you, and your ego's, you should be here." Roni smiled.

"I doubt that Abby, I have a pretty big ego, and hers is catching up quickly." She smiled, and I gave a smirk.

"That's okay, we also have a frigging huge garden." Birch gave a giggle, and Roni sighed.

"I am not going to win here, am I?" I stood next to Birch, and slipped my arm round her waist.

"Nope, failure is a good character building experience, live with it Roni." She burst out laughing, and looked at Birch.

"You have a lot on your plate, we just did not want to put you out, I shall talk to Will." Birch nodded.

"Just tell him you are staying here, mum we miss you, if you are here, we will have more time."

"Well I hope the food is good, you will have a hard time beating the Chef at the Hunters?" I looked at Birch.

"We mastered the beans on toast thing, haven't we?" She started to giggle, Roni walked up and pulled us both into a hug.

"Okay you win, I will get William to go and get our things." Birch smiled at me, as Roni turned towards the hallway.

"Thanks Sweetie, I was losing, you pulled it back for me."


William went to the Hunters, and explained to Andrew the situation and checked out, and arrived back with their cases, Chloe in her dungarees, helped him unload the car.

"This Mr D, it's a nice big room you will like it, Edwina always has her head phones on so it will be nice and quiet." His eyes twinkled.

"I take it you will be at the other end of the house?" Chloe gave a saucy smile.

"It is okay, I have padded my headboard, the others were complaining about the endless beat of drums on the wall." He gave a giggle as he lifted his bag, and shut the boot.

Roni and Will were here until Monday night, Roni wanted to be there on the open day, as well as the first official day of business. Once settled into the guest room, life returned to normal. Edwina sat in the library working, I hung out in the kitchen working with Birch on a meal, and Chloe disappeared into her studio. Debs sat out in the garden with Roni and Will and talked of her wedding.

"I was not keen at first, I mean the Church Hall is hardly romantic, but it has a great stage, and Jimmy has some friends who are doing the music, so a live stage show is cool. Katie is helping with decoration, she has promised me I will not recognise the place when it is finished, and there will be loads of space for dancing, so I sort of swung round to the idea, and I am little excited about it." I yelled out from the kitchen as normal.

"COME AND GET IT!"

The table was laid, and everyone appeared looking hungry, Birch and myself had excelled ourselves, and made a huge cheese and onion pie, which we served with hot buttery potatoes, and veg. Birch sprinkled the green stuff as usual all over it, I am not good with herbs, but it always tastes good when she does it. William loved it, and Roni was satisfied, so it was a win for us.

It was still warm, and so with glasses of wine we headed back outside and sat in the garden to watch the sun set. Bedtime grew close and we headed to Birch's room and snuggled up together, she curled round me, and softly kissed my neck, I got goosebumps.

"Birch, is it okay to have sex in the house with your mum here, I mean, she knows right, so it's okay?" Birch moved down my back and I squirmed.

"Dead's we live with Chloe."

It was a good point, I rolled over and she worked onto my tummy, I gave another wriggle.

"Who is it tonight?" She kissed a little higher.

"Ryan, or Brian, I don't know, something like that, I mean seriously, the girl should just put a turn style on her door." I giggled, she moved higher, and my toes curled, as I tingled.

Thursday brought clouds. The morning was chaotic, we all got up in various stages of dress, wandered around, and then headed for the kitchen. I wandered into the kitchen to find William stood at the hob cooking, he was wearing Birch's red Apron. Debs, Chloe, Edwina, and Birch were sat at the table with Roni eating. Chloe looked up, and spotted me, she pointed at her plate with her knife.

"Abby these are banging, Mr D has outdone himself, I am telling you Mr D, you can stay anytime if you are going to make these."

I yawned, Birch got up, she was in her business suit, and carried her plate to the sink. She poured me a fresh coffee and steered me to the table, I was not good in the mornings. I sat down and lifted my cup. William arrived with a plate and I smiled, Chloe looked up at him.

"Is there any more?" He gave a chuckle and took her plate.

Breakfast this morning, which was courtesy of Will, was bread dipped in beaten eggs and then fried, Chloe, who loved eggs, had devoured two plates full already, and was eagerly awaiting her third, and she was eyeing my plate.

I sipped my coffee, and then lifted my knife and fork, just so I could see the disappointment on her face. She was right, they really were good. I chewed, watching Chloe drool, Roni gave a titter.

With breakfast over, it was time for work, Birch with her mum and dad, kissed me, and left, Deb's scuttled off behind them, and Edwina headed into the library to start her day. Chloe was in her studio, and I stood by the sink, as it was my turn to wash up. I was happily enjoying the soap suds, when I heard Edwina stomping down the hallway.

"Chloe! How many times have I told you, not to put your fucking dick pics on my flash drive?" She looked round the edge of the studio door.

"I didn't, I used mine." Edwina looked really pissed off, she scowled at Chloe.

"YOURS IS THE FUCKING GREEN ONE, MINE IS THE RED ONE!"

"Okay.... Sorry I made a mistake." Edwina, gave a snort.

"You filled my whole fucking drive, I almost uploaded them to my website."

"I said I am sorry, my phone memory was full, so I moved them over to save them. God Edwina it was a mistake, you can tell someone here has not had one for a while." Edwina narrowed her eyes.

"Well are you surprised, have you any idea, how hard it is in the south of England, to find a male... YOU HAVE NOT ALREADY FUCKED?"

She turned and stormed out, Chloe looked at me watching and giggled, I had to ask.

"Why do you have so many, do you get that many guys sending them, I have never had one?" She walked into the kitchen.

"They don't send them, I take them. I have a picture of every guy I have slept with erect." I was kind of impressed, and disturbed by it, and more than a little curious.

"Don't they mind?" She shrugged and grabbed the coffee pot.

"Abby they are guys, no guy will refuse to let you have a dick pick. I use them in my art, to be honest to really get the detail on a picture, it takes time, and so far, I have not met anyone who can stay hard long enough for me to draw in all the detail, so I ask them for pics." It kind of made a strange sort of logic, and therefore made sense.

"How many do you have; I mean you filled the whole flash drive?" She shrugged.

"A lot, I don't take one, I get it from every angle with each guy, they love it, I suppose they see it as me worshiping and admiring their manliness, and then when I have what I need, I fuck it, no one has complained yet."

"You are kind of a genius and a raving pervert; you know that right?" She gave a little giggle, and winked at me.

"I love sex Abby, what can I say, I live it, love it, and paint it, that is my life, it is all I have ever wanted, to fuck and paint, it makes me happy." I lifted the clean plate out of the water, and put it on the drainer.

"I guess that is all that matters really, it's simple, yet sensible." She took a sip of her drink.

"Think about it. What if whilst you were writing, Birch went under the desk and spread your legs, and then went to town with her tongue, you would be pretty fucking happy wouldn't you?" I had to chuckle.

"I would not be able to write if she did that Chloe, I would lose focus." She grinned at me.

"Yeah, but what a great way to lose focus, see, sex and art, because writing is art too."


The day was underway, Wotton was awake, and life around the village, was in full flow. Colin and Angela were serving in the bakers, Mary was behind the Post Office counter, and Amanda was filling her flower containers with water.

The Tea Rooms were already doing a good trade, it was the start of Summer, and Green Street was blocked off, and the tables were out in front. Louise and Stacy could be seen in their little aprons, long black skirts, and white blouses, delivering coffee, tea, and cakes to the tables, and Marjorie, who appeared much happier than normal, was sat in her usual place, watching the street.

There was the rumble of an engine, and a large purple, single decker bus, came round the corner from Station Road, and turned on to the main street. Everyone stopped to watch, as the bus with large letters, on the side, revealed it was a 'Mobile Library.' It pulled into the curb, and parked right outside the bookshop. The doors swung open, and Bethany Goodwaters, stepped off with a beaming smile, and a handful of leaflets.

As people approached, she handed out the flyers, which were headed. 'Why pay, when you can read for free.' Quite a few who were heading for the bookshop, took a leaflet and looked at it, then stepped onto the bus. Bethany smiled, looking at the shop, as people climbed on the bus. Deb's came out of her shop, and looked at the bus, then Bethany.

"What is going on, why is this outside my shop?" Bethany gave a smirk.

"This is a public service, and it has only wholesome books on it, some people around here have no interest in filth." Deb's did not really know what to do.

"I know it is a Library, I used it all the time until it was closed down as being too expensive to run, and they stopped it, why is it back, and my books are not filth? I stock a wide range of all types of books. Bethany this is going to take trade from my shop, can you not park it in another place, what about in front of the church like it used to do?"

"This Debbie Wheeler, is a public service to this community; it can park where it likes." Deb's was starting to feel upset.

"I pay for that bus, I pay my taxes, but that is having an impact on my trade, all I am asking is you park it in another location, it is not a lot to ask Bethany."

She continued to hand out leaflets to people who were walking up. Nine out of ten looked at it and then got on the bus. Deb's held out her hand.

"Let me see that." Bethany handed her leaflet and she read it; she felt a lump in her throat.

"This is a deliberate attack on my shop and on me, FIVE HOURS! It was only ever two?" Bethany smirked.

"And that is three days a week, that is what you get for peddling trash and smut." Deb's eyes filled with tears.

"This is Marjorie isn't' it, this is deliberate to make me fail? This is because she does not want any of us younger ones to do well, she wants us to fail, and leave here, so she can run everything, that is what this is about isn't it?" Peter Saxon came down from the Post Office, he wove through the crowd that was forming.

"What is going on here, the library bus never parks here, it always parks near the church, why is it here Beth?" She straightened herself up.

"We can park wherever we choose, this is a public service." Peter looked at Deb's.

"Do you know about this Debbie?" She gave a snort and tried to wipe her tears away.

"I just found out Mr Saxon, look at the leaflet, it is going to take all my trade away, and I have put every penny I have into this place." She gave another sob. Peter looked upset.

"Don't cry now Debbie, I will sort this out, the Parish Council, have heard nothing about this, but I promise, I will get to the bottom of this."

Deb's gave another snort and wiped her eyes. Having heard the commotion Birch came out, she saw Deb's in tears, and came quickly down, and put her arms round her, she looked at Bethany.

"You are Marjorie's friend are you not? Get this bus out of here, before I lose my cool." She looked at Deb's. "It's okay Sweetie, we will sort this out." Bethany scoffed.

"You can do nothing about this, Miss High and Mighty, this is a public service that has been privately funded, to help it return to serve the community." Peter Saxon looked confused.

"Privately funded, why do I not know anything about this, who is this private financer, can I talk to them?"

She handed out more leaflets, Birch snatched one, before a customer could take it, she looked at it and read through it.

"This has Marjorie stamped all over it." Deb's looked up.

"This will kill the bookshop." She burst into tears. Birch looked at Peter.

"Is there anything we can do about this?" He looked at her and gave a sigh.

"Sadly, not today, but I will look into this, I promise you both, I will get to the bottom of this, for now I am afraid you will just have to tolerate it."

Peter turned and walked off back to his shop, he had calls to make. Birch's eyes burned bright green with her anger as Deb's sobbed. She slowly released Deb's, and wiped her eyes with her hand.

"Go into your shop and make a coffee, I will be in shortly."

Deb's gave another sob, turned, and walked back into her shop. Birch spun round and walked right up to Bethany, she leaned in very close to her, her eyes burning with anger.

"Tell me Bethany, do you love your God, and does he love you?" She stepped back, looking nervous.

"My lord is my Shepard." Birch leaned forward, and looked really scary, as her anger rose up inside her.

"Tell me little Christian, are you afraid of witchcraft?"

Bethany's eyes opened wide, and leaned back more, as Birch leaned right over her, she was clearly very angry.

"God is my saviour; he protects me always." Birch glared at her, and Bethany took a step back and swallowed.

"I hope so, because the worst thing you can ever do is piss off a Wiccan witch, and you have just about ticked every box I have, if you don't believe me, ask your vicar." Birch moved closer, and Bethany grabbed the bus door rail.

"If you would rather avoid something unnatural, I would suggest you move this purple monstrosity, over to the church where your god can protect it, are you understanding me?" Bethany turned pale, and shook.

"I do not fear you; the lord is my shepherd; I shall not want." Birch smiled.

"Good to know, because you will be wanting him to remove the hex I am saying in my mind as we speak, run to your church little Christian, you need your god more now than you ever have."

She gave a slight squeak, nodded very fast, and stepped back onto the bus; Birch stepped back.

"Trust me it's safer."

Birch headed back into the shop, where Denise, her new twenty two year old, assistant was comforting her. The bus outside rumbled into life, and began to pull slowly away.

"Are you alright, they are leaving for now, I convinced them it is in their best interests to move close to a church, you know a pissed off Wiccan and all that." Deb's smiled.

"Thanks Birch, I really panicked." She smiled.

"Any time Sweetie, look I have to get back, we will talk later."

The bus rumbled up Church Rise, as Birch came out of the bookshop, Roni was stood outside the practice doors.

"Is everything alright?" Birch shook her head.

"It is that witch and her brood looking to cause yet more pain for us, she has targeted Deb's, I can only wonder who will be next."

Birch saw Marjorie make a sharp exit out of the Tea Rooms, and march up Green Street towards the bus, as it pulled in outside the church.

"I knew it, is there no lengths that bitch will not go to?"

Birch walked quickly into the road, and headed across the green; Roni saw Marjorie approaching the bus.

"Oh shit." She hurried to catch Birch, and try and stop her before she did something she would regret.


Marjorie walked with a face like thunder towards the bus. "Why is this not down there, I specifically told you to park it in front of that shop?" Bethany looked terrified.

"I cannot do this Madge; I will not risk my soul for a bookshop."

Marjorie frowned.

"What the hell are you blabbering on about?" Bethany saw Birch approaching at a fast pace and squealed.

"I want nothing unnatural to happen, I love Jesus, and I am staying with him. I would not survive a hex Madge, please I beg you, save your soul before she takes it."

Marjorie was lost for words; Bethany squealed, and ran round the bus, and in through the church gates. Marjorie stared at her.

"Have you gone mad, what the hell are you blabbering about.... Where the hell are you going.... Bethany.... BETHANY COME BACK!?"

It was too late, she was at the church doors, and screaming.

"I AM WITH JESUS!"

Behind Marjorie, Birch stood in the road glaring with hate.

"Is there no end to your hate, can you not just let us get on and live our lives?" People stopped and watched, as Roni came panting up behind her, as Marjorie turned.

"Your life is nothing but deviance, and disgrace, I will do everything I can to uphold the decency of this village. How dare you even stand there in your fake clothing, pretending to be anywhere near as respectable as the rest of this village." Roni grabbed Birch by the hand.

"Jemi do not do this, please sweetheart you will regret it, there are ways to deal with this, and a slanging match with her will do you no favours. Walk away sweetheart, be the bigger person, please Jemi, trust me."

More people were already stopping to watch; Roni knew her daughter.

"Jemi, you are upset, your friend is hurt, but look at the people, if you do what I think you are going to, it will work against you. Please sweetheart, don't give her the satisfaction, not here." Birch glared at her.

"YOU MARJORIE WALLACE, ARE THE REASON THE YOUNG LEAVE THIS VILLAGE. YOU AND YOUR CRONIES. THIS VILLAGE WILL DIE, AND THAT WILL BE ON YOU, WE ARE WORKING WITH FELICITY TO SAVE IT."

Birch gave a long sigh, and turned round; Roni breathed a sigh of relief.

"Good girl, well played, you used your brains. You are a doctor here, you must be seen to be aiding the community, thanks, I wanted to batter the bitch too, but it would have served no purpose, you did good Jemi."

Birch walked across the grass holding her head up high, Peter Saxon stood outside his shop, he smiled and gave her a nod, she noted it, so did Roni.

"Jemi, this is a chess game, play carefully and deliberately, but never rush at the queen, set up your bishops and knights, then strike."

"I already am mum, and have been for a while." She smiled as they reached the practice.

"That's my girl."

Chapter 23

# Called Out.

The previous day had left Deb's upset and down, and that had
its effects on all of us. Birch was nervous, it was her open day
for the practice, and all of us, in a show of support, went to the
practice as volunteers for the day. I was on wine and coffee duty,
as there was free wine and small eats, Chloe and Edwina were
helping promote the youth program, and the counsellors were
free to mingle, and explain their roles within the organisation.

The doors were propped open, and all we needed was villagers
to enter. Roni and Will were on hand, and even my mum showed
up to offer her support, she made the most of cornering us, she
had Village Fete places to fill and handed us the forms to take
part in the competitions. We had not really done it since that year
we won places, Anthony had continued, but we had avoided it.

We gathered as a group, and it was decided, we would repeat
our entry as of five years ago, and so we were set, on flower
arrangements, jams and cakes. Mum was happy and badgered
the two new receptionists, Megan Sutton age twenty, and
Alexandra Davis Thomas age twenty two. It was yet another two
young people kept in the village through employment, of which
Jim Sutton, was very pleased. As a local farmer he had three sons,
and two other daughters, and whilst his sons stayed on the farm,
his daughters had left for work, keeping Megan at home was a
welcome relief for him and his wife.

It started slow, but as the morning got closer to lunch time,
people started to arrive, and the place filled up. Birch and Roni
stood side by side, welcomed everyone as they walked in, and
they were allowed free access to all areas of the practice. Rodger
and Pat walked people round, Izzy floated all over, and Gill spoke
from reception, with the new receptionists, as they observed, and
got a feel for the place.

Chloe and Edwina were in the back meeting room, with flyers

and leaflets, talking to adults and the young. I smiled and handed out glasses of wine, or made coffees, and also helped by following Gill's lead, informing people of the full services available.

It appeared to be going well, and Birch looked relieved and very happy, when four black suited men came in, and walked to the reception desk. One of them showed a card to Gill, as I watched from a few feet away.

"Donald Islington, Inland Revenue, and these two gents are Customs and Excise, can I speak to the proprietor of this establishment?" Gill looked at the credentials, and looked across the room.

"Dr Dixon?"

All three of them turned and looked at her, I sniggered. Birch came behind the desk, and looked at the man.

"I am Doctor Jemima Dixon; how can I help you?" He looked at her with cold eyes.

"Are you the proprietor of this business?" She smiled.

"I am, is there something I can help you with?" He pulled a sheet of paper out of his small case.

"Yes, you can close this place down, and clear the building, we are shutting you down, pending a review and audit of your accounting and personal service practice."

I stopped dead, and looked at Birch, who was momentarily lost for words, she took a few seconds trying to fully comprehend what he had said.

"Excuse me, this is just an open day, the practice does not commence trading as a therapeutic centre until Monday." He looked a little surprised.

"You are not trading?" She was trying to understand the situation.

"No, as I just stated, we do not open until Monday, this is a brand new start up. You have everything you need to know about this practice on your files, I submitted all the paperwork required months ago, it is all on your system." He turned, and looked at one of the other men in a suit, and then turned back to Birch.

"I apologise Dr Dixon, but we have been given information that this is a front, for a sexual operation, and I have to follow through with a full review and audit of your finances and paperwork. Until this is complete, you have to empty the building and close this establishment." Birch looked up; she was clearly upset.

"Mum?" Roni came up to her side.

"What is it Jemi?" Birch's eyes filled with tears.

"They think this a sex parlour, and they are shutting me down." Roni held out her hand, and turned to the man.

"I am her mother Doctor Veronica Dixon, head of the Dixon Therapeutic Group, this is psychotherapy clinic registered with the NHS, I will need to see your full identification and paperwork. If you would care to follow me, we can discuss this matter in private... Jemi, William."

She guided them through the doorway towards the offices. I felt my anger rising as I looked at my mum.

"Frigging Marjorie, yesterday Deb's, today Birch, mum you need to fix that bitch before I do, because if Birch loses this place, I mean it mum, I will burn the church and the vicarage down."

My mum looked shocked. Izzy came through from the back room, and walked up to Gill and me.

"We have to shut up shop, orders of the Inland Revenue, and Customs, can you help get everyone out? I am sorry guys, looks like your friend has pulled a lot of strings. Roni is on the phone to Bradley, Jemi will need legal representation." I swallowed hard, and felt my heart beat faster.

"They have not arrested her, have they?" Izzy smiled.

"Not yet, but someone has made a report that this is a front for a massage and sex parlour, and a high class call girl operation, it is going to take a little time to sort all this out. Deads, Jemi asked that you do not do anything rash, her mum and dad are helping her."

I nodded, although my blood was boiling, people appeared through the doorway from the back, and some headed out across reception, and out onto the street, some hung around watching us. Chloe and Edwina came out from the back, both of them were looking upset, Edwina looked at Izzy.

"Rodger and Pat are getting their things, everyone else is out, and the back is clear, Izzy this is fucked up, it's that nasty cow again, isn't it?"

The practice front area was full of people who were watching silently, I probably should have not done it, but I could not help myself, I looked at Izzy.

"You know what this is don't you Izzy, it's that witch Marjorie Wallace? She will do anything to stop the young in this community from being successful. All she cares about is her own fat ass, and running this village in a state of fear. She does not give a shit about anyone living here, all she cares about is fixing the vote, and skimming the cash off the top, to line her own fat pockets. This centre is a great thing, that would really help this community, Birch has worked her ass off to make sure she can help everyone, and that fat ugly bitch hates us for it. I am telling you now, she will drive everyone with a different opinion to hers out of this village, it is not right, Birch deserves better than this, she is trying to help this village, not destroy it."

"ABIGAIL THAT IS ENOUGH!" I looked at my mum.

"Is it mum, I mean, really is it enough? She has bullied and blackmailed too many into suppression in this village, well I for one, will not back down. Birch and me are on the side of the people, and if no one else has the guts to face her, then I will, if it saves this community."

It had the desired effect; it was too late now. I had declared war, and mobile phones would be lighting up all over the place, because if there is one thing I know about this village, it is the gossips move faster than e mail. The word was already out, and it was too late to stop it. Izzy smiled and winked, she understood me, so did Gill, who was quietly smiling with her head down. Mum turned to help everyone leave.

When the place was cleared, Izzy, Gill and my mum sat behind the reception desk, when one of the men in suits came out and looked at us.

"Everyone out, that includes you lot." Izzy looked at him.

"I stay, I am first in and last out, I am the practice manager of this facility, Public Liability, and our insurance demand it, so as long as you are here sonny, so am I." she sat down, he looked at us.

"Alright you stay, the rest go."

We all walked out and stood outside, mum looked flustered, I looked at her.

"Mum it is time to choose a side, it is us against her, and you need to make a choice of who you are backing?" She glanced at me.

"Don't be absurd Abigail, I don't have to choose, I am behind you and Birch, and you know it." I smiled.

"Good because for my next trick, you are going to really hate me. I will not stand by and watch Birch be destroyed, if she wants a fight, fine, I will bloody well give one." She looked very concerned, and had that panicked look in her eye.

"Oh god, what are you planning now?"

"Mum I love Birch, I really do, I know it is not what people want to hear, but it is how I feel, and no one is going to attack her without facing me. I have had years of her shit, well I am done, this will end now." I took a deep breath. "Follow me." Gill looked at me with a smile.

"No idea what you are doing, but I am coming, and I am helping, she is my boss, and a mate." I winked.

"Let's go, we need the Post Office."

I walked off up the street towards the Post Office, my anger was rising, and with each step, I felt even more pissed off. Mum trotted just behind me to keep up, Gill appeared to be really enjoying herself. We arrived at the Post Office, and I marched in. The anger inside me was growing, it had been for over five years, but even I had not really understood just how much I had trapped inside. Everything that had happened to me, to Deb's, Chloe and even Hatty, had happened for just one reason, and it was time, someone made a stand.

I grabbed a pad off the shelf, and a packet of biro's, the place was busy. Peter was behind the partition, and Mary was behind the till serving, there were two queues of people waiting. I opened the pad and wrote quickly. I signed the letter and tore it out of the pad, and folded it neatly.

The gossips were already working, the news was spreading fast. I walked up to the Post Office queue, where Annie Baxter was buying stamps. I stood at her side, and smiled, she looked at me and gave a wide smile.

"Annie, I really am in a huge rush, would you let me jump in front for one minute, and I will happily pay for those stamps." She gave a grin.

"Abigail, oh yes please do, I have heard about all the goings on, it's shocking." I nodded at her.

"Isn't it just? I mean, picking on a young bright doctor, it is disgraceful if you ask me." I slipped in front and looked at Peter Saxon through the glass partition.

"Mr Saxon, I know you to be a true and honest man, and so I want to hand this to you. This is a letter, calling for a vote of no confidence in Marjorie Wallace, as Vice Chair of the Parish Council. As a life time member of this community and property owner, I believe under section 62, clause 9 of the Parish Council Constitution, I have the right to call for an explanation under section 12, clause four, which is when a council member deliberately risks the livelihood of a resident, they should be called into disrepute and removed from office. If the vote is carried at the next public meeting, I need a council member to accept it, and have it seconded, before it applies. Please accept this on my behalf." He looked shocked.

"Abigail, do you know what this means?" I gave a nod.

"I do, I have been reading the constitution, as I would like to run one day." He took a deep breath; the place was completely silent.

"I have to say Abigail, you have guts, but I still need a second."

"I will second. Felicity Watson, Chair of the Parish Council."

I turned to see her looking terrified, at the back of the shop with her hand up. I gave a sigh of relief and smiled, the buzz of conversations instantly started, I turned back to Peter.

"I would also like to pay for these, and Annie's stamps." He gave a long sigh.

"That is £8.25."

I held my contact card to the machine and it bleeped, he handed me the receipt.

"Good luck, you know what will come at you, be careful Abigail." I smiled.

"I have taken nothing but abuse from her and shouldered it all, so has Birch, and our friends, we will handle whatever she does."

He nodded. My heart was racing like an express train, and I was sweating, he gave me a nod, I think he understood.

"You will have your meeting, you can withdraw it anytime up to 24 hours before, just so you know, and if I may add. I actually think whether or not you or your friend Birch apply, you would be inspirational council members." He smiled. I handed Annie her stamps, and she gave me a big smile.

"I voted for your mum, and I would vote for you too Abigail." Murmurs reverberated round the shop.

I walked out holding a pad and a pack of biros, Gill followed with my mum, she looked really worried as she looked at me.

"This will get really dirty Abigail, and I am not saying it will be easy. I texted your dad, he told me he will back you 100% so that is two out of the seven members with you, it will not be easy to get the other five, we all fear her."

I understood, I had been watching village politics all my life, I knew how things worked, and as predicted, bang on time, the work of the gossips did its job.

I smiled, as Marjorie came storming out of the Tea Rooms, she was red in the face. She marched across the road towards me. I saw my mum tense up, Gill was loving all of this. Marjorie came right up to my face and leaned into me. I could see the Tea Room empty out as everyone wanted to watch.

Okay at this point I want to point out, I was shit frigging scared, this woman is very powerful. Before acting, I had asked myself one question, which was are my feelings for Birch strong enough to overcome my fear of Marjorie? As she leaned in on me, my legs were trembling, but I was not going to back down. All I could think of was, Birch would do it for me, and I knew the answer was yes. She screamed at me in a rage.

"HOW DARE YOU MAKE SUCH ACCUSATIONS TO THIS COMMUNITY." She lifted her arm and pointed at the post office. "NOW GET IN THERE AND TAKE THAT LETTER BACK!"

Honestly, how I did not pull a Chloe, and piss all over the pavement I have no idea? I gritted my teeth, and stared right back in her face, her breath stunk.

"NO.... Call off your dog's first." My mum stood behind me, utterly terrified and holding her breath.

Yep, I was about to pee, but I was so angry, I could feel it boiling inside me, and it was too strong for me to control. She stared at me, and it was pretty bloody intimidating.

"You have a nerve Abigail Watson, trash like you has no place in this village. Now get in there and withdraw that letter."

I leaned back, a crowd was forming all around us, as the Post Office emptied. I stood my ground, and clenched my fists, and I felt a surge roar up inside me.

"TRASH LIKE ME... YOU MEAN UNDER THIRTY AND FORWARD THINKING?" I laughed and smiled.

"Yeah, that is it isn't it; you cannot control us as easily as you can the others, can you, that is why you call us all trash because of what? You cannot blackmail us like you have everyone else, well guess what MADGE, everyone in this village is tired of your shit, and us young ones aim to do something about it. We are the future, and it will be us giving back to these people, not taking back handers." She was almost purple.

"HOW DARE YOU, YOU HAVE NO PROOF, AND YOU MAKE RANDOM STATEMENTS, FOR WHICH, YOU HAVE NO EVIDENCE TO PROVE IT!"

God her breath was vile, I wafted my hand in front of my face.

"Phew Madge, suck a mint; it smells like rotten shrimp. I do not have proof, but my dad does, there is still the matter of Birch's five hundred pound cash donation to resolve, and I can prove you set up the mobile library to hurt the bookshops sales, and hurt Debbie Wheeler. You see Madge, just like this, you were shouting your mouth off, and quite a lot of people heard you scream at Bethany, for moving the library away from the bookshops front." I leaned in and lowered my voice.

"I also have something hanging in my wardrobe, which I found in my cellar, and you will never guess whose name was in it, and I am not talking diving suit, but you know that don't you?" She snorted out of her nose like a bull.

"You will regret this, Abigail Watson; you will withdraw that letter before I am done with you. I will make sure you never sit on the council." I stepped back; her breath was awful.

"Call your dog's off Birch, and leave us alone. That is all we have ever wanted, which is to come home from Uni, and live our lives. Let us do that without interference, and I will withdraw it, carry on this five year old vendetta, and I will face you at the next public meeting, challenge you, and have you replaced." She smirked.

"You don't have the guts, all you whores know how to do is how to fornicate, you will not last the month." I shrugged.

"Good to know one of us is getting laid, just you try me and see Madge." She spat on the floor at my feet.

"Look at you shaking like a leaf, that is the problem with your generation, none of you have a spine."

She was not lying, I was terrified, and my legs were shaking, and at this point, even I was not aware of how long I could keep this up.

"Yes Madge, I am scared, I am just like everyone else in this village, we are all scared, but someone has to make a stand. As your favourite target, who is tired of being shamed by you with your lies about me, I want to set an example to this village. So call off your dogs, or I will not stop until you are ousted."

She screamed in my face and I almost peed, my pants were damp, there was definitely some leakage.

"NEVER!" I stepped back.

"Then we are done talking."

I turned, and walked away in a straight line, and just left her standing alone, as everyone stared at her. I was breathing rapidly, as everything in my brain crashed, what the hell had I done? The tears came. I was walking as fast as I could, I heard Gill, behind me.

"I seldom swear Mrs Watson, but 'Fuck' that was terrifying, how the hell did she do that?"

My bravery ended, and panic surged into me, I started to run, my mum called out to me, but the tears were flowing. I could see the blurred sign of the bookshop, and I tried to keep it in my sights, I ran for all I was worth, and crashed in through the door sobbing, Deb's saw me and rushed out to meet me.

"ABBY WHAT IS WRONG?"

I dodged past her, hitting the book cases, scattering books everywhere, as I tripped and stumbled. My heart beat was thumping in my head, as I ran to the back, where I knew the toilet was, but it was too late. I smashed in through the door, and my bladder gave way, and I pissed my pants. I pulled them down, and sat on the toilet, and just burst into tears. Deb's knocked on the door sounding terrified.

"Abby.... Abby talk to me please, I am scared, what is happening?"

I was shaking violently, and pushed my legs up against the door and just sobbed, I had never been as scared in my life. I looked down at my wet shaking legs and hands, and just wailed in fear, what the hell had I done? I needed Birch. I sat there for a while, trying to calm down, there was a gentle tap on the door.

"Abby, sweetheart, please come out. What you did took immense courage, I have never been as proud of you as I was watching you. Come on darling, come out." I sniffled.

"Mum I can't, I pissed my pants. I was so scared, and now I am sat here not knowing what to do." I started to cry again. "Mum I am sorry; I didn't mean to pee."

"Alright darling, I will text one of the girls, to go and get you some clean ones, don't worry, you are safe here." I was still shaking.

Chloe showed up fifteen minutes later, I opened the door, and she stepped right in and hugged me.

"You are a fucking legend, that is the coolest fucking thing I have ever seen, fuck you are the maddest of all of us. Shit Abby, I am so proud of you, God I love you so much at the moment." I had no idea what she was talking about.

"Chloe how did you see it, I thought you were at home?" She smiled.

"Hatty was with me. One of the villagers live streamed it, and we all watched it as it happened, although you know what those social media fascists are like, they cut the stream when Marjorie called you a whore, but fuck, what I saw was blinding. Edwina is trying to find out who streamed it to see if it was filmed, I hope so, I really want to see it again, my god you were awesome." Her eyes were wild, and dancing she was so happy. I looked down.

"Chloe I was so scared I pissed my pants."

She looked down, and then realised, she handed me the pants, and a pack of wipes.

"Fuck Abby, I would have pissed myself the moment she came at me."

Wiped down, and with clean pants, I came out, which is a good thing as my bum was going numb, sat on a cold toilet. Mum hugged me so much I thought I would suffocate; Deb's had been filled in by Gill and Mum, as she cleaned the books up. Gill took my hand, and squeezed it.

"What you said was right, she called my sisters so much, they left the village. I really admired you today, I rang my mum and she told me she would back you at the meeting, and I know my dad will."

I smiled and took a deep breath; my heart was still fluttering. All I really wanted to do was go home.

I stayed and had coffee with Deb's, and then I walked out of the shop with my mum and Chloe. I did not look back, but once again, I could feel that sensation, and I knew my name was on everybody's lips. I just wanted to get home, I wanted to feel Birch's arms round me, and once I made it in, my whole world collapsed to find she was not there. Edwina had got hold of Izzy and was getting regular reports.

Birch was still there in the meeting room, the Inland Revenue were on her office computer going through every item accounted for in the set up, and checking all the paperwork. Some of the other men had conducted a thorough search of the place, and found nothing to suggest anything along the lines of a massage parlour.

They checked Roni, William's, and Birch's credentials and education history, and took copies of all her leaflets, they even contacted the NHS registrations to ensure it was legit. They were to say the least thorough. Birch sat for seven hours answering questions with her mother, before they were finally satisfied, she looked exhausted and pale when she finally got home.

Everyone rallied round her, but she just walked upstairs to her room, Roni nodded and I followed her. William and Roni took the others into the room to fill them in. Her door was locked, so I entered through my room, and was relieved to see the partition door was still open. Birch was lay face down crying into her pillow.

I climbed onto the bed, and lay by her side and slipped my arm round her, she turned to face me, her eyes, red and swollen. No words were spoken, I just pulled her close and held her as she cried.

Seeing her like that, I think I hated Marjorie more than I have ever hated anything. This was her dream; I had known that since

I first went to Uni. It had been her single ambition in all that time, and today should have been a glorious day, and it had been destroyed for her. Birch fell asleep, and I slipped off her blouse and slacks, and pulled the duvet over her, I felt exhausted and emotional.

I came down stairs, Roni looked straight up as I walked in, I tried to smile.

"I have put her to bed, let her sleep for a while."

I looked round the room, it had filled up. My mum and dad were there, so were Bradley and Ellen, and also Derek and Margret Pemberton, Hatty was leaning against the wall. I shuddered as I saw the Shredder sat in the corner, reading through some papers. Derek Pemberton smiled at me

"How are you Abigail, that was quite a face off you had?" I flopped down next to my dad; he slid his arm round me.

"I am tired, and honestly Mr Pemberton, I am scared, but what choice did I have, she has pushed us all too far this time?" He gave a gentle nod.

"You did not say anything the rest of the village has not thought in private, but hell girl, you told her right to her face. A lot of people were bloody impressed."

I didn't feel impressive, I leant into my dad, and he tightened his embrace. It felt nice, I was glad to be home, and once again out of sight. I looked round the room.

"I have always run away from fear, I have always hidden from it. When I came home from Uni with Birch, I wanted to run away again then, but Birch called me out on it, and she stood by my side. When Martin tried to hurt Chloe, it was Birch again who gave me the courage to face him, and tell the police about what he had tried to do to me. Birch has taught me so much, and so today, when they went for her, I stood up for her, I was not brave, it was the right thing to do. I wanted her to know I was there for her, and I had her back, like she had mine, and Chloe's, and Deb's and also Edwina's. This is who we are, and what we do, we stand, fall and fight together, no matter what, and it is time the village learned from us." William smiled and raised his glass.

"I have total respect for all of you, and Abby... Thanks for standing up for her, I owe you." I smiled.

"I only did what you and Roni taught her, because she taught us the same." Roni gave a nod, and smiled, Derek Pemberton raised his glass.

"We are behind you girls all the way, and we will help wherever we can. Birch and yourself have been great friends to my girls, it has not gone unnoticed. We both owe you a great deal, having our daughters here in the village means everything to us, even if they do not visit as often as they could." Chloe rolled her eyes.

"God dad, embarrass us much?" He chuckled. Hatty leaned off the wall.

"The problem is Marjorie has a lot of connections, I think it is obvious that her sister in law is involved, she is a high up in the Inland Revenue. She also has that slippery snake of an MP in her pocket, plus most of Oxendale Council. They would have to of approved of the mobile library, she will not back down, you pretty much declared war on her today, and it will divide this village, but you have the best ace Abby." I looked up at her.

"How... What ace do I have?" She looked at me.

"Birch got a resolution passed by the Parish Council, to protect the young, and help them to remain here in the village. There is not a parent out there that is not grateful that finally someone is doing something to keep their children close. I have to give Birch her due, that was an act of genius, and it has resonated through the whole village, if this does come down to a vote, you have substantially increased the odds in your favour."

"It does not feel like a great deal to be honest Hatty." She disagreed with me.

"How it looks is what is important. Birch has three in her practice, Deb's, has taken on one, Celia has given her two girls full contracts, Norman is interviewing for four, even Mary and Peter have a young assistant for the shop in mind, who knows how many more people will consider it. The thing is every time one gets hired, that is one more grateful parent. Even Derek Werrington from the antique shop, has been singing your praises in the Hunter's, and we all thought he was a bigger fan of Madge. No, I think your support is growing, and all I can say is keep encouraging more."

It was all very well to say, but for five years it had been me on the receiving end, and yes, I had faced her, I am still not sure how, because I was petrified, and actually, I was even more afraid now it was all over. I stood up.

"I do not wish to be rude, but I am really tired, I am going to go and lie down for a while, and check on Birch."

I walked upstairs and undressed, and then slipped into bed, and snuggled up to her. I slid my arms round and cupped her boob, the way she always did mine, somehow it always made me feel safe, and I hoped it would help her. Her hand slid up and held mine against her boob, and I relaxed, feeling her warmth, it is all I had wanted all day, just to be close, just to feel safe.

I closed my eyes, and listened to her breathing, I loved the sound of it. Birch's breathing always reminded me of the sea, that constant rhythm of the waves rolling over each other before racing to the shore. It felt peaceful, and relaxing, and I felt myself drift, all warm, cosy and snug.

Tomorrow would be another day, what the hell would she do next?

Chapter 24

# Curio Life.

"Hello, I am Jemima Dixon, My Curio friends call me Birch, you know, the hair and all. I am 25 years old, and I hold a doctorate in Forensic and Clinical Psychology. I am also a qualified relationship and sexual therapist, living in Wotton Dursley, a small village in the South of England. I want to welcome you to Curio Life, a website dedicated to young adults under the age of 30, who are struggling with issues of Bullying, Victimisation, Sexual Identity Issues, Acceptance, and so many other aspects of life today in Modern Britain, we are here not only to tell our story, but to give you a platform to tell yours."

"CUT!.. Brilliant Birch, okay we will move on to the rest of it."

And suddenly our house is a film set, so let me rewind back to last night, when everyone was dealing with the fall out of Birch being investigated by the inland revenue, and then my encounter with Marjorie.

I went to bed, and snuggled up with Birch, and after a lot of legal talk, it was clear that a lot of things would be hard to prove. After everyone left, Deb's Chloe and Edwina were sat with Roni and William, feeling very frustrated, as we all knew that Marjorie was behind everything, we just had no way to prove it, and it felt unjust.

Edwina had been online, and had followed up on leads given her by Hatty, and she found out that Marjorie did indeed have a sister in law, who was pretty high up in the inland revenue. To top that off, Marjorie was the single largest donator to the local MP. She also had several seats on high up committees with Oxendale Council, and it was one of those that approved the mobile library. All of this was printed out by Edwina, and laid out on the large table in the library. Roni was impressed, and Edwina was frustrated, she was sat in her seat looking at her monitor as

Roni commented, and Edwina's response was.

"Never underestimate the power of the internet, most people hit social media, but there is so much more when you use it properly, nothing can hide on the internet." Roni looked at her and gave a wide smile.

"So why not use it then, use it to all this groups advantage?" Edwina had frowned unsure of what Roni meant.

"How do you mean use it, I am doing, that is how I have found all that?"

Chloe was watching blankly, trying to follow, but not really sure. Roni shook her head.

"Edwina you are a computer wizard, use your magic, tell me, what is your biggest problem at the moment?" She stared at her screen.

"That old witch." Roni chuckled.

"Okay so why are you all so frustrated?" Deb's was sat in my chair at my desk.

"Roni, no matter what we do, she always finds a way to overcome us. No one knows the real truth of what we have suffered, if they did, they would speak up, and stand with us." Roni Smiled.

"So, tell it... Tell them, all of them... Let the world know what it is like to be a what do you call it, A Curio?" Edwina jumped in her seat.

"Roni you are a fucking genius, oops... Sorry, my bad." Chloe looked blankly at Edwina.

"We all know that, she has like two hundred million views on her vid... E.... O's HOLY SHIT RONI!"

The penny dropped, and as Edwina went to work, Chloe grabbed her camera and lights, and within an hour, the house was a film studio, and all while Birch and I slept, and Curio Life, was born.


Breakfast this morning was crazy, ideas were popping, I was sat sipping my coffee, and Birch was watching Chloe on her laptop.

"Hi I am Chloe, I am an artist, and I am 24 years old. It is so tough being a young artist, I live for painting, and er... Well sex too, it inspires my work. I have been skint for ages, really trying to stay afloat, and I can tell you guys, god, it has been so hard, and that was when I ran into my group of friends, who we call the Curio's." She gave a really sweet smile.

"You see guys, the problem is, here in my village I want to belong, but there are some here who hate me, because I don't really fit in. I like life and modern stuff, I don't wear clothes a lot, yeah, I really dig the nudist thing, but if I have to wear clothes, I want them to reflect me, not some old bores idea of what I should be like, and for that I get called slut, trash, and whore. I laugh it all off, but I can tell you all, alone in secret, I have done a lot of breaking down, and shed a lot of tears."

She stopped for a second, and her face clouded over, almost as if remembering something painful.

"I am young, so I'll ask all of you out there, why is it wrong to just want to be me? I know you guys really get it, so hey, why not make me a video, and let me see your story, I think that would really be brilliant. Come on don't be shy, I shit myself filming this, but you know what, I am really glad I have done it."

Birch looked up from the screen.

"Wow Chloe, that is really touching. Edwina, you have something really worthwhile here, so tell me more."

Deb's had the bookshop to open, and Izzy departed with Chloe, to head to the practice to clean up, it still had to open on Monday, no matter what was thrown at us, and the men from the revenue were not tidy.

Edwina moved into the library and showed us what she had, it was just a basic site, but had a blog attached, and a video section. There was an introduction page, and help tab for resources. Birch looked at each part carefully, her eyes combing over the site, inspecting every aspect of it, before she looked up at us gathered round.

"This could really work, we could talk to every villager via this, and get the truth up, but I will warn you guys, we will have to step very carefully, I don't want a liable or slander case tossing at us. But yes, this could help not just us, but so many more. Right, I am in, what do you need from me?" Edwina smiled; Roni looked over the computer.

"Jemi this could really serve as a vehicle for youth, it is a perfect vehicle for your program to keep young adults in the village, I think you should add that too, and document the progress of the program, it may inspire others."

It was Saturday, and we had nothing better to do, so we headed out into the vast garden and picked out filming locations. Chloe had filmed herself alone in her studio, and with a lot of space and a big house, we knew we could film just about anywhere.

A blog was needed, and who better to write it, and so I sat with a pad, and started to write, whilst Birch stood in the garden, in her business suit, surrounded by large flowering shrubs and looked into the camera. Edwina stood behind the camera, and lifted her hand.

"ACTION!" Birch smiled.

"Hello, I am Jemima Dixon, My Curio friends call me Birch, you know, the hair and all. I am 25 years old, and I hold a doctorate in Forensic and Clinical Psychology. I am also a qualified relationship and sexual therapist, living in Wotton Dursley, a small village in the South of England. I want to welcome you to Curio Life, a website dedicated to young adults under the age of 30, who are struggling with issues of Bullying, Victimisation, Sexual Identity Issues, Acceptance, and so many other aspects of life today in Modern Britain, we are here not only to tell our story, but to give you a platform to tell yours."

"CUT!.. Brilliant Birch, okay we will move on to the rest of it." It was a rap, and Roni watched on with approving looks. Edwina turned to Roni.

"Do you remember your speech that you did here at the hall, could I link it to this site?"

"Yeah, no problems, do you need the links?" Edwina chuckled.

"Roni, it's me, do you not think that I don't already have them?"

I was writing away lost in thought, William was sat back from me, reading what I was writing, he leaned forward.

"Abby, you need a cover name for her, something all of you could use, that will ensure you do not get into any legal problems. This will be live online, so cover your bases." I understood, I had been trying to think of one, on my notes I had put a star every time I mentioned her.

"I have a long list, you know, Cow, Witch, Bitch, Gargoyle, Harpy, and the like, I just think they are too obvious." He gave a grin.

"What about Shrew? An animal that is mouse like, with razor sharp teeth, and is known for being fiercely territorial, as it drives off its rivals. They also only come together to mate only, and if what I have heard is true, that does sort of explain what does Jemi call him, the Bell Twat?" I started to laugh, he was so right, it was perfect.

"The Shrew it is, yeah I love that Will, it fits her perfectly, tiny little eyes, and a long nose, and a nasty bite. Phew, I am amazed I survived her, although I did piss my pants." He patted my shoulder.

"I watched the video, Abby, the fact you did not in the first minute, was a miracle, she is pretty bloody intimidating. I think you stood your ground fantastically, you put yourself down, but you deserve the praise you got. Stronger people than you have fallen to her, if what I hear is true. Hold your head up Abby, standing up for what you believe is a noble act."

It was nice to hear it, especially from William, I sat back for a moment, the sun was really nice today, not too hot, as there was a breeze, and it felt nice, on my legs. They had all seen the video, but Birch had said nothing, although today had been pretty crazy. I was strongly aware that Izzy had told me Birch wanted me to do nothing, but instead I had gone off half cocked, and I wondered if she was secretly angry with me, I needed to talk with her.

Chloe came walking out through the patio doors, she held something up, it looked like a piece of paper.

"Have you guys fucking seen this?" Edwina swung the camera round and hit film. "That bitch has done it again, I got an £80 fine." I looked up from my pad.

"What the hell for?" She stormed down the garden.

"I was parked outside the practice, and a copper rolled up level with my car, got out of his car and started writing a bloody ticket. I ran out, but it was already stuck on my window." It made no sense, I stared at her, she had tears in her eyes.

"But why Chloe, we all have parking passes because we are residents?"

"The fucking post code is wrong." She flopped down on the grass in front of me.

"I had to sell my spare laptop, my game console and the designer handbag, my mum bought me, to pay for it, it's not fucking fair guys." She looked at me as her eyes sparkled with tears.

"I told the cop I had filled in the paperwork, I told him I was just waiting for the new one. Abby I sent it in three weeks ago, I really struggled to get that permit, and he did not even look at the one on my window, it was like he knew I had not got the new one." She looked down, and her shoulders shook. "This is not fucking fair; I have done nothing wrong." I reached out and took her hand.

"Hey come on, this is not like you, look, I will talk to mum, I will get her to find out who has your form. Chloe it will be signed and dated, so once she has it, she will talk to the police, and sort this all out." She gave a sniffle.

"It won't make no difference, it's her, we all know it, she fixes everything in this village, it is why everyone leaves." She looked up at me. "Abby you are so brave, she has attacked you for years and you have taken it all. I am not that brave, I am not, I fucking hate her, I do, I was so happy, and she is ruining it all."

I got on my knees, leaned over and pulled her into a hug, she burst into tears and wept. Edwina stopped the filming.

"If that does not get some attention, nothing will." Chloe looked up with tears in her eyes.

"Fucking hell Edwina, did you film that, you bitch?" Birch walked up.

"Chloe, one part of this site will be us telling our story, and that, is exactly what we need to make the villagers see what is really going on out of sight." I agreed.

"As long as we keep her name out of it, she can do nothing to stop us. I am writing the intro blog, and I have named her, 'The Shrew,' she can only come at us if we actually name her, so from now on, we use that." Everyone agreed, Edwina shouldered the tripod.

"I am off to film Deb's in her shop, and I am going to talk to Anthony, he is aware of what is happening, he is really busy, but I hope he will put his name to this. When I get back, Abby, I want your footage, and then Chloe you film me, once I have all that, I will be able to code it all and upload it. I want this site live as soon as possible. Birch I need everything you have on the youth program; I want to build those pages later. Right, I am off to film." I looked up at her.

"Edwina, be careful… Deb's, Birch, Me, Chloe, there is only two of us left, and you are one of them." She gave a nod and smiled.

"I am so aware of that Abby, you have no idea, it is on my mind, and I am keeping my guard up." I gave her a soft smile.

"Okay then, watch yourself."

I watched her leave, and I felt that sinking feeling in my stomach, it reminded me of that summer, when I tried to hide at home, because I knew to venture out, would bring attention and nasty comments I did not want to hear. I wanted to think that by owning a house, and writing my books, I had brought change, but after yesterday it was clear, nothing at all had changed. Well actually there was a small change, it had not been Birch fighting for me, I had fought for her, and even though, thinking of it made me feel sick to the stomach, I was glad I had done it.

Chloe was so right, it is strange in a way, she can be a real liability at times, and she was possibly the most perverted person I know, but she also was spot on. All I had ever wanted was to just be left alone to be me, and yet Marjorie was obsessed with trying to prevent it. I am sure Birch could give me some long complex psychological explanation, as to why Marjorie felt the need to destroy us, but honestly, I am not that interested.

I had hoped challenging her would make her back down, and I think the feeling I had in my stomach, was me denying the fact, that she would call my bluff and see this through to the end. That meant there was going to be even more trouble, and maybe that was my fault, a part of me wished I had done as Birch asked. Another part thought it was time to bring the fight, and finally end this, after all, this had been going on for five years, and all I really wanted was for it to end. Like Chloe, I was so happy, and all I wanted was to be who I was in the house, out there, I wanted simply to be me.

With the practice clean and ready for business, Izzy locked up, and took out her phone to message Birch. She was absentmindedly walking up the street, towards the Post Office, when there before her, loomed the larger than life, Marjorie. She stopped still holding her phone and hit send. Marjorie looked her up and down, Izzy felt no fear.

"Say what is on your mind, I am busy." Marjorie looked at her like she was disgusted.

"So, you are Isabella Johnson, born in Clayton, worked for the Dixon Group for fifteen years, and then moved here? I have heard disturbing things about you. Did you or did you not attack a man with a bow and arrow?" Izzy gave a chuckle.

"Is that what you want to know? Oh dear, your contacts are slipping, if that is all they can find. Come on woman I expected better of the terror of this village, to answer your question, I will tell you. I shot my fiancée up the ass, because he shot me in the leg, he also burned my car and my flat down, he was mentally unstable. I think you would have liked him; I am sure you two could spend days in the Tea Rooms finding fault with me. It is no secret, I wrote a blog for Roni about it, you will find it on her site, just search 'Stalker'." She stared at Izzy, who was not in the slightest bit afraid.

"I am watching you, all of you, I do not like your kind, and you will put a foot wrong at some point, and when you do, I will be there to catch you." Izzy shrugged.

"That is a fair deal, I have no issue with that, if I fuck up, you have every right to call me out. I mean, let's be honest, it is better than what you have been doing, like getting your sister to make a false report to the inland revenue. Or how you got your council and MP friends to try and kill little Debbie's business, not that you would ever admit that, but we all know it was you." She gave a smug smile.

"As you can see then, I have a lot of contacts, and I am not afraid to use them, it should be a lesson to all of you. Tell that little whore you are hiding, that I want that letter removing from the council, otherwise it will just get worse." Izzy nodded.

"More inland revenue, police and council problems I take it?" She smirked.

"I am glad you see how far my reach is, finally someone who understands." Izzy nodded and smiled.

"You really have us all in your clutch, but beware, these people you call in favours from, all have deep pockets. I hope it has not stretched your finances too far?" She gave a look of pride.

"Let me put it this way, their pockets are not so deep it will have any bearing on my lifestyle." Izzy smiled.

"I like the fact you can admit it, in a weird way I respect the fact you are happy to do bribes so openly, it takes spirit, as well as cash."

"I am glad to see at least one of you understand how things round here work." Izzy gave her a big smile.

"I will as you have informed me pass on the message, but you know Abby and Jemi, they are both strong willed girls. I may not convince them, but I will say this to you as a warning. I am polite to most, and equally as respectful, but you see I have no care about who you own in the council, or what politician you have in your pocket. I manage that practice, and if you come anywhere near it again, trust me, fear of a little arrow will not be your biggest concern. Leave that practice alone, it does good for this community, hurt it again, and I will hurt you ten times more." She stepped back and looked at Izzy.

"Are you actually threatening me?" Izzy gave a nod.

"Yes, I am, so be on your guard, and leave the place alone. Fuck with me Marjorie, and I promise, you will not last long enough to pay anyone… Okay we are done, I want a nice pretty cake to devour, so I will excuse myself."

Izzy barged past her and walked on, she lifted her phone and looked at the voice recorder, she smiled, and pressed save. Then headed towards the Tea Rooms.


Chloe drifted off to paint, and I had enough on my pad, and so I left Birch with her mum and dad, and headed for the quiet space of the library to write. I like the idea of blogging, but I have never really seriously got into it, and so for me this was a whole new experience. I was going to write it on my computer, and then copy and paste it into the blog feature on the web site. I have a camera filled with pictures from my Uni days and my time here, since coming home that summer, so I had plenty to work with.

Writing for the blog, I felt a new sense of freedom, even though I had completed the book manuscript, of the story of that first summer with the Curio's. I had been constrained by the fact that I had to change everything, and build a make believe place. The blog allowed me to be less censored, and I found that very motivating.

Edwina returned with Deb's, she had spent the afternoon talking with her whilst the shop was open, and as soon as it closed, they stayed back and made a short film feature for Deb's, about what happened to her and her mother, and how she felt, and how she had completely reinvented the book shop. Edwina thought it not only showed who she was, but also what young people could do if they put their minds to it.

I hammered away feeling inspired, and soon had what I thought was a good first blog, explaining the meaning behind the term Curio. I loved it so much, I headed to my room and started another.

I had a list that plotted the journey we had all been on, and I aimed to work down the list, and write a blog for each event. My soul focus was the Curio's and telling their story, and the shaming and suffering they had to endure because of it. Downstairs Edwina was in serious mode, building the site and adding the videos to the vlog section, all that was left was for me to film mine.


I had been at it for some time, when Birch appeared with the tri pod and a camera, she smiled.

"Hi sweetie, it is time for your slot, but I want to do something a little different, will that be okay?" I was unsure, this was Birch after all.

"How different?" She put the camera next to the bed, I was concerned. "You want to make a sex tape?" She giggled.

"No, although…. Would you, I mean could we, should we, oh god Deads, I want a sex tape now, with us?" I shook my head.

"You spend way too much time with Chloe." Birch looked excited.

"Oh wow, do you think she has one, I cannot deny I would love to see it?" I tried to steer the conversation back to the purpose we had in mind.

"When you say different, how do you mean, I thought I was just going to sit in front of the camera and talk?" She sat on the bed.

"Deads I know you; I have seen the attempts you made to film earlier, I mean come on let's be honest, you will avoid a lot of things. I thought we could do it as an interview, you will introduce yourself, and then I will ask a few questions, to lead you into what we think is important for the site." It appeared fair enough, so I agreed.

Birch wanted me to sit cross legged on the bed, and she would use my desk chair, behind the camera, and ask the questions, it seemed simple enough, so I saved my work, and then headed to the bed to get comfy. She nipped off and returned with drinks. I took a big swig, as she sat down and set the camera.

"Just be you talking to me, and answer with what comes naturally." I nodded and took a deep breath. She gave me the signal.

"Hi, I am Abigail Jennifer Watson, I am 24 years old, and a writer, author, and now a blogger. My friends that are close to me call me Deadly, because I have this hair, I love black eye makeup, and I mainly wear black clothes when I am out, I also write gothic fantasy vampire novels. I am here on this site, because the person you see is not who I used to be, for a long time I was naturally blonde, and was the perfect ideal for the village I live in. I was sheltered and protected, and had no idea about life outside, but all that changed when I went to university in Manchester, and there I discovered who I really was." Birch cut in.

"When you say who you really were, is that different from who you were here?" I nodded.

"You cannot be you living in this place, not the real you, if you do not conform, people you have known and loved all your life turn against you." Birch smiled.

"So, I take it at Uni, you could be the person we see now, so I suppose coming home was hard, especially if these people you loved turned on you, what was that like for you?" I suddenly felt emotional, and my voice dropped, and lost its confidence.

"It was hard, I felt so alive when I was at Uni, I was scared coming back, I know these people, and I know how they treat outsiders. I had changed so much; I knew they would see me that way, and I was dreading it. I was right though, people who I had always talked to and cared about, shunned me. One person in particular really attacked me, she has been ever since, she calls me whore to my face, and in front of everyone else, it really hurts me, because I am still me. I have not changed much on the inside, my changes were in my mind, and how I thought, and obviously outside I looked different, but I was still me."

You know you think this stuff goes away, but it doesn't, you deal with it better as times move on, but every now and again, it hits you right in the heart, and it hurts all over again.

"I would imagine that was really hard for you, can you tell me what was it like walking down the street knowing that?" I felt a jerk inside me.

"I wanted to hide, I did not want to be seen, I just wanted to disappear. I could hear my name being whispered, and I knew they were calling me. I wanted to run back to Manchester and never come back. It really hurt, they have no idea how much it really tore me apart inside, I tried to be brave and hold my head up, but the things they were saying were not true. I was not trash, I was well raised, to be decent and respectful, okay so my hair is now black, but I was still the person they knew."

Why was this hurting so much? A tear formed in my eye and ran down my cheek, before I knew it, my other eye filled. Birch sat there watching, she was cool and calm.

"Deadly, that was five years ago, surely it must have changed for you now?" I swallowed hard, and shook my head.

"It has and it hasn't, it is worse now, some people in the village will hate me forever. There have been days when I felt so alone and isolated, I sat on a wall and they all ignored me, and walked past saying bad things, it felt like they would never forgive me for being me."

"How bad did it get Deadly, how low did you go, can you tell us, will you share that?"

I felt the sob in my throat, I did not want to remember that. My whole insides twisted as I tried not to think back to that, I never wanted to remember that time, not ever. I looked at her and shook my head, her bright eyes clouded as she saw my reaction.

"Don't ask me that Birch, you know how bad it was, please don't make me say it." Tears rolled down my face, and my lip started to quiver.

"Deads Sweetie, don't you think they should know what they did, isn't it time they saw how far they pushed you, they were hateful towards you? How many others have they hurt who have not had the guts to stand up to them, tell them Deadly, show them how vile they were?"

I gave a huge sob as the pain flooded into me, and looked down at the bed where my tears dripped.

"I cannot, please Birch, this is so painful, how can I tell anyone something that even I am ashamed of, I am sorry, but I cannot."

"It is alright Deads, I will not force you, I think it is clear how far they went, and the damage they did. All that matters is you made it through, and you are here today, and others will see this and understand, are you alright?" I nodded, and gave a snort.

"I am okay, can I stop this now?"

Birch hit the stop button, she crawled onto the bed, and pulled me into her arms.

"I am sorry, I am so sorry, but they need to see the truth Deads, we have to show them, because you have suffered more than anyone, and this village needs to see what Marjorie has done to you, please forgive me."

I rested on her shoulder and calmed down, she squeezed me tight and just held me. I was glad it was over, but I know I will never watch that video, I have tried so hard to overcome it all, and yet even now I still struggle trusting people and I actually still do not really want to leave the house alone.

Building the site had taken most of last night and all of today, Edwina worked none stop, and by eleven thirty that night, she was ready to go live.

"Right, it is linked to the village site, Roni's site and the practice site, so as soon as we go live, we will see who is out there watching. The next thing we need is a social media presence, so we can share all this stuff around. I suppose guys, now is the moment when the fight back really begins. This summer will be our summer, a Curio's Summer, if all goes well."

Edwina hit the button and the site was published and went live, she sat back and gave a sigh of relief. Birch sat at her desk and typed in the URL, and the site came up on her computer, and it looked amazing, God Edwina was good. I stood by Birch's shoulder as she clicked the links, the blog came up, and looked amazing, it was neat, crisp, and the pictures were really high quality.

Deb's was sat in the living room with her laptop as Roni and Will leaned in, looking at it with her. It felt exciting, and maverick, and it was also really wonderful to know it had been a team effort. It was done, we had achieved our goal, but as happy as we were, suddenly, all of us felt emotionally drained and exhausted. All I wanted was to curl up alone with Birch. We collapsed into bed, and that really is all I remember.

The following morning, Chloe came hurtling into the room, and bounced onto the bed. I jolted awake to her loud voice.

"GUYS WAKE UP, GUYS! TEN PEOPLE HAVE UPLOADED THEIR OWN VIDEOS LOOK!" I sat up in bed and rubbed my eyes.

"Christ Chloe what time is it?" She shrugged, her eyes were wide and wild with excitement.

"Not early, the church bells have been ringing... Sod that Abby, look Gill put a video up, and Stacy, and some other random people. Guys, people are looking at it, see we have had ten thousand views, they are sharing the shit out of it on social media, it is on the walls of every young person in the village, we did it guys, we found a way to talk."

Chapter 25

# Shrew.

The Curio's Life website appeared to be a local hit. I sat at my desk looking at it with my ear phones in, as Edwina built a forum to add to it. Birch was at the practice on its first official day open, and Deb's was in her bookshop. Izzy acted fast, and was busy setting up a group session for all the young who were ringing in to talk, and Chloe was painting, lost to the world, humming to her music.

I cannot deny it was pleasing to see the response the site had got, and I looked at the faces of young people, some who I knew, and quite a few I did not. I clicked on Gill's video, she looked awkward and nervous.

"Hi my name is Gillian, and I am 23 years old. My life is not that bad, I actually just started working for Birch, and I have got to know Deadly a little, as I live in the same village. I have two older sisters, one in Bristol, and one in Nottingham, and I really miss them. My sisters left this village because they were shamed and bullied by the same person who is attacking the Curio's. The blog named her 'The Shrew' so I will use that, she is the most mean spirited person I know of, she is cruel, and hateful to anyone who will not live up to her standards, and I am really terrified of her. The thing is, I do not want to live and act like I am forty, I am only young, and I want to enjoy my life. It is hard living here and being hated, I am so glad I got a job, so I can stay and support my friends the Curio's, I am not brave, but I am with them."

I clicked on the comments box, and saw Birch had already been on, I smiled, she was so on the ball. Birch commented. 'You are exceptionally talented, be you, and be happy, we are with you.' It reminded me so much of my time in Uni, I sat back and closed my eyes, and I could see her sat there on her bed, naked and holding a raspberry gin.

"If you are so unhappy Abby, change, look you cannot be ruled by them forever, why wait, only you can live your life? Don't make the same mistake your mum did, she was like you, blonde hair, pretty floral dresses, and a perfect lady in every way, and she still is, but they broke her spirit. Look Abby, you have the hair dye, you have bought the clothes and you have not even worn them, for god's sake Abby, become something, become that dark beastie you have been talking about for so long, stop pissing about and just do it."

I opened my eyes, and looked at all the pictures of the videos, of desperate lonely, and isolated, young men and women, and all their eyes looked the same, lost and dead, that was me five years ago. I knew these people, I understood them, and it was not much, but I would do something for them. I started to click each video, and at its end I wrote a comment. 'We care... You are not alone... I was you and look at me, it can be done.... Do not lose hope... Be you, and they will have to get used to it." Every video, every face, every lonely soul got something, and to each of them on all of the video's comments I added. 'We are building a forum, soon you will have a chance to talk to each other.' It was the best I could do, to ease their helplessness, but at least it was something.

The keys were clattering as I took out my ear buds, Edwina was focused and yet smiling, she glanced at me, and gave me a smile.

"One word from you and Birch, and all of us is enough, you did good kid, the forum is almost complete, give me an hour and it will be live, and I am also adding a photo gallery and expanding the storage, at the rate this is growing, we will need a hell of a lot of server space." I felt good, and positive, as I got up from my seat.

"I am making coffee; do you want one?" She gave a gasp.

"Please, I am parched, I want this up, so have slaved through it." I wandered into the kitchen.

"COFFEE CHLOE?"

"PLEASE"

I gave a slight smile, I could see her sat naked, and cross legged on the floor, covered in paint, and happy, that was how Chloe should be. There was a tap on the glass door, and I leaned back, the door slid open and my mum looked in, she saw me by the kettle, and smiled.

"Hi can I come in?" I frowned at her.

"Daft question, you are always welcome." She gave a giggle.

"Saw the website, I wondered if the enemy is allowed in these days."

"Mum you are not the enemy, you are with us, mum this is not a war on the older people, it is us reaching out to others who feel the same as we do." She came in and sat down.

"Yeah, I saw the video's, some of them made me cry... I did want to say Abby, I think all of you are very brave, it takes guts to stand up for what you believe in. I never had them with my mum, she was just like Madge, she terrified me."

I understood, gran scared the shit out of me too. I took the coffee to Edwina, and came back, to find Chloe sat with mum, she was smiling, as Chloe wiped a lump of paint off her left boob.

"Yeah Mrs W, it gets bloody everywhere, although I really love this colour." She giggled.

"I would love to paint naked; I would imagine it is so freeing." Chloe gave a happy little giggle as she wiped the paint off.

"I love being naked, I was so hooked up on clothes and makeup, and now I hardly wear any, I have saved loads of money, especially on makeup, that stuff was expensive. It makes me calm when I paint naked, you know you should try it." She gave Chloe a smile.

"Maybe I will." Chloe lifted her drink, and looked at her.

"I paint every day, if you want come join me, I would love to watch you paint, and just so you know, I am so straight it's weird, so you will be safe." I gave a giggle as I reached for my cup.

"Now that is something no man will ever be mum, safe in Chloe's studio."


Mum had been busy, the summer program was in full swing, and she was heavily involved in the events taking place on the village green, and organising the fete. In a show of good faith, she had brought in two volunteers, aged 19 and 21 to help out. Simon Renshaw, and Oscar Holdsworth (Ozzy), and they mucked in with Molly and Sophia. They were both good strong lads, which was a great help moving tables etc. She was also looking into Chloe's parking issue, and had been in contact with the police, who were looking into it.

Marjorie walked into Milton's study, where he was as always looking at his computer.

"Milton, you need to talk to your son, Gabrielle has turned down his invitation again, this really will not do, her parents are very happy for the match, and yet he keeps spoiling everything by being Nigel. Can you not give him some tips and pointers, after all you are his father?"

She walked across the room holding several envelopes, she placed half the stack on his desk, and saw his monitor, it was something she seldom did, after all in the past she had seen some of his club photos, and had found them disturbing. Today he was looking at a house, she frowned.

"What on earth are you looking at the Baker Harding's old place for?" He looked up.

"Well, I am somewhat curious, I was talking to Bradley last Sunday, and he mentioned his company was renovating it. The barn has been converted into a separate accommodation, it is not too large, but I feel large enough for a small family, and the farm house is looking somewhat delightful, I was considering buying it." Marjorie looked horrified.

"What on earth is wrong with you, why would you buy a house so far from the centre of the village?" He looked uncomfortable, like he was looking for the right words.

"Marjorie, this war between you, the Birch girl, and Abigail is going too far. Now I have always tried to allow you to live your own life, and I do not interfere, but I feel changes will come whether we like it or not. Marjorie, I have spoken to all those girls, and they are not really doing anything untoward, they are young ladies with high spirits, nothing more, but this vendetta with you is not doing this village any good, it is dividing the parish. I am the Vicar here; it is my job to administer to all the flock. So, I have been talking to the bishop, and I am thinking of taking an early retirement."

"YOU ARE DOING WHAT?"

He jumped in his seat, and recoiled back slightly. She glared at him with angry eyes, he puffed and panted trying to find the right words.

"I am 61 Marjorie, it is going to happen in the not too distant future anyway, and this property will be a good place for us. It is private, set back from the road, and peaceful, and with the extra accommodation Nigel will have his own home and family." She was actually shocked, as she stared at him in disbelief.

"Milton we are in the heart of this community, this is our home, we cannot just move to the back of beyond, I need to be here in the heart of everything. No, I simply will not allow it." He gave a sigh.

"Marjorie, sadly you have no say in this, it is not just about you, it is about doing what is right for all of us, and that includes myself and Nigel. Whether you like it or not, this is going to happen one way or the other. In four years, who knows what will be available, I think now is the time to prepare. The bishop is going to allow the new vicar who is temporarily based at St Bartholomew's, to join us in two weeks, see the parish, and get a feel for it, and if all goes well, I will stand down, and hand over the parish after Christmas." Marjorie looked mortified.

"BUT SHE IS A WOMAN, HOW DARE YOU EVEN THINK OF SUCH A THING?"

"Marjorie, I have told you, the church is modernising, it has to, and if it does not it will die. Congregations are falling all over the country, and I actually think it is a fine idea for this community. My mind is made up." She folded her arms.

"Well that just about says everything doesn't it? Just because that Birch witch covered up your little hobby with Gwenda and co, you have gone soft on women? Well this will not do, oh no indeed this will not be tolerated, you will singlehandedly destroy this parish, and I for one will not allow it." He gave a long sigh.

"You are being ridiculous, this property is a good choice, you can continue your activities here, it will just be a two minute drive that is all, and I will have more time, to do the things I like. You know administering to the parish is a lot of work, I will enjoy a little more time for myself." She narrowed her eyes and curled her lip.

"Well yes I can see that, more time sulking around getting up to god knows what with those leather clad hussies." He felt insulted.

"I have told you before, it is not like that, we do not do anything that would break our vows. Apart from that one time with Monica, and that was hardly my fault, I was chained to the bed, it was all her." Marjorie walked towards the door.

"Milton, I cannot allow this, I simply cannot, if I have to, I will fight to the death with you to prevent it." She slammed the door and he shuddered.

"Well you may as well Marjorie, let's face it, you are at war with everyone else in this village, you may as well add me to the list."


Birch walked through into reception, holding a green file, she opened it up and looked down at the paperwork.

"Mr and Mrs Pilkington, Hi I am Jemima Dixon, would you like to come through please?" Elizabeth gave him a nudge, and he reluctantly got up off his seat, with a heavy sigh. Birch held out her hand.

"Lovely to meet you both, if you follow me, we are in the lower counselling lounge."

Birch walked through and Elizbeth gave him another nudge, he looked very uncomfortable, and slipped his flat cap off. They followed Birch down the corridor, she turned back and smiled.

"I suppose this is a busy time for you both, what with the fete on the horizon?" Geoffrey Pilkington nodded.

"Aye it is." He looked at his wife. "Not much time for messing about, too much to do." She smiled, as Birch opened the door.

"This way please, it is a nice relaxed setting. Sit down and get yourself comfortable."

They both entered, and headed across the room, he appeared very uneasy, and she noted it. Reluctantly he sat on the large sofa, and Birch moved over to her single seat, set back a little, next to a small table. Behind her was a desk with a computer on it, she sat down and faced them. Geoffrey was obviously very uncomfortable, he was an older man, with thinning grey hair, but looked to be healthy and in good condition, he frowned.

"I heard you were called Birch or Beech or something like that?" She gave a little chuckle, as her green eyes twinkled.

"Birch is my nick name, it's because of my hair and the birch bark look of it." He gave a nod of understanding. She sat back, relaxed, and smiled.

"Okay how can I be of help to you?" Geoffrey swallowed hard, looked at his wife and then back at Birch.

"I will be honest, I am here under protest, this is... Well, it is not the sort of thing I think should be spoken of. It is private you see, but she is insisting, and it is hard when she gets like this. I won't hear the end of it, so I am here, but I will not deny, I am not thrilled about this." Birch gave a smile.

"Firstly, you should know, that I am a qualified doctor in this field, and anything you say will be held in the strictest confidence, there is no shame here, if that is what you are concerned about?" He gave a long sigh, and Elizabeth looked at Birch.

Elizabeth Pilkington was a slender woman, with a good tan, it was clear she worked outdoors, and looked to be in really good condition, for her age she had a lovely figure. Her hair was long and well cared for, even though she tied it back, although she had quite of bit of grey streaked through her black. She smiled a kind and warm smile, and her dark eyes sparkled.

"The thing is Doctor Dixon, we have eight kids; we have always been active in the bedroom." Geoffrey leaned back and gasped, as he lifted his hand and wiped his face.

"Oh Christ!" She ignored him and continued.

"The problem is Doctor Dixon, things of late have slowed down, it has lost its abilities, if you understand me?" Geoffrey rubbed his hand on his face, and he rolled his head around on the back of the sofa.

"Oh bloody hell Liz!" Birch gave a nod.

"How old is your husband Mrs Pilkington?" He lifted his head forward.

"I am 61, and still as fit as a fiddle, I just work long hours, that is all, there is nowt wrong with being a hard working man. It is her, she is too bloody demanding, I cannot just click my fingers, and have everything ready, I am not a bloody tractor." She smiled, at Birch.

"I do not think three times a week is demanding." He looked at her red in the face, and horrified.

"Bloody hell Liz, why don't you just tell her everything, some things should be sacred, you know?" She looked back at Birch.

"I like to dress up for him, that usually works, he really likes the nun, but loves the prostitute, I think it's the crotchless panties." He gave a gasp and leaned back, turning bright red in the face, as he gasped.

"Oh, Christ woman!" Birch gave a smile.

"Look this is a normal thing for a man of your age, and the good news is I can speak to your doctor, and I can arrange for a little medical help." He suddenly looked panicked, and sat up straight.

"Medical help, hold up a little." He shook his head. "I am having none of that, there is nowt wrong with down there, and no bugger is cutting into it." Birch understood, he was starting to sweat, and looked really panicked. She gave a soft smile.

"You are mistaken, I am sorry, I should have been more precise, I was thinking of a pill, that is all. We have some wonderful things that can help you, just one pill, and you will see a big change. Your doctor will have to monitor your blood pressure, just to make sure, but I can assure you, that should be all it will need." He looked at Birch, and then Elizabeth, he gave a little chuckle.

"What that is it, just a frigging pill, after the months of nagging it will go away with a pill? Bloody hell Doctor you are good, I was wrong about you. I thought all this was mind games and mumbo jumbo, but bloody hell, if all it takes is a pill for some peace, that will bloody do me." Elizabeth slapped his leg,

"I have told you, no swearing in front of the doctor." Birch looked at the file.

"Your GP, is Doctor Jake Williamson, I will need you to sign a release so I can speak to him about you, but apart from that, if he thinks you are fit enough, I can get the prescription delivered to your door. I have some leaflets on relaxation techniques, you may find they are helpful, and if you use scented oils, they can be a lot of fun."

Elizabeth smiled, and they both got up, and shook her hand, Birch guided them back into the corridor.

"Thank you, Doctor Dixon, I have been promising him Wonder Woman, and if this works, I will get it for him." She gave a shy smile, Geoffrey looked back her.

"Christ Liz, not in the bloody corridor." Birch led them to reception, and looked at Gill.

"Gill I will need a release signing for an approach to a GP, would you help Mr and Mrs Pilkington fill it in please?" She smiled as she shook their hand.

"It has been lovely to meet you, and anything else you have an issue with, please do not hesitate to come and see me, either together or alone."

Gill took over, and Birch turned, and walked back to the office, she placed the file on the completed stack, and stretched.

"I think that's me all done for today, how are Rodger and Pat doing?" Izzy looked at the monitor.

"It has been steady, your mum has been sitting in with them and monitoring their performance, she appears to be really impressed. We have a way to go Jemi, but it is a good start." Birch stretched.

"I cannot wait to get home, and get out of these horrible clothes."

Marjorie was having a very strange day, first Nigel appeared to be ruining everything, and then Milton, and his revelation of the prospect of a female vicar, and then there was something else, something bizarre. The post man had arrived tipped his hat and said, "Shrew," then walked off. The milk boy did it as well.

When young Gordon dropped off the vegetables from Oxendale, he also did it. She had arranged a meeting of Bethany and Marion at the Tea Rooms, in order to brain storm how they could prevent a female vicar, and hurried out and down the street. She had not even stepped onto Green Street when two girls came out of the salon with red streaked hair, looked at her and gave a nod. "Shrew." They walked off quickly.

She was utterly flummoxed, was this some new sort of greeting, because if it was, she most certainly did not like it? In the tea rooms Celia filled the trays and nodded to Stacy, she came to collect the tray, Celia smiled.

"These are for the Shrew."

Lillian gave a joyful titter, and Stacy, who had let them in on the secret, and showed them the site on her phone, which had Abby's blog post on it, chuckled as she lifted the tray.

She crossed the room with a smile and placed the tray down, and then stepped back, she nodded. "Shrew," she turned, Marjorie looked up at her.

"Just a minute young lady." Stacy turned; Marjorie looked at her suspiciously.

"You are unusually happy today, and what is this shrew business about, I am hearing it everywhere I go?" Stacy was finding it hard not to laugh.

"It is the language of the young Mrs Wallace; we use it as a mark of respect." She sat back in her seat looking surprised.

"Really I had no idea, but that hardly surprises me, everything today is about slang, why we do not teach correct English these days amazes me, okay you can go." Stacy gave a nod.

"Shrew." She walked off with a huge smile, towards the chuckling Lillian and Celia.


Birch came in and the door banged, she dropped her bag and keys on the table, and walked into the library unbuttoning her blouse. I looked up from my computer, and smiled, Birch walked round the desks, and came behind me, she leaned round my neck.

"Hi Sweetie." I kissed her arm.

"Good day?" She slid her hands down over my breasts.

"MMM... I need a hot bath with a hot woman." I giggled as she played, oh god I hate it when she does this, but it feels so good. Her arms slipped lower. I leaned back into her.

"Not in front of the children dear." Edwina giggled, Birch smiled and took my arm.

"I have a need as a hard working wife, run me a bath and I will thank you for it." I giggled as she pulled me up out of my seat.

"Back in a while Edwina." She tutted.

"I want a wife now, I hate you two at times, you won't even let me watch." I laughed as I passed, and leaned down and kissed her on the cheek.

"Maybe we will film it, after all the camera is still in my room." She started to laugh as Birch dragged me out of the door and onto the stairs, she shouted back.

"I STILL HATE YOU BOTH!"


Edwin was home and Felicity was in the office as they went through the mail, and over the arrangements for the coming weekends guest speaker. The Choir night in the church had been a resounding success for Peter Saxon, and this weekend Edwin was to be in control as Anthony Bancroff, Explorer and Adventurer, did a presentation and slide show. Tickets were sold out, much to the relief of Edwin.

Felicity was opening her endless piles of letters, and placing them on the relevant pile, some were trader confirmations and final payments, some exhibiting confirmations, and some more applications to enter one of the many categories in the fete. She opened a brown envelope and frowned.

"This cannot be right?" Edwin looked up, and saw her reading the letter.

"What is it?" She looked up.

"It says there is a wiring fault in the Church Hall, how can that be, it was passed as safe and up to date just last month?" Edwin held out his hand.

"Let me see."

Felicity could not understand it, she handed it over, then got up, and went to one of the boxes on the floor and pulled out a file, she brought it over to the desk and went through its contents.

"See, here it is, we got full certification." She handed it over to Edwin, he compared the two letters.

"There is something not right here at all, and if the wires are unsafe, why is the Church Hall only being closed from August 28th, until September 10th. Why not immediately?"

"Oh god, Edwin, this is Marjorie's doing." He looked up from the letter.

"I know she has caused a lot of problems Felicity, but you cannot blame everything on her." She looked at him with a fixed stare.

"Oh really, Edwin what is planned for Saturday the 31st?" He could not remember and opened his desk diary. He gave a long sigh.

"Oh, bloody hell!" Felicity nodded.

"How do we tell her Edwin; she is going to be broken hearted?" He put his head in his hands.

"This is going too far Felicity; people are getting hurt."

"Edwin there is nothing we can do until the next meeting. If Abby does not take back that letter, and withdraw her complaint, this will continue, because that is what this is all about. I mean honestly, can you see any of those girls backing down? Marjorie has pushed them too far, and I am sorry, but after what I saw last Friday, I am not asking her to withdraw, I think she was right."

He sat back, and leaned his arms on the chair, and placed his palms together.

"Abigail will not back down, she has had years of abuse, and she is very strong minded, and I have to admit Felicity, I was really proud of her standing up. She has really surprised me with her knowledge of the constitution. I actually think she would be a wonderful addition to the council." Felicity got up.

"If I have to go over there and tell Debbie her wedding reception is cancelled, I am having a stiff gin first."

Birch lay back on the pillows, and gave a long soft moan, her legs were wide apart and I was softly kissing between them, her legs stiffened, as I moved inside.

"Oh God Deads!"

"OH MY GOD...! Oh ... Oh I am so sorry."

My mum had arrived, heard we were in the bath, and had come straight up to us, she walked into my room and was confronted with my white, waving naked ass, as I worked my tongue between Birch's legs. Birch looked at her mid moan, smiled and waved.

"Hi Flick."

My tongue froze, firmly implanted between Birch's legs, I slowly withdrew, and looked back, she had turned her back, and I was not sure who was redder, her or me? I slid up the bed and under the duvet, Birch closed her legs.

"Sorry mum, I did not know you were here."

She turned round looking very embarrassed and upset, she was holding some papers in her hand, I thought they were Chloe's passes.

"Girls I really am so sorry; I should have knocked." She looked really flustered.

"Girls we have a huge problem, if it had been anything else, I would have rung, but I felt this should be faced in person."

I knew instantly by her tone, this was a huge issue, mum had that I am so sorry, and I am afraid tone.

"How bad is it mum?" Her face sort of contorted, and then the tears formed in her eyes, her voice went instantly higher.

"Oh Abby, Oh Birch, I have no idea how to say this, so I will just get to it and say it out loud, because I am trying really hard to control my emotions, but I am so...."

"Flick, just say it." Tears dripped off her chin.

"She has closed down the hall from Aug 28th, I do not know how she has done it, but she has, and the council are shutting it down until the repair work is done. I mean it makes no sense; we got a full bill of health for the place just last month." I closed my eyes and leaned back into the pillows.

"Oh bollocks! She has screwed Deb's wedding reception; my god, is there nothing she will not do?" Mum came over and sat on the bed, Birch looked at her.

"She will not stop, until that letter of no confidence is withdrawn, let's be honest, if she hurts Deb's, she hurts all of us, and that is her plan, well screw that bitch, we will find another way." I opened my eyes and sat up.

"How, I mean come on, seriously, where will we find another venue big enough to handle the guest list, the Hunters is not big enough?" Birch turned and looked at me, her green eyes twinkled with devilish delight.

"The show field is though, if it can host a fete, then it can bloody well host a wedding." I looked at her with astonishment.

"Are you off your tits, you cannot have a reception in a tent?" My mum looked at Birch, and smiled.

"It is a big task, you will need permits, and you will also need the Pilkington's on board, it is their field. But you are right, it is possible." Birch gave a nod.

"I need to make a phone call, give me a second." She grabbed her phone off the dresser and slipped out of bed, and dialled. It took a few moments, and then connected, Birch smiled.

"Katie you slag, how the hell are you... Oh you very naughty, and actually, really dirty girl. Look something has come up and I need the biggest favour ever... No, it's bigger than that.... Screw you bitch, she is mine, you dangle your red pussy elsewhere ha ha ha. Nope she won't sleep with you, you will have to ask for something else." She looked at me and winked.

"Katie, we need to put on a wedding reception, with a stage big enough for a couple of bands, in a field." She laughed, and held the phone away from her ear.

"Yeah, for Deb's, that shrew has gone and found a way to have the place closed down before the event... Yeah... Right so you have seen the site, and you understand what is going on?" She walked round the room, stopping and nodding.

"Look I know it's a huge ask, I will throw 200k in the pot to start it, will that help? Okay I will transfer the money tonight, and

I want a bloody invoice, I have the IR up my ass. Okay look into it, and get back to me as quickly as possible, because we have not told Deb's yet, and this will break her heart. Okay talk soon, you old slapper." Birch chuckled as she ended the call, I took a long breath.

"Can she do it?" Birch looked at mum and me.

"This is a big ask, I mean her equipment is all over the country, just getting it here is a logistics nightmare. I won't know for sure until she calls back, but you know this is Katie, and she fancies Deb's, so that is a good sign. If anyone can pull this off it is her, Deb's will have something, she has promised me, as to size and scale, we will not know just yet. The good news is she will get a reception." My mum gave a huge sigh of relief, Birch sat down next to her.

"Flick, go and see Bradley and Ellen, let them know what has happened, and get them here, I want them here when she is told, it is probably better if they are the ones to do this. I am going to get Edwina to work, and we will see what we can find for the event, and try and do a little leg work for Katie." Felicity stood up.

"Birch you are a god send; this village has no idea how lucky they are to have you." I sat there listening, and all the time I was feeling worse inside. I looked at them both.

"This is my fault, isn't it, if I withdraw the letter all this will stop?" My mum turned sharply.

"Don't you dare Abigail, it is the best thing anyone has ever done for this village, and you are quite wrong, according to this letter Mr Johnson visited the Hall at 10 in the morning Friday, you did not hand in that letter until after lunch, this was going to happen regardless of anything you have done." I nodded, my mum can be a bit scary, when she is forceful.

We slipped on our robes and followed my mum down the stairs, Debbie was stood in the living room doorway, mum grabbed her and kissed her forehead.

"Debbie my dear, you are adorable and priceless." Debbie looked at her strangely as she exited.

"Your mum can be weird, I mean ten minutes with you two, and she goes all weird and old hippie." I gave a giggle at her.

"Well, you would know, you live with us." She giggled.

"I love you guys; you know that right?"

Chapter 26

# Pressure.

Bradley Wheeler lifted the phone. "Get me Margret Stuart." He held the phone to his ear, whilst he looked at Felicity, Ellen was in tears, there was a voice on the end of the phone, and Bradley looked at his pad on his desk.

"Margret, we have a problem, and I need you to look into the contract with Ian Johnson... Yes, the electrics inspector... He is not a straight player, and I want him out. I realise we have a contract, so find me a way out, I have sent you some scans of letters, look at them, and find a way. I do not want his feet on any property we are working on, and I will find someone who cannot be bought, to replace him." He listened as she spoke to him, and nodded his head.

"I have to see my daughter Margret, but I will have my mobile on me at all times." He put the phone down and looked at Ellen.

"My daughter will be married, and she will have everything she planned, it might not be in her hall, but one way or the other I will not let her down, I promise you Ellen. Now dry your eyes, I don't care if it costs millions, no one will spoil her day." She gave a sniffle and nodded at him, he had never once let her down, and she trusted him completely.

When Bradley and Ellen arrived with mum, Birch had already been online with Edwina, and was putting together a plan in her mind, on how to resolve this problem. I was sat at my computer, already writing my next blog, and deep down inside my stomach was twisting. I felt really bad, Marjorie started this war, because five years ago, we refused to backdown, and very shortly Deb's would be told her special day would be destroyed. I loved Deb's; she was my oldest friend, and she had already been through the ringer once, I know, I was there at her side during school, and witnessed it first hand.

It looked like Marjorie had reached into those deep pockets again, and targeted her for no other reason than she knew, Deb's was the weakest link, she was soft, caring and respectful, and the easiest to hurt. Chloe was loud and brash, Edwina was very clever and not easily intimidated, and as for Birch, Marjorie knew hurting her would be the hardest, because no matter what she accused her of, Birch always shrugged it off with a 'so what?'

It was unacceptable, and impossible to prove, like most of her dealings, they were done behind closed doors with no witnesses, we had no hope of finding out the truth, but that was not going to stop me from writing about it. I could not directly accuse her, but I could skirt around it enough, that it would be suggested, and so that was my goal tonight.

With the arrival of her parents, we stopped working, got up, and walked through to the hall, to meet them. Edwina showed them through to the living room, my mum hung back and took my hand.

"Bradley is very angry Abby." I was surprised she said that, and looked back at her.

"Wouldn't you be if this was my wedding?" We walked in, and Deb's looked up surprised.

"Mum, Dad, what are you doing here?" She saw Bradley's face, and picked up on it straight away.

"What has happened, why are you upset dad?" He sat down at her side and took her hand, Deb's suddenly looked really frightened, he smiled the best he could.

"Debbie, we have some news that will upset you, but I want you to know, no matter what it takes, I will fix this, I promise." She looked to her mum, her face looking panicked, I felt the knots twisting in my stomach tighten.

"Mum?" Bradley squeezed her hand as Ellen's eyes filled with tears.

"Debbie, there has been a problem, and it looks like the Church Hall will have to close on Aug 28th for two weeks, they say it is a wiring problem." Deb's face turned pale.

"But my wedding reception is on Aug 31st, Dad does that mean I cannot marry Jimmy?" He shook his head, and smiled, tears formed in his eyes.

"No sweetheart, you will get married in the church, and I will find somewhere for the reception, we have everyone booked and ready, I just need to find a new place." She filled up and started to cry, and it tore at me inside, I felt the pain twist inside me, as I heard her weep.

"Dad Jimmy wants the band to play, that is why we booked it, he needs a stage."

Bradley gave a sniffle, and pulled her into his arms, it is so hard to believe seeing them together she is his step daughter, I mean hell my own dad has never been as loving as Bradley is with her.

"I will give you a stage, don't you worry, one way or another you will have one."

I turned to Birch and she was gone, Debs carried on weeping into his shoulder. I cannot deny, in this single moment, I hated Marjorie more than ever. I leaned back and saw Birch on the phone, she was walking up and down in the kitchen. Birch was nodding and talking quickly.

I walked slowly down towards her, she turned on the spot, she looked focused, and yet I could see the strain on her face. She walked back up the kitchen, she saw me and smiled, it was not the smile I knew, she stopped on the spot, and listened very carefully, and then gave a sly grin, as she nodded into the phone.

"You are a goddess; we all owe you so much thanks."

She ended the call, and gave a massive sigh of relief, she looked at me and her eyes danced, as she broke into a smile. Birch walked over and grabbed me by the face, she leaned in and gave me a long slow passionate kiss, I felt my breath catch, and my heart flutter, as she pulled away, her eyes were dazzling and filled with life.

"Do you know how much I love you? Deads, if you want to, and only if you want to, you have my permission to screw Katie." I took a deep breath of shock.

"What... I mean... What? No, absolutely not, I mean, I get she is good looking and all that, but I have told you, I am not interested in other women."

She chuckled and kissed me again, she broke the kiss, and I was gasping for air, wow what a kiss, I was actually wet. Birch grabbed my hand.

"Come on, let's tell Deb's the good news."

She almost dragged me off my feet, my legs had started to tremble, and I found it hard to keep up with her. We arrived at the living room where everyone was around Deb's. Chloe was stomping around behind the sofa cursing Marjorie. Roni and Will were talking quietly in the corner. Birch stood in the doorway.

"Bradley, stop worrying, the event is going ahead, and it is happening in Wotton as planned, regardless of what that Shrew thinks, I have spoken with Katie. It is a short time frame but it can and will be done." He looked confused.

"How?" She smiled at Deb's.

"I love you Sweetie, we all do, so do you honestly think we will let her win?" Deb's swallowed back her tears and smiled.

"You will have an even better wedding reception than the one you had planned, trust the Curio's, we will ensure it, so no more tears." Bradley was still waiting for an answer.

"A little elaboration would be good at this point Jemi." Birch nodded and her eyes sparkled as she watched Deb's.

"When we found out, Edwina and myself got online, I called Katie, and asked what was possible, and Katie got hold of Jimmy's management in Singapore. Tomorrow is their last night of the tour, and then they have some press days, and a few days off before heading back to the UK. They will be sending the stage from their outdoor gigs, back home after it is dismantled tomorrow, and then it will go back to their hanger, be checked over and maintained, and then it will be brought here and erected the day after the fete ends. She has also been in touch with a specialist company, and they will be providing high class Victorian marquees, these things apparently are huge, and they will lay them out in a completely Victorian/Steampunk decoration. It will not be cheap, the Curios have already lobbed 200K at it, but yes Bradley, there may be extra costs."

He gave a huge smile, and pulled Deb's into his arms, and almost crushed her.

"Spare no expense, and send me the bill." Ellen got up, and walked over to Birch, she took her by the hands.

"Thank You." She kissed her on the cheek, Birch smiled.

"We love her Ellen; she is one of us." Roni got up and walked over, she pulled Birch into a hug.

"I really have no idea why I am surprised, but I have to say

Jemi. I am immensely proud of my daughter tonight." Birch wrapped her arms round her.

"I love you too mum."

It was a bitter sweet moment, Roni and Will would be leaving in the morning, and heading back to Manchester, and to be honest, it was clear Birch did not want her to go, but just like Birch, she had a practice to run, and she had to be back.

For the rest of the night as the adults talked, we manned the computers, and updated Curio Life, I finished my blog post, and Edwina uploaded it, we decided that there would be no mention of our plans to save the wedding for now, just in case, we would let Marjorie think she was winning.

It was late when we finished answering comments and emails, as well as spending time on the forum. I was surprised to find Chloe had been on and off all day talking to people, and cheering them on. I do find her surprising at times, I just get to think I know her, and another side to her pops out. Tired and a little drunk, we all made it up the stairs towards our beds, I flopped on the bed and lay on the cool duvet, it felt glorious.

Birch came in and climbed in behind me, she giggled, she was a lot happier than she had been these last few days. I felt her lips on the back of my legs and wriggled, as she slowly made her way up, she reached my bum, and I was already tingling, and I gave a giggle, I rolled over with a smile.

"It's not fair, you know all my weak spots now."

She said nothing but just smiled, and swung her legs round over me. She backed up to my face, and pulled my legs apart.

"We have never done this before."

She gave a giggle and lowered her head, I lay there looking at her exposed rear, inches from my face, how could I possibly refuse, I leant forward and started to pleasure her.

It was early morning in the home office of Bradley Wheeler, Margret Stuart was already there waiting. His phone gave a buzz and Marie his private secretary, announced.

"Mr Johnson is here to see you." Bradley looked at Margaret.

"Send him through." Ian Johnson, came in looking very angry, he slapped a letter down on the desk.

"What the hell is this, we have a contract with your company, you cannot back out on a whim?" Bradley pointed at the chair.

"Sit down Ian." He was red in the face, and he flopped into the chair.

"Bradley this is one of my most important accounts, it makes up a large part of my business, why now, why so suddenly are you determined to back out?"

Bradley looked at Margret, and she stood up and walked forward, she placed a sheet of paper on the desk, on which was a highlighted paragraph, Bradley pointed at it.

"That clearly states that if you or your employees, act against any member of this organisation, or place this organisation in danger or any form of disrepute, then your contract is forfeit. Last night we were handed information that clearly shows you worked against the interests of a member of this organisation, and have risked the good name of this organisation. We deal hard, but we deal fair, and you have proven our confidence in you was ill placed." He shook his head.

"What is this bullshit, I have done no such thing?" Margret placed copies of the letters of the electrical reports on the table.

"Can you tell me why, when you gave a full clean bill of health last month, you felt the need to revisit the church hall, and deem it unfit, but not so unfit, as it could remain open until August 28th?" He looked worried and lifted the letter.

"The stage is dangerous; we found the wiring sub standard." Bradley gave a nod.

"So, the hall could be used, as long as the stage is not used?" He gave a rapid nod.

"As the report shows, it is the stage wiring that is the problem, so yeah, you could use the main roof lighting." Bradley sat back.

"So why August 28th, from what I can see there is a talk on Saturday with an explorer, and he will be on stage, and the week after is the brass band concert, they will be on stage, and the weekend after that is the end of the fete, and a celebrity guest will be on stage, as well as all the participants to collect their prizes. Surely such use of the stage at those events is dangerous?"

He swallowed hard, and he started sweating heavily, he looked down, and tried to avoid the fixed stare of Bradley. Margret placed another document down.

"This is a copy of a report by yourself, that shows the completion of a complete upgrade and rewire, to modern safety standards, done by your company three years ago in February. If this wiring done by you is so unsafe after only three years, why should we trust your company?" He looked up at her, and closed his eyes, and slowly shook his head.

"Please don't do this." Margret looked at him coldly.

"A shareholder of this organisation, had a major event planned for Aug 31st, and that is now ruined, because your company either supplied bad wiring three years ago, or you changed your mind, for some unknown reason. I will warn you Mr Johnson, if you cannot convince me of which, I will expire this contract on behalf of this organisation."

He was caught in a trap, whichever one he admitted to, it would expire his contract. He was clearly panicked as he looked at Bradley.

"Bradley, we go back a way, I have handled thousands of jobs for you, I need this work."

Bradley reached for his phone, he opened his MP3 player, placed it on the desk and pressed play, Marjorie's voice, followed by Izzy's came out of the phone.

Marjorie: "I am glad you see how far my reach is, finally someone who understands."

Izzy: "You really have us all in your clutch, but beware, these people you call in favours from, all have deep pockets, I hope it has not stretched your finances too far?"

Margret: "Let me put it this way, their pockets are not so deep, it will have any bearing on my lifestyle."

Izzy: "I like the fact you can admit it, in a weird way I respect the fact you are happy to do bribes so openly, it takes spirit, as well as cash."

Margret: "I am glad to see at least one of you understands how things round here work." Ian flopped forward, and put his head in his hands.

"Oh fuck." Bradley sat forward in his seat.

"I have enough here Ian, to void your contract, and bring in the authorities, you are stood on the edge of ruin, and I would think very carefully before you speak. I am a fair man, and your record until today has been exemplary, it is why we hired you. I want all the details Ian, if not, Margret will shred the contract, and all your people will be ordered off the jobs they are on, within the hour." He shook his head.

"Bradley you have no idea what you are asking, I have a whole work force dependant on the work I have, if I tell you the truth, I will lose half of them, and if I don't, I will lose the other half." He looked up and gave a slight laugh. "Whatever I do, I am screwed." Bradley was emotionless.

"Start talking."

He had no choice, he was hanging by a thread, and Bradley hit the record button on his mobile recorder, as Ian explained how the head of Oxendale Council, and local MP Walter Parkinson pressurised him, by threatening to take his Council contract away, unless the Church Hall was closed on August 28th, until September 10th. He was instructed to meet Marjorie at the hall, and hand her the paperwork, without doing another inspection. He looked at Bradley.

"I didn't want to do it, everyone knows I am as straight as a die, but this time Bradley they had me. I cannot lose the contracts, my men need their jobs, I have forty men working on those contracts, if this place opens before September 10th, all of them will be unemployed on the 11th. Those are good men who work hard, they all have wives and kids, how can I take their livelihood away from them?" Bradley gave a nod.

"So, Marjorie Wallace was quite specific about the dates, she actually told you what to write on the form?" He nodded.

"Yes. I am really sorry, but I was looking at destroying good men's lives, I had to protect them." Bradley leaned forward and pressed stop.

"You can leave the place closed; we have looked into other options. I am going to warn you Ian, if you get any heat again, and those people try to force you to fake reports, you will be through with this organisation forever. This is your one and only chance, we deal straight, and we only deal with straight companies. Go back to your work and say nothing of today, I will deal with this." Ian gave a huge sigh and sat back in his seat.

"Bradley you are indeed a fair man, and I will never forget this, I won't, and for what it is worth, that scum bag MP gave me £200, and I have not touched it, I feel sick looking at it. I will send it in with a courier, give it to your daughter for her event, and give her my best."

He stood up, and gave a nod to Margret, and then walked towards the door. He came out of the main building on the Bradley estate, and leaned against the wall, and closed his eyes, the sweat was running down his face.

"Hell, that was not good, whoever is watching over me, I am grateful, and so are my lads." He stood for a moment, and then gathered himself together, and headed for his van.

It had been a rough few days, and to be honest, none of us were looking forward to the week. Saying goodbye to Roni and William felt hard, having them in the house we got used to it, and suddenly, parts of the house felt empty.

Anthony appeared after work and made a video, and it was uploaded, and really hit a chord with a lot of people. Edwina was in control of home base, she had the long table laid out with paperwork, and was building a file on her computer. The Curio Life site was getting regular updates, and more and more videos were being uploaded. Chloe was sat on the spare computer on the site, and she was really engaging people on the forum, and talking openly and honestly to them, and the word 'Shrew' was growing at a fast rate, and was being adopted all round Oxendale.

The days slipped past, Birch worked, Deb's opened the shop, the mobile library, stayed close to the church, and so far, all was smooth. Chloe's updated pass appeared in the post, and my mum managed to get the fine removed, and as Friday rolled in, Izzy conducted her first session in group therapy, with young adults aged between 18 and 30, and she left feeling very positive, except me.

I cannot explain it all, but I felt responsible for everything, and was really starting to doubt myself. All of this had begun with me coming home with black hair, and now everyone connected to me was being targeted, and if I withdrew my complaint, everything would return to a more peaceful way of being. I sat for hours at my desk starting to question everything, was I really doing what was right for everyone, was I even doing what was right for me? My life felt like one long line of bad decisions after bad decision, and deep down inside, I began to question every single aspect of me. Everyone was working so hard, and yet as I watched, it felt a little pointless.

Birch was working every night with Katie, monitoring the progress of how the reception night organisation was going. Bradley took over the permits, he wanted to deal with the council himself, and made it really clear, he would not take no for an answer. It was a huge load off Birch, all she had to do now was get an agreement with the Pilkington's.

She left the practice, and jumped into Petal, and drove up to the large farm estate. It was a massive place, far bigger than she had realised, she walked to the door and rang the doorbell, Liz answered, and was delighted to see Birch. She excitedly shepherded her in, and was all chuckles and smiles. She sat in the kitchen, where Elizabeth made her a tea, she excitedly sat down, and looked at Birch across the table.

"I have to say Doctor, with you being so young and all, I was not sure at first, but oh my dear, you are a miracle worker." She fanned herself with a tea towel, and grinned as she turned a little bit red.

"He is like a wild beast, we have done things we did not do when we first got married, and as for the wonder woman, well!" She gave a wild giggle. "It has brought out the wonder man in him." Birch smiled.

"I am so happy for you both, and yes, I may be young, but I have spent years studying for this, it has been something I have always wanted to do. The practice is there for people like you and your husband, so I am delighted it has been a positive experience for you." Elizabeth beamed with delight.

"He is so happy, it has been so nice to see it, his problem was getting him down, he will be in shortly for his cup of tea, so you will see for yourself."

True to her word, ten minutes later he arrived, and was completely different to the way he was at the surgery. It was a startling change, he grabbed Birch' hand with both of his, and shook it hard.

"I won't deny Doctor Birch, I had my doubts, but bloody hell you are good, anything, anything you ever need just let me know."

Birch sat down, and explained the situation to Geoffrey, and he sat smiling, and listening very carefully, he nodded as she gave him an idea of the set up. Birch sat back, her heart was beating, as he considered it.

"Well, I have to say, it sounds bloody fishy to me, are you sure that bloody interfering woman has not been involved, you know, I am not sure if you know this Doctor Birch, she is no fan of yours?" Birch nodded.

"I have heard that." He laughed.

"Aye, you would be a good card player, I heard what little Abigail did, and I won't deny, she will have my vote. I have always dealt with Peter, he is a good sound bloke, and to be honest, I feel Liz and me, owe you big time, so aye, I have no problem with it, this little Debbie is Bradley's kid, isn't she?" Birch nodded.

"She is his step daughter." He smiled.

"I like that about him, richest bugger in the area, and he goes and marries an outsider. I know Ellen, she took good care of my dad, I reckon I owe her too. Look the field has a few issues, and to be honest the backhoe is not really good enough for the job, so I will make a deal with you, get Bradley to offer me some of them big fancy machines he has, so I can level the field more, and it's yours, no fee. I like a gentleman's agreement, so if you shake my hand, it's a deal."

He spat on his hand, which bothered Birch, but in good faith she spat on hers, and they shook, he smiled.

"Right, that is done, the field is yours, and Bradley has to help with his machines, that is good fair business that is. It's how the whole village should work, none of this lurking in dark corners, it should be out in the light. I have to get on, but I want to say again Doctor Birch, I am indebted to you, for Liz and me."

Liz sat happily smiling, and Birch sat for another cup of tea before leaving. She jumped in Petal, fitted her phone to the dash, plugged it in, and started the engine, and wiped her hand on a baby wipe, and shuddered, some aspects of country living she found a little unsettling.

She drove back towards the village talking to Bradley, and explaining her deal, and he told her how grateful he was for all she had done. She came back through the village, and headed towards home, she was exhausted, and was feeling the pressure of her long hours of extra work planning at night. As she drove onto the lane, and she looked to home, she saw it, and pulled in on the opposite side of the road, and just looked in disbelief.

Her beautifully painted stone garden wall, which had been painted the same yellow as the guest house, had the word 'Whores' painted on it, in large red letters. She lifted her phone, flicked on the phone camera, and took a shot. Sat in Petal with the engine running against the curb, she burst into tears. Was this woman ever going to stop?

Hatty was on her way to Flicks, Edwin was out at the hall working on the final set up for the following days talk, she saw Petal parked on the opposite side of the road with the engine running and then the wall.

"Oh Fuck."

She hurried up to the side of Petal, and looked inside, where Birch sat sobbing, she opened the door.

"Birch are you okay?" She gave a sniffle, and looked round with tear filled eyes.

"Hatty that is my home, look what she has done to where we live, it is my home Hatty, it is the only place Deads feels safe, and she has done that. Hatty all we have ever done is just be ourselves, we don't hurt anyone, we just live our life. I am so tired Hatty, I just don't think I can take anymore." She gave a giant sob, and Hatty climbed into the car and pulled her into her arms.

Birch leaned into her, and wailed into her shoulder, and all she could do was stare at the wall.

"Birch you cannot let her get to you like this, this is what she wants, she will push all of you to breaking point, now do you understand how she became so powerful? Birch you cannot show weakness, you have to face her, and not bat an eyelid." She sniffled and sat back and took a deep breath.

"I thought I was strong, but she is hurting all of us, and I hate seeing them like that. How do you stay so strong Hatty, she has been at you for years?" Hatty sat back in the passenger seat and smiled.

"I face the bitch, I am disrespectful, and then I go home lock the doors, and have a dammed good cry." Birch turned and sniffled.

"You cry, what, you mean all these years, you have gone home and broke down?" She gave a nod.

"Birch don't do it on a lane where people can see it, and then tell her. Do it alone where no one will see it, that way she never knows she is winning." Birch nodded, and gave a huge sniffle, and took a long breath in.

"Okay Hatty, I understand that, I am sorry, I just saw it and it really hurt, you know, this is our home, Deads will be heartbroken when she sees it." She understood.

"Birch, all of you should come out, stand in front of it, and post it to your site, let the world see what she is doing, expose her for what she is, a vicious and scheming old shrew." Birch gave a sniffle and nodded as she wiped her eyes. She took a big deep breath.

"Yeah, you are right. I will show them, but honestly, I do not know how much more I can take."


Thirty minutes later, I stood with Hatty and mum, alongside the Curio's, looking at the wall, and I felt horrible inside. No matter how we all looked at it, this was my fault, it was a direct result of my letter, and she had told me she would make my life hell, until I withdrew it, and I was starting to wish I had listened.

"She really wants that letter withdrawing." Hatty leaned on my mums' wall.

"That is why you must not back down Abby, you have her cornered, and she is dangerous, but no matter what, stay your course." Chloe was sat on the curb in front of me.

"I fucking hate that Shrew, but you know what screw her." She stood up, looked back and smiled. "I have an idea."

In her big baggy dungarees, which to be honest did nothing to hide her boobs, she wandered back into the house, as we all stood by mum's house looking at it. A few minutes later she returned shaking a can.

"Edwina, film this."

Edwina lifted the camera and focused, then started to film. Chloe looked at the wall and then turned to face the camera.

"Do you honestly think this will put us off Shrew? It won't."

She turned, faced the wall, and then in bright blue paint, in big letters, under the word 'Whores,' she wrote, 'Welcome.' She turned and smiled a big beaming smile.

"If I am a whore, and I am this fucking cool, then screw it, any other whore is welcome to come visit." She folded her arms and smiled. "What do you say guys, because I say fuck you Shrew?"

I started to laugh, there are days when I love Chloe so much, it staggers me to think we were ever enemies. Birch crossed the road and pulled Chloe into her arms.

"Thanks Sweetie, I really needed that." Chloe smiled.

"Not gonna let you screw me; you know that right?" Birch giggled.

"What, you being all straight and that?" She smiled a big smile.

"Oh, Birch I am so fucking straight, it's unbelievable." She giggled, and Birch hugged her hard.

Chapter 27

# Cold Reality.

Marjorie held the phone to her ear. "Well, I am sorry Bishop, but I cannot agree, I think I know this parish far better than any, and I have to say, I feel this will all be met with a lot of resistance." On the other end of the phone, the bishop was trying his best to be as patient as possible.

"Marjorie, I am sorry, the wheels are already in motion, and Milton has given his full approval. He knows his flock, and I have taken him at his word. Gail Linley is a wonderful woman, and she has done wonders for the numbers at St Bartholomew's, and she was only a temporary replacement there. I think she will fit in very well at Wotton, and let's be honest, the numbers have fallen in the last few years, Milton is right to look to reinvigorate the flock. I am sorry Marjorie, that you oppose this, I truly am, but when Milton retires, she will be his replacement. She will be there tomorrow, to get her introduction, and she will be helping out, to ease her transition." Marjorie was outraged.

"I will of course be writing to the Arch Bishop, and making my strongest opposition to this appointment, and will advise this parish to do the same."

"That is your prerogative, and I will not prevent you, but I think Marjorie, that at some point, you will have to accept, that even the church has to come up to date. All of us have to move on, it is those who live in the past that ultimately get left behind." Marjorie screwed up her face.

"We shall see, this is not the end of this matter, so I will bid you good day Bishop." She put the phone down, and scowled at Bethany.

"If I hear the word modernise one more time, I think I will scream. Tradition is exactly that, and it is for a reason."

It was Saturday, and I had not left the house for days, to

be honest, I really did not want another slanging match with Marjorie, and I was avoiding the village. Our latest upload, which featured the pictures and Chloe's footage of our wall, had been another hit, comments of support were pouring in, but my main task had been getting my Seeds of Summer manuscript finished. I leaned back in my chair and gave a long sigh of relief.

"It's finally done." Birch was sat in the bed reading, she looked up and smiled.

"It is really good Deads, I loved it. It is funny and bright, and gritty, I really think this will get some attention." I hoped so, I stretched as I stood up, and walked slowly over to the bed.

"I am tired, I don't know what it is, but as soon as I finish writing anything, I just feel exhausted." I slipped under the duvet. "I love Saturdays, lazing in bed with you, it's the best day of the week." She smiled and put her book down.


The doorbell rang, Edwina came out of the library and opened the door, to find a tall scruffy looking guy. He had long dark hair, a very unshaven square jaw, kind dark eyes and a lovely smile. Edwina looked at him and smiled.

"Please be here for me." He frowned.

"I am sorry... And you are?" She gave a shy grin.

"I am Edwina, and you are who exactly?" He looked a little confused.

"You are aware you only have knickers on, and you are standing in full view of the street. Looks like I am at the right house, I was told Jemima lived here?" Edwina gave a sigh.

"You want Birch?" He nodded, and smiled, and held out his hand.

"Hi I am Kev; I am a good friend of hers." Edwina swung the door open.

"BIRCH WHERE ARE YOU?"


I was lay face down on the bed, as Birch sat on me, and massaged the fragrant oil into my back, Birch turned round.

"IN MY ROOM EDWINA." She pushed up my spine, towards my shoulders.

"Oh god that is so nice Birch." She giggled.

Edwina pointed. "Straight up the stairs, it is the door with the birch trees on it." Kev nodded, smiled, and looked at the stairs. Birch leaned down and kissed the base of my neck, I felt the shivers run down my spine, she gave another little giggle.

"You like that don't you my dark little beastie?" She put her hand behind her, and ran it up the inside of my thigh, I quivered.

"Oh god Birch, stop it, you are driving me wild, don't start something you are not prepared to finish… Oh god, that is so naughty."

"HOLY FUCK!"

I jumped with shock, and Birch twisted round, the moment froze for a second, as she stared at the outline of Kev stood in the bathroom partition doorway. Her voice was filled with shock, I was pinned face down, into the bed, with Birch sat just above my waist. I heard the words, and my heart gave a massive jolt.

"KEV! What the hell are you doing here?" He stared at her.

"I am starting to wonder… I missed you, but it is pretty clear you have not missed me."

Birch slid off my back, and I pulled the duvet over me, as I turned round, he looked at me, and honestly, he looked like he hated me.

"Deadly, holy fuck, I did not see that coming." He looked at Birch.

"Is this why I have spent over a year without a word, just a message saying, sorry, but I am fucking off to another part of the country?" Birch pulled her robe off the floor and slipped it on.

"We can talk through here, in my room." She walked right past him, and into her own room, he stared at me.

"So, is this what Uni life was really about, all secret lesbo's together, you have been fucking her for all this time?" I shook my head.

"It was not like that, you're being a prick Kev, get the hell out of my room." Birch glared at him as he walked into her room.

"What the hell are you doing here? It was a lot more than just a short message, I bloody well told you, there was no future for us, you had too many frigging groupies." He stood in her doorway, and glanced back.

"Well I don't know Jem, it looks to me like you had a groupie of your own, how long have you been fucking her for? I mean, we have all been out of Uni for four years." Birch glared at him, and her eyes burned with anger.

"If you must know, just under two months, wow you know Kev, you have a real bloody nerve just showing up out of the blue, and then lecturing me on who I screw. I mean just how many have there been, do you even remember, after all you have been touring none stop?" He looked at the floor, and gave a long sigh.

"Look I am sorry alright, it caught me by surprise, I did not come here to fight, I had no idea you were a lesbo." Birch sat down on the bed.

"Don't say that word I hate it, and just for the record I am not." He gave a laugh.

"No offence Jem, but I could only see three fingers, you were pretty much exploring your little Uni friend there with some skill." Birch shook her head.

"It is just something between Deads and me, it has nothing to do with other women, she is different. Look Kev, why are you here, no disrespect but you just buggered off on tour, without saying a word, and then just reappeared when it was all over. Now you come here and start slinging shit at me. I must admit, I am struggling with the irony a little?" He walked closer to the bed and crouched down.

"Jem, I have been thinking a lot of late, we have finally got a deal, we are in London making our first album, and I really miss you. I wanted you to be a part of it, you know, like we were back then?" Birch shook her head.

"There is no going back Kev, there is too much between then and now, it is why I walked away. How the hell did you find me anyhow?" He gave a sigh.

"I was in the village, and I bumped into that lesbo friend of yours, she had just got back from France, and she told me you had moved down here, although she said nothing of Deadly being here." Birch nodded, she understood, Bev did not really know the circumstances, it was not her fault.

"Stop calling her a lesbo, I hate it, Bev is a really nice person. So, she told you I was here, and you just happened to be in London, so what, you thought hey, I will go and bang Jem for old times' sake, is that what this is?"

I was a little freaked out, I won't deny, Kev seemed really different from the guy I had met at Uni, not as calm or sedate, more edgy and a lot more aggressive than he used to be. Birch had looked panicked, and it worried me, I slipped out of bed and put on my robe, and snuck quietly into the bathroom. Kev had moved from the door, so I crept closer. He was crouching on the floor in front of her sat on the bed.

"Jem I am getting fixed up with a deal, we have a shot, come on girl, you know we were always good together? Come to London, no strings, and just be a part of it, and see how it is now. Jem, I have really missed you, look." He put his hand in his pocket and pulled out a small red box. "Jem, I came to ask you to marry me."

My heart stopped, I could not think, my brain was in melt down, and just swirled, I as felt my breath trap in my windpipe. He opened the box and it sparkled. I felt the tears in my eyes, and I had no idea why? Birch jumped up, and moved back from him.

"What the hell Kev, get that thing away from me."

She looked up and saw me standing in the doorway, tears rolling down my cheeks, she shook her head.

"This is not frigging happening; you know how I feel about this Kev. YOU HAVE NO GOD DAMMED RIGHT DOING THIS KEV!" He stood up.

"Jem think about it." She looked terrified, and backed away from him.

"What the hell is wrong with you? I told you, it would never happen, I told you Kev time and time again. I am not the kind for you, I will not tolerate all that bullshit, with the drugs and the week long parties and groupies. I don't want that, I have never wanted that, now put that bloody thing away, and then get the hell out of here." He moved closer.

"Jem, just calm down and think about it, we were good, we could be again." She shook her head, and started to cry.

"No Kev, that was then, before the coke, and smack, you are no longer that guy. I told you all this before, it can never be. I once thought maybe, but not now, not after all that." She looked at me stood in the doorway, and she smiled, her bright green eyes locked onto mine.

"I am with Deads, I really love her, she is my whole world, I realised my mistake in letting her come home from Uni alone, and I came back here a few months ago, to be with her, and make up for it. I have built a new life here, and I am staying here at her side. I am sorry Kev, you had your chance, you blew it, when you started on the coke, and screwing hundreds of groupies. I told you that was not what being open was about, you abused us."

He slipped the ring back in his pocket, and his mood instantly changed, and it scared me, as his voice turned hard and coarse.

"You are fucking stupid Jem, you are wasting your life on a tart from Uni. Fuck, you used to be cool, what the fuck has happened to you?" Birch pointed to the door.

"Just leave Kev, you wasted your journey, I am sure there is a coke snorting groupie out there somewhere for you, we are done, so please just leave." He shook his head.

"Fucking lesbo's, fuck Jem, you blow my mind." He glanced at me and smirked, his eyes looked hateful. "God she is not even a good looking one, either." I stared back at him with hate.

"You heard her, piss off." He walked to the door, and pulled it open, Izzy stood there waiting, he laughed.

"Fuck, they get even uglier." Izzy pointed.

"Stairs are there, walk down them, or I will throw you down them, either way, you are going down them."

He sauntered across the hall, Edwina and Chloe were staring at him, he shook his head, and walked onto the stairs.

"Fucking house full of Lesbo's, fuck this place."

Izzy followed him down, and Birch sat on the bed, she looked down and started to cry. I moved over to her, and sat down at her side and pulled her close. She shook her head.

"You remember him Deads, he was such a nice guy, I really did care about him, that bloody manager Robert, got him into all kinds of shit, and look what it has done to him. They killed him Deads, they took the best of him and killed it." I held her tight as she sobbed, what else could I do?

I have always been scared of drugs, I mean, I have had a few totes on a spliff occasionally, but I have heard so many things about drugs, some good and some bad. I know for some, limited use brought them out of themselves, and helped them understand themselves better, but those stories were always seldom. At Uni there were groups who did coke and smack, and God knows what, and they always scared me. That dead look in their eyes, I found frightening, I knew Kev at Uni, and I really liked him, he was soft and gentle, and loved music, and he was always so lovely with Birch.

I honestly thought Birch would marry him back then, sat in our dorm she would smile, and fill with life, just talking about the fun they had experienced together. I have so many memories of that time, sat on my bed listening to her, and wondering if I would ever find someone as perfect for me.

Today hurt me, it hurt me deeply, as much as it had Birch, because somewhere in the back of my mind, I had always thought that at some point we would stop sleeping together, and just end up the best of friends, and she would probably end up with Kev.

The guy I saw today, was not the guy I knew, and it was heart breaking to see it. The change in him had been so complete, it was as if someone had sucked the real him out, and put someone else inside his body. I was scared by that, probably more than I will ever admit. At this moment, considering everything that has happened, I think life is really cruel, and it is yet another reminder of how trusting people is not always safe.

Izzy came back up, and I knew she would be more help to Birch, so I left them alone, and came down to the kitchen. I sat with a coffee alone, and just drifted, reality sucks, maybe that is why I became a writer, after all, I can hide with my vampires, when I need to.

My life felt like it was unravelling again, and I was so unsure as to what to do, it had felt perfect, but sitting alone in the kitchen sipping my coffee, I was starting to wonder if it had all just been one big fantasy driven unrealistic dream. I live in Wotton, this was not a place for happy people, my life here had always contained a false reality and an air of sadness, and suddenly it felt like nothing had changed in the last ten years of my life, and I was starting again, for the third time in two months to question myself and the life I was living.

In my mind I could hear her words, and it felt like they were caught in a loop, as I saw her face and eyes filled with tears. "I once thought maybe, but not now."

I was right, she had always thought she would marry Kev, so why had she denied it that day in the bath, why had she said, it was not love, and only a FWB thing? I sat there alone with her words going round in my head, it was clear, it had been a lot more than she had said.

Bradley Wheeler ended his phone call, and buzzed through to Marie.

"Marie, I have just finished talking to Milton Wallace, he wants the old Sutton's property, can you get Margaret to finalise the paperwork, and send it over to him, and we can close the deal? If anyone else enquires, the property is off the market. When you have finished, call it a day, and thanks for coming in today, it has been a big help." He sat back in his chair and looked at Ellen.

"Getting her away from the village could be a blessing for everyone, the word is not out yet, but tomorrow, you will meet the future of this village. I won't spoil the surprise, but honest love, I think you will enjoy it." He smiled, sat back and gave a long sigh, he was really hoping this would be the start of Marjorie's demise.

It was Saturday night, and the Parish Council, had been unexpectedly summoned to the vicarage, they all assembled in the living room, under the guidance of Marion, which was probably a good thing, considering the way Felicity currently felt. Edwin wandered round looking at the artwork. Celia sat with Marion, and across the other side of the room, sat Peter and Phillip. Milton walked in with a young woman, she was around mid thirties, had short black hair, dark eyes and a friendly smile.

Milton stood at the end of the room and faced them all, the young woman stood beside him, she had on a big baggy jumper and jeans. He gave what looked like a smile as he looked round the room.

"I must apologise, Marjorie has a bad migraine, and so will be absent tonight. I have asked all of you to attend here tonight, as I have a somewhat unusual announcement to make. I think it is fitting that those who have served this community with such valiant efforts, should be the first to be informed." He smiled, as everyone waited for him to continue, Edwin frowned.

"Well, what is it that we should be informed of Milton?" He gave a somewhat gassy sounding laugh.

"Oh yes of course, how silly of me. I have decided, having spoken to the bishop, to hand over the baton as it were." Celia looked blankly at him.

"Baton? I am sorry Milton, I may be missing something here, what baton, and to whom?" He gave a chortle.

"Oh dear, yes, yes, I am so sorry, I am feeling a little giddy with all this excitement. I have decided to retire, yes that is the job, and so Gail here, will be stepping in with me as of tomorrow. You know, just to get the flow of things, and all that, and then she will take command of the ship when I pop off." The young woman gave a warm smile.

"Hello everyone, it is nice to meet you all, I have heard some wonderful things about you all, and how dedicated you all have been. I hope we all can carry that on in the future."

Felicity looked at her with wide eyes, and then gave a smile, she stood up and offered her hand.

"I hope I am right in asking, but are you saying that you will be taking over as vicar of the parish, when Milton retires? I am Felicity by the way, Felicity Watson, chair of the parish council." Gail took her hand with a huge smile.

"Oh yes, Felicity, Milton has been immensely flattering about how you have become such an invaluable part of this parish, I am thrilled to finally meet you. I am Gail.... Gail Watkins Linley, and one day vicar of Saint Augustine's." Felicity could not believe her eyes, and she felt a wave of joy run through her, as she smiled and turned.

"This is my husband, Edwin; he is Parish Accountant."

Edwin stood up, looking somewhat bewildered, and took her hand with a smile. Slowly each member of the council shook hands with her. Milton opened a bottle of wine, and they all stood around holding glasses, and talking, as Gail slowly got to get to know each of them. Milton was all smiles.

"Yes, yes, Gail will be joining in the services as of tomorrow, so I want all of you to help her to get to know everyone, and give her a warm and friendly welcome. I realise this may seem as being very modern for all of us, but actually I think this will be very good for the village." Edwin leaned into Felicity, and lowered his voice.

"The crafty old badger shafted Madge right under her own nose, no wonder she has a migraine, I am surprised she has not had a stroke." Felicity bit her lip.

"I just texted Hatty, she is in hysterics, I sent her a picture, she thinks this is absolutely hilarious." Edwin sniggered.

"You know, I am quite looking forward to church tomorrow, the old battle axe will have to make an appearance, and I am dying to see the look on her face." Felicity patted his shoulder.

"Really Edwin you are terrible." Celia stepped back. and leaned into Felicity.

"I must say Flick, she is a bit of a looker, she has a great ass, I would do her." Felicity sniggered, and looked at the Wilton carpet.


The doorbell was ringing, and ringing. Chloe gave a sigh. "OK, OK, KEEP YOUR KNICKERS ON!" Deb's came up the hallway and chuckled as she looked at Chloe.

"They will be more dressed than you then."

Chloe looked down at her nakedness, and side stepped the door, she pulled it open, and leant round, Hatty exploded inside with a huge smile on her face, and gasping for breath.

"Where is everyone, I need all of you here?" I walked up the hallway holding a bowl of cereal, as I crunched.

"Hey Hatty, what is with the sudden arrival?" She looked at me and smiled.

"Oh, Abby I have such news, I ran all the way round here. Fuck, I need to cut down the cigs, where is Birch?" I looked at her.

"Birch has had a really rough day; she is taking some time out alone." Hatty shook her head.

"Abby she must be here, trust me, she will want to be in on this." I shrugged.

"I will ask, but don't get your hopes up, she has had a really tough time."


I put my bowl down on the hall table, and walked up the stairs. Birch's room was in darkness, the blind was right down, I carefully crossed to the bed and sat down.

"Birch, Hatty is here with some big news, she wants you to hear it with all of us." Birch rolled over; I could just make her out in the dark.

"Deads Sweetie, I need a little time, I am alright, honestly, but

I need to be alone for a while, I am sorry, this must be as hard on you as it has been on me?" I smiled in the dark and reached out to her, I felt her face, and cupped her cheek.

"I almost fainted when he asked you to marry him, but actually I am okay, I just wish he had not come here and hurt you. To be honest Birch, I hate saying it, but I always thought you would eventually leave me, and go back to him. I cannot deny, I was scared when he showed up, I mean, one day you will want kids and stuff, I am not stupid, but…" She swept up off the bed, and dragged me into her arms.

"Oh, you silly little beastie, there will never be a day when you are not in my life, you must never think that." She was crushing the life out of me, and I patted her arm.

"Birch, sweetheart, you are crushing me." She lessened her hold, but just held me.

"I am sorry Deads, I did mean to tell you, but what with Melody, and then finding out how bad you were suffering, I just got side tracked, and never got around to it. His drugs were the reason I was ignoring him, and on top of that, I realised that yes, I did actually love him, but not as much as I loved you." She slid back in the dark.

"This probably sounds crazy, because I am the one who is supposed to know everything, but suddenly realising how much you meant, how deep it was, was pretty scary for me. I have always seen myself as straight, but I had all these feelings and desires whenever I thought of you, it took me a while to accept that, and once I did, I came straight here." I understood some of it, I had been questioning myself since Uni.

"Birch you were not alone, I was going through the same thing, honestly, I could not believe I was turning into a lesbian. I didn't want to be one, I saw what the others went through, and my life here was bad enough. I could not explain why you and no one else, it made no sense to me, hell it still doesn't, but you showed me it is okay, and that is all I care about, but that is also why I was so scared when he showed up like that." She leaned into me, and placed her forehead on mine.

"It does not matter Deads, we are just us, possibly the most curio of the Curio's, and we are here now, I don't care about the future at the moment, this is all that matters." Chloe shouted up the stairs.

"IF YOU TWO ARE SCREWING AGAIN, I AM THROWING COLD WATER ON YOU." Birch sniggered.

"See, they accept it, and that is all that matters. Come on, let's find out what has got Hatty so wound up."

She got up, and got herself sorted, and we walked towards the door, and out onto the top of the stairs, but as we came down, all I could think of, was she broke up with Kev because of the drugs, that was the real reason, and she did actually love him, so, why had she not admitted that before when I asked? It really bothered me deep down inside, and I know it is crazy, but I felt she had lied to me, and this was a person who prides themselves in never lying, and yet she did to me, and it hurt to know that.

Ten minutes later we were all sat in a line on the sofa, as Hatty bobbed up and down on her feet, grinning like an idiot. We looked at her, and Edwina gave a gasp.

"Well... We are here, what is so big a deal that you come running round like a maniac?"

Hatty looked like she was fit to burst, she opened her phone, flicked to her pictures, then turned her phone round, and held it in front of her, it was a picture of a woman, it was no big deal, Edwina leaned in.

"She is pretty fit, who the hell is she?" Hatty gave a chuckle, and then broke into a huge smile.

"That girls, is the new vicar." We all looked at each other then back to Hatty.

"Huh?" It suddenly hit me, and my mouth gaped open.

"NO FRIGGING WAY?" Hatty gave a nod and smiled.

"Oh yes girls, big fucking way, the old prick has decided to retire, and this woman is his replacement. I have got to tell you guys; I cannot wait for church tomorrow." Deb's looked at me with huge eyes.

"I am bloody well going to church." Birch sat up, and looked closer at the picture.

"Well, well Milton, you screwed your own wife over, and I have to admit, I think I am starting to like him. I take it Madge is having a fit about now?" Hatty started laughing.

"I bet she has had several, the batty old dog has really screwed her over, if he is retiring, she will have to move out of the vicarage." I sat back and my mind reeled.

"This will be a massive blow to her guys, holy shit, this is going to really look bad for her, she has spoken out against female vicars a lot in the past, how the hell is she going to face the village now?" Hatty shrugged.

"This is Madge, no doubt she will find some way to make this look like her work, she will end up getting all the credit, but no matter what, this is going to wound her, and we can use that as a weapon."

Chapter 28

# Party people.

I woke to the smell of cake, just for a moment I thought I was back at home with mum, I rolled over, and the bed was empty, I sat up.

"Oh, Christ not here too?" I slipped out of bed, and headed for the door, moments later, I walked into the kitchen, and was greeted with a very happy.

"Hi Sweetie."

I yawned, and looked round, there were six cakes in a row, yep, I had been dragged back into fete hell, Birch had gone full on Felicity on me. She had fete fever, and as I headed for my coffee, she was filling a huge pan with fresh fruit, and had several bags of preserving sugar on hand. I was dubious, was this going to be yet more weird curd, or was she actually making jam. I peered over the edge of her pan, I saw blueberries, damsons, and passion fruit and gooseberries, I looked at her.

"You really like weird jam, don't you?" She smiled.

"I like flavour, a good jam needs to identify itself to the eater Sweetie, it shouldn't need a label, you should just know." I looked back in the pan.

"Then why not make strawberry and apple, everyone knows that?" She nodded in agreement.

"Yes Sweetie, but everyone will be making those, I want mine to stand out."

It was hard to argue, she made a logical sort of sense, I grabbed my coffee, and headed into the garden for some none cake smelling air, and to wake up slowly, and gently. Across the village the bells began to ring, I slid down in my chair, and smiled, inside the kitchen, the muttering started.

"Really, I mean fucking really, hundreds of thousands on soundproofing, and an open door lets the Bell Twat in?"

BANG!

I jumped, and looked back, the door was shut, I slipped back and smiled, and then sipped my coffee.

"I have missed that."

Most of the church congregation were not aware of what was coming, the council had said little, and so when the service began, and there was an extra attending, most of the parishioners were confused. When it came time for the sermon, a moment when most of the assembled settled in the seats, and got comfortable, and ready for the long drone, they were very surprised to hear Milton announce from the pulpit.

"My dear flock, I have stood here for almost thirty years every Sunday, and it has been a joy for me. Yes, yes, it will become a fond memory when I move on later this year." There were sudden murmurs, Deb's smiled at her mum.

"That was a surprise, they are awake now." She gave a quiet giggle. Milton looked out over his flock from high up.

"Sadly, I feel my time is drawing near, to hand you all over to another shepherd, and so I must tell you, that I have made the choice to retire early, and have informed the bishop." Deb's watched as they all looked round at each other confused. Ellen leaned into Deb's.

"It has baffled them, they cannot understand why the village gossip network has let them down, they have forgotten who leads all the gossip, and she does not want to talk about it." Milton continued, unaware of the stir, in his audience.

"I have watched this village in recent times, and I have seen entrenched views, clash with more modern views, and it has been saddening to watch, for I believe there is room for both. Our village is changing, oh the outside will always look the same, this will always be a place of great beauty, but I must declare, I have failed, in my task to lead you all. So today, I would like to introduce a new more balanced and modern figure, to take this church forward. Gail Watkins Linley, will replace me later this year." He walked down from the pulpit, and Gail walked up the steps. Hatty leaned over Felicity's shoulder.

"That is the first time that bloody idiot has spoken from up there, and made sense in thirty years." Felicity Sniggered.

"Hatty we are in church you know; the lord hears all." Hatty giggled.

"He is probably as relieved as we are, the old badger is nearing his end." Even Edwin smiled. The Rev Gail Linley, looked out across the church.

"I am so thrilled to be here, but I will also add, I am not here to make waves either." Hatty coughed.

"Says the tsunami that has swept Madge off her feet." Felicity sniggered.

"The world is changing, and we will see new ideas, and new ways of meeting in our spiritual union, which is why I have joined this church earlier than my appointed time. Whilst the Rev Wallace is with us, I want to use him as my guide, so that I can get to know all of you better, and use this time to understand the parish. I hope to be involved with everyone, and would say to all of you, that I want to hear your views on the direction of this church." Hatty whispered.

"Probably better off she does not ask Madge, I am not convinced she will get the answer she was looking for." Felicity turned round.

"Will you behave, this is church?" Hatty smiled.

"God likes the honest, I wish Birch was here, she would love this." Gail looked out from her pulpit and smiled.

"I will be around the parish daily, and I hope to visit all of you at some point, so please, guide me, for the sake of the future, of this church." Hatty sniggered, Felicity turned.

"What?" Hatty looked at her.

"You told me to shut up." She rolled her eyes.

"Don't laugh and then say nothing, tell me." Hatty leaned forward.

"She wants to be guided, if I was her, I would be careful, because Madge will probably guide her off the canal bridge." She sniggered, and Felicity faced forward.

"You have a wicked mind Harriet Barker."

"I know, that is why I am in church, I need to be saved."

Gail played an active role in the rest of the service. It did not go unnoticed, that when she stood to give out the communion, Marjorie remained in her seat. She scowled for the whole service, and after it was over, rather than stand at the doors and talk, she walked down the path with Bethany, and headed for the vicarage, several of her minions followed. Ellen and Deb's came out, and Milton smiled.

"Debbie, would you mind if I asked you a favour?"

Deb's worried a little, ever since the whole cellar incident, she had avoided him. She looked nervous.

"What is it Vicar?" He gave a smile, or at least that was how she interpreted it, after all his teeth did move a little.

"I was wondering, and considering you are to be married here at the end of the month, if you would consider allowing Gail the honour? I will of course be on hand, but somehow I feel, you more than most, would appreciate a younger more modern spiritual guide on your special day, and it would set a standard for others to follow." Deb's was very surprised, Gail smiled at her.

"I would love that; I mean are you okay with this Rev Wallace?" He nodded his head.

"I would be delighted to be a part of it, but you would be doing this church a huge service, by allowing Gail to take the leading role." Gail winked.

"So, you are the girl who ran off with his hat, I have been dying to meet you?" Deb's was blown away.

"You listen to Jimmy too?" She giggled.

"I may be a reverend, but in all other aspects I am a normal woman, I can assure you." Deb's gave a huge smile, Gail leaned forward. "I have a huge crush on Floyd, will he be there too?" Deb's nodded.

"He is playing the intro on his guitar." She chuckled.

"I want a copy of the wedding video, okay?" She held her thumb up, Deb's was delighted. Milton interrupted.

"Gail this is Mr and Mrs Walton Hopkins, they have played a very active role in our dramatic company." Deb's walked down the path with her mum, feeling more relieved than anyone would ever truly understand.


She returned home very excited, and told us all about it as we made pints of jam. Chloe and Edwina had joined in, and we all had different flavours, Birch, had the award for the weirdest.

The cakes were sealed in plastic tubs, the way we saw it, they all turned out well, and to be honest, the jams within them would be different, so the fact remained that they would all taste different.

Birch noted, we all had to sprinkle our own flavour of magic on them, just to complete the process.

With cakes and jams made and stored, we went online to answer questions and emails, and update the site, and then we were free to lounge around the garden, and that set the theme for the rest of the week. Birch hired a painter to come and paint the outside front wall, and Deb's opened the shop each day with Denise, and Sweetie's Retreat saw an influx of new clients as the NHS contract kicked in.

It was notable how quiet things had got on the Shrew front, she was keeping a low profile, although it was noted that she had once been overheard referring to Gail, as that tart in a collar. I was nervous, I had avoided the village, the letter had not been withdrawn, and yet she had backed off completely, and it really bothered me. It made no sense at all, but it was there in the back of my mind with all my other doubts. I tried to keep busy, but all of it was slowly eating away at me, and I was really not sure what to do.

The week moved slowly by until Thursday evening, without anything unusual happening, until at half past six that evening there was a knock on the door, and Birch went to answer it. She opened the door to the tall figure in a top hat, and smiled.

"Jimmy, you made it."

"Alright Birch my darling?"

He stepped in carrying a large stuffed bear, which was wearing a flying helmet and goggles. He stood in the hall, and then yelled.

"OI! WHERE THE HELL IS MY GOGGLE BEAR, I WANT MY HAT BACK?"

There was a wild scream upstairs, and Deb's came flying out of her room, she stood at the top of the stairs with a huge smile, and Jimmy looked up at her.

"There you are, so what are you waiting for girl, I am back Doll?"

She tore down the stairs screaming, and leapt into the air, and he caught her with a wild laugh, as she wrapped her arms and legs round him.

"JIMMY!" He giggled.

"That's me girl, and don't you forget it." It was kind of sweet to watch, as he held her tight, Chloe leaned into me.

"If that is a goggles bear, why the fuck are the goggles on its head, shouldn't they be, you know, lower down?"

Birch and me giggled, and left them to it, the way we saw it, this was going to go one way, and we were not wrong.

Twenty minutes later we all sat on the floor in the hall outside Deb's room, eating ice cream. Chloe leaned against the door, and pressed her ear up to it, she waved her arm, and we all got ready. Chloe counted down on her fingers, as the dull moans came through the door, three... Two... One. We all leaned back our heads and screamed.

"OH JIMMY!"

Laughing like lunatics, we grabbed our ice cream, and legged it, the door opened, and Jimmy popped his head out, we were all peeping from Chloe's door, sniggering, it was such fun, he wagged his finger at us, smiled, and went back in the room.

It was at least two hours before they came down, Jimmy got his bag from the hall, and walked through, Deb's was all smiles. We were sat round the island as he looked round the place.

"Got yourselves a nice pad here girls, I was looking at your website, been sorry to hear of your woes. If there is anything me and the lads can do, let me know, we like a good hag roast.... Anyways, I think you lovely ladies need cheering up, and so... Pressies all around." He smiled as he lifted out silk kimonos from his bag.

"I hope you don't mind, I figured it was fair to get you all the same, I mean like, they are different colours an all, but I grabbed these at this cool little place in Tokyo."

Jimmy handed them round, and we all stared with lust at them, they were stunning, Birch stripped on the spot.

"Oh, Jimmy this is pure silk, I am having this next to my skin."

Suddenly it was strip tease time, he sat back and smiled, well I mean, he had five naked girls to look at, who wouldn't? Mine was deep green, I slipped it on, and felt the cool softness of it against my body, it felt divine. Birch got a golden one, Chloe red, and Edwina blue, Deb's was white, and all of them had beautifully embroidered patterns of flowers all over them, these were really high quality garments. We all lined up looking like we had stepped out of a Japanese bathroom, and kissed him on the cheek, we were very happy.

Within the hour, the rest of the band showed up, with the roadies, the support crew, as well as the caterers, and before any of us really understood what was going on, we had a full on party flowing.

Chloe being Chloe, hit the text, and Louise and Stacy from the Tea Rooms, accompanied by Denise from the bookshop, and Gill, Alex, and Meg from the practice, were at the door, and Chloe welcomed them in, they also had a friend none of us knew with them, she smiled and introduced herself as Gail.


There is something I did not know about bands, which is that they travel with a mobile booze supply, I mean these guys play serious. They had at least forty bottles on our island in the kitchen, five kegs of larger, with taps, and enough plastic glasses to build a transparent Eiffel Tower.

The furniture slid back to the walls, opening up the whole room, and soon enough, the joint was jumping. Having had the weirdest month of our lives, this was a much needed experience, although the five of us were dressed just in Kimono's and nothing else, but as I was about to find out, this was a rock band party, and soon the floor was littered with bra's panties, and some great designer clothing.

Chloe was in cock heaven, and the studio was very busy, Birch was dancing, with a roadie called Max, and Edwina was doing very well, with the bass payer Emerson's fiancée. Battered Taco boomed out of the stereo, and I wandered round watching, and not actually enjoying myself. Birch came over to me.

"Are you okay Sweetie?"

"I am fine, this is a good party, I just don't seem to feel like I can connect with anyone, Birch, Max, seems like a really cool guy, go on and have fun, hey you might get lucky." Birch smiled.

"It is no fun if you are not having fun too Sweetie, and yes he is yummy, but I do not want to, if you are not." I looked at her.

"Birch the night is young, go have fun, I am sure in this lot I will find something to amuse me."

Birch returned to dancing, Edwina was pretty much naked on

the sofa, with whatever her name was, and people were pretty drunk, and horny all over the place. Just about everywhere, there were little pink bums, bouncing up and down. I made my way up the stairs to my room and unlocked the door, I have no idea why, but I was not really feeling the vibe.

I sat at my desk listening to Birch bang away in her room, actually out in the garden, there was more squealing than a brood of peacocks, the pool was full of naked people. My mind was elsewhere, it had been for a week now, as I had thought deeply about every aspect of my life.

I felt confused and mixed up, and very unsettled, I had endless thoughts going round my head, and felt I had no focus as I tried to work, just what it was exactly I wanted out of life. Kev's visit had compounded on to what had become an episode of self doubt, and it had been there in the back of my thoughts.

My door was open, and Kyle the keyboard player in the band leaned in with a bottle of vodka.

"You not feeling it either?" I turned and looked at him, and gave a smile.

"I guess I am not really in the mood, not sure why, I have always loved a good party, but recently I have been spending so much time alone. I guess with a house full, I am struggling, so I thought I would hide up here." I gave a slight laugh.

"Pretty pathetic yeah, how come you are not down there, I thought you guys loved the groupie scene?"

He walked in with two glasses, put them on the desk, and poured the vodka into each of them.

"I don't do groupies, I always pick a girl before the tour, and take her with me, with the understanding that it will only be one tour of the rock and roll lifestyle, and then we go separate ways. I like company on the road, but also like to know who I am with."

It fascinated me, he talked of life and the road, the joy of travelling, and sharing those experiences with someone special, someone who understood the quality and the meaning of it all. God I really got that, and was captivated by his thinking, as I watched his bright twinkling eyes, he had no idea how his words resounded deep inside me, I sat listening to every word he said, whilst I sipped my drink. He had a deep rich quiet side, and he was so softly spoken, and all I could do was marvel and listen. He gave me a shy smile.

"I guess it all sounds mad considering our reputation, but yeah, I like the one girl approach, I think it suits me better." I nodded, and lifted my glass in salute.

"To be honest, I like your thinking, it sounds so wrong, no offence, but I did think that all you guys just did was booze and screwing, and did not really do a lot of thinking. Shit, am I a bad person?" He sat down on the carpet.

"Nah, you are not a bad person, that does sort of really fit the rest of the band. I mean they are clever enough when writing the music, well not lyrics, if you get me?" I laughed.

"Yeah, fuck me till I cum, not the most inspiring lyric, I have heard." I looked down at him, sat next to me.

"You know, I have to ask, what the hell are you doing with them, I mean you come across as being a little more on the ball?" He took a drink and giggled.

"I am in it for the money, I have a good nest egg put away, and let's be honest, how long will we run for? Big bands never stay together, I mean look at the past, how many with the original line ups made it? You get the fame, and then the money, and then the bloody ego's kick in. I reckon the band has a couple of years left, Jimmy is doing well, Floyd is getting a rep, how long will it be before they clash?"

He made a lot of sense; history is filled with great bands that broke up. I have to admit, I was becoming more and more curious about him, he looked at me as I stared at him.

"What?" I gave him a smile, as I was trying to work him out.

"So why Battered Taco, and the whole steam punk image? I mean look at you with the waist coat and stripy pants, and all the belts and leather boots, I must admit I have always wondered about it?" He lay back on the floor, and stared at the ceiling.

"I guess my parents, my mum has a book shop, next door to my dad who has a music shop, that is how they met. They got together, and knocked a doorway through to each shop, that was my playground growing up. I would read books and play music, I guess I love the classics which are considered Steam Punk. I have read Wells and Verne all my life, my mum then introduced me to Tim Powers, K W Jeter, and James Blaylock, she even got me into Pullman, and Shelly's Frankenstein." I blinked, what did he say, I stared as if offended.

"Frankenstein is not Steam Punk, it's gothic horror." He looked up at me, and frowned.

"I thought you were a writer, shit Abby, it's Victorian fantasy, filled with electrical machines and futuristic devices, and you don't think it fits the genre, are you crazy, of course it is?" I was lost for a moment, as my mind boggled. He sat up.

"The doctor uses power through all types of futuristic devices for god's sake, he brings life to the dead with them, if that is not punked up Victorian what is, it's a no brainer?"

I just sat there looking at him, loving his mind, I was not completely sure I agreed with him, but just the thought of it blew my mind. Was this where I crossed over from Shelly to Wells, was that the attraction that made me a fan of both genres? I had no idea, but there was one thing for sure, I suddenly felt really aroused. I slipped off my chair and looked him in the eyes.

"I am going to screw you."

He lay back and laughed. I grabbed his belt and undid it, and pulled down his zip, he lifted his head and looked alarmed, as I slipped in my hand, to find his manhood.

"Holy shit you meant it?"

It was too late, I found what I wanted, pulled it out, and I had every intention of devouring it, my robe was open and ready to slip off, as I opened my mouth, and swallowed him, and it had the desired effect.

He lay back and groaned, and I pulled his pants down to his thighs, I felt an overwhelming urge to have him, was this an intellectual turn on? I had no idea, all I knew was I was soaking wet and fiery hot, and had a need for this man inside me, and within a few minutes I had protection on him, and was sat on him, leaning back and writhing in ecstasy, and heading towards orgasm.


Chloe was exhausted, she lay on her bed with the lights out, she had successfully avoided Zac all night. A very drunken Jimmy and Deb's, both naked, guided him towards her door. Jimmy giggled, he opened the door and shoved Zac in.

It was pitch black, Chloe lay there naked her legs open, and drifting in sexed brain mode. She blinked and looked down, she could see nothing, but she felt everything, as the mouth began to work its magic on her. Her toes curled, and she bit down on her lip.

"Oh god, I have no idea who you are, but Christ, don't stop."

Jimmy and Deb's giggled outside, as they heard her moaning loudly. Zac was moving up her, and she opened her legs wider, she looked down.

"I hope that frigging thing is protected, I am a no cum zone?"

He stopped in the dark, and looked down at her.

"I know you."

Jimmy opened the door and leaned in; Zac was staring in the dark trying to focus on her face. Jimmy slid his arm along the wall, found the switch, and clicked it on, Chloe looked up into the eyes of Zac, she gave a loud gasp, and looked down at his huge stiff manhood.

"Oh fuck, not again!?" She looked down and bit her lip, and gave a little whimper.

"Oh god, I know how good that is, this is so not fucking fair… Zac, stick it to me, I love your cock, but I got to tell you, I fucking hate your face." She closed her eyes, and Deb's and Jimmy giggled.

I was thrusting into my last second, as I leaned back and wailed out a long moan, and started to cum, Kyle pushed up hard, and jerked, which sent me completely into space.

I gave a huge gasp, sucking in air, and flopped on his chest, it was strange to be naked on a clothed guy, well his pants were round his thighs, but the rest of him was dressed. I lay my head on his chest, and saw Birch's feet in the doorway, my eyes followed her legs up, to her face, she was simply stood staring. I smiled up at her, Deb's and Jimmy staggered in, Jimmy looked at Kyle.

"Why am I not surprised, I should have known you would go for a book geek." He looked up and smiled.

"Hey man, I did not get a lot of choice here, I got attacked, she caught me off guard."

Outside there was a lot of noise, I slipped off Kyle, and staggered to my feet, Birch walked over and looked out of the window.

"Wow, Floyd has his hands full; she is going at him hard."

I staggered over to her side, and unlatched the door to the balcony, down below, Floyd was lay on the glass garden table, a woman straddled over his groin. She was riding him like he was a wild horse, and she was not quiet, as she pushed hard onto him, Birch gave a titter.

"I think I am a little bit jealous; I would not have minded a crack at him myself. I tell you what though, she knows how to screw, wow she has what it takes to make a man cum, look at her go." Jimmy giggled and Deb's looked at me and gasped, I frowned, she pointed at Floyd.

"Abby, that is the frigging new vicar."

"Huh?" Birch burst out laughing.

"Well halleluiah, praise the lord." I shook my head in disbelief.

"Guys, what the hell is a vicar doing screwing the shit out of Floyd, Jesus, is this place a bloody magnet for vicars to screw?"

By midnight we were all sat in the library on the floor with drinks. All over the house people were either passed out or still having sex, the sounds of groans and moans littered the background. I have to say, have you any idea how weird it is to sit on the floor opposite a naked vicar? She noticed me staring and smiled at me.

"I am glad you are as interested in me, as I am in you." That bothered me more than a little bit.

"I am with Birch full time." She gave a chuckle.

"Abigail, you misunderstand me, I am a straight girl, what I meant to say is, I have been reading your website, and I cannot deny, I really wanted to meet all of you, and talk." Birch was dubious.

"You are still a Bell Twat, so if you are looking for converts, you are wasting your time with me, I have issues with your beliefs, they do not work for me." She smiled.

"I am not here on a spiritual quest, to be honest, you both fascinate me, you two have seen the good and the bad of this place, your posts on the website forum are forward thinking and insightful. It will be my responsibility at some point to understand how this community works, and I hope to resolve issues within this community." Birch chuckled.

"If you want a white flag between us and Marjorie, I am sorry Gail, but that will not happen. I can work things out with most people, but having to live with what she has done, there is no way back for me. I have accepted her position, and I know it will never change, the two of us will never really have peace." She understood and gave a nod.

"I must say she is confrontational; I have felt a little of her wrath, I think it is clear I am not wanted by her, the bishop has advised me there is opposition, and I have heard there is a petition to remove me."

I sort of felt bad for her, I mean let's be honest, few know what it is like to be on her receiving end, like we all do. I raised my glass.

"You're drunk, naked, and love to screw, I got to say Gail, that is all good in my book." Edwina nodded.

"I got to say, you are a good looking woman Gail, and the nudity is comforting, I cannot deny. Although I have to ask, because you are here naked around us and men, and you appear really at ease with all this." She gave a chuckle.

"You know Edwina, vicars are just normal people, despite popular belief, we can be very open minded. My parents are naturists, and I have grown up pretty much naked all my life, this for me is normal." She shook her head.

"Maybe, for you, but you are here now Gail, and if they find out you like to live naked, you will be on the next train home before you could blink. This place has some nice people, but it also has some demons, and they are stuck in their ways." Gail took a drink, and looked round the library.

"You guys have so much to offer, you have no idea of how much change you could bring?" Birch looked at her.

"I mean no offence Gail, but you have not been here long enough to really understand this place, well at least not like we do. You are right about us, we do have a lot to offer, and probably more, and we have made changes here, but we are not on a crusade. If you think that is what the Curio site is, you are mistaken, that site is about listening, and understanding those who have been hurt, and sharing that experience, so they know they are not alone, like we have felt here. All we actually want is to be left alone, to live our lives our way, you see, we can accept the villagers, and their beliefs. I understand Marjorie, hanging on to her ideals, she feels threatened. I get it, the problem is, she refuses to even try to understand us, and so she will never accept us, and the same goes for her cronies." Gail sat back, and she looked at Birch.

"I am not here to recruit you Birch, all I want is acceptance too, and I have to say, I have really enjoyed tonight, you are all really lovely people, I hope I can visit, and be accepted here and in the village." I had no issue with that.

"You can visit and join us any time, we pretty much live naked, and we can offer that, we all want to be a part of this village, and we do join in when not attacked, in that respect we have brought change. We go at our own pace in our own time, I am sure we will be involved in many things together if you survive. If I am honest Gail, I personally am not in a huge rush at the moment, I am going with the flow and watching." She nodded as she watched me.

"I cannot say fairer than that Abigail, Milton has given me some idea of what you have suffered with here." I laughed.

"I have suffered alright, especially at the hands of his wife and his son. It amuses me that now he has so suddenly stepped up, when he could have done that five years ago. Personally, I think it is a little bit too late, if you ask me, he is trying to run away before everything blows up."

Gail left just after one in the morning, and we all made our way to bed, stepping over the bodies, I let Kyle have my bed, he grabbed my hand.

"You know you could stay for a while; I feel we really connected, I would like to talk more." I smiled.

"I am with Birch; we are a couple." He shrugged.

"You didn't come across as that tonight, you were here alone, if anything she appeared pretty cool and off the boil around you, but it's cool, see you in the morning I hope."

I do not know why it bothered me, had he picked up something I had not? I left him, and wandered through to her room, and slipped in with Birch. We lay in the dark, and she curled around me, and cupped my boob. I could feel her breathing, and lifted my hand to hers.

"Are you alright, you are not a fan of Gail, are you?" She was silent for a few minutes.

"As a woman, I have no issue with her, her pathological need to be liked by everyone bothers me. As a vicar, the way I see it, I think she is someone who wants to use us, actually I see her more as someone who wants to use you, as a tool for change. I am not into that, and it bothers me a lot more than you would think. I do not like you being misled for the purpose of someone else's agenda, there is too much of that going on here at the moment. I am sorry Deads, but I think she wants change too fast, and here, that could lead to disaster, if she wants to burn things down, that is fine, but I won't allow her or anyone to use you as the spark."

I could understand that, I had wondered as we sat in the library. It bothered me she saw the Curio site as a crusade, I never have, and I could not deny, the last thing I wanted was a crusade of the young against the old. We had worked hard just to gain the small amount of acceptance we had to date, and I lay there hoping, she would not just wade in and destroy it all. It was yet another thing for me to worry about, and honestly, I was starting to lose track of it all, as my thoughts got more and more confused.

# Chapter 29

# Eyes Opened.

It took a while for everyone to wake up, and there were a lot of furrowed brows, and heavy heads around the place. I grabbed a coffee and headed to my room, where Kyle was pulling his boots back on.

"Thanks for letting me crash here last night Abby, it will save me some time on route to the airport." I span round on my chair and looked at him.

"Are you heading off somewhere, I thought all the band were heading home for a week, before coming back here for the wedding?" He smiled.

"I am taking some time out from the band, and doing a little touring of my own. I am off back packing with a couple of friends to Thailand then India, call it a bit of a spiritual quest for inner peace." He stood up, and lifted his jacket off the bed, and slipped it on.

"I want a little bit of simplicity and some peace for a while, Doug Collins is playing at the wedding." I don't know why, but I felt really disappointed, I stood up, and faced him.

"Well, I suppose this is goodbye then? I was looking forward to talking more to you, I am a little sorry you are leaving." He walked over and smiled, and then slipped his arms round my waist.

"Yeah, me too, last night was really nice, I really thought we connected, you know, same vibes and stuff? I won't deny, you really surprised me, but I enjoyed it, although, I sort of wish you had stayed in here last night, I would have liked to have woken and seen you there besides me. I lay awake thinking of you and wishing you had stayed." He lifted his hand and cupped my cheek; I felt a flutter, as his eyes locked on mine.

"I could wake to this beautiful face every day, wow, you are one in a million." The crazy thing was, it had been in my thoughts too this morning. He smiled.

"If it is okay with you, I would like to stay in touch, and when I return, I would like to see you again? Just to be clear here, not for sex, although if it ever comes up again, I will take you up on it, but no, I would really like to know the real you, maybe hang out a little? I really feel, I need to get to know you much better, call it an instinctive thing."

I smiled at him, he had such gorgeous light brown eyes, and I felt my heart flutter when I looked into them, I think I liked his sincerity. I had last night, I am not sure why, but I just felt the need to get closer to him too, and that was why I had jumped on him. Our eyes were locked together, and his gaze held me captive, so he too had felt a connection, why did that please me so much?

"I would really like that, as I said I am sorry you have to go, maybe I should have stayed with you, maybe one night I will, you never know. Have a good trip, and keep me posted, and when you get back, you can show me the shop where you grew up." He smiled, and gripped his heart with both hands.

"Now I really don't want to leave, but I will definitely come back, if only for that. I know it probably feels strange, but I think maybe you could be my Weena." I had to chuckle.

"I am not that innocent, although I do think I could live with the Eloi, I like their calm, garden like world." Kyle leaned in.

"This is goodbye for now, but I will return."

He slowly came forward and kissed me so softly on the lips. I instinctively lifted my hands to his head, and held him there, and continued the kiss, and I felt a warmth fill me inside. Oh God, I wanted so much more of this. We finally parted and he raised his eye brows, his voice was so soft, and it felt like it had a little sadness to it.

"Wow, I really think I may regret leaving now." He stepped back, and took my hands in his.

"Got to go, time is always ticking, but I will message you when I fly."

He grabbed his coat, and walked to the door, turned back and smiled, I smiled back. I suddenly felt really sad, he winked and left. By the time I had blinked, and snapped out of it, and made it to the top of the stairs, all I saw was the back of his coat, as it flapped through the door, and I felt a strange kind of loss within me.

Birch came out of her room, and stood beside me, her arm slipped round my waist.

"You could have stayed with him last night, those moments are fleeting, and yet appear special."

I glanced sideways towards her watching those green eyes watching the door.

"You heard then?" Her head turned to me and she smiled.

"I did, and I envy you Sweetie, what you two had in that briefest of moments, I have only ever had with you, and you appear to have had it twice in your life. You are lucky, and so special, I am glad, I really hope he got to see you as I do, I really do."

It is strange, because I wanted to cry, she had a sadness to her eyes, something I had never seen in her before, I lifted my hand to her cheek.

"You are the love of my life, and you always will be, no matter what the future brings, that is one thing that will never change, not ever." She smiled, and her voice was so soft.

"I love you too, my dark little beastie."

She smiled, and I slipped out of her arms, and headed back to my room, Birch stood still staring at the door, her voice was quiet.

"You are so like your mum Deads, even now after five years, nothing has changed."

Later that night I got a message, with a picture, showing the coast of England, as Kyle flew over it, he was in the air, and on route to Thailand before travelling on to India, it simply read 'Waves to Weena' I smiled when I saw it.

Everyone finally went home and the house fell silent, Deb's took a bag and went back to her house complex on the Wheeler estate, she would be living with Jimmy up until the wedding. Chloe slept most of the day away, Edwina wandered round in her kimono, and Birch sat out in the garden, and read a book. After a massive clean up, because the house got trashed, I lay out on the lawn and sunbathed, as my mind tried to work out, why Kyle had affected me so much.

It may sound strange, but I felt like I had cheated on Birch, we have both had sex with other men whilst being together, and yet Kyle felt different, and it made no sense to me. How could something so short, and so fleeting mean so much to me, and why did I get so emotional when Birch told me she loved me? I really had no answer, and finally I drove myself bonkers so much, I grabbed a book from the library, and sat on my bed to read.

Monday came, with five messages from Kyle, which I read smiling many times, and it was also another work day, the fete started Saturday, and so it was all hands on deck. I headed over to mums with Chloe and Edwina, and we all joined with Oscar and Simon, to load boxes in Petal, and transport them to the centre of operations at the Church Hall. That could only mean one thing, the scowl and dark looks from Marjorie all day. As Vice, she was in charge of the allocation of exhibition passes, and she was curt and impatient when she sorted out, Birch's and mine.

"You can access earlier to the event if you a stewarding, make sure your exhibits are placed by 10pm Friday."

She pushed the card passes into my hand. I gave a nod of thanks, and smiled, said nothing, and walked away, the quiet whispered words of 'Trash' clearly met my ears, but I kept on walking.

I found Oscar, or Ozzy, as he preferred, quite irritating. He was tall, stocky and attractive, well, he certainly loved himself. I suppose to most he was dashing and smooth, but honestly, I found him nauseating, and I hated the way he oozed over everyone, especially my mum. I mean wow talk about an ass kisser, he called my mum Flick, and I did not like it, I know, weird right?

I have always used the correct terms of Mr, and Mrs, I just feel it is more respectful, and after a day of his ass kissing, I cannot deny, I was glad to get away from the creep. I was glad when the day was over, and I found three more messages from Kyle, in my inbox, I sat in my room, and smiled as I read them, oh God he was such a good writer, and his use of words left me breathless.

The week ran like clockwork, the field was opened, the gravel trucks arrived, the radio set up on the green, all the shops had outside display stand's, even Deb's had a book rack on wheels.

On Wednesday the marquees arrived, and Peter, Phillip and my dad, supervised the placement and erecting of them. Thursday was table day, and Chloe and Edwina joined me, again with Ozzy and Simon, under the supervision of my mum, we carried and lifted tables, into all the tents and set them up. I was so close to hitting Ozzy, it was unbelievable, God he was such a suck up to mum. I was knackered when I slipped into the spar at home, with Chloe that night, to soak away the aches and pains.

I lay back in the bubbles, and read more messages on my phone, Kyle was true to his word, and keeping me up to date. He had sent endless messages, and he shared a lot of deep dark secrets, he was so bright, and told me even though he was not with me, he was missing me, and he felt this strange feeling in his chest, it felt special and precious, and really cheered me up.

Birch was working long hours, with the retreat and the reception for Deb's, she lived on her phone or was sat at her laptop organising with Katie, or sat on the lawn quietly talking with Izzy. She looked tired and worn, and was unusually quiet.

Friday was flower arranging day, we were to be stewards on Saturday, so we just needed to set up our flower arrangements, jams and cakes. Birch bought plastic covers to place over them on the stand, which would be removed minutes before judging, just to ensure they remained moist and fresh. We had a wedding rehearsal in the middle of everything, so it felt like a busy day, and at 2:30, we all met in the church, as Gail walked us through our paces, and did a run down of the service. Floyd sat on the alter steps bored, there was not really that much for him to do, he played his bit, and then sat down.

Once that was done, which took forever, as Milton constantly butted in, and talked bollocks for what felt like an endless age. We dashed home, sorted out our arrangements, and headed back at high speed, in order to set them up on time.

By the time we had finally finished, and were ready, we all sat curled up on the sofa in the living room, and had a beer. It had felt like an exhausting week. Birch took my hand, and walked me upstairs, where she was running a bath, and we slipped in together and relaxed, where she caressed by breasts with soapy hands, which led to me turning round, and screwing her half in and half out of the water, God I loved this huge supersized bath.

Having pleasured each other many times, and jumped out of

the cold water, we both collapsed with our hair still wet, and fell asleep curled together, under the warm duvet, I felt we had hardly seen each other all week, and so it was a fitting end to an exhausting week.

Saturday morning was a scorcher, by eleven o'clock it was so hot it was unbearable, and we changed into vests and shorts. Our shift was not to start until one, when we would relieve the Parish Council, Ozzy, Simon and Molly, would go to the vicarage for a lunch.

Just before we arrived, an exhibitor crashed their car, by reversing into a large water butt, spilling it everywhere, creating huge puddles in the main floral tent. My mum and Ozzy, headed to the rest tent, grabbed two bales of hay, and returned, the area was covered, to create a mud free zone. Mum stayed back, as the others went for lunch, and decided to bring some more hay to keep on hand just in case.

She arrived at the tent with Ozzy, and as she looked at the bales, enjoying the few moments of shade and cool. Ozzy appeared behind her and grabbed her hips.

"You rest a minute Flick." He leaned in. "You have such soft delicate skin, and in this summer dress, you will easily overheat."

Ozzy leaned in and started to kiss her neck, he had spent the week flattering her, and she had to admit she had enjoyed it. Considering her marriage, it was nice to be seen as female, he breathed softly into her ear, Felicity shuddered.

"Ozzy I am married; you have to stop that." And yet she did not move, and he continued. "Ozzy this is ridiculous, look this is going too far, compliments are one thing but..."

She closed her eyes, oh god, her body was alive and aching. She tried to snap out of it. "Ozzy stop, I have a daughter older than you for god's sake, this is absurd."

He slid his hands up to her breasts and started to massage them slowly, she felt her breathing increasing. He was not going to stop, and he moved to the back of her ear.

"I want this Flick, I have for a while, don't tell me you have not enjoyed it, we are alone, and no one will come here."

She turned to stop him, and he went straight into a kiss, it had been ages since anyone had kissed her with such passion, and she started to respond. Her body was on fire, as she broke apart, and looked at him, her voice was breathless.

"Ozz this is wrong, I am married, and you are so young, let's just walk away, and forget this happened."

He slipped his hand under her skirt, and leant in to her low top. Felicity was torn, he was kissing the top of her breasts, and his hand began to run between her legs, and she was trembling.

"Ozzy, we cannot do this... Oh god!"

He rubbed his fingers over her short lacy panties, and her body ignited, no man had been there for a long time, and she knew he could feel through them, and how wet she was becoming. He slipped the thin straps of her dress down, and pushed her back against the wall of stacked hay.

"I want this Flick, I want you."

His hand pulled, and her top slipped, and with one swift move, he popped her breast out of her bra, and was on it, she gasped and felt weak, his hand was still moving between her legs, and somewhere in all of it, she got lost in the feelings. Her dress came up, and her panties came down, and suddenly his head was below her waist, and he was using his mouth to pleasure her, Edwin had never done that.

She felt dizzy, unable to focus and breathe, her whole body was on fire, this was so wrong, and yet, she could not stop. How many times had she fantasized about a man doing exactly this, well in her head, he was older, and yet Ozzy wanted her?

She could not hold back, she was heading towards something she had missed, some moment from years ago, and she knew she was going to orgasm.

"Oh my god, Oh god, oh, oh, oh, oh, oh, Ozzy, oooohh!" She flooded out and into his mouth, and lost complete control.

Before she was even able to move or speak, she was lay on a bale, her panties were gone, her skirt was completely up revealing her neatly groomed sex, and he was stood between her legs, unzipping his pants. She could do nothing but stare, he slid them down, and she saw his erect manhood, and swallowed hard.

"Holy Moses!"

Her mind spoke to her, 'he may only be 21, but my god he was huge.' He came down to her and pulled her bra down popping out, her other breast, and then he leaned in and began to kiss them. She was tingling all over, and then she felt him at her entrance, this was so wrong on so many levels, but she knew she wanted it. She lifted her legs to his butt cheeks, just like she had done all those years ago with Edwin, and then pulled him towards her, and he slid inside.

"OOOH!"

It was glorious, he looked up from her breasts and smiled, and then began to pump, in and out, and with each thrust in, he increased the power, and she was in tenth heaven, her back arched, and her eyes rolled back, and her whole body was alive for the first time in years, she had forgotten how wonderful it could feel.

Molly looked at me like I was dirt, it is good to see some things don't change.

"They have all gone for lunch, here are your duties." She pushed the clip board into my hands, I gave a grin.

"Enjoy your lunch, try not to choke, I hear young babies are filled with small bones."

Birch giggled, and took the clip board off me to read it. Shorts, vests, and a big baggy yellow Stewards vest, are uncool and annoying, especially when it is this hot. Birch read the list.

"We need a bale of hay for the floral tent, there has been a flood and it is getting boggy. The radio stand wants drinks delivering, and we have to remove the judging signs, and open the flaps at two, apart from that, we walk round, look important, and generally piss about." Chloe was fanning herself.

"I will grab hay, you two do the drinks, that DJ is fucking creepy, he always tries to grab my ass." And so, we separated, and our shift began, and it was going to be a long hot time.

Chloe had hay on the brain, the rest tent was her favourite place in the fete, in the last few years, many young men had fallen foul to her vagina, and her lust. She walked into it through the side flaps, and gave a smile as she heard the familiar sounds of youth, it had to be Edwina or Deb's?

With a sly giggle, she tiptoed along the hay walk, to what was lovingly referred to, as the shag spot. The sound of a guy grunting and female moaning was soft, but she knew what that meant. At the end of the long wall of stacked bales, came the familiar sound of slapping, and wow he was going fast, it would not be long before whoever it was came. The moaning grew a little louder.

"Oh god, oh god, oh god, OOH GOD!"

She turned the corner and peered round, just as Ozzy gave a loud grunt, and went rigid. Chloe's eyes almost exploded in her head, as she saw Flick, red in the face, with her eyes rolling back into her head, arch her back and cum like crazy, 'holy shit!' exploded in Chloe's head.

Chloe came out of the rest tent at high speed, and walked down between the tents talking to herself.

"Oh fuck, oh fuck, oh fuck, ooh fuck!"

She moved quickly, weaving through the tents, towards the radio station set up, Abby was still up there on the platform emptying the tray, she saw Birch, and yanked on her arm, and pulled.

"I need you, holy fuck Birch I am in big fucking trouble... No, we are in big fucking trouble." Birch pulled her arm free.

"Ow Chloe what the hell?" Chloe looked desperate, as she looked at her.

"Chloe what the hell are you talking about?" Chloe looked to the radio stand.

"Not here... Birch you have to come."

"I am waiting for Deads." Chloe grabbed her arm again.

"OH FUCKING NO WE ARE NOT!"

She pulled, and dragged Birch between the veg and jam tent. She took a deep breath, she was sweating like crazy, she pointed back up the field, Birch looked at her like she was a maniac. Chloe tried to find the right words, she was slightly breathless. Her finger was still pointing at the top of the field, and her eyes were huge in her face.

"Birch we have trouble... Oh fuck we have big fucking trouble... I just went to get hay, oh shit I forgot the bale... OH SHIT I FORGOT THE BALE!" Birch shook her head.

"What the hell is wrong with you, just go get it will you?" Chloe shook her head.

"I am not going in there alone; you have to come with me." Birch frowned.

"Jesus Chloe they are not that heavy." She was still pointing up the field, she looked Birch in the eyes.

"Birch please I need you, Ozzy is in there fucking." Birch smiled, and gave a sly giggle.

"Wow, you want to screw that creep?" Chloe shook her head, she looked left than right, lowered her voice and then leaned into Birch.

"It is not about him fucking me, it is who he is fucking." Birch gave a giggle.

"Is Stacy up there... Holy shit it's not Gail, is it?" Chloe shook her head.

"Oh fuck.... Worse!" Birch leaned back and looked at her, she was as white as a ghost, and sweating heavily, Birch frowned.

"Not Anthony or Brent?" Chloe looked desperate and panicked.

"Birch, he is fucking Mrs W." Birch blurted out a laugh.

"Piss off Chloe, don't be frigging stupid." Chloe shook her head.

"I know right, it's madness, but Birch, I saw it, he was fucking her, and I think he came inside her, and the fucked up thing is, she was loving it and cumin faster than a freight train. Birch what the fuck do I do?" Birch suddenly looked serious.

"Holy shit, we need to find Deads, and then keep her the hell away from that tent."

Chloe nodded vigorously, she leaned forward and rested her head on Birch's boobs.

"Birch is it wrong, that I was so turned on, and I wanted to watch and frap, seriously feel my panties, they are fucking soaking?" Birch grabbed her shoulders, and pushed her back.

"Stop that Sweetie, it unsettles me, and it is seriously messed up."

Birch and Chloe made their way up to the rest tent, Chloe was really weirded out.

"Oh god I have no idea of what I am going to say if they are still at it, I mean Abby will be really pissed off."

They approached the tent, and the flaps burst open, as I walked out with a bale, Chloe gave a gasp and.

"AAAAARRRGGGGHHH!"

Birch leaped up in the air with a squeal, and I jumped out of my skin and dropped the bale, Chloe started breathing really fast, her head bobbed, and she looked at either side of me. I picked up the bale.

"What the hell is your problem Chloe, you scared the shit out of me?" I watched as she nervously looked past my shoulder to the open flap, and dithered on the spot.

"Are you okay, you are acting weird as hell?" She looked at me and smiled, and tried to look innocent.

"Nope… I am fine… Yep completely fine." She leaned back, and checked inside again. I shook my head.

"I got to get this to the floral tent, it's got a huge muddy puddle, and someone forgot the straw." Chloe smiled.

"Sorry, I got side tracked."

I shook my head, and wandered off towards the tent lugging the huge bale of straw, it was hot, and it made me itch, and I was not best pleased.

Inside the tent, out of sight behind the bales, Felicity sat squatted, quietly sobbing to herself. Not quiet enough for Birch not to hear, Birch pulled back the bale, and looked over, and gave a sigh. She pulled back another bale and stepped over, and then crouched down in front of her. She slipped her hand in her back pocket, and pulled out a small pack of tissues, and slid one out.

"Here… Ozzy is still leaking out of you onto the grass."

Felicity took it and put her head down, she slid it under her dress and wiped, and gave a huge sob. Birch leaned forward and put her arms round her.

"You are not the first, and you won't be the last Flick, all of us at some time lose our heads, it is pretty normal you know, it proves you are human?" She shook her head.

"I am such a fool; I should know better at my age." Birch shrugged.

"There is no age limit on wanting to be desired Flick, isn't that what all of us want, to be seen as beautiful and be loved for it?" She looked up and gave a sniffle.

"It was wrong Birch, I told him it will not happen again, and he just shrugged, said fine, pulled up his pants and walked out. It was like it meant nothing to him. Oh god, I have ruined everything." Birch looked back into the tent.

"Chloe, give me your knickers." She looked at her and frowned, then shook her head slowly.

"I have told you, I am so fucking straight, it's unbelievable, and to be honest, I like you, but what the fuck Birch?" She stared at her and sighed.

"Flick needs some, she is in a short dress and you have shorts on, and I need to get her out of here, and home, and you are standing on hers." Chloe gave a look of sudden understanding and unbuttoned her shorts.

"Oh, right yeah, I get you."

A few moments later she handed them over, they were pretty damp, Birch shook her head, and wrapped another tissue round them, and handed them to Flick.

"Here, slip these on, I will drive you back, run a bath, and sort yourself out. I will tell the others the heat has got to you, have a stiff drink as well, you will feel better." Felicity stood up, and looked very embarrassed.

"I am sorry Birch; you have enough troubles without me trying to pretend I am a teenager again. Honestly I feel so ashamed of myself."

She pulled on the panties, and straightened her skirt, and took a deep breath. Birch looked at Chloe who was buttoning her shorts back up.

"Let the others know Flick has a touch of sun stroke, and I have taken her home, I will be back shortly, and Chloe... Not a word to anyone about this." Chloe looked insulted.

"Screw you Birch, I am not like that, I have fucked up loads, I know how it feels, and if I am honest, I don't think Mrs W did anything wrong. I like it when guys tell me I'm pretty, it makes me feel good too."

Birch drove Felicity home, and as she went to get changed, she ran her a bath. Felicity came out of her bedroom wearing a towel, and took a deep breath, Birch stood by the bathroom door and smiled.

"Don't beat yourself up, how many has he had? You have not betrayed anything; Edwin did that for you years ago. Have a bath, there is a gin on the side, a good wash and you will be like new, and Flick.... No matter what you may think, it was a good thing you got to feel like a woman, even if only for a little while."

Chloe told me, and I was worried, but knowing Birch was with mum, I knew she would be fine. I was hot and sweaty, and busy, but I was for the moment in charge, handing out pamphlets talking to visitors, and ensuring everything was going according to the list I had on my clip board.

I was high profile, smiling and polite, just like my mum always was, and even though I was hot and in need of a drink, I was actually enjoying myself. My break finally came, and I handed over to Celia, and wandered up towards the only cool place I knew, the rest tent, when I bumped into Ozzy. He smiled at me.

"I have been looking for you, I got you a drink."

It was good of him, and I gratefully took it, I unscrewed the cap, I was parched, I lifted it up, and took a massive swig, it was ice cold, and I gulped, he smiled.

"You have dribbled a bit."

Ozzy ran his hand down my neck, and onto my left breast, he smiled as he rubbed in the moisture into my vest, and then he tweaked my nipple, his eyes fixed on mine.

"Wow you are hot, and I do not mean overheated."

SMACK!

He went sideways and fell to the floor, my head snapped round, and there was Birch, her eyes were glaring down at him with hate.

"Birch what the hell, he was giving me a drink." She leaned in, and her eyes burned in a fiery green.

"Deads just leave, I want to talk to him." I looked at him as he sat up.

"What the hell, I thought we were not doing jealousy, is this about Kyle?"

"I SAID LEAVE, NOW JUST GO DEAD'S, IT IS NOT ABOUT THAT."

I stepped back quickly, she was really angry and was kind of scary, Chloe took my arm.

"Come on Abby, it is better you are not here." I looked at her.

"Chloe what the hell is going on?" She shook her head.

"It's best you don't know, trust her Abby, Birch is right, now come on."

She pulled, and I looked back as I started to walk, Birch pushed Ozzy back on the floor, and leaned over him, her eyes burned with real anger.

"I know what you did, you were seen, so what was that, you

wanted the bloody set? You go within forty feet of Abby, or her mum again, or you say one word about what you did in that tent today, I can assure you, a whole world of pain will come your way, and if you don't believe me… ZAC?"

Zac came out from between the tents, he was in a vest, and his large tattooed muscles were more than evident. He walked up, he was tall, wide, and was as ugly as hell. He wore a grisly smile, Ozzy swallowed hard; Birch looked back at him.

"You want something to play with Zac, you know, a little amusement to practice your swing on?"

He gave another wide grisly smile, he looked scary as hell. Ozzy shook his head, and lifted his hand up, as he sat up.

"I won't say a word, I promise, no one will know, please don't let him hurt me." Birch stood up.

"One word, and Zac will be there, and I can assure you he is frigging terrifying in the dark, keep your mouth shut, and you won't need to look over your shoulder at night." Birch lifted her leg, and pushed him hard, he slammed back into the grass, she turned.

"Want a pint Zac, come on I am buying?"

He smiled, and she slipped her arm round his wide waist and walked off, Ozzy swallowed hard, and sat forward, and put his head in his hands, his nose was slightly bloodied.

"Fuck, she can punch, and she is scarier than Zac."


We didn't win any prizes this year, most of our stuff came last, which was a little disappointing, but as Birch pointed out as we drove home in Petal, Marjorie was a judge, and she was also allocating the numbers to every exhibitor. It was pretty clear, all she had to do was mark us down, and convince the other judges it was not of a high enough standard, and that would be it, we would all be out of the rankings. It felt unfair, but this was after all Wotton, what were we expecting?

The good news was, we had a year's supply of jam, we would all have cake Monday night, and for the rest of the week, the house would look pretty, because we could put our arrangements on the small tables dotted about the place.

I was hot, sticky, itchy, and flustered still over Birch's behaviour, which had really pissed me off, and I was starting to think Kyle was right. I walked into the garden, stripped, and dived into the pool. I swam a few good lengths, it was great for getting rid of frustration, and helping me think.

Birch dived in, and swam beside me, I did a few more lengths, and then grabbed the side out of breath. She swam up to me and rested at my side, I looked at her, I was angry with her, I thought she was well out of order.

"I don't like jealous you, you acted like Kev." She looked really shocked.

"That was not jealousy, it was anger."

I shook my head, and pulled myself up on the side, and grabbed a towel.

"Call it whatever you want Birch, but shout in my face like that again, and I am moving back into the guest house. Don't pull that frigging lesbian tantrum shit on me. I am going to my room, stay the hell out of it." I walked off across the grass. Birch pulled herself up on the side of the pool.

"Deads listen to me, that is not the reason, honestly it is nothing to do with that." I stormed across the grass; Chloe stood watching on the patio. Birch climbed out of the pool, and ran behind me to catch up.

"Sweetie honestly, it was not like that, I told you it was not about Kyle. I cannot deny, his endless bullshit messaging is frigging annoying, but it is nothing to do with that, please Sweetie, listen to me." I stopped and turned.

"So, what the hell was it about then, because it looked pretty much to me like you were staking your claim, if not that, what was it Birch?" She stared at me, and bit her lip, and then shook her head, her eyes sparkled.

"Please Sweetie you have to believe me, you have all of this wrong, I will not deny, I don't want to lose you. So okay, yes, I saw you with Kyle, and just for a moment, and the way you read his messages, I thought I might. But I would never stop you from being happy, I promise you, I would never stop you. I wouldn't."

She gave a sob, and tears rolled from her eyes. I stared at her; my impatience was growing inside me. I had never for once thought she would be possessive, but Kyle was right, she was treating me like she owned me.

"So, tell me then, what is so frigging important to you, that the moment a guy even looks like he is going to touch me, you go all frigging ninja on his ass?" She took a step forward.

"Deads, I cannot tell you why, I promised, just please trust me. He was lucky, because I could have done worse. Actually, he was squeezing your nipple, so he was touching you, and trust me he deserved what he got." I stared at her, and shook my head.

"Not good enough Birch, and so what, I saw Max last weekend almost gnawing yours off. I didn't push him off, or hit him. Ozzy was my call, I knew he was on the make, I am not the innocent girl who started at Uni anymore Birch. If I wanted to screw him, because let's be honest, that is what he wanted, I would have done, because that is my call." She shook her head, and sobbed even more.

"You don't understand Deads, it was not like that, I promise you it was not like that." She gave another sob. "I am sorry, please trust me." Her shoulders shook, and she looked down. I was done and that was enough.

"Not good enough Birch I am done with this bullshit."

I turned to walk away and leave. Chloe loomed up in my face, and BOOM! I felt her arms push my chest, went sprawling back onto the grass.

"YOU ARE BEING A REAL PRICK AT THE MOMENT ABBY."

I slammed into the grass, and just for a moment, I thought it was school all over again, she leaned over and looked down at me, Edwina appeared, and pulled back on her arm.

"Chloe whatever this is, don't." She pulled her arm free.

"You're a prick, she loves you, she has defended you, and she has never fucking lied to you, and what one sweet dick inside you, and a couple of fucking sweet talking messages, and that's fucking it, she is ruling you? Grow the fuck up Abby, it's not about fucking you?" I felt a wave of anger surge up into me.

"Oh, yeah, and suddenly you are miss frigging all seeing and wisdom? If she is so frigging right, then why won't she tell me, come on smart arse, answer me that?" Chloe gritted her teeth.

"Abby I really fucking love you, you are one of my best friends, please let this go. Honestly, I have never asked you for anything, so please, listen to Birch, and trust her." I lay on the grass staring at her, and even angrier.

"Yeah, thought so, you know sod all, you are just protecting your assets." Chloe screwed up her face, Edwina looked at me.

"Wow prick much Abby, that was low even for you?" She pulled on Chloe's arm.

"Leave it, it's not worth it." Chloe looked at Birch, and Birch gave a sniffle.

"It is alright Chloe, it's fine, leave it, let's all walk away from this." Chloe breathed in through her nose, I could see she was really pissed off, and I just had to.

"Yeah Chloe, just leave it and walk away, maybe you could go find Ozzy and fuck him for me, I mean let's be honest, that is your forte."

Her head bobbed, she looked so pissed off, Birch yelled, and Chloe looked right at me, and our eyes met.

"YOU STUPID FUCKING BITCH, I CAUGHT HIM FUCKING YOUR MOTHER, IN THE FUCKING RESTING TENT. YOU SHOULD HAVE LISTENED TO BIRCH, YOU FUCKING ARSE!" Edwina gasped and stepped back.

"What... Holy shit, you mean he...."

Chloe looked at me, and shook her head, and then walked off. I sat up, I felt the air running out of my lungs, I could not breathe. Edwina looked in shock, Birch fell to her knees, and sobbed, my head had flipped right out. What the hell was she saying, I looked at Birch knelt on the grass, and gasped for words.

"She is lying... I mean... Birch... Say something... It's not true, it cannot be, I mean..."

She looked up at me, and I saw the streaming tears flowing from her eyes, and I knew, but I could not grasp it, my eyes clouded, I gasped in air, as tears flowed.

"Birch... Birch say something please." She just stared at me sobbing.

"I am so sorry Sweetie, I promised her I would not tell you; I gave her my word." I swallowed hard and tried to gasp in some air.

"He played her didn't he, all that bullshit all week, he wanted both of us, it was a frigging game to him?"

I felt shocked and disorientated, what the hell was happening? Edwina knelt down and pulled me close, I couldn't handle this, what the hell had I done? I pushed her back hard.

"I am fine... I am fine, really bloody sorry, but I am fine." I got up off the floor. "I need to see Chloe; I was a total bitch, and she was looking out for me."

Chloe sat on the floor in the corner of her studio crying, as I walked in, I felt like a complete cow. I was so out of order, and had no idea what to say. I crouched down and took her hands in mine.

"I am so bloody stupid and so sorry Chloe, you are right, I am an arsehole. I am so screwed up and sorry." She looked up at me, and then reached out, and pulled me close.

"She wanted to protect you, she loves you Abby, honestly, I get jealous, I wish someone would love me that much, you have to trust her, she would never hurt you, that twat is fucked up, and he hurt your mum. Honestly, she wanted to stab him, and then she saw how he touched you, I mean holy fuck, she really lost her shit, and punched him, she is a tougher bitch than I ever thought. I love you Abby, I love all you guys, we are all in this together you know, and we do watch each others back, next time remember that." She kissed my cheek.

"Just for the record, that was a straight kiss." I gave a chuckle and giggled. I pulled her out of my arms and kissed her head.

"I wish that was a straight one, but actually, holding you naked like this, is really turning me on." She straightened.

"You are fucked up, you know that Abby? This pussy is men only, you keep that tongue away from it." She smiled. "Abby, go to her, she loves you so much, go hold her, she really needs you."

I smiled and let her go and stood up, I felt so awful inside, how could I be so wrong, what the hell was happening to me, I felt so confused and like my whole world was falling apart?

"I am, oh boy, I really need to grovel to get out of this one." Chloe shrugged.

"Yeah, this one is at least ten orgasms, I hope your mouth can handle that?"

She smiled, and it was if it had never happened. I walked into the kitchen, and Edwina pointed upwards, I nodded, and turned right into the hallway, boy when I get things wrong, I really do screw everything up big time.

Chapter 30

# Growing Pains.

Walking up the stairs, felt like the longest walk of my life, talk about climbing the hill of my own anger and stupidity? I walked into my room, my bed was made, the sheets were clean, but she was not there. I walked through the bathroom, to her room, she was lay on the bed, her long white hair, with those beautiful black patches splayed all over, and I felt like shit. Chloe was right, she had never really lied, had always protected me, always defended me, and yet even now, I still refused to believe her, I still found it hard to really believe that someone could actually really love me, my god how fucked up was I?

Is this what I had learned from my parents, is this how they are, was this the reason my own mum, who was so unloved, got played by a boy, simply because he had been nice to her? She deserved better, and so did Birch. I watched her as the low sun came through the window, and illuminated her bright white hair. I felt like an absolute shit inside. What was wrong with me, why could I not trust her enough to believe her?

"For what it is worth Birch, I am sorry, I truly am."

I left the room, walked down the stairs, and out of the door, I crossed the street, and walked through the side gate. It looked so small, and yet for me, it was safety, it was protection. When I was young, this was my escape before gran came, this was where I hid when the truth was too painful, let's be honest, I was twenty four, and I was still hiding.

I walked down the garden, and grabbed the door handle, it turned, the door swung open, and I walked inside. The sun set streamed in through the window, the small table and two chairs were by the window as always, and I found that comforting.

The door to the bedroom was closed, I took a breath and walked through it, the room lacked clothes on the floor, but there it was, the bed that had been my haven for five years. The duvet was rolled up, with the pillows stacked neatly at its side. I felt relieved, and tired and shitty. I tossed the pillows to the head board, and unrolled the duvet, there were no covers, but I did not mind, I was still wrapped in a damp towel, it was insane, I dropped it to the floor, and crawled under the duvet, and gave a sigh of relief.

I fluffed up the pillows, and lay back, and memories flowed through my mind, I was such a fool, such an idiot, she was a much better person than I was, and she did deserve a Kyle of her own. The voice of Roni echoed from some past moment, just like it had on the train all those years ago, I saw the table in Uppermill, her bright green eyes looking over her cup, she saw something all that time ago, that I did not even see today, her voice echoed in my head as I drifted into sleep.

"I am not sure if you are aware, but you are pretty naïve for city life, Jemi has been carefully controlling your exposure to new things, so it does not freak you completely out. She is an extraordinary girl who has formed a deep bond with you, I am not sure you are fully aware of how important you are to her, but as her mother, I can tell you, that girl will have your back for the rest of your life."

Somewhere in my dreams, I wish I had listened, but it was too late now.

My night was weird, my dreams surreal, my insides were trying to talk to me, but it felt like it was all in a different language. I woke up feeling disorientated, and yawned lay on my side. I felt warm and snug, and just lay with the heat radiating out of me, with my eyes closed, and let my thoughts swirl. This was nice, it felt familiar and real, and safe. I lay there drifting, my mind still playing tricks on me. Outside was Sunday, and bells began to ring out across the village, I just lay there in silence, drifting. The bed moved, or I dreamt it did.

"You have got to be fucking joking, fucking Bell Twat, God, I fucking hate that church, why don't country people ever fucking sleep?" I rolled over, she turned and looked at me.

"It's a bloody liberty, that's what it is, it has to be some form of discrimination to all us none Christians, we are oppressed you know that? We have no rights when it comes to the Bell Twat, we should lobby the Church of England, and tell them to shut the fuck up on Sundays." I stared at her with utter disbelief.

"Birch what the hell are you doing here?" She blinked, and rubbed her eyes.

"What do you mean, we sleep together, and you were not in your bed over there, so I came to your bed over here, I wanted to cuddle you. I find it hard to sleep when I don't, why Sweetie?" I sat up, not quite understanding.

"Birch, I made you cry again, I did not believe you, and that upset you, I came upstairs and you were flat out, and I felt so bad I came here." She yawned.

"I know, but we always sleep together, I just told you, I can only sleep when you are there, and so I came here, because this is where you were. I was sleeping nicely too until that twat started. One day I am going to hang him on his own rope, noisy fucking twat, it's a liberty you know, that is what that is?" I flopped back on the bed.

"Do you like practice stalking or something, is this what you learn from your patients, you know, tracking me down?" She slipped back in the bed and yawned.

"Sweetie I am sleepy, it is too early to think, well at least not with all that frigging racket out there."

She snuggled into me, and lay her head just above my right breast. I gave a sigh and stroked her long hair; she gave a happy little moan.

"This is nice, we should come here for holidays."

She lifted her leg, and slid it over mine, and snuggled in closer, and soon I heard her soft breathing, she had gone back to sleep.

I have no idea why it surprised me, we once sat on a bench outside Manchester Cathedral, and she fell asleep on me, we were supposed to be feeding the pigeons, but she just leaned back, closed her eyes, and off she went, she is an enigma, that is what she is. I suppose one day I will get used to it, well maybe, I don't really know.

I lay on my back, staring at the ceiling, trying to understand my complicated life. Had anything actually changed, or was this it, was this how the rest of my life was going to be, days of confusion, sex, and getting drunk?

It was clear I was as untrusting now as I was in the days before

Uni, Birch had never lied, and yet when she told me I was wrong, I just could not believe her. Why was I so shocked that my mum had sex with someone not my father? I knew he has had affairs; I had seen him with one of them, what bothered me most, was it the fact she had screwed someone else, or was it his age, holy shit was I ageist?

My mind swirled with an endless list of self doubt, why could I not trust anyone, why did I feel I had to be on my guard, why did Birch really leave Kev, was it for me, or was it the drugs? The list of questions just kept on growing, and it was getting longer and longer, I was sure that at some point my head would explode.

I closed my eyes, I felt so weary, so tired, so God dammed frigging lost, the mist rolled into my thoughts and I drifted. Birch's soft breathing bounced around inside my head, I felt like I was floating, water lapped against the boat, the mist was so thick. I could not see, but somewhere in the distance, two green lights shone through the thick grey swirling waves of mist.

"Sweetie, it is time to paddle, you have drifted out of the current, you're drifting away, and I am losing you, paddle my dark little beastie, paddle to me, I miss you. Deads, you have to paddle, I am losing you."

I didn't want to move, I was warm here, I couldn't see anything, I just wanted to stay here safe and warm. Kyle spoke in my head.

"I will come back, you are the one, you know you must never question love, you just feel it and I really feel it Abby." That soft voice flowed through the air; it was further away.

"Sweetie... Lift the sail."

"You are my Weena, I will return for you, I will be back, and then I will show the truth of real love."

"Deadly don't leave yet, I need you, come back to me Sweetie, you have to pull up the sail, Sweetie.... Sweetie... Sweetie... Sweetie... I love y..."


"NOOOOOOOO! BIRCH... BIRCH... BIRCH DON'T LEAVE ME!"

I sat bolt upright in bed, filled with panic and fear, as my heart raced and my head thumped in rhythm with it. I was tangled in the duvet and crying, God I was crying so badly, my eyes were cloudy like they were still in the mist. I lurched out of bed, tangled in the duvet and crashed on the floor, sobbing and wailing.

"Birch... Birch... don't leave me, I want you, don't leave me."

My legs were tangled, and I could not remember where I was, as my eyes looked wildly round the room, trying to focus. My heart was thumping inside my chest, I grabbed the mattress and pulled myself up, she was not there, she was not on the bed.

I pushed my face into it, and just balled my brains out, sobbing and muttering, was anything real anymore? All I knew was I was so tired of everything, nothing made sense, nothing felt real, nothing felt worth the effort. So, I just buried my face in the mattress and wailed.

A familiar warmth came around me, and pressed into my back.

"Sweetie... Sweetie what on earth is happening?"

She was knelt on the floor, pressed into me, and hugging me from behind, my mind was everywhere, was this real, or another horrible dream, I sobbed into the material.

"I thought I had lost you; you were not here and I was terrified, I don't want this Birch. I don't want us like this, I want it all as it was. It is all too much, and I cannot take anymore, I just cannot keep doing this." I shook as I cried, and she squeezed me harder.

"Deads, it is okay, I just went for coffee, that is all. When I woke up you were asleep, and I really needed a pee and coffee, so I walked up to the house. It's fine, I was here all night, honestly, you just started overthinking and misread everything, it's what you do. Sweetie I am here, I am not leaving, I mean hell Deads, I spent six million quid to be here, honestly why would I leave?"

I sniffled, and tried to calm down, I could not control the feelings of fear and dread that were spiralling out of control inside me. I did not understand any of this, I did not want to be this, what the hell was going on, why did I feel this way? I had no answers, it was just how I was, and nothing at the moment made any kind of sense to me. I leaned back into her, and she slid her arms round my tummy.

"Birch, I feel I am losing control, and I am so frightened, I am so utterly frightened."

She slid back away from me and then reached for my hand, and gently pulled, I slowly turned round with red watery, puffy eyes. She slid her arms under my armpits, and started to lift, I helped, and sat on the edge of the bed. Birch knelt on the floor and looked up at me, her green eyes filled with concern.

"Okay so talk, it does not matter if you make sense or not, just talk to me Deads, tell me what is going on in your head, let me see your truth." She lifted a cup, and handed me a coffee. I was shivering or trembling as it lifted it to my lips.

"I had horrible dreams."

She gave a slight nod of recognition, and flicked her head, so her long hair slipped back over her shoulder.

"Tell me about them, describe it as you saw it." I looked into her eyes, they were so deep and full of life.

"I don't know where to start, it was misty, and I felt like I was in a boat, and I could not see you, but I could hear you in the distance. You were calling me, but I felt unable to move, and then Kyle started talking and confusing me, so I was floating away from you."

She sat and listened, as suddenly I was talking, about fear, love, feelings of isolation and abandonment. I talked of the pain I felt before Uni, how I wanted to die to be free of it, and the terror of coming home with black hair, and all the hateful comments. I went on and on about how I did not understand why I was sexually attracted to her, but not Deb's or Chloe, or even Edwina. I talked of her love for Kev, her telling me it was his drugs that ended it and it was not for me, I talked of Kyle, and how it had stirred up feelings inside me, and how I felt I had cheated on her, and felt really guilty about that. She said nothing, she just sat there and listened, her gaze never leaving me, but her nods at specific moments, assuring me she was understanding my weirdness.

I think it is the most honest I have ever been with anyone, and she was so patient sat listening to every word. I think I talked myself into a coma, and took a huge breath and relaxed, I was feeling so much calmer now, she smiled.

"Feel better?" I gave her a nod, she knelt up and pulled me into a hug.

"Thank you for sharing that, it must have been hard for you to talk about it, and I am happy you did." She let go and stood up and offered her hand.

"Come on, let's go home, eat, and talk more, I like this part of you best, because I get all of the answers to the millions of questions, I wanted to ask you." I looked up at her.

"Birch, we are naked, where are your clothes?" She frowned.

"What clothes, I got out of bed and came looking for you?" I stared at her in disbelief.

"Are you saying you walked here naked?" She smiled.

"Yes, why is that a problem?" I stood up, and looked round the room.

"Well yeah, people don't like seeing that, it sort of offends them. Jesus Birch, we live in Wotton." She shrugged, and picked up my towel and handed it to me.

"I have a nice body, and I am not ashamed who sees it, if these great tits, and my killer ass offend people, screw em, we all come to this world naked and we leave this world naked, it sort of makes it pointless to worry in the middle." I wrapped the towel round me, and she smiled and took my hand.

"Come on Sweetie, let's go home."

Hand in hand we headed home, I was wrapped in a towel, but not Birch, she walked with me at a leisurely pace across the road, without a care in the world. In the house I sat in the kitchen, Birch insisted she cooked, and I cannot deny, I was starving. We headed up to the bedroom to eat, and sat on my bed.

It felt strange, I had told her so much, and yet she had not responded to any of it, and I won't deny, it was driving me mad, I watched as she sliced her egg, and lifted it to her mouth, she noticed. She chewed and then swallowed.

"I can read your thoughts Deads, you want to know why I have said nothing?" I forked in a mouthful of beans, and then nodded.

"I expected your response, I somehow thought you would tell me something."

"Yeah, I figured you would, which is why I was just there for you, and stayed quiet. Look sweetie, I have no need to tell you how I feel, you already know that. I am not here to lead the way, I am here to share the journey, and honestly, at the moment you are unsure of where to walk, so I will stay by your side, and match your steps." I gave a sigh and put my fork down.

"Birch I am so screwed up at the moment. What with mum, and all the shit we get, Kev plus Kyle has just messed with my head, I feel stuck in a mire, and I cannot pull myself out. You are not at question here, that is the only decision I have made that is right for me, but its everything else." Birch slid her empty plate to the unit, and lifted her cup.

"Deads Sweetie, we work, this, whatever it is, us, we work well, but you have to look inside and really think about you. Look Sweetie, Kyle conflicted you, and that says something, and you need to ask what that is, I cannot answer that for you. You know how I felt about Kev, and yet when he showed up, I knew how I truly felt about everything. Deads you spent a few hours with Kyle, and so I think you really need to ask, is that really enough to know him, and I mean really know him?" I shook my head.

"This is all so confusing, I don't know what I should feel for anything, that is why I feel so screwed up."

She looked down and looked really sad as she looked at me, I felt a twinge deep inside, and knew, somehow, I had hurt her, but I did not understand how.

"Honestly Deads... I had hoped you would say something else." I had lost my appetite.

"This is so hard Birch, and I am not dealing with it very well, Marjorie is never going to leave us alone, and I have no idea what is going to happen with my mum and dad, and honestly, a two hour talk, sex and shit load of messages with Kyle is not exactly the best way to plan my future, he just upped and left right after for a back packing trip." She understood.

"Maybe so Deads, but you know, I left you too, you packed your bags and came home. You have no idea how much I have thought of that, and I regret it. I should have asked you to come live with me whilst I was finishing Uni. It took me a while, but it gave me clarity, you need to be certain, and I mean completely certain about your true deep feelings, they are there if you look for them."

I had no idea what to say, she came back, and spent a fortune to stay close, and I loved that about her, she needed to understand, this was not about her and me. I was happy with that, it was everything else that felt like chaos, and my biggest fear was... I voiced it.

"Birch we are fine, but what if all this hate, all this chaos, and all these shitty people, cause so much more shit for us that it just becomes too much to cope with? I am so scared that it and everyone else that will drive us apart?" She looked at me and then just shrugged.

"So, Izzy takes on the practice, we sell the house, and piss off somewhere nice."

My jaw hit the bed. "Huh?" She smiled.

"Sweetie it is just money, we can spend that anywhere, being happy is far more important than cash, if this place is too much, we will just pack up our girls, and all piss off to somewhere nicer. Deads a house is a brick box, it is good for storing memories, but life is about making them, if you really cannot take any more of round here, then we can move." I was stunned.

"Birch how can you be so sure about things? You know people don't just uproot and move? I have so many doubts, can I really write enough to live, will I ever be accepted here, do I want kids, honestly, I am not sure, will you fall in love and leave, is Kyle coming back, will mum and dad divorce? There is just so much to consider, I cannot be like, oh, yeah, I will sell up and piss off, I am so unsure about everything, and it scares me." Birch leaned back on her pillows, and sipped her drink.

"I am not, I wait to see what happens, and then I think about it and deal with it. Deads you do not need all the answers, some things are best left to just unfold, you don't have to be successful to be a writer, you just need to enjoy it. What happens between your parents will happen, you have no say in that. Kyle is an unanswered question. I left you once, I hated it, so it is not in my plans, as for kids, if you want them, cool we will go get some, and I don't need to fall in love, I am already in love, and no matter what happens, that will not change, and so I just go with the flow." She put her cup down.

"Deads you have to decide what you want, because at this moment you clearly don't know. I already know what I want, and to be honest, I want to relax in the spar, it is a nice day. The girls are on the grass, and I want to be out there with them, so you sit here and think, or join us, it is up to you."

She slid off the bed, grabbed her plate, and went downstairs, and I sat staring at the door, not really sure of what to make of it all. I sat on the bed trying to really understand what I should do, and just figured that this was something that would take some time to work out.

I really want to be able to sit back and let things go with the flow, but so much had happened, that I was finding it hard to find my way. Birch was right, I could see her point of view, and it made sense, she was right, I had to decide what I wanted, for myself.

I went down to the garden, it seemed pointless sitting in my room, it was our day off from the fete, so I wanted to enjoy it. Chloe and Edwina were stretched out on the grass with Izzy, Birch was relaxing in the spar with her eyes closed. I walked down the grass, and stopped as I looked down.

"Holy shit Izzy, what happened to you?" She rolled on her side, and smiled.

"I made it into the club, I got my initiation last night."

I gave a shudder, she had red wields all across her back, and they looked really painful. I sat down by her side.

"Doesn't that hurt, it looks really painful." She sat up.

"Pain is the game Deadly, and to be in the club, I have to prove that not only could I take it, but also that I could get to my sexual high from it. Unless you understand the joy of the experience, you will not get why it is such a big turn on."

She was right, I really did not understand it, looking at her back made me shiver, I could not imagine that kind of pain. If someone hit me and asked me to cum because of it, I would batter the shit out of them with something very big and very heavy. I already had scars on the inside from my exes, and could not handle them on my skin.

"I actually admire you Izzy, I really could not handle that level of pain, I think I am a coward, I do avoid painful situations." Izzy understood me completely.

"Deadly I have studied sex and sexuality in great detail, so would it surprise you if I was to tell you, that when Jemi told me she was sexually attracted to you, but no other woman, I thought that was really strange? I talk to people every day about their kinks, but could not understand Jemi, and then I met you and we spoke, and suddenly there were two of you, and you are the only two I have ever met who feel that way. I have been looking into it, as it fascinates me as a kink counsellor." That really surprised me.

"I think I am pretty normal Izzy, I think I just fell in love with the most least expected person, and it took me a long time to admit or accept that, because I did not want to be different. I wanted to be just an ordinary person, and actually I think I am." Izzy gave a slight nod as I spoke, she smiled as she watched me.

"I actually think you are an extraordinary person Deadly, nothing about you is ordinary, you are complex, and deep, and you have a very rich hidden beauty within you, and do you know how I know that?"

I was a little thrown by her comment, and I did not know how she could see all that.

"I am a little curious Izzy, so yeah, tell me how you can see that." Izzy gave a little chuckle, and looked behind herself.

"I don't see you that way, she does, and I know her really well. I have worked with Jemi for a long time, and we have seen too many tough times together. Deadly you captured her heart, and you did it simply by being you, and you achieved something no one, not even Kev could do. Trust me she was so broken without you, and coming here made her whole and happy again, and only a very extraordinary person could do that."

I turned, and looked at her, relaxed with her arms stretched out across the top of the spar, her eyes were closed, and she looked serene, and beautiful. I felt emotional, hearing Birch tell me of her life without me was one thing, but hearing it from Izzy somehow gave it more impact. I lay back in the sun and closed my eyes, and felt the heat on my skin, it felt nice, and I drifted within myself, and tried to puzzle things out.

Even now after all this time I was still doubting myself, was this huge feeling I had for Birch even real, was this true love? I had thought so, but then Kyle came along with his sincerity and heart felt deep insights, and now I was so confused. Was this what it had been like for mum, is that why she chose dad, oh god, was I becoming her, was I really screwed up by all their mistakes? I had no idea, I just knew that I was struggling to understand me, and when I thought Birch would talk and offer advice, she had said nothing, and I felt crushed by it. If she really did love me as much as she says, why was she not helping me like she always had? My brain felt like it could not take much more, I felt I was overloading.

We ate late, all of us had just enjoyed a quiet peaceful day, and

Chloe ordered pizza, so we all sat out on the patio, and ate, and talked about the fete and the wedding, and I drank beers. Birch was silent for most of the evening, she sat back on a lounger, wearing her darkest glasses, and sipped from her tall glass of vodka, as the day slipped towards sun set, she sat forward in her seat.

"I have some messages on the web site to answer." Edwina gave a sigh.

"Yeah, as much as this is nice, I have to do a few things on the forum."

She got up and followed Birch in, I arrived last and sat at my desk, Birch was typing away responding. I opened my website inbox, and there was a long list, and so I got stuck in, and began to respond to each of them. The site had grown far more than we ever expected, and with four of us responding it was still a lot of work.

My eyes strayed to Birch, as she focused on the screen, the way her eyes moved as she read, the slight smile when she read something she liked, there was no denying she was beautiful, not just outside but inside.

I reached the end of my list, and then the two more in my personal box, both were from Kyle on his travels. I responded with a smile, it made me feel good, and I wrote a really long response, grinning like an idiot.

Finally, I was done, and closed the email down, and stretched, as I sat back in the chair. I had drunk a lot of beer, and felt a little light headed, it was getting late, and we were all on duty tomorrow for the last day of the fete. I got up from my chair.

"I am off to bed; I will see you soon." She looked at me and smiled, and I staggered a little out of the room.

It was twenty minutes later when she came up, she walked into my room and sat on the end of the bed, I lay on the pillows, she gave a sigh.

"I listened today, I listened very carefully to everything you said. Deads I am certain in the choices I have made; I have no fears or questions, I made the choices that I felt were right for me. I have thought very carefully all day, and I think you do not have the certainty I have, if anything, I heard a lot of doubt."

I looked at her sat there, she looked so self assured, but I felt nervous, she smiled.

"I love you Sweetie, but love is not enough, you need to reflect on what it is you want, and so I think for now, until you know, we should sleep apart. We should stick to our own rooms, and when you can answer all those doubts, we will talk."

I felt my stomach twist and a lump came up in my throat as she stood up, my eyes followed her towards the door. I took a huge breath, trying to hold back the sudden wave of emotion that was crashing over me. I struggled to talk.

"Birch, are you breaking up with me?" She stopped but kept her back to me.

"No Sweetie, you cannot break up a one sided relationship, you need to seriously decide what it is you want. I cannot leave what I do not already have. You have the space, use it, and then we will talk."

The tears filled my eyes, as she walked through into the bathroom, I heard her door close, and then the lock clicked, it was the first time I had ever heard the door close, and it sent a cold chill down my spine. I slipped down into the bed, pulled the duvet up, and turned into my pillows and wept.


It was a rough night, I slept little, even full of booze, it was hard. I was awoken by Chloe with a coffee.

"We have to get a move on, or we will be late." I sat up feeling rough, and took the coffee.

"Have you got Birch up?" Chloe gave me a funny look.

"She had to go into work, I thought you knew, she will not be available today... Okay what is going on with you two?" I shook my head, and took a sip of my coffee.

"Yeah sorry, I vaguely remember her saying something, ignore me I was drunk last night, and I am not awake yet." She stared at me.

"You guys are alright; you have not had a fight, have you? I mean she was pretty quiet last night. Abby you are not still pissed about the Ozzy thing, are you?" I lifted my hand.

"No, I was the one who screwed up there, I talked it out with her, it is all sorted out."

"Okay Abby, I am glad to hear that, because she was so right in that. Abby, can I say something and you will not be pissed off with me?" I frowned.

"Why would I get pissed off with you?" She shrugged.

"I am not sure, you have been pretty volatile recently, and a little weird at times, but you know I love you? I care about you, in a totally straight way of course. Abby you may not see it, you might even doubt it, but just trust me on this, if you let her go, and fuck off with Kyle, you will regret it for the rest of your life. I just wanted to say that." I looked up at her, and somehow felt there was a 'but?' Yet it did not come.

"Chloe, do you know something I don't?" She gave a slight smile.

"I know a real relationship when I see one, and I ain't seen one around Kyle. I get he is a cool guy; he is a well read, and I could see how that would appeal to you, but throwing something as real as Birch away, I think that would be madness. That is all, and I just wanted you to know."

It stayed in my mind all day, the fete was hot, and busy, and I felt rushed and pressured all day. When it came to the end of the day, I cleared all our exhibits into Petal, Birch had left Edwina the keys, and then we started to fold up tables, and stack them on pallets so they could be loaded.

By seven o'clock the marquess were already coming down, and I was exhausted. I wandered into the large Village Hall and sat down at the back, the special guest had finished, and prizes were already being awarded. Deb's gave me a big smile as she sat beside me, Jimmy was a few rows in front with the band. She looked so happy.

"Jimmy loves the place; he says it is a really great home. Abby it has been so nice being alone with him, I cannot wait for next weekend." I slid my arm round her and pulled her close, and hugged her.

"I am really happy for you."

I was, and yet inside I felt a pain in my chest, Birch's last words were stuck in my head. 'I cannot leave, what I do not already have. You have the space, use it, and then we will talk.' I sat back and zoned out, we were all there, all the Curio's bar one, and it did not feel right. Even Gill and Denise had joined us, although I had not realised, Anthony was not there, but since Brent, that had become sort of normal.

The final prizes were coming up, and I was relieved, I wanted to see her, and could not wait to get out. I could see Marjorie handing out prizes, and I knew we had all been excluded, because she knew our numbers, and I really wanted to be as far as I could from her. Even at the back she could see me, and as she gave away the prizes, she knew she had yet again got at me. God, I hated her so much, I was so tired of her shit.

The last prize was given, and my mum walked up to the mic, she looked good, I had not spoken with her, but how could I? She thought I did not know, and if Chloe had not said anything I wouldn't. Ozzy was nowhere to be seen, whatever Birch had done, it had worked. My mum tapped the mic to get everyone's attention.

"Ladies and gentlemen, before we end tonight and wrap up the fete for this year, we have one more item that was unscheduled to add to our program. Vice Chair Marjorie Wallace will address it."

She walked away from the mic and Marjorie approached it, I was so sick of seeing and hearing this bloody awful woman.

"Good evening all, thank you for your patience. It has probably come to all of your attention that my husband Milton, who has served as the vicar of this parish for almost thirty years, has decided to take early retirement. We shortly will be moving out of the vicarage to a new local property, the old Suttons farm estate, and your new vicar Gail Watkins Linley, will be taking up residence, as she prepares to take over the parish. I have given this much thought, and I cannot deny, I am absolutely opposed to her becoming the vicar of this parish."

I looked up at the stage, holy shit did she actually just say that? Deb's looked shocked, and there were many rapid conversations started instantly, and a low rumble began around the hall. Marjorie stood poker faced, and looked out on everyone, she tapped the mic for quiet.

"Please let me finish... Considering my opposition to her placement, and after much consideration, I feel very strongly, that my opposition to this appointment, is a conflict of interest, that compromises my work as a Parish Council member. So I have decided to join my husband, and relinquish my position as Vice Chair, as of tonight. Under the ruling of our constitution, my seat will be filled by the longest serving member of the existing council, until such time as a new Vice is assigned the task from the chair. So I would like to congratulate Celia Thorpe Willingham, as new vice, and I wish her well in her role. Thank you." I was in shock, Deb's leaned into me.

"You got to give it to her, she has found her way out of an impossible position." I turned to her.

"How do you mean?" Deb's chuckled.

"That letter of yours is worthless, she put us all through hell, and yet you did not withdraw it, you beat her Abby, you finally forced her into a position where she had to fall on her sword, and she has."

Marjorie stood at the front of the stage and wiped her eyes with her hankie, as a large amount of the crowd stood and applauded her, in a way I had to laugh, even defeat for her became a victory. She stood there dabbing her eyes and offering thanks, and honestly, it made me sick, I got up and walked to the door, Deb's called me back.

"Abby are you not going to saver the moment?" I looked at the stage, and then back to Deb's.

"I have seen all I need to see, I need some air, and I want to be alone."

I left the hall, and walked out into the cooler air, I slipped my hands inside my short's pockets, and walked slowly down the green, the lights in Sweetie's Retreat, were out. Birch must have finished. I walked slowly towards home.

Had I won? I was not sure, Marjorie did not attack me from the seat of the council, she attacked me from behind closed doors, from secret meetings no one saw. I was not convinced this was the end. I really wanted it to be, she had swayed public opinion for far too long, and I could use the break.

I took a long deep breath, and took in the nights air, and looked around the village I had known all my life, and nothing looked any different. The fact was the loss of Madge from the council meant nothing, and that was the saddest thing of all, because at the end of the day, it was the one thing all of us shared in common, all of us loved, and wanted to protect the village.

I had never wanted to ruin it, neither had Deb's, her shop was modern, and it was greatly improved, and yet outside it looked as traditional as ever, even the practice blended in. The Curio's wanted to live in peace, and be a part of this place, why had no one ever understood that? I had dyed my hair and it started a five year war, and if it came to an end, I would not complain, but even that would have no bearing on village life.

I think I was really starting to understand Birch, she knew, she was always aware that we come and go as we age, and the village would remain as it has for the last two hundred years. It would always have a well maintained green, always be a place of great beauty, and always attract tourists, it really did not matter who was on the Parish Council.

I arrived home and walked in, Anthony sat on the sofa with Edwina, I had not even noticed her drive past me. I had not seen Petal parked in front of the garage. Anthony was holding a wad of tissues, and had very red eyes, I walked into the living room.

"Anthony are you alright, what has happened?" He exploded into tears; Edwina looked up at me.

"He was at the door crying when I got here, it appears Brent has been sleeping with Peter. He sold his house to move in with Peter, and they have broken up, he has nowhere to go Abby." I gave a sigh.

"Yes, he has, he is one of us. Anthony it is fine, you can stay here, we have the space, I am sure Birch will not mind, I will go talk to her, and explain things." Edwina frowned.

"Is Birch home, because Anthony said he had been ringing the bell for half an hour? When I got in, the house was empty, I called her, but got no reply."

I did not understand, the retreat was dark and locked up, and she was not at the hall. I turned and walked out of the living room, and up the stairs, I felt panic flood inside me, and I was not sure why? I opened her bedroom door; the adjoining door was still closed and her room was empty.

I felt my stomach twist, I turned to leave and saw the wardrobe door open slightly, I went over and opened it, half her clothes were gone, my heart started to beat rapidly. I turned and crossed the room, and opened the door from her room to mine, and hurried through. My room was as I left it, apart from the envelope attached to my monitor. I felt a lurch in my chest, and hurried across the room, and pulled it from my screen, I tore it open and unfolded the sheet of yellow paper.

*Dear Abby.*

*You have your space; I need some too. Deb's wedding is completely done and arranged, I have asked Denise to step in, the marquees are all organised, and everything is set and ready, Katie has everything in hand.*

*It is time for you to grow up, and finally decide what exactly it is that you want, you are losing control again, and I cannot watch you self destruct, so make the choices you can live with, and then we will talk. Until then, give me some time and space, this is so hard for me, so please think very carefully, because not everything is as you thought, talk to your mum. This is not a game; people are going to get hurt.*

*I love you. Jemi xxx*

My world completely crashed; she was gone.

Hatty poured out a scotch and turned. "Here, this will help." She handed the glass to Birch. She took the glass and held it in her lap.

"Thanks for this, I am sorry to just text out of the blue like that, I really appreciate this, I was unsure of what to do." Hatty stood by her fire place and looked at the lost sad face of Birch.

"It's fine, honestly, this is the best place at the moment. Sadly, we both have something very much in common, both of us fell in love with a Watson, and have suffered because of it." Birch looked up and tears formed in her eyes.

"I just need a few days, I am going home next week for a couple of weeks, I just need to sort a few things out at the practice, but I want to give her the space to make her mind up." Hatty gave a long sigh.

"Take as long as you want, I have a spare room that hardly gets used, and I am in the studio more than the house, just do as you need, you can stay as long as you like. I am here Birch, and possibly the only person alive, who truly understands. Take your time, and if you need to talk, we will."

Chapter 31

# Hard Facts.

I sat on the bed staring at the letter, downstairs it was all hands on deck, Deb's arrived with Jimmy, and some of the crew. Chloe held Anthony's hand, and talked quietly to him, Deb's did her best, and Jimmy and the boys offered to go beat the shit out of Brent and Peter. Deb's gave them all a disapproving look, Jimmy looked sheepish.

"Sorry Goggle Bear, we are just trying to help." Edwina chuckled.

"It is greatly appreciated guys, there is beer in the kitchen, we will handle this." Jimmy gave a big smile.

"Come on lads." He turned, and they all followed, leaving the girls alone, to deal with Anthony.

It is strange, I felt numb, I wanted to cry, it had hurt so much when I saw the letter, and yet now sat on the bed, all I could do was stare at it. Deb's came in, and walked across the room.

"Abby I just got a text." I looked at her, she had tears in her eyes.

"What is happening, why has she told me she will not be at my wedding?" I shook my head, I did not know what to say, accept.

"She has gone." Deb's sat down on the side of the bed, and stared at me.

"How... Abby I don't understand, she loves you more than anything, how can she go?"

"Obviously not, she left." Deb's shook her head.

"I don't believe that Abby, Birch did all of this just for you, she would not just leave, it is not like her." She slipped the letter out of my hand, and read it.

"What does this mean, you have your space, did something happen Abby?" I stared blankly at her.

"I guess you cannot be in love with her, and screw other men, she got weird after Kev came here, and then again after the party, she became all protective, controlling and it freaked me out." Deb's frowned.

"That does not sound like Birch, she is a free spirit, she would not do that to anyone, especially you. Abby she really cares about you, what exactly happened?" I gave a sigh.

"Deb's I am tired, it has been a really shit few days, can we do this another time?" She smiled and handed the letter back.

"Alright Abby, but I want to know what happened at some point, we need to talk."

She left, and I slipped into bed, I curled up under the duvet, and lay in the darkness and stared at the wall.


Chloe looked stunned. "Well, where the fuck is she, I need to find her, she will need us?" Deb's looked at Chloe.

"I want to know what has happened since I was at home. I want to know everything, there is something really messed up going on, and if those two are apart, that is the worst thing that has ever happened to all of us. If you guys know something, you all better start talking, because this is Abby and Birch we are talking about, not some casual couple." Edwina looked at her, and nodded.

"My room, it is too public down here." Izzy came in through the door, she stood in the doorway and looked at us.

"That look says you have heard, so come on, what the fuck are you doing about it?" Deb's gave her a shrewd look.

"I think you know more about this than any of us, what do you know? This is all wrong, and they need us, we are going to Edwina's room, there are no perverted teddies in there. We are going to work out what the hell has happened, and then find a way to fix it." She gave a smile and nodded.

"Good, let me grab some scotch, I missed a club meeting in hope you would say that, get up there, I will be up in a sec."

Deb's, Chloe and Edwina headed upstairs, and Izzy went in search of her bottle, and a few minutes later, Edwina sat at her desk chair, whilst Deb's and Izzy sat on the bed, and Chloe sat on the floor, with her back to the wall.

Edwina had a long table with three large screens, and a massive set up of wires, a computer and a large server. Her keyboard and mouse flashed different colours on the keys. She turned round in her seat.

"Okay we know something happened the night of the party, and whatever that was, it was the start of all this, Abby has been weird since. After that there was the Ozzy thing, and Abby exploded over it. That night she slept at her mum's house, and Birch went to her, they came back and were quiet, actually Birch has been unusually quiet since the party. They came back, went to their room, and it looks like they slept apart that night, which is really messed up and weird for those two. Birch got called into work, and Abby did the fete, and we came home to find Anthony in tears. Abby went upstairs and has not been down since, and Birch is nowhere to be seen. Okay is this everything?" Izzy took a deep swig from the bottle.

"What was this Ozzy thing, I don't know about that?" Chloe looked up.

"I caught him fucking Mrs W in the rest tent." Deb's gasped and looked at her.

"What the hell Chloe, no frigging way?" Chloe shrugged.

"I know what I saw, he was really going at it, and she was fucking loving it, trust me, she needed that. Anyhow, I panicked and went to get Birch, when we came back, I freaked out because Abby was in the tent. Luckily Mrs W hid, and Abby saw nothing. Birch helped her, apparently once he had done the deed, he blew her off. Birch took her home, and came back, she saw Ozzy hitting on Abby and feeling her boob, and she just fucking lost it. She marched up to him, and smacked him in the head, and I mean, she really packed a punch." Deb's looked mind blown.

"Why didn't you tell me, I would have come straight to Abby?" Chloe shrugged.

"Birch cleaned up the mess, covered for Mrs W, and promised she would not say anything, Abby knew nothing. We came back here, Abby was pissed off, she gave Birch a mouthful about being jealous and controlling her life, and I pushed her on the floor, and told her she was out of order. Birch was really upset, she was crying her eyes out and begging Abby to listen, but you know Abby, she is stubborn, so I told her the truth, and she just fucking died on the spot." Deb's was lost for words, Edwina continued.

"Abby went up to say sorry to Birch, and a few minutes later she left. A couple of hours later I saw Birch walk across the road and go into Abby's mum's, I assumed she knew Abby would go there. I think they talked, they came back, cooked, and ate in their room, and something happened, and here we all are." Izzy took another long swig.

"Birch knew that keyboard player was a fraud, he tried to fuck her in the kitchen at the party, she told him to piss off, and ended up with Max, in her room. She heard Abby with a guy, and was happy for her, later on she went into her room and found it was the keyboard player. She was upset, but did not have time to talk, because everyone heard Gail screwing the guitarist, and Abby came down stairs. You all talked, got pissed, and went to bed. Birch wanted to talk to Abby about it, because when she went into her bathroom, on the morning after the party, she heard him and Abby talking, and she knew, Abby was falling for him, but Birch knew he was a liar, and using her. Max had told her the truth, and she did not know what to do. She called me in my room and asked me, I told her to let it play out, he was lying to her, and she needed to discover the truth herself." Deb's gasped.

"Well yeah, he has quit the band, and gone off to Scotland to marry a girl he has been seeing for ages. Jimmy is not happy at all, luckily, he got Doug to replace him. He asked Kyle to reconsider, and at least do the wedding, he refused and left." Chloe put her head in her hands.

"What a twat, Abby thinks he is backpacking round Thailand and India, she showed me the picture of the plane leaving the country. He has been messaging her none stop since he left here, Abby told me he told her he was falling in love with her." Izzy looked round the room.

"Jemi already knows, she tracked him down, and told him to stop messing with Abby, he told her to fuck off." Edwina stared at Izzy.

"Why the hell didn't Birch just tell her?" Izzy looked at all of them.

"Look guys, even now you really do not understand her, Jemi is so tough on the outside, but she is so full of love and kindness, honestly she is the nicest person I have ever met. Abby is the love of her life, honestly you guys have not seen what being without her does to her, I have, and it is painful. Jemi has done all of this with the house to protect you guys, but most of all to protect

Abby. The problem is, Abby started to question her feelings for Jemi, and it has really hurt her, she is struggling with it because Jemi is 100% sure of her feelings for Abby, there is not a grain of doubt in her. For Abby to say that, it has torn her to pieces. She has given Abby a chance to really decide how she feels, if Abby does realise her love for Jemi, all will be fine, if not, get used to living without Jemi, because she will not be able to live in this house, and not be close to her." Edwina closed her eyes.

"Oh bollocks... Poor Birch, but Izzy Abby loves her, can she not see that?" Izzy shook her head.

"She is so hurt I don't think she can, honestly I spent four hours on the phone with her, she is falling apart, and has gone to a friend to stay for a while." It looked really bleak; Deb's understood.

"Abby needs someone to open her eyes." Chloe shook her head.

"That is no easy task." Deb's stood up.

"You lot are no good, I am the only one who can fix this, she will listen to me, and I really hope not hit me, I don't want to be married with black eyes." Chloe lifted her hand and rubbed her face.

"No... Been there, it hurts like fuck and takes bleeding weeks to heal, Abby packs a punch when she is pissed off." Deb's gave a loud huff.

"Right, I need a few things, and then I will sort this." Chloe got up off the floor.

"I will be there with you, if she punches, duck, a bridesmaid with a black eye is not that big a deal." Deb's looked at Chloe and took a deep breath.

"Let's do this." Deb's looked determined, as she marched downstairs and looked for Max, Chloe followed.

"No offence but why Max, he is just a roadie?" Deb's walked down the hall with her voice lowered.

"Max and Kyle were good mates, they used to share girls on the road... I know, it's messed up, I try not to think about touring. Max actually told me; Jimmy did not touch a single girl on tour this time round, apart from he kissed one steam punk fan for a photo in Japan." Chloe shrugged.

"I cannot say anything, I shared Zac with Edwina... Oh fuck I regret that." She chuckled.

"You did him alone the other night." Chloe shivered.

"Shut the hell up you are freaking me out."

Debs walked into the kitchen, the boys were all sat on the floor, drinking and playing cards, and talking tour stories, she walked up to Max, he was a big guy, Chloe sized him up for later. Deb's looked down at him, and put her hand out.

"Lend me your phone." He looked up at her and smiled.

"Okay Goggles you are freaking me out, why, I told you once, he was a good boy, and I was not lying?" Jimmy smiled.

"Go on, give it her, I ain't got nothing to hide." Deb's smiled at Jimmy.

"I love you Jimmy Bear, but this is not about you, it's Kyle, he has lied to Abby, and I need to show her the pictures to prove it." Jimmy pursed his mouth, and breathed in.

"Is she alright, I mean it Goggle Bear, if he has hurt her in any way, I will deal with that fucker personally." She smiled.

"This will be enough, but thanks." Max gave a nod, and slipped his phone out of his pocket.

"Here, go help her, but be aware, I am a total slut and do fucked up shit, and I am sorry you might see that, I like how you see the good in me." Chloe smiled.

"I am gonna screw you at some point, you are my kind of cool." Jimmy laughed, and Max looked her up and down.

"I got my bridesmaid lads, hands off, she is mine." Chloe beamed a big smile, and winked.

"I am wet just thinking about it." They all burst into laughter, Jimmy looked at Max.

"I think you just met your match mate; I hope you can handle her?" He looked up as Deb's flicked through the pictures, and smiled.

I sat in my bed lost to the world, just drifting in the darkness, drinking vodka from the bottle, I figured numbness on top of numbness would help. I wanted to sleep but couldn't, and I was hoping at some point I would, after all, it had worked in the past. The lights flashed on, and I screwed up my eyes.

"What the hell?"

I shielded my eyes with my free hand, and saw Deb's staring at me with her hands on her hips, Chloe was stood to her side.

"Deb's piss off with the lights, will you?" She looked really pissed off.

"I told you I wanted to talk." I gave a long sigh.

"Deb's not now, I am not in the mood."

"Then get in the mood, because we are talking, whether you like it or not, what the hell did you tell Birch?" I shook my head; she was starting to piss me off.

"What the hell do you care, you got your singer to screw, leave me the frig alone Deb's." I could see her swallow hard, and her lip trembled.

"I have always cared, you know that, for a long time I was the only one who cared, and that is why I am here. I know it's swearing, but Abby, you are being fucking stupid, and you are about to lose the best thing that ever happened to you, and for what? A few soft words from a book reader, one I may add who is a lying sack of shit." Okay that really pissed me off, I looked at her and laughed.

"Wow, you screw one vocalist, and what, you frigging know everything about the band, wow, I didn't know Jimmy was that good a shag?" Deb's eyes teared up.

"I will let that go Abby because I love you, and you are my best friend, and you are drunk, and hurt. Kyle lied, he lies to everyone as he screws his way across continents, everyone knows that, except you apparently, it looks to me like you and your mum have a lot in common when trusting men." Chloe screwed up her face.

"Fuck Deb's."

Yeah, Deb's knew what she was doing, we had been friends long enough for her to know all my buttons, and that particular one, was currently one of my most sensitive. I sprang up off the bed, Chloe jerked, as I launched myself at Deb's, and she grabbed Deb's and yanked her out of the way. I came up swinging and suddenly Chloe was there, and before I could do anything, her arm came up and BAM!

I saw stars, and went flying sideways, and crashed on the floor in a heap, Deb's lifted the vodka bottle that was spilling out onto the bed, Chloe stood with her teeth gritted, and shaking.

"Abby please don't do this, please, I love you and I don't want this, but I cannot let you hurt another person, it is bad enough that you have torn Birch apart.”

I lay on my back and looked at her, my face was throbbing, I could actually feel something. I chuckled.

“Well, we are even now, same frigging eye as well.” I sat up and grabbed the bed, and blinked my eyes.

“I didn't hurt Birch, she frigging left without talking.” Deb's stared at me with tears running down her cheeks.

“She really loves you, how can you not tell the difference, you honestly think Kyle does, he is getting married tomorrow in Scotland, to his fiancé of five years?” I shook my head, and looked up at her, and started to laugh.

“You stupid bitch, he is in Thailand back packing, why the hell would he go to frigging Scotland?” Chloe stepped between me and Deb's, she lifted the phone, and opened it up.

“He is in Scotland Abby, he is marrying into a rich family, everything he told you was lies. Birch knew and wanted to tell you, but you had already accused her of being jealous. It was breaking her heart to see you thinking you were in love with Kyle, and not her, so she stayed quiet. Birch knew you would not believe her if she told you, because let's be honest, you just don't trust anyone do you, because you think you know it all, because you have been picked on? When the hell are you going to grow up and actually face the fact you completely screwed up?”

I stood up, and was very unsteady, and swayed, I had just about had enough of this shit, I could feel the anger building in me.

“You are talking shit Deb's, that's not how it was.” She shook her head, and more tears streamed from her eyes.

“No Abby I am not, see for yourself.”

She held up the phone, and there was a picture of Kyle having sex with a Japanese girl, she slid the screen right and there was another, he was in bed with three girls, and there was another. They went on and on, picture after picture, until finally she stopped at a really pretty girl with long brown hair, nice eyes, and a soft smile.

“That Abby, tomorrow will be his wife, it was sent to Max two hours ago, and as you can see, that is not bloody Thailand or India. I am sorry Abby, but he played you, just like Ozzy played your mum.” I had enough, I was not in the mood for any of this shit, I stared at Deb's.

"Keep my bloody mother out of this."

I lunged forward, and swung out hard, I was not pissed enough to miss, and hit Chloe full on in the face, she folded backwards, and I headed for Deb's, as I screamed.

"IT'S NOT TRUE, IT'S NOT, HE TOLD ME IN ALL HIS LETTERS, HE LOVES ME MORE THAN BIRCH EVER COULD!"

My legs trapped, Chloe was on the floor bleeding, but she had managed to twist round and grab my legs with hers, blood poured out from her nose. I crashed to the floor again, and it took the wind out of me. I rolled back on the floor, and lay back gasping, trying to breathe. Edwina appeared with a towel and dragged Chloe out of the way, and covered her face.

"You daft bitch, why didn't you dodge her?" Chloe gasped in pain.

"Abby loves Deb's, she will really regret hurting her if she does, I am sorry Edwina, I could not let that happen."

I gasped for air, feeling like I was going to suffocate, Deb's stared at me her tears falling to the floor.

"I am so sorry Abby, you would not believe Birch, how could you even think anyone could love you more than her? You are such a stupid bitch, and you have screwed up everything. I am sorry, I really am, but I don't want you at my wedding, do you hear me? We are through."

I breathed in, and sucked the air back into my lungs, another voice shouted behind me.

"EVERYONE GET OUT!"


I closed my eyes, oh Christ not more, I lay back on the floor, my face hurting, and just trying to breathe again, air was slowly filling my body, as I heard everyone moving around, and they all left me alone. I just lay there trying to understand it all, nothing made sense to me anymore, as my mind just swirled in a mush of uncertainty. Why was the world so God dammed screwed up?

"People lie and cheat and pretend, why is no one ever bloody honest anymore, why is it they cannot just be honest, and tell the God dammed truth? Oh god, why did I believe him? I knew it was bullshit. I knew no one could love me like she does, I love her the same way, I am a liar too, she means everything, she is my whole frigging world, and I have screwed it all up like my mum has."

"Yep, pretty much."

I opened my eyes and sat up, Hatty was sat on my bed. I looked at her and shook my head.

"Hatty I have blown the best thing in my world to shit, and I don't know what to do to fix it, is this what mum did to you?"

Now the tears came, with the sudden explosion of reality in my life. She smiled and leaned forward.

"You probably don't want to hear this, but honestly Abby, you are her fucking double, doing all the same shit, in the same fucked up way. This Kyle, he is exactly the same as your dad, and Birch knew if she told you, she would end up the same as me. Because I lost to Edwin and his smooth lies, the same fucking way she lost to Kyle." I brought up my knees and hugged them, and just cried.

"I cannot believe after all my fighting and resisting, I have just become her. I never wanted that. Hatty I love mum, but I don't want her miserable life, it is the one thing I hate the most about here, they are all the bloody same." I pushed my hurting face into my knees and just sobbed.

"Then it is not too late is it Abby?"

I lifted my head and wiped my eyes on my sleeve, my eye hurt like a bitch, and I winced.

"Hatty I have lost her, and I love her so much, but I do not know what to do, she will never forgive me for this, she is so beautiful and kind, but honestly, I am not worthy of her. I cannot be like her, I am flawed as shit, and I really screw up a lot, but I do really love her, I cannot imagine my life without her." Hatty smiled.

"Then all is not lost is it Abby, because your mum could, and it took her a long time of pain and mistakes, with a cold hearted man, before she truly understood that she made a huge mistake. To be honest, it took a brave young kid with black and red hair, and a crazy friend, for her to really understand everything. Abby you are twenty four, you still have time, so what the fuck are you going to do about it, because it is not too late?" I sniffled into my jeans, and just wept even more.

"I don't know what to do Hatty, I am so stupid, she never lied to me once, she was always there, she will never know how much she changed my life. From the day I met her, I think I was in love with her. I never really understood why, but today when I read the note I knew. I knew for sure; she is me, it does not show, but we are the same on the inside deep down. She hurts like I do, and feels like I do, and she is as afraid of losing me as I am her, and I screwed it all up because some arse, tried to convince me my love for her was not real. But it is Hatty, and it is really hurting me, because I threw her away." I lifted my head and looked at her.

"Hatty I don't want her to suffer like you did, I want to fix this, I want a life with her, tell me what do I do to make this all right again?" She smiled.

"Abby just tell her all this the way you are telling me now, it does count, trust me." I shook, and the huge sob came out of me.

"I don't know where she is Hatty, I want to see her so badly, but I don't know where to look." She smiled.

"Try behind you." I gave a sob and frowned.

"I don't understand."

Two soft long slender arms came round me, and I felt her, Hatty smiled and stood up.

"You know what to do?"

I just started to shake as a huge wave of emotion crashed over me. The tears shook me, I gave an even bigger sob, and I could not speak, the pain was so great. I just sat there on the floor, shaking and crying, as she leaned into me and wrapped her arms around me, her voice was so soft, and so quiet, I could hardly hear her over my sobs.

"I am here... Now we talk."

It is hard to explain that moment. In years to come, I will see it as possibly as one of the most important turning points of my life. I sat on the floor crying and bawling my brains out like a smacked baby for at least an hour, she cried too, she held me tight as years of hidden pain just flowed up out of nowhere. It was probably the most painful moment of my twenty four years of life, because it was then that I truly understood the life I had lived. Eventually I went calmer and quieter, and I sniffled a lot, and Birch did not move, she knelt there holding me, and letting me just release it all.

We finally sat crossed legged on the floor, and we talked, and talked, and talked. I told her of how hard it had been to grow up, with a father who was so strict and so emotionless. I talked of

his affair, and how he had punished me for telling Hatty, and as
hard as it was to admit, I told her how I had hated him so much,
especially after Martin. I loved my mum, I had seen her suffer,
I had seen her turn her whole life into the focus of the village. I
told her what it was like as I watched as Marjorie took control
of her, and changed her, into a sterile clean freak, who was most
concerned about how it looked to the village, than how it actually
was in the house. I explained how disappointing it was to see my
own mother change, and turn against me.

I told her the full truth of how it drove me to that night in the
bath with the sleeping pills, where I wanted to die, because she
had told me she would never allow me to go to Manchester for
Uni. I talked of how waking up in the cold water shivering, had
been the most disappointing time in my youth, as I realised I was
even too stupid to even kill myself properly. Throughout all of it
she smiled and listened, and occasionally quietly cried.

I reached out and took her hands in mine, as we sat face to
face, and I talked of how I finally got into Manchester, and kept
it secret, and then left disobeying them, and how I then talked of
how I stayed at Uni rather than go home on my first term break,
and how when I did come home, I had been punished severely.
I told her how I got a roommate who changed my life. I told her,
how she gave me the strength to dig deep inside and find the real
me, and how wonderful that was, and how it had meant the world
to me. I looked into her big green tear filled eyes, and told her
how I fell so hopelessly in love with her, and how it challenged
me on every level of my being to admit it, and how painful it was
to have to leave her behind and come back here alone. I talked of
the isolation, the victimisation I suffered, and how desperately I
missed her to the point of wanting to die, but I passed out.

I talked of the night she did not call, and how I got drunk in
my abject misery, as I sat there with the bottle, swigging away,
looking at the bottle of pills. I honestly thought I had lost her
forever, and how it made no sense to be in love with a girl, and
yet I missed her so much I would rather have died than endured
much longer. I told Birch of the morning, and of how I had woken
up, terrified to be in the house alone, just in case I tried again. I
had walked into the village and just wandered around for hours,
because I was afraid to go home, and how when least expected,

she drove into the village in a lilac coloured jeep, and held up a funeral, just so she could hug me, and how wonderful that was. She giggled through her tears at me, and I smiled.

"You saved my life Birch, you saved me, and I have no idea how to repay that." She gave a sniffle and wiped her eyes.

"If I could have my way, I would ask just one thing." I looked at her.

"What can I give you, what is that one thing?" She gave another sniffle and her voice was croaky.

"Be this, be this for the rest of your life Deads, this here, this honesty, this is my dark little beastie, this is who I fell in love with back in Uni. Stop doubting this, and analysing this, just accept that this is who we are. I have never lied to you and I never will, so if I tell you something, love me enough to trust it, do that and we are even, because when you look at me and doubt me, it is like being stabbed with a thousand knives, and honestly, I cannot handle it, it kills my soul."

I felt my lip trembling, and sniffed up to clear my nose, I hated myself so much at that moment, just sat there looking into her bright sparkling eyes and seeing the love and pure honesty of her, made me feel like an utter shit for ever doubting her.

"I promise, I am so sorry for screwing everything up, Deb's hates me, and I hurt Chloe, Oh Birch, I have really made one hell of a mess." She smiled.

"It is what we do, we bring madness and chaos, they will get used to it, it's a Curio thing." Still holding my hands, she stood up. "Come on, it's time to face the music."

Hand in hand we walked down the stairs and into the kitchen, Max was lay on the floor, with Deb's and Edwina leaning over his face, and dabbing his eyes with damp cotton wool balls, looking very concerned. Chloe was knelt at his head looking really worried, I felt guilty, she had two black eyes and a swollen nose, which was packed with cotton wool. Birch looked at them all, and then Jimmy stood at Max's feet.

"What the hell is going on?" The rest of the band sniggered over near the table; Jimmy gave a laugh.

"Well, the thing is, Max here felt sorry for Chloe, so he goes into her studio to like cheer her up. Now the way I see it, is he is good at his trade, if you get me? So, whilst she is lay on that bed thing she has, all naked and looking tasty, Max decides to put a smile on her face, and in between those legs he went, with his very magic tongue." Chloe looked up looking really guilty.

"I didn't mean it, but he took me by surprise, and he just went straight to my spot, and oh my god, he is so fucking good." Jimmy gave a laugh, the rest of the band sniggered and started laughing.

"So, you see guys, Chloe here, well, she kind of came really bloody hard, and them there cotton things in her nose, were full of dried blood, and they were as hard as missiles. So, she cum's like crazy, gasps for breath, and Max here, looks up with a prideful look, and them fuckers fired out of her nose, and hit him in the eyes, and we think she has blinded the poor bastard."

The guys at the back fell about laughing, Birch sniggered as Chloe looked down.

"I am so sorry Max, but you really made me cum." He smiled and lifted a thumb.

"Any time girl, but I think if it happens again, I am best off wearing my goggles." Jimmy walked over and looked at me, he smiled.

"You look like shit... Look love, she didn't mean it, I told her you were both angry, and she already regrets it. I told her fuck Kyle he is not worth it. I also said if she isn't by your side, then there isn't no wedding." He smiled and lifted his hand to my face.

"I want you there, you belong here with all of us." I felt the tears again, God have I not cried enough today?

Birch slipped her hand round my waist, Jimmy just smiled and leaned in, and kissed my cheek, I flinched, he stood back and gave a giggle.

"I bloody well hope that was pain, I just risked a divorce before I even got married to kiss you?" I giggled.

"Yeah, Chloe has a good right hook, it is sore, but I needed it, she was defending Deb's." Chloe stood up, God she looked a mess, I felt so guilty, I filled up with more tears.

"I am so sorry Chloe." She came over and pulled me into a hug.

"Yeah, me too, we should leave this shit back in school. I love you Abby, I really do." I pulled her in and hugged her hard.

"Me too, god I hate myself tonight." She gave a gasp.

"Abby if you squeeze any harder, I may shoot you in the tits."

I gave a gasp of a giggle, and released her. She smiled, and then flinched, her eyes were really starting to blacken.

"Fuck Abby, we are going to need a shit load of makeup come Saturday."

Chapter 32

# Girls Night.

It had been possibly the worst, and the best of days in my life. Birch and I sat with Anthony, and did what we could, but he was broken hearted, and just wanted some space, to come to terms with it. He thanked us both, but to be honest, we had not done that much.

When it came to bedtime, I suddenly felt very nervous, I changed the bed, and then I started to undress, and Birch made her way to the partition door, I felt my heart jolt, she noticed, and looked back and smiled.

"Sweetie, I need a pee, I will be back I promise."

I slipped off my jeans, and climbed into bed, and slid under the duvet. I heard the toilet flush, and she reappeared, I watched as she stood at the end of the bed and stripped, she smiled and lifted the duvet, and slid in under it, and then moved over towards me. Birch straddled over me and leaned forward.

"Are you alright, it has been a rough day?"

I lay back looking at her, with her alabaster white skin, and her long white and patched hair, and those intense green eyes. I took a breath, and gripped her waist, and then slid my hands slowly up her body, I moved to her boobs and felt the softness of them and just enjoyed feeling them in my hands. I gently rubbed her nipples and felt them grow, she closed her eyes and smiled, as her breathing quickened.

"I need to touch you, I need to know you are real, it has been a shitty few days, I need to know this is not another awful dream." She opened her eyes and leaned forward.

"Does this feel real enough for you?"

She slipped her hand behind my head, and lifted it slightly, and her mouth met mine, I opened my mouth, and felt her lips match mine. She pulled back slightly sucking my lip, and I felt my whole body warm up, I kissed her back, and we matched the rhythm of each other. It was soft and warm and passionate. Never before had a kiss made me tingle between my legs, I still had my hands on her boobs, and was exploring them.

Birch moaned in my mouth, as she kissed me, she grew faster, like she needed to devour me, and I felt the desire in me rise, as I really got into it. We broke apart and she flew to my neck, and started to kiss, gently biting it. Oh god I was so turned on, it was like she had just switched off all her controls, and she was ravishing me, I felt a massive pulse run through me, as she slid down to my breasts, I was losing my breath.

"Oh Birch, Oh Christ."

She slid her waist slowly, down my legs, and I could feel the dampness from her on my tummy, she slid in between my legs, and I didn't wait. I spread my legs wide, the need to be touched was burning inside me, she started to move lower kissing my tummy, I had never in my life been this turned on, or wanted anyone more.

My heart was racing, my breathing was rapid, as my whole body was on fire and tingling, she was not even there yet, and I wanted to cum, I reached up for the head board, as my toes started to curl.

"Oh Christ Birch, I am on fire, I think I am going to cum."

I heard her giggle somewhere at the base of my tummy, I looked down and she was watching me, our eyes met.

"Oh shit, Birch, don't drag it out, I cannot take it." She smiled as my legs trembled.

"I am going to make you pay, tonight my dark little beastie, I am going to eat you alive."

Just the sultry tone of her voice, that smouldering sensual look in her eyes, I could not look away. I yearned for her, her eyes never left mine as she lowered her head, and then she moved forward, and made contact, my whole body exploded, I breathed in deeply, and spasmed, my legs went taught, my back arched, and my head rolled back into the pillow.

I felt like I was being electrocuted, it was unbearable and wonderful, I gasped for air, and gripped on the head board with all my strength.

"OOOOOOOOOOH!"

Hatty sat back in her armchair and looked at Felicity, she gave a slight smile as she sipped her whiskey, watching her oldest friend in the world try to make sense of her life. She rested her glass on her lap.

"Oh come on Flick, what the fuck does it matter, you are acting like it is the end of the world, it is not, hell, it is about time you had some fun." Felicity gave a sigh.

"I should know better, Hatty he was only twenty one, I am thirty four years older than him, hell, Abby is even older than him." She shrugged at her.

"You came, he came, it appears to me both of you enjoyed it and it did you both good, and what the fuck has age got to do with it?" Felicity looked up at her.

"It's wrong, that's what."

"Says who... Marjorie? Jesus Flick, you are acting like you are dead, for God's sake, it was just a shag, and one I may add that you bloody well needed, I mean, it is not like Edwin has been up to the mark is it. You know what your problem is, you are still way too involved with what those old prudes think, if you ask me you should look to Abby and follow her lead, and be more like her." Felicity frowned.

"How do you mean?" Hatty sighed and leaned forward in her seat.

"Flick, look at you, I hate to point it out, but for your age you are still a pretty good looking woman, I mean, you have a great ass. You know it is alright to feel sexual and want to be desired, do you think Abby cares, when she is lay back and knackered because Birch made her cum? I can tell you; she is not lay back worrying what that fascist and her brood of dried up old prunes are thinking, she is there in the moment, feeling alive and happy because she made love to someone she desired, and Birch made her feel great. So, okay, Ozzy was a young guy, but honestly, tell me, what did it feel like looking at him fucking the shit out of you, don't tell me you were worrying about Madge, because we both know that was bollocks, you were fucking loving it."

Felicity looked down and felt her cheeks pink up, Hatty gave a happy chuckle, her eyes danced and she lifted her glass.

"Yeah, I remember that look too, you looked the same the night after we fucked each others brains out in the tent in Scotland."

Felicity shook her head, as she looked at the floor.

"It is not the same Hatty, I have never regretted that." She looked up at her. "I regret a lot of things, but never that, never you, I hope you believe that? I know I screwed everything up, but never for a moment think I have regretted what we did, because I haven't." Hatty smiled.

"It is nice to hear you say it Flick, you know I love you, I always will, and honestly, I think you are going overboard with all this Ozzy stuff. The way I see it, you got to feel all those wonderful feelings again, and honestly, it was not with Edwin, I get it, I do, but look at how he has treated you, seriously Flick, he has fucked half of his office staff, personally, I think this has done you good." She gave a scowl.

"How the hell has this done me good, I feel terrible and ashamed?" Hatty gave a shrug.

"Yeah, for now you do, but give it time, and that will change, honestly, he may be young, but at least Ozzy saw your worth, he saw you as desirable, which let's be honest, is more than that dull shit you married does. Maybe now you can actually see the difference between Edwin, and how other men perceive you, and let's be honest, I have told you a thousand times, out there is a man who will make you feel like a goddess when he looks at you, maybe now you too will see that. Flick, Abby is grown up, you no longer have a reason to stay, isn't it time you seriously thought about living for you, and kick that cheating slippery old shit out?"

I was convulsing, unable to stop, my body wasn't in control, it was on auto pilot, and Birch was soaking wet, I flopped down and collapsed onto the bed, I could barely breathe as I sucked air desperately in. I felt amazing and horrified at the same time, I was completely out of control, and just lay quivering, shaking, and exhausted, Birch stood up with a smile, her hair dripping. What had she done to me, I had never seen so much liquid come out of me, and I was unable to stop it?

"You okay Sweetie?" I just looked at her unable to speak, as I breathed hard. She just smiled.

"I am going to run us a bath, although I think I just had one, thank you Sweetie, I have wondered if I could do that, it was insanely amazing."

I had no energy at all, I just lay there panting, covered in sweat and smiled, I simply was incapable of speech.

What had she done to me, it terrified me, I had lost all control, did I cum, or was that pee? I was soaking wet, as was the bed, I mean, I had heard stories at school about it, but I never once thought I would be able to do that? It was amazing, and yet really terrifying at the same time, Birch had complete control of me.

I had been rendered unable to stop myself, and yet for her, it had been an amazing thing, her face had been so happy, it made no sense at all. I lay there wet, control slowly returning to my body, my vagina felt massively sensitive if I moved, and little pulses still tingled into my stomach, I had never experienced anything like this before, and strangely enough, it made me really happy, as I lay flat on the bed still twitching.

Birch ran a bath, my god the bed was drenched, but I was so knackered, I could barely walk. She helped me in, and slid down behind me and I leant against her.

"Birch, you have broken me." She giggled as she pulled me back and softly washed me.

"I wanted to, I wanted to show you the truth of my feelings, my desire, my passion. I have done a lot of thinking Deads, and maybe I should have made myself clearer, and been braver with you. I stood behind you today as you talked to Hatty, I heard what you told her, you said things about how you really feel I did not know, and it made me see that we are both afraid of what we have. You were right, it does go against everything we thought we were. Tonight, proved to me, it is alright to show it more, maybe that is why we felt like we were drifting. I want us to be more open, and talk about our fears, I think only then will both of us feel complete. Communication is everything Sweetie, so now we have started, let's not stop." I leaned back into her, and I closed my eyes.

"I have missed this, we have been too busy, I want more time with you, let's find a way to just walk away from everything at times, and be us alone." She leaned down and kissed the top of my head.

"Okay Sweetie, we will do that, all I want is for you to be happy." I gave a long happy sigh.

"This makes me happy, just being alone together."

One hour later, I was curled up in Birch's bed, mine would need a good washing, I had two sets to wash now. Birch was happily curled around me, I lay warm and contented, glad to realise how dangerously close I had come to losing this. I closed my eyes and just relaxed, it felt a little like old times, like that crazy summer so long ago, and it was nice.

Deb's was right, it was time to grow up, I could see now how childish all of this had been, the truth was I had not wanted to grow up. I was afraid of being my parents, I wanted to stay that crazy nineteen year old filled with crazy ideals, but the facts were that growing up is inevitable, no matter how hard you fight, you cannot stop. Age comes whatever your thoughts may be, one day you look in the mirror, and a different you is looking back, and that can feel scary, but really why should it?

I thought of May, swearing like a trooper, not really aware of who or where she was, a crazy old lady with long white hair, who no matter what people told her, defied everything. Even with her mind deteriorating, she still hung on to a piece of herself, a piece that had once been nineteen and far ahead of her time. No one understood her, and yet Birch had, and now I think I do.

"Birch?"

"Yes Sweetie?"

"I want to go and see May; I really like her." She moved slightly, and I felt her head lift off the pillow.

"I have been talking to her on video chat, she is really lovely, isn't she?" I turned to look at her.

"You have been talking to her, when?" She smiled.

"Ellen lets me know when her shifts are, and she sets up the laptop on the table, and when May sees me, she smiles and says 'Slut,' all happy and bright, she remembers me Sweetie. I talk to her every week; I have been since our visit."

"Birch that was five years ago, why didn't you tell me?" She smiled.

"I thought I was the only one who saw that she was holding out and fighting to stay her. I didn't realise you got her too, I am really glad you do Deads, she is proof we can be us forever and never apologise for it." I gave a smile.

"I like the idea of being some crazy old lady with long white hair, it really appeals to me." She giggled and kissed my cheek.

"Yeah, me too, although to be honest, I think I am already half way there." She giggled, and it was nice to hear it.


The Tuesday after the fete, is clean up to the point of exhaustion day. And so still tired and worn out, dressed in jeans and vests, we all joined in to help out. Mum took one look at Chloe and me, and completely freaked out. It took a while to calm her down, as Chloe explained we had been pissing about at the side of the pool, and tripped, and during the fall, we had head butted each other. I was impressed she bought it, and was so grateful to Chloe, although she flustered and inspected us both thoroughly, before letting us work.

Chloe had two large black eyes and a red nose, I had a black left eye and large bruised cheek, we looked a right pair. The tents were down, and we did the usual site walk, making sure not a single piece of litter was missed.

By dinner time we all headed to the Church Hall, and the endless files that had to be boxed up, and then transported to storage for another year. By the time we finished, we were exhausted, but Chloe, Edwina, and myself called into the salon, under the pretence of talking about getting our hair redone on Friday evening at home. It was nice to say at home, and that also meant Anthony, I had missed him in the group, and suddenly it felt more like us again.

Delphine helped him move all his stuff into our house. We all mucked in, and soon he was settled. We left him to unpack and sort out his room, it was nice having him home with us, it felt right and proper, and now he had four women to take care of him, and I felt that was a good thing.

I swam a few lengths, and tried to relax on the grass, Chloe brought out some ice packs, and we lay on our backs in the sun, and covered our wounds to bring down the swelling as quickly as possible.

Over at Sweetie's Retreat, Izzy walked into reception, and smiled at Gill, as she handed her a file. Gill handed her another one, and she opened it, read the name and looked at the new clients waiting.

"Felicity Watson, hi, I am Izzy, would you like to come

through?”

I had no idea of course, but Birch had arranged a series of special sessions for her, so she could talk openly and honestly, to let out all her hidden thoughts and fears. Izzy was also aware of what had happened, and so her reaction would not be one of surprise.

On Wednesday morning Katie arrived in town, and her crew took up residence in the Hunters Arms. Four large trucks moved onto the show field, and the start of the wedding officially commenced, as the crews went to work, on the secret plans of Birch and Katie. Deb's was now officially banned from the site until Saturday, although Jimmy was on site for the erecting of a stage.

Wednesday night was girl's night. The band were booted out, the garden and patio got decorated with streamers, and big blown up penis's, I am not even going to ask Birch where she got them from. Katie showed up with five girls from her new crew, and we all mucked in before Deb's arrived.

Hatty, Mum Ellen, Gill, Denise, Celia, Lillian, Stacy, and Meg arrived. It was a really warm night, and yep, we were naked, much to the joy and love of Celia and Lillian. Chloe broke out the body paints, and soon, Hatty and Mum were naked painting each other, which got the mood going. Gill soon joined in and a very red faced Denise looked shocked, but smiled as she was also painted up. Birch smiled at Celia and Lillian, as she lifted her arms and gave them a spin, she was covered in brightly coloured butterflies.

“Ladies, I hope you approve?”

Lillian was quite overcome, Celia was really enjoying looking, it was like her birthday had arrived, Birch winked.

“So, ladies, will you be joining in?”

Ellen was stripping with Stacy in the background, Lillian gave a wicked giggle and looked at Celia.

“Oh my, should we dare?” Deb's walked up painted with exotic vines and flowers, and winked at Lillian.

“You seen my vagina, get yours out Lilly, you owe me for the day you cleaned the floor under the table.” Birch giggled and winked at them.

Within the hour everyone was painted, free, and dancing in the garden, I must admit, it was without doubt the best Hen Night I have ever been too. It was wild, and the drinks flowed, and talk of naughty sex was high on the agenda. The highlight of the night was when Anthony arrived home and joined us. I painted him, with big flowers, and found out he was very ticklish, and his shrieks, and howls of laughter got everyone going.

It was such a wonderful experience, and after a lot of drinks and dancing, I sat down next to Birch, and giggled watching the others. The door banged and from nowhere came a familiar voice.

"YOU THERE JEMI?" Birch sat upright, Chloe, Edwina, Anthony, and Debs, snapped round.

"Guard your vagina's." Everyone stopped, and looked round mildly panicked.

She came bouncing through, dragging a really attractive girl with her, she stopped and looked round at all the naked women.

"Hello, what is this?"

Deb's covered her lady parts, and looked terrified; she had 'Bride' painted across her boobs. Birch stood with a huge smile.

"SWEETIE!"

She walked over and hugged Bev, and looked at the young girl smiling at her side.

"Bev who is this delightful guest?" She gave a big smile.

"This is my bird, she is French, she is called Breeze-Yet, it's proper frog language that." Birch smiled.

"Sweetie she is beautiful, I am so happy for you."

She turned to Bridgette, and smiled, and then she spoke French, I did not even know she could. Bridgette smiled and looked relieved, she answered, and Birch introduced all of us, and she smiled and waved, Bev was very impressed.

"Fuck Jemi, when did you learn frog, oh wow I am impressed."

Bridgette seemed very happy, she spoke to Birch, and she smiled and answered, and with that, she lifted her top and took it off, and suddenly Bev was stripping and Chloe and Hatty were there with the brushes and paint. Roni came out and gave a big laugh as I hugged her.

"I might have known with you two, oh well, when in Rome."

She took off her jacket, and unbuttoned her blouse. It felt like the best night ever. As I stood at the kitchen door and watched everyone with huge smiles dancing on the lawn, especially mum, it was so nice to see her smiling, painted with rainbows and clouds. Celia came in through the other door, and opened another bottle of wine.

"I must say Abigail, your friends live a remarkable life, is this normal for all of you, as you are all so at ease? I have only ever been naked in front of Lillian, this is new and extraordinary, I wish I had done it years ago?" I chuckled.

"You are right, in the house we seldom dress, and through the summer we spend as much time naked outdoors as possible, I am glad you enjoy it. We obviously do not advertise our naked life, but if you ever want to stretch out in the sun, you will always be welcome." She gave a big smile.

"You know, I am so glad that you came home with Birch, we think the world of you two, you know? You are both very special, and for this village, we both think you two are vital. Abigail, you know I have been made Vice Chair, well part of that is to appoint two new members as officers, Marion is stepping down, and I was wondering if you two would consider a position?" I looked at her and gave a sigh.

"Celia, I am not ready for that yet, but I would like to make a suggestion if you don't mind? Actually, I think Edwina for her technical abilities, and for an open minded, free thinking person, I actually think you should ask Anthony. He could use something at the moment to boost his confidence." Celia gave a big smile.

"Abigail, you are amazing, I actually think Antonio would be wonderful, and we could use the extra tech support, I am really glad I asked you, you are quite an inspiration."

Outside there was loud singing and lots of laughter. I walked out, and watched them having so much fun. I walked over to the pool where Roni stood talking to Birch, she smiled at me as I approached and Birch turned.

"Hi Sweetie." I walked up and I slipped my arm round her waist, Roni smiled.

"You two look lovely together, I heard about the eye, ouch, but maybe it is a good thing. You know Abby, I see you as another daughter, that is how important you are to Will and myself, to us you are family, and always will be." Birch leaned in and kissed my cheek.

"See how much you mean to us?" I understood. Roni looked across the garden.

"You two do have a way of opening people up, I think I will look into naked therapies, it does bring out the positives in everyone." I turned, and Bev was dancing like a maniac, Roni giggled.

"I take it you have found out Bev speaks French now?" I sniggered.

"Bless her, she is lovely, do you know Roni, I think it is wonderful she has a girlfriend, and I think it is cool that she is putting in so much effort to learn French. For her, it must be like the world is opening for her, and I find that beautiful."

Like all hen parties, we all ended up drunk, hugging, and expressing our love for each other. Slowly the party quietened down, and I sat by the pool as the darkness descended, and the pool lights came on. Deb's walked over with a smile and sat down, she leaned into me, and I slipped my arm round her.

"Thanks Abby, it was an amazing night, I am so happy." I gave her a squeeze.

"Good, this was all for you, we all love you Deb's. I cannot deny, I have missed you this last week, it has felt odd not having you living here." She leaned her head over onto my shoulder.

"Are you going to be alright Abby, I worry about you a lot? We have all moved on so much, and I have felt you were in danger of getting stuck. I guess I need to know you will be fine. I mean it is silly I know, I will just be up the street like always, and I am in the shop every day, but I cannot help it. Promise me Abby, you will stop hiding things from me, talk to me more, I really need to know you will be okay."

God she really knew how to pin me into a corner, I lifted my glass and held it in my hand, and rolled it in my palms.

"I have been afraid of so much Deb's, it may be awful to say it, but I do not want the life my mum has. Yet I have felt I was becoming more and more like her, and I was afraid to move on because of it. These last few weeks have been hard for me, I have looked at myself and not liked what I have seen. I have hurt everyone here, especially Birch, and I am still coming to terms with that." I think she understood, she gave a sigh.

"You have always been way too hard on yourself; you took

on everyone's problems Abby, and made them your own, give yourself a break. Birch loves you Abby. I know for you two it has been hard to come to terms with, I remember you two that summer trying so hard to play straight, it made me laugh. You two belong together, you work in ways none of us ever will. For what it is worth, I love your mum to bits, but I do not think you are capable of being who she is today. I actually think you are who she was meant to be, I think you have it all back to front. I have watched her tonight, and I have seen more of you in her, than her in you. I don't know if that helps, but think about it."

I looked down the garden to where mum sat with Roni, and Hatty, Deb's made an interesting point, one I had never really thought about, and yet in a way Hatty had pointed out some of it. I gave her a squeeze.

"You are going to make a great wife, and a good mum you know that?"

"If I have kids, they will have two very crazy aunties, should I worry about that?" I gave a chuckle.

"Aunty Birch, secretly handing out sweeties, and letting the kids run wild, and naked, are you sure you could handle that?" She giggled; I gave a sigh. "I don't want kids Deb's, I do not want to create a perfect human being, and then screw it up like my parents did me. I have thought about it a lot recently, am I a coward, dodging the responsibility of life?" Deb's sat up, and looked at me.

"What has Birch said, or have you not told her?" I leaned forward rolling my glass in my palms.

"I mentioned it, because if we stay together for the long haul, we will not be able to, and she just told me, if I want some, we will just go get some, like there is a shop you just nip to and pick up a kid. I did not press the point any more than that." Deb's nodded, and thought for a few moments.

"I think you two have loads of time to talk about that, I mean it is probably not a bad idea to talk about it. Abby we are all still young, we have time, I am not in a rush, I want to enjoy just being me for a while. We all change Abby, we are not the Curio's we were back then, all of us have changed in some way or another, that is life, no doubt when we are all thirty, we will all be different again. Birch is right, if it comes up deal with it, it is what I have learned from her, Abby enjoy now, live for a while and let go of the past. You have such an amazing person at your side, stop asking so much, and just let go and live." I smiled, when the hell did she become so wise.

"You sound like Birch." Deb's turned and looked at me.

"Birch has taught me so much Abby, I think if I had never met her, I would be sat at home reading a book, after spending all day in a lab I hated, with no hope of a future. It was Birch that scared the shit out of me, and pushed me into a tent with Jimmy, because I have got to tell you Abby, I was not ready to lose my virginity that night. I was terrified, if it had not been for her, I would probably still be a virgin. She opened up a world I did not know existed, trust her and let her do that for you, because you are so blind, and you do not see it, but we do." I turned, and frowned at her.

"What do you all see that I don't?" She gave a chuckle.

"You are so hopeless at times Abby, can you not see, she is you, she has all the same feelings and concerns, and it is you who opens up the world for her too. When she is with you, she finds the courage to live, just like you do when you are with her. Hell, when you two put your heads together, you empower each other so much, you can do anything. I mean seriously, you two are bloody chaos with vaginas, and you are the perfect complement of each other, why do you think we all fought so hard to keep you together? Abby no man will make you happy like she will, and there is no man to match you for her, that has always been the point. God, you have no idea how many text streams went on five years ago, about why you two were not sleeping together yet, there were days we thought you two would never bloody do it."

It was surprising to hear it, and I did not really know what to say, she just smiled.

"You know what, when Jimmy puts that ring on my finger on Saturday, I hope I radiate just half the joy you do when you stand next to her, because I want everyone to see how happy he makes me, and if I do, no one will doubt our love." I was stumped.

"Really?"

She rolled her eyes, and picked up her phone, she opened it up and flicked through her pictures.

"Look at that, now you tell me, how happy are those two?"

I looked at the phone, and there we were, stood side by side, talking to Roni, both us naked and painted, and both of us smiling, with our arms round each others waist. I looked really happy, and so did Birch, it was probably the best picture ever taken of us.

"Can you send me this, I really love it?" She smiled at me.

"See what I mean?" I nodded at her.

"Yeah, thanks Deb's."

Deb's was special, there was no doubt, she had been my friend since school, and she had always arrived and delivered joy when I had least expected it, she was without doubt the best friend I had ever had. So few saw how incredibly clever she was, and how much depth she had. She was smart and witty, and actually one hell of a lot braver than most people realised.

I sat there looking at her and listening, and she was yet another sign of us all growing up. It was hard to realise that here she was, sat naked and painted, and about to marry a rock star, she had come so far from that shy, scared little girl, I had first befriended.

"I am really happy for you Deb's, and I am happy you will be alright, that is all I have ever wanted for you, I think considering everything, you deserve it more than most."

"Everyone deserves to be happy Abby, and she is right there in front of you, never forget that."

Our glasses were empty, so together we walked across the long lawn, back to the house. The guests were thinning out. Katie and her girls had an early day and had left, Gill and Denise were passed out on the sofa, Edwina had disappeared, so I assumed Katie was one staff short. Hatty and Chloe were in the studio, and Celia and Lillian had disappeared for an early night together. Bev and Bridgette, were happily snogging each other in the kitchen, and Birch was leaning on the patio door frame, wearing nothing but her large happy smile. She pulled Deb's into a hug.

"Oh Sweetie, I am so wondrously happy for you." Deb's looked back at me, and winked.

"Close your eyes Abby, there is something I really want to know."

She turned to Birch, stood up on her toes, and pulled her into a kiss, Birch went a little stiff, as Deb's smooched her, she broke apart and winked at Birch.

"Sorry, but you have no idea how much I have wanted to know what that was like, I will marry knowing I did it all."

I started to laugh, the look of shock on Birch's face was priceless, Deb's gave a huge beaming smile and winked at me.

"Wow that was good, oh you are a lucky girl Abby."

Deb's headed up the stairs to bed, grinning from ear to ear. I slid into Birch's arms chuckling.

"Wow she totally caught you out." She looked at me a little lost for words.

"That was a little unsettling, I never expected that." I shrugged.

"We did once shave her vagina for her." She thought about it for a second, and smiled.

"Yes Sweetie, but you were the one that got her wet as I remember?" I gave a shudder and she started to laugh. "Not so fun now is it?" That was a night I really wanted to forget.

It felt like forever, but we showered and finally made it into bed, we curled up together having had a really wonderful night, I snuggled back feeling the heat from Birch, I was happy inside, as I relaxed.

"Birch did you ever dream of getting married when you were a little girl?" She snuggled into me.

"Not much really, I suppose living with my mum and dad and hearing them talk of all the marriages they counselled, in a way I was fearful of it all going wrong. I remember a girl called Shelly, she got married just before I started Uni, she was pretty wild back then. I met her not long after I left Uni and was working with mum, she was a client, this wonderful and perfect guy she married, turned out to be an abusive control freak. I think maybe that scared me a little, because I was already seeing the change in Kev. I remember at the time how lucky I felt, because it was the day after, I left to come here to be with you, it has stuck with me, and I often wonder how she is." I lay there relaxed and calm and thought about it.

"I have always been terrified I would marry a man like my dad, it really scares me Birch, so much so I am not sure I ever want to, I am happy with this, just me and you, I feel safe with you." She kissed my neck.

"You always will be, I could never harm something so precious to me."

Chapter 33

# Deb's Day.

I was asleep, and somewhere in the warmth that surrounded me, I could hear the distant breathing of Birch, I was warm, safe, secure and happy, as I drifted through the idyllic land of dreams.

DING A LING A LING A LING!

My eyes were wide open, I was sat up, and my head was exploding, Birch was also sat up, holding her ears, and screaming at the top of her voice.
"PISS OFF, YOU FUCKING BELL TWAT!"
Anthony smiled as he lowered the large brass bell in his hand.
"Really ladies, that is how you say good morning to a friend? It is the big day, there is hair makeup and dresses to fit, and we do not want to be late, do we?" I looked at the clock."
"ANTHONY IT IS ONLY TEN O'CLOCK YOU TWAT!" He gave a smile.
"Abby darling, I am an artist, I need time, now come on ladies, we have work to do." He walked over towards the bed, and reached out for the duvet, Birch lurched forward, and spoke through gritted teeth as her eyes blazed at him.
"If you even touch this bed, you and your fucking bell are going off the balcony, you get me?" He stepped back, and looked at her.
"I always wondered which one of you was the grumpy one when waking up, and now I know, Birch darling, you are quite scary first thing in the morning." She glared at him.
"You ever frigging ring that in this house again, and I personally, will hang you off my balcony, and ring you by the neck. Now take that fucking bell away and destroy it, before I do." He gave a titter.
"There is coffee and food waiting downstairs, now hurry, we have lots to do."

He turned with flare and walked out; Birch looked at me, her hair was sticking out in every direction.

"I love him, I do… But I also frigging hate him… Hi Sweetie."

With little choice left us, we slipped out of bed and walked downstairs, Chloe met us rubbing her eyes in the hall.

"What is with that fucking bell?" My eyes were still only half open.

"Frigging Anthony." Was pretty much my entire vocal range before coffee, she gave a nod.

"I fucking mean it Abby, if he rings that fucker again, he will have a smile and detailed knowledge of the inserted handle. Oh, fuck my head is banging."

We walked into the kitchen, to be met with a screech that exploded our heads, from Delphine. I stared at her with half closed eyes, as she fussed.

"Ladies, ladies where are your robes?" I looked at Birch, she shrugged.

"Fuck knows?" Delphine had her hands over the eyes of her two female assistants.

"A lady should keep her feminine wile's hidden from view at all times, and ladies should curtail their language." Birch reached for a cup that Edwina was pouring.

"I am not a lady, so we are good thanks."

Delphine looked panicked, I sat down and grabbed the next cup, Chloe sat at the side of me, and pushed her forehead into the cold stone surface of the top, and groaned. Delphine gave a gasp.

"I feel today will be far harder than I thought." I sipped my coffee and closed my eyes.

The wedding was at four, and it was just gone ten, why the hell was I even awake? I mean, how hard is it to brush your hair, slap on some eye makeup, and then put on a dress? In my mind, I could get up at two, slouch around, get ready, and still be there before everyone else. What is this weird messed up day of preparation thing, everyone does for weddings?

Waking is a process of nurturing, it requires, soft calm consideration and coffee, lots of coffee, all of which should be done with great care, after the hour of eleven o'clock. My suspicions of these young Delphine wannabe's rose, when Edwina offered them a drink, and they both asked for tea, who were these alien creatures who were devoid of all respect for humanity?

One was named Michelle, so I did not trust her for starters, I have never met one yet that was not a complete cow, the other was Amanda, and she looked scared stiff of Birch, so I could live with that, the girl obviously had good intuition.

We sipped our drinks quietly, and calmly, trying to ignore the whole room, which is the correct etiquette for the morning. Amanda tip toed towards us, she came round the front of the island, with a plastic carrier case filled with cans and tools, and looked at Birch.

"Would you like me to do your hair for you, it is really lovely and unusual?" She reached for a can in her holder. Birch glared at her.

"Touch my hair bitch, with any of that chemical laden shit, and I promise you, I will drag you out in to the garden, pin you down, and shave your head bald. I use only natural products on my hair."

Amanda swallowed hard, and stepped back, she had gained sudden wisdom. Anthony stared at us, and gave a dramatic sigh, and rolled his eyes.

"Oh ladies, will you please, just let them help, they are here to make the day run smoother." Birch looked at him, she was still seething over the bell.

"They touch my hair; they will be one hell of a lot frigging smoother than they wish to be. I do my hair, you colour it, Deads brushes it, and that is it, let them go play with Deb's, and keep them the hell away from me." He gave another dramatic sigh.

"Birch darling, you are impossible." He clapped his hands, and Chloe recoiled.

"We shall go see Ellen and Izzy, leave these grumps to wake up."

He marched off towards the library, and left us alone. Edwina filled Birch's cup again.

"Go easy on them guys, they are doing their jobs."

Birch stood up with her cup, and headed for the patio, and the silence of the garden.

By twelve we were fully awake and functioning more like us.

Deb's came down in a strapless white lace bra, that gave her a cleavage you could park a bike in, a white lace thong, with suspenders, and thigh high white pullups. She looked at us, her hair all curled and looking insanely fantastic.

"Guys please, be nice to the hair girls, you have scared the shit out of them. Please guys just do this for me."

We saw her large hazel eyes, which looked like baby rabbits, and both suddenly felt guilty, I looked at Birch, and she gave a long sigh.

"I hate people touching my hair, but just this once... For you Deb's, they can help, but if they come anywhere near me with all that spray poison, I am striking a match and toasting the bitches, with their own chemicals." Deb's looked relieved.

"Thanks, poor girls, fancy having to work Saturdays and getting you two, talk about drawing the short straw." I giggled, and Birch gave a sweet smile.

Birch's idea of letting them help was, she sat in front of the mirror, and handed pins to Michelle, Amanda was still too afraid to come near us. She handed Michelle the curling iron, picked up the brush, and looked at her.

"Watch."

She brushed her hair, gathered it up at the side, took several pins off her, and then pinned her hair into place. She then took the curling iron, and with one side of her hair up, she pulled down the other side and curled it into ringlets, and dropped it on her shoulder. The whole thing took but a few minutes, and she looked stunning, she smiled at me.

"So, what do you think Sweetie?" I was impressed.

"I think I am wet."

Michelle screwed up her face. She became very nervous around me after that. Amanda did my hair, it was swept back and pinned into place, and then had two really nice clips put in, with feathers and cogs on them. I really liked the effect, Birch leaned in, and kissed my exposed neck, and I shuddered, and got goosebumps, and Amanda was suddenly happy to leave us alone. We each had a small top hat, which would be added on a clip shortly before we left the house.

Next was makeup, and a girl called Janet. She was actually

pretty cool, she asked us what we wanted, and we showed her pictures on our phones of what we usually did. She gave it some thought and went to work, both of us got black eyeliner, and soft skin tones for our cheeks. I have to admit, I have never really done huge amounts of foundation, and I felt like I had paint on my face, but it did look good, and although not the heavy dark goth I was used to. The good news was she hid my black eye, I liked it.

Next came dresses, and the struggle, of having our boobs fondled and cupped, as we slid them up, Birch had bought white lace panties, and I found it really weird looking at her in them. She was very uncomfortable, and kept pulling at them, and scratching in a most un-ladylike way.

With the four of us finally ready, we stood in the living room and waited for the bride, trying to look like the Victorian fantasy women we were supposed to be, and yep, we failed miserably at it. We felt awkward and uncomfortable, and not at all like H.G. Wells would have imagined us.

Bradley arrived and we all gasped, wow he looked good, in his long brown jacket, cream shirt, gold filigree waistcoat, and long brown boots. Chloe stared at him stood in the hall.

"Guys is it weird that I am looking at Bradley and I really want to frap?" Birch shook her head.

"Is that all, hell Chloe, if Ellen was not here, I would take him upstairs and totally screw his brains out, he looks really hot in that get up."

I had to agree, a part of me wanted to time travel back, and hang out with guys dressed like that, it was really sexy.

Anthony was pacing about, he was dressed not unsimilar to Bradley, and looked like he had stepped out of a Jane Austin novel, the time was drawing closer. Ellen came down looking flustered, and wow she was breath taking, although she did look like she had stepped out of some high class wild west whore house. Bradley was all eyes, and he pulled her close.

"Oh, Ellen darling, you look ravishing." Edwina leaned in to us.

"Is it messed up that I would totally do, Deb's mum? I cannot look at her, it's really turning me on." I looked at Edwina.

"Be honest, your family is all hormones. You are to women, what your sister is to men?" She gave a wide smile.

"Pretty much... Yeah."

We were all stewarded to the front door, and Deb's appeared at the top of the stairs, wow what a staircase to have for her, she looked a little nervous, but stunning, Birch breathed out.
"Wow guys look at her, she is so beautiful."
All of us agreed as she elegantly walked down the stairs to her father, who was clearly blown away. Anthony lifted a tissue to his face and blubbered. I nudged him in the ribs.
"Pack it in you will set me off."
Deb's got to the bottom of the stairs, and looked at me, I put my hands on my heart and smiled, I really was lost for words, and doing my best to fight back the tears. Anthony wiped his eyes and looked at his watch.
"Right, we are on time, so that is good, the cars are here so let's go."
We were unceremoniously pushed out of the door by Anthony, as Bradley pulled Deb's into a soft hug and told her how stunning she was, whilst Ellen wept.

Outside were long golden, open topped, American cars, I am not good with cars, so your guess is as good as mine. They were vintage, and had all sorts of extras attached to them, they looked like they had been driven out of a Jules Verne novel. I was pretty impressed. Jimmy, I know, had paid a fortune for these, and they were absolutely perfect for the job. We stepped on the running boards and climbed in. Anthony, Edwina, and myself sat with our back to the driver, with Ellen, Birch, Chloe sat opposite. I felt like I was on a movie set, it was pretty thrilling.
Deb's and Bradley got into the other car behind us, and I could see her smiling, some of the neighbours had actually come out to watch, which in itself was amazing. I had lived here all my life, and I had no idea what half of them looked like. In the distance the bells of the church struck up, and I looked at Birch, who had suddenly sat up straight.
"Today is for Deb's, Bell Twats are allowed."
She looked disappointed, but sat back and conceded, they were for Deb's, not God, so that was fine. Chloe and Edwina both sniggered, Ellen looked confused.

Inside the church, Jimmy stood looking very nervous. He was wearing a brown jacket with tales, a white shirt, of which the lace cuffs came through the bottom of his jacket sleeves. His waist coat was the same as Bradley's, and he had a black neck tie, he stood holding his black top hat under his arm. A professional barber had done his moustache and beard, which he had grown especially for his wedding, and looked very much like that of a Victorian country squire.

His groomsmen all wore shirts, with leather sleeve bands and waistcoats to match. They had brown striped pants in two shades, and wore boots. The way they all stood in a line, they almost looked like an old western barber's quartet. Gail and Milton were ready, as the signal was given that the cars were arriving, and Jimmy gave a sigh of relief. Outside the Vicarage, the cars slowly pulled up, and we all climbed out and prepared.

It was interesting the attention we got as we slowly drove by. Saturday was a busy day in the village, and there were a lot of people around. A lot lifted their phones and took pictures, and walked along the green following us, there was a lot of people gathered to see Deb's slide out of the bridal car. She stood as Ellen straightened her dress, and then slowly led by Edwina and Chloe, we headed for the church doors.

Inside the dress maker checked us over, to ensure everything was perfect. Anthony organised the flowers and bouquet, and offered his arm to Ellen, and with one last big smile, she walked through into the church, and we lined up, ready. I looked at Birch at my side.

"You are not like going to burst into flames when we walk in are you?"

Chloe and Edwina both sniggered, just in front of us, Birch looked at me and smiled.

"You know what Sweetie, I would frigging love that." Bradley burst out laughing, Deb's suddenly looked really worried.

"Please don't Birch, oh shit, I am terrified of going in now."

Suddenly the riff of a guitar, sounding very like Van Halen erupted into the church, and ran into a squealing long note, and then the music began, and I looked back at Deb's and winked.

"Go get that new hat."

She giggled, we all faced front, and the doors opened, and to a wild screaming version of 'Here comes the bride.' We stepped into the church, and Birch did not burst into flames, obviously the good lord felt, Deb's could not handle it, and so passed up on his chance to nail a Pagan.

The service was beautiful, she looked so stunning, and yet innocent, Jimmy was so caring and gentle, and the way he looked at her as he gave his vows, it was so beautiful, it brought tears to my eyes. Birch wiped hers, and passed me an extra tissue, and I sniffled as Deb's radiated joy. Gail handled the service so well, and gently guided them both, I found her care and attention touching. They were pronounced man and wife, and I handed her the bouquet back, and smiled, and quietly whispered.

"For you Mrs Battersby. I love you Debs."

The guitar struck up, and Floyd played as the bells rang, and together, Jimmy and Deb's walked for the first time as man and wife down the aisle, and out into the sunlight.

Then began the exhausting round of photos. Family, friends, and so forth, we were hit from every angle by a zillion cameras, and I thought I was going to go blind, or have a fit, it was like standing in strobes. After what felt like an age, Deb's asked.

"Can I have one of the Curio's, I really want one of us?"

How could we refuse. Anthony joined us and we all stood together at the church doors, just like we had behind Petal that last day of our crazy summer, and suddenly I felt really emotional. Birch pulled me close, almost as if she sensed it, and leaned into me.

"I know Sweetie, hold back the tears, just for a little while longer."

I swallowed hard, was this going to be our last time, or would there be more? The simple fact was we had no way of knowing. It had taken five long years to get us together again in one spot after that summer, and I did not want us to wait another five years, before we were all together again like this.

For most of the summer, Anthony had been missing, as he was living with Brent, but now he was home with us, and yet Deb's had returned to her house as Jimmy came back. It appeared impossible to keep us all together, and maybe I missed that. Was it selfish that I loved them all so dearly, I wanted them close to me at all times?

Stood together as we all giggled and cracked jokes, the bond was there, the love and deep trust we all had. I could feel it in the air surrounding us, these people were so special and so unique, each of them had such a huge place in my heart. Each of them had a place in life, a purpose, a meaning, a huge significance, they were family, my brother and sisters, and I would put my life on the line for any of them.

The moments we had shared together, went beyond anything I had shared in my life before. The closeness I felt towards them was indescribable, and my biggest fear as we aged, was knowing life moved on. Just like Deb's, one by one they would leave the coup and fly free, into their own lives and futures, and the truth was, I did not want them to leave me. Stood here as the cameras flashed, I knew ultimately this moment would be repeated each time, one of them did.

The pictures were taken, and Deb's was so happy, and in a way, I was really happy she asked. Once again, we broke apart, and all made our way together, down the gravel path, towards the gate, and out of the church.

Katie stood by the gate in a suit and top hat, and gave a regal bow, as we walked towards her.

"Mr and Mrs Battersby, your guests are ready and seated, if you would care to follow me, I shall escort you."

I had no idea what was planned at this point, it had been a secret project. We were taken on to the fete site, where there were three huge marquees, that formed three sides of a square, on the fourth side was a stage. We entered through the side to find a long table, dressed fit for a queen, it looked like a palace banquet. All of us gasped, as Victorian style waiters walked up and down. The flowers, the silverware, everything looked Victorian and elegant.

The inside of the marquees, had billowing burgundy cloth, that was pleated from the centre, and hung down to hide the structure, like a high vaulted ceiling, it looked so high class, all I could do was stare. Each marquee had the side removed that faced the stage, creating a large square. It had been covered in a hard shiny floor, surrounded by elegant rails, into which flowers, cogs, and ribbons had been woven. The whole area created a huge dance floor, and above it from the stage, running to each of the marquee tops, was thousands of lights, all suspended like twinkling stars, it was breath taking.

This was Victorian style, taken to the extreme, and it was mind blowing, we were guided to our seats, and then an army of waiters and waitress descended, and champagne corks fired into the air, and food was supplied on mass, and it was a full on banquet. I ate so much I thought I would explode.

With the meal over, the speeches began and the toasts, I was slowly getting pissed so much wine had been served, and then it was Jimmy's turn for a speech. He stood and took Deb's by the hand, and walked her onto the dance floor. They crossed it, and he led her onto some steps, and took her onto the large stage, instantly two side screens came to life, and there was Deb's sat on a stool. Jimmy stood at her side next to her, and leaned into the mic.

"This feels familiar, I think I have done this before."

Floyd walked onto the stage with two guitars and handed one to Jimmy, he looked out at all the guests.

"Five years ago, a mate of mine told me of this bird he had just F.. Er talked to, and told me that her mate was a mad fan of mine, and so I naturally wanted to meet her. He took me to meet a girl called Birch, who told me all about this girl called Debbie, who was my biggest fan in the world. Well, obviously, I just had to meet her, so I had a beer and hung around, and she turned up with her mate Deadly.

Well, I took one look at her and thought wow, what a stunner. I won't say what happened next, but it changed my world forever, and I gave her my hat. I saw her the next day, but the event ended, and I had been so caught up in her, I never got her number and thought I would never see her again, and yet I could not stop thinking about her." He looked to the guests, and nodded.

"It ruined the tour, because I tried everything to try and find her, and then one night Floyd says, for fuck sake Jim, write a fucking tune. Yeah, I moaned that much I drove em all mad with it, and so I wrote a tune, and it became a top five hit.

Last year at Glastonbury, I was in the middle of a set, and I saw my hat, and I cannot tell you how crazy that moment was. I looked at Floyd and yells, that is her, she is bloody well here, and he walks up still playing the tune, and gave this long sigh, and he says, for fuck's sake Jim, go and bloody well get her then, or we will never hear the end of it. I did, I dived off the stage and fought my way through, and there she was, I was blown away." Deb's giggled as he smiled at her.

"Look at her folks, she is the most beautiful woman in the world, and I should know, I have toured all over it, and she has just become my wife, how good can life get? Deb's my little Goggle Bear, I love you, and I wrote this with Floyd just for you."

The melody started and Jimmy with Floyd strummed along together, and slowly the other band members appeared and started to play. Jimmy began to sing a soft ballad, as she sat there, it was nothing like any of the band's tunes, it was poetic, and lyrical, and surprisingly beautiful, and entitled the rose amongst the weeds.

I sat there watching the screen, watching Deb's, her eyes never leaving Jimmy, and I started to cry, it was possibly one of the most beautiful things I have ever seen. He finished, lifted his hat, and bowed to her, and she wiped her eyes, and all around me the tissues were being passed round, and the love between them was so real, so strong, and I was really happy for her, she really deserved it, more than anyone else I knew.


Jimmy escorted her down to the dance floor, and Floyd was joined by the rest of the band, and a few musician guests, played 'I want the girl in my hat back' and together they had their first dance. Jimmy was actually a really good dancer; he was proving to have many hidden talents. After the tune, selected special guests came to the stage and played a whole night of classic rock music, and more wine flowed, as people got up to dance, as the night moved on.

I danced with Anthony, and he was happy, he danced with great elegance, and I do not know why I was surprised by that. The music played and as I walked off the floor smiling at Birch stood watching me. Jimmy took my hand.

"I would be honoured if you would grace the floor with me madam."

I giggled, as he smiled and led me back onto the floor, and took my waist, and held my hand.

"Abbs, I wanted to talk before we leave. Firstly, I want to thank you for all you have done for Deb, she loves you so much, and when she has felt worried or insecure, you have always been there for her, and that means a lot to me." He smiled, his eyes had such depth and kindness, I had never really noticed.

"I love Deb's, we have been through a lot together, she is my best friend, I will always be there for her." He gave a gentle nod, but I could see he had something on his mind.

"I really do love her Abbs, this is not a game to me, I am completely serious… Look I know the band have a bit of a reputation, and I am not going to stand here and pretend to be an angel, I am not. I have had a pretty fucking wild time, but you know what, I am changing Abby. I am twenty six, and I have had a wild time, but I want something more. I want meaning in my life, and it is important to me, that you know I am on the level with Deb. Endless touring has knackered me out, we have a shot now, we have a chance as we are getting bigger, and I can slow down more and take some time out, and I want that time with Deb." It is funny, just when you think you have seen it all, someone surprises you.

"I am glad to hear that Jimmy, I really am, because this is not a game to Deb's, she really wants this, you are her dream, and if you stick with it, she will make you so happy. She is one of the most amazing people I have ever known, let her show you that, and you will never regret it, I know, she is massively important to my life." He smiled and we slowly glided across the floor.

"Are you going to be okay now, she is worried about you, and I am too? You know Abbs, me and the lads, we think the world of you lot, and we talk, and we worry. We are not as stupid as our lyrics sound, and we see the things that happen. I probably should not say, but you are kind of a bit of a pin up with the boys, they all fancy your arse off, and I am telling you Abbs, they will be there if you need them. If Deb gets upset because you are hurt, they are all there for you to help, as I said, we really love all you guys."

It was sweet to know, it is silly really, they all looked a bit comical in their top hats, and they do have a really bad reputation from some of their road activities, and yet they were all really kind. He winked at me.

"We look out for our own Abbs, and you guys are part of that with us lads, just so you know. Look I just wanted you to know, no matter where we are or what we are up to, if you need us, me and the lads will be there, for all of you, we are there. And if I may say so, fuck Kyle, no one will ever love you as much as she does." He gave a chuckle. "She has not taken her eyes off you all night, even now she is making sure I behave."

He gave a loud chuckle and spun me round, as I giggled and the music came to an end. Jimmy stopped and let go of me, and gave me a huge smile as he bowed to me, he was so respectful, and I liked that, I gave a regal curtsy, and smiled.

"Thanks Jimmy."

"The pleasure was all mine Doll."

He took my hand, and escorted me towards Birch, she was all smiles stood holding her phone, her camera had lots of pictures, Jimmy bowed to Birch.

"I entrust this good lady into your care Madam." She gave a chuckle.

"Why Sir, you are without doubt, a true gentleman, and I am in your debt."

He laughed as Birch slipped her arm round my waist, and he bowed again as he withdrew.


I was light headed, it had been a long day, we had both danced with so many people, even Birch got a dance with Floyd, and surprisingly Zac, he appeared to be very protective of Birch, which was strange. The evening moved on, and I was feeling a little bit more than tipsy, and tired, but around us everyone appeared to be so happy and smiling, and the wedding had been a huge success, and that was all that mattered.

I had just finished another dance with Birch, we kept sneaking them in whenever we could, when Deb's appeared, dressed in jeans and a pretty top, it was time for her to leave. She pulled us both into a hug and smiled at us, she looked at Birch.

"I am glad the hall was closed down, Katie told me all of this was you; she just did as you asked. Birch this was so special and magical for me, just as you two are. It is the best night of my life, and I want to say so much but I just don't know how to, except to say, I love you, I love you both, you made this day better than ever, and Jimmy and me want to thank you." Birch smiled.

"We love you too Sweetie, and I am happy you liked it, I thought a good start sets the trend, and so you had the best we could give." She pulled her into a hug, and almost squeezed the life out of her, I did the same.

"Go on, go and enjoy Bali, and be happy." Jimmy appeared, and hugged us both.

"You two are the best, you know that, I owe both of you big time, and I will not forget what you have done for us."

Hand in hand they walked out of the tent, as everyone crowded round, and wished them the best and hugged them. It had been an amazing day for both of them, and they now faced a long life together.

Birch took my hand and walked me back onto the dance floor, she took me in her arms, and we danced softly and slowly, her bright green eyes watching my blue, she smiled, I was melting in her arms.

"Deads, as you know I am against marriage, but I am not afraid of commitment. I love you; I mean I really do love you, and here and now I know, I never want us to be separated, and I want to make a commitment to you." Her eyes sparkled so brightly, I was completely lost in them, she gave a soft smile.

"Deads, be mine completely, and I will be yours completely, be my Lillian, to your Celia, I want this to never end, us to never end, forever and beyond, could you do that?" She was so sincere, and a little bit scared, and she was beautiful, I smiled at her.

"I am already yours, I have been since I first knocked on that dorm lost, but yes Birch, I will be your Lillian, if you will be Celia, we will never end, because this summer, that is what I learned about me. I will never allow this to stop, I will always be yours forever and beyond."

She smiled, leaned in, and she kissed me softly, and slowly, and I felt a fire rage within me. I gave a chuckle, and she looked at me.

"What?" I gave a giggle.

"My Dad is watching, I think the cat is out of the bag, but I don't care, I will never hide or deny this ever again, not ever Birch."

She smiled and her eyes sparkled with devilish delight. She pulled me close, and we danced on, laughing and talking, and suddenly my world was changing again.

I remember sitting with Birch in those first few weeks of Uni, when I did not really know her that well, she sat on her bed and looked at me, smiled and told me something which really opened my eyes. Birch told me, that most people referred to life as a journey, and that it annoyed her that it was always referred to as a path of life, in her book, it was a river, and she had dropped the sail, and was enjoying the journey, bobbing along, and going with the flow.

As I stood there in her arms dancing slowly to the music, and looking into those beautiful green eyes, I think I really understood what she had meant. The last few weeks had tested me so much as I questioned everything, when what I should have been doing was just accepting that life has a lot of bumps in the road, and so it is so much easier to just jump in a boat, and drift along with the sail down. Birch has always been my boat, all I needed to do was drift along with her, simply drifting in the flow of life, and I would be fine.

Is it me or is it really screwed up, that five years ago, I hated this place? Honestly if it had not been for Birch, I would have got right back on the train, and gone back to Manchester, and probably never set foot in Wotton again. Yet here I am, with these admittedly insane friends all around me, living in a house I half own, and writing fiction novels that I cannot deny, are not selling that well. I am held in the arms of the craziest, and most beautiful person I have ever known, and I am so frigging happy about it, who the hell would have seen that coming?

The world is changing my friends, new trends, new faces, and new ways of living. Even Wotton is changing, the Parish Council now has two Curio's on it, and Marjorie is moving out of the village and taking a back seat from political life. Although, her public and private life have always been different, and I will not deny, her behind the scenes behaviour still concerns me.

Wotton will always remain as beautiful and as idyllic as it has always done, but tides are turning, and opinion is shifting, and yet somehow, I do not think it will be in the direction of Birch or myself, but who knows, stranger things have happened.

It is a curious thing, and it has been a curious summer, and I will probably always think of this moment exactly like that. It took us five years to really come back together, and I am so glad we did, and yeah, I get it now, this will always be our summer, the Curio's Summer. I really do think I like the idea of that?

"Birch?"
"Yes Sweetie."
"My dad looks really pissed off."
"Maybe Sweetie… But look how happy your mum looks."

# More Author's
## From
# Violet Circle Publishing

## Mike Beale. (Children's Book)

Crumble's Adventures.
ISBN: 978-1-910299-06-7
Digital ISBN: 978-1-910299-08-1

## Colin Smith (Play)

Heaven knows I'm Miserable Now
ISBN: 978-1-910299-16-6
Digital ISBN: 978-1-910299-23-4

## Ted Morgan. (Poetry and verse)

Wordsmith's Wanderings.
ISBN: 978-1-910299-04-3
Digital ISBN: 978-1-910299-09-8
Peregrinations of the Wordsmith
ISBN: 978-1-910299-18-0
Digital ISBN: 978-1-910299-21-0
Silhouette Soldiers
ISBN: 978-1-910299-19-7
Digital ISBN: 978-1-910299-22-7
A Menu of Memories
Digital ISBN: 978-1-910299-32-6
Digital ISBN: 978-1-910299-33-3

Robin John Morgan. (Fiction/Fantasy/Slice of Life)

## Heirs to the Kingdom.

Book One, The Bowman of Loxley.
ISBN: 978-1-910299-00-5
Digital ISBN: 978-1-910299-10-4
Book Two, The Lost Sword of Carnac.
ISBN: 978-1-910299-01-2
Digital ISBN: 978-1-910299-11-1
Book Three, The Darkness of Dunnottar.
ISBN: 978-1-910299-02-9
Digital ISBN: 978-1-910299-12-8
Book Four, Queen of the Violet Isle.
ISBN: 978-1-910299-03-6
Digital ISBN: 978-1-910299-13-5
Book Five, Crystals of the Mirrored Waters.
ISBN: 978-1-910299-05-0
Digital ISBN: 978-1-910299-14-2
Book Six, Last Arrow of the Woodland Realm.
ISBN: 978-1-910299-07-4
Digital ISBN: 978-1-910299-15-9
Book Seven, Bridge Of Sequana.
ISBN: 978-1-910299-17-3
Digital ISBN: 978-1-910299-20-3
Book Eight, The Circle of Darkness.
ISBN: 978-1-910299-26-5
Digital ISBN: 978-1-910299-29-6

## The Curio Chronicles.

Part One, Abigail's Summer.
ISBN: 978-1-910299-27-2
Digital ISBN: 978-1-910299-28-9
Part Two, Curio's Summer.
ISBN: 978-1-910299-34-0
Digital ISBN: 978-1-910299-35-7

Find out more about our authors and their books at
www.violetcirclepublishing.co.uk

Violet Circle Publishing Manchester UK